"WELL AND TRULY
offers a realistic and app
Hatch, newly widowed
cope . . . Maggie strugg
of passivity and the rigid structures of the insular New England community . . . and her search for redefinition is both believable and engrossing."

—*Publishers Weekly*

"WELL AND TRULY
is a fetching tale, written with exacting ease, that serves up a rich slice of small-town Vermont life . . . Bright flashes of humor and delightfully fresh characterizations enliven this touching novel of self discovery."

—*Booklist*

"WELL AND TRULY
is an exciting new novel in which Evelyn Wilde Mayerson has adroitly interwoven two strong stories of a recently widowed woman who serves on the jury in a deplorable murder case and must judge not only the fifteen-year-old accused but also her own behavior and values. . . . The little accused-murderess is perfection . . . it is a fine novel that makes for compelling reading."

—James Michener

WELL AND TRULY

EVELYN WILDE MAYERSON

A SIGNET BOOK

SIGNET
Published by the Penguin Group
Penguin Books USA Inc., 375 Hudson Street,
New York, New York 10014, U.S.A.
Penguin Books Ltd, 27 Wrights Lane,
London W8 5TZ, England
Penguin Books Australia Ltd, Ringwood,
Victoria, Australia
Penguin Books Canada Ltd, 2801 John Street,
Markham, Ontario, Canada L3R 1B4
Penguin Books (N.Z.) Ltd, 182-190 Wairau Road,
Auckland 10, New Zealand

Penguin Books Ltd, Registered Offices:
Harmondsworth, Middlesex, England

Published by Signet, an imprint of New American Library,
a division of Penguin Books USA Inc. Previously published in
an NAL Books edition.

First Signet Printing, July, 1991
10 9 8 7 6 5 4 3 2 1

PUBLISHER'S NOTE
This is a work of fiction. Names, characters, places, and incidents either are the product of the author's imagination or are used fictitiously, and any resemblance to actual persons, living or dead, events, or locales is entirely coincidental.

For Maryanne Colas, my agent, my friend,
who has been with me from the beginning

I am grateful to all whose expertise has led to the development of this novel. Myra McPherson's work, *Long Time Passing,* provided valuable insights, as did the clarification provided by Doris Buchanan, clerk of the Vermont District Court, and the forensic possibilities outlined by Gene Man, Professor of Chemistry at the University of Miami.

While there have been many who have helped, the following individuals have been especially generous with their time: Janet Reno; William D. Wright; The Honorable Arthur J. O'dea; The Honorable Theodore S. Mandeville, Jr.; Geoffrey Alpert; Thomas Wills; Andrew S. Jonas, M.D.; Steven Zeidman; Bruce Swaffield; and, always, Don.

CHAPTER 1

Summons

MAGGIE HATCH'S PRINTED SKIRT had a raspberry stain. She tried unsuccessfully to rub out the blemish with her finger in the persistent, involuntary manner one uses to rub an itch from the eyes or a pain from the temples, and made a mental note to take the skirt to the dry cleaner with Kristen's winter coat and Alan's only suit, the gray pin stripe he wore to conferences.

Someone cleared his throat. The sound had a cranky, sick-bed urgency that demanded attention. Maggie looked up and brushed aside the strands of curly, coppery red hair that fell across her forehead and veiled her glasses. Lester Perkins sat before her across a clawfoot mahogany desk that had been worn to a polish by generations of elbows; he was arranging his large, round face into an expression of sadness. With his mouth and eyes turned down, he looked like a cookie with the raisins picked out.

"Don't worry about a thing, Maggie," he said. "Leave it all to me. All you have to do is sign this slip of paper giving me permission to pick up the body."

Maggie looked at him in bewilderment. She was puzzled by two things. First, what she was doing indoors on a white, sunlit summer day when she would rather be outside hiking through maple-bordered pastures of chicory, or rummaging through tag sales for a discarded, tattered canvas or a piece of verbena-scented lace, mellowed by generations of female fingering into an ancient sepia. Her second question was why Letitia was sitting beside her like a warden, holding her elbow as if in a vise.

Something else was hurting besides Letitia's long, bony fingers. Maggie looked for the source. She concentrated on her mother-in-law's thin, tightly pressed lips in the way that she had tried the week before to focus on the northern lights through Alan's homemade telescope. Maggie had thought that the long, quivering streamers looked like ribbons, but seventeen-year-old Kristen said she should be seeing an arc. Kristen's boyfriend, Ranger, who squeezed the cardboard tube so tightly he made a mirror pop out, told Maggie not to feel bad because he didn't see any arc either.

"Maggie, Lester is waiting," said Letitia. "Sign the paper."

A box of Kleenex, with a tissue puffed and ready at the perforated opening, sat conspicuously on top of Lester's desk. Alan had ragged Lester about his profession. Last winter he and Peter Bouchard appropriated a carton of false tuxedo fronts from the rear of Lester's funeral home, and they wore them all season, tied like hospital gowns, over their ski clothes. He also needled Lester about his heavy, flat-footed tennis game, and would only play with him when neither he nor any of his tennis cronies could get a fourth. Lester, who knew this but held no grudges, led Alan's mother and wife to a dimly lit room to show them a display of caskets.

Maggie was told to feel a certain quality of satin lining. It slipped between her fingers, reminding her of the silken contents of her mother's dresser drawers. She thought about Alan resting his head forever on Sybil's lingerie cases. "What about a beeper?" she asked.

Letitia took her daughter-in-law's elbow and guided her back to Lester's office, where the heady scent of new-mown hay drifted in through the open Palladian window. "Was Alan forty-three or forty-four?" asked Lester. "He went to school with my sister Norma, but it depends on when his birthday falls."

Alan was three years older than Maggie. That and his medical education had given him an edge in their twenty-year marriage, resulting in short arguments and long instructions. Maggie, bent on a stability she never knew as a child, was a willing, if not chafing, subordinate. "Forty-three," she said.

"I don't know if that's accurate," said Letitia, with the glint of a tear. "My son would have been forty-four next Thursday."

Maggie raised her voice, though she did not mean to. It was something that Alan's family never did, like leaving napkins unfolded or smoking cigars. "Close doesn't cut it," she said, "I didn't even get a chance to wrap his birthday present."

"I'm afraid she's right," conceded Lester. He scribbled on a yellow pad, then looked up. "Just out of curiosity, Maggie, what did you get him?"

"A Wilson Profile," she replied.

They continued to compose the notice that Lester assured Letitia the *Banner* would run. Alan, survived by mother, brother, wife, and daughter, was also vice-president of the county orthopedic association. "Don't forget to mention," said Letitia, "that my son's great-great-grandfather Hatch served side by side with Ethan Allen in the Revolutionary War. In fact, he was with him when they seized Fort Ticonderoga."

Lester tactfully chose not to argue the point. According to his sources, largely his grandmother, who heard it from her own grandmother, it was not Ethan Allen but his cousin Zimri with whom Hatch fought side by side. Instead he said, "I knew someone in your family was a Green Mountain Boy," then knit his brows. "What about Captain Burton? I remember hearing my grandfather say that he owned a hosiery mill."

"That's not important," said Letitia, whose grandfather's mill once sustained the entire village. "The main thing to say about Alan's great-grandfather Burton was that he became an aide to Calvin Coolidge."

Lester handed Maggie an estimated bill. It was required by law. He had folded it in half. She continued to fold it in increasingly narrow widths, the way her father taught her to make fans when she was six. At least she thought it was her father. Or maybe it had been the Puerto Rican janitor who lived in the basement of their New York apartment in an aroma of cigars and bay rum, and who broke down cartons with a machete while speaking to her of bougainvillea, tree frogs, and evil American sugar corporations.

Maggie finally put the bill in her purse. A moment later, crushed beneath some enormous weight from which she could not free herself, she forgot what she had done with it and scrambled through the pockets of her yellow nylon windbreaker.

Lester and Letitia looked at each other in somber commiseration. "It's in your purse," said Letitia.

Lester dropped his voice deep into his chest. It came out as a dismal basso. "Would you like me to pick up Alan's burial clothes?" he asked. "Or will you bring them by?"

What burial clothes? Maggie wondered. Alan didn't own any burial clothes. In the summer he wore white tennis outfits or green hospital fatigues. In the winter he wore ski clothes with false tuxedo fronts. "I don't know what to bring," she said.

"A suit will do nicely," said Lester. "A white shirt, a nice, conservative tie."

"I have to take his suit to the cleaner's," she replied. "With this skirt. I don't know how this stain got here." She began to cry, with the easy outrage of a little girl whose mother has thrown her best paper fans into the incinerator.

Letitia, who at sixty-nine bore no sign of the calcium depletion that was supposed to bend her into a question mark, sat tall and straight, a pylon of stoic resignation.

She seemed to carry her grief purposefully, skillfully, reflecting her sobriety in the loft of her chin, her sufferance in the pained expression of her slate-gray eyes. "You must bear up," she said. "Think of Kristen."

Where was Kristen? Most likely with Ranger, bumping over the stony trout stream in an inner tube, or drying somewhere, febrile and fumbling under a blanket. Unless she was crying. Maggie and Alan had discussed the continuum of intimacies between their beautiful seventeen-year-old daughter and her boyfriend. Alan, in the puritanic obbligato of fathers of daughters, said no way. Maggie disagreed and said every which way.

What was a cerebral aneurysm, anyhow? Alan would have explained it to her—in layman's terms, as he always prefaced any explanation—but he could not because he was the one who was dead. Why wasn't he there to help her, to tell Letitia to let go of her elbow, to chip away the cement that was beginning to harden in her chest?

Maggie told Lester she had to do her husband's shirts over. Alan had complained the day before that they didn't have enough starch. "It doesn't matter," said Lester gently. "I made them too soft," said Maggie, who began to cry again. "The collars flop."

"I imagine you will want a viewing," said Lester.

Letitia said of course.

Maggie hesitated. "You don't have to worry about the aesthetics, Maggie," he said. "We restore the remains." What was there to restore? she wondered. All he had to do was wipe off a little clay.

"Will the family sit or stand through the viewing?" he asked.

Letitia said they would stand.

Burial, of course, would take place in the family burial grounds, which were no longer attached to Letitia's property but protected nonetheless behind a stone wall, where bronze griffins stood guard on the ridge behind the Bonny Peter Motel. Maggie remembered when Alan's father died, Alan had shown Kristen the elm trees planted by his great-grandfather, even tracing the outlines of their roots which sprawled over headstones lying flat among the weeds.

"What are widow's weeds?" asked Maggie. "I knew but I forgot."

Lester diverted her shaky attention. "You may want to consider," he said, "what memento you wish to deposit in the coffin. A picture of yourself, perhaps, a ring, something that he cared about."

Alan was over six feet and muscular, the tectonics of his body clearly defined in mesomorphic plates that gleamed under the shower. Maggie thought about what he would have liked beside him for eternity and wondered if there were room. Alan was interested in everything and, unlike his older brother, Owen, successful at almost anything he tried, as evidenced by the gear and trophies of his achievements which cluttered the hall closet and spilled out into the mud room. She decided it was a toss-up between Alan's letter to the editor of the *New England Journal of Medicine,* supporting the use of fetal tissues with characteristic logic as crisp as ice-cold lettuce, or his birthday present. "Would a tennis racket fit?" she asked.

Letitia looked worried. She knit her brows into a *V.* "Might Margaret have a glass of water, please?" she asked.

Mourners attended the viewing in a never-ending stream, like airline passengers going through an arrival gate. Most were from the village and nearby farms, while others had come from towns beyond the county line. Although everyone presumed a first-name basis, the equality that such conventions implied did not exist. In fact, the mourners were as stratified as the layers in the igneous rock through which their highways were cut, their hierarchy disclosed in their speech, the polish of college education that changed the sound of their A's and added a hard edge to their R's, and in the measured distance at which they stood from Letitia.

Maggie kept looking over her shoulder for the familiar

dark, tousled head, then remembered that Alan was not coming, which was too bad, since he was better at this sort of thing than she was.

Alan's body, laid out in a silver-handled walnut casket, did not look lifelike, as Lester had promised. It looked different. His stocky sister-in-law, Jenna, thought otherwise.

"He looks natural," she said. As squat and as spatulate as a woodchuck, Jenna was a part-time barn manager at a riding stable, and preferred man-sized Spandex breeches with suede knee patches and field boots to the shirtwaist with a wide, gathered skirt that she now wore. Made the night before, its short sleeves, trimmed at the cuffs with contrasting piping, bulged over her deltoids. "Don't you think he looks natural, Maggie?"

Alan had been vital and intense. Even when sleeping, flinging himself from side to side like a person in a hurry, his eyelids fluttered as if moving across some urgent, private video. The man wearing Alan's pin-striped suit lay as inert as his unstarched shirt, his face dredged as if floured for deep frying, the quizzical smile that had given him a perpetual frown pressed smooth and filled with wax.

"He's got on too much powder," said Maggie. She put her fingers to her neck and felt a strand of pearls she did not remember owning, much less putting on.

Jenna, smelling like a harness, shook hands with the line of callers as if she were priming a pump while she advised Maggie, whom she considered at the moment as a liability, to keep a strict accounting of gifts and givers. "You have to be on top of these things. People expect it of you." Then she said that they were all as proud as a pig with two tails of Kristen, who was holding up real well, behaving like her father's true daughter, which was to say, like a brick.

Maggie, suddenly reminded, searched for Kristen in panic, in the way she might have checked for an umbrella or a purse. She found her daughter drifting like perfume in and out of little clusters of mourners, making twists and bends and graceful dips to the brittle, knobby elderly who sat banked against the wall like a hickory trellis. Kristen's pale blonde hair was woven into a French braid and she moved like Sybil, which was strange, since she had spent so little time with her other grandmother.

Someone escorted Alan's great-aunt from her place along the wall, a centenarian of relic status, paper-thin and deaf, whose survival from one day to the next brought dumbfounded clucks from her caretakers, and whose last birthday had been announced on national television. "Willard Scott has my picture," she said. Then, prompted by an unseen voice, she added, "If there is anything I can do, please let me know."

"I bought two hundred stamps for my thank-you notes," said Maggie. "I don't know where I put them."

"You've got to get a hold of yourself," said Jenna. She hurried to get her sister-in-law a glass of water, her hips shifting like saddlebags, while Owen took Maggie aside to discuss selling her house and moving in with Letitia. His suggestion was as unthinkable as the fact that Alan was dead.

Maggie felt light-headed. She studied Alan's brother, Owen, whose angora rabbit farm had failed, like the string of ventures before it, and she thought, in the secret place where one is allowed to have such imaginings, that he should have had the aneurysm. It made more sense.

The only time Maggie wept was when Anne Bouchard appeared, slipping sideways, smiling and apologetic, through a tangled knot of mourners with her husband, Peter, behind her. The sight of elegant, solicitous Anne, with saddened Peter, worked like a floodgate.

The Bouchards had been Alan and Maggie's best friends since the March when Alan brought Maggie home to the six-mile-square town where he was born. Maggie remembered that it had been the sugaring season, with cold, snappy nights and daytime thaws, when she and Alan made love in Alan's room beneath a Lone Star quilt. They were across the hall from his parents and she had to keep her sighs to herself. Alan had taken her to a nearby farmer's sugar shack, where sweet steam rose from the boiling maple sap. The farmer had been old, or at least he had looked old to Maggie. He was probably dead now, she thought. Then Alan rose one morning to begin his residency, and Maggie was left with Alan's parents. What should I do all day long? she asked. Alan told her to watch the spring climb the hillside. "One hundred feet a day," said Alan's father. It was Anne who rescued her from the tedium of picking up coffee cups and setting them down, of looking through old photo albums, of searching for meaning in long, unfamiliar Yankee silences.

Anne's sleek ash-colored hair was secured at the back of her neck by a Chanel bow, which made it easier to whisper into her ear. "Why did it happen to him?" asked Maggie, crying into black grosgrain.

Everyone looked tactfully away as Anne pressed her friend to her narrow chest as if she were trying to pass through her. "I don't know, Mag. I wish I did."

"It's not fair. Someone actually said that it was part of God's plan. That makes no sense." Maggie's voice became strident, contentious. "How can it be part of God's plan when Alan has five patients still in traction?"

Anne reached behind her head to straighten her bow while keeping indulgent eyes fixed on her friend. "You don't know what you're saying, Maggie."

"Yes, I do. I know exactly what I'm saying." Then Maggie confided in a whisper as sudden as a draft beneath a door that Letitia, consumed by heroic mourning kept molten in some metallic inner core, was driving her up a wall. "It's not Letitia," counseled Anne. She looked to Peter for confirmation. He nodded. "You want your own mother, Maggie. That's the reason Letitia is getting to you. She's here and your mother's not. By the way, where is your mother?"

Sybil, contacted at the Canyon Ranch Spa between loofah scrubs and herbal wraps, was on her way to provide solace, but Maggie was doubtful. Selfish, unpredictable Sybil was the last one to turn to when you were hurting. Maggie learned this in junior high when she was in a field-trip bus accident in which her jaw had to be wired shut right over her braces, and it was Sybil who had to be sedated.

"That's who you really need to turn to at times like these," said Anne.

"What kind of time is this?" asked Maggie.

"Maggie, are you all right?"

"No," she sobbed, "I'm not."

The fragrance of mid-summer chicory and Queen Anne's lace had given way to the smells of rotting leaves and musty, wind-fallen apples as dead leaves blew in rolling hoops and blizzards of dried grasses drifted into barns and sheds. It was the hunting season, with mornings of opal woodsmoke haze, gleaming, frost-filmed thickets, and red-capped hunters trudging through rocky pastures and fields of scarlet sumac into nearby woods. All day long village folk and farmers heard the crack of rifles until late afternoon when the hunters rode into town with deer strapped to the fenders of their cars and pickup trucks, to record their kill at the Mobil station. Five weeks before, a hunter had found a decomposed body of a woman in a lonely ravine. It was a yearly occurrence and the reason that the three-man police force never began any missing-persons search in earnest until after November.

The news had percolated so quickly that by the next day everyone in a twenty-mile radius knew that the woman was wearing an apron with a packet of Burpee squash seeds in the pocket, just as they knew that Win Dyer paid $4.75 at a tag sale for a 1934 pop-up toaster, that the chicken pies at the Presbyterian church supper were made with too many vegetables, and that Alan Hatch hadn't left his widow as well fixed as he might have considering he was a bone doctor.

Maggie pedaled her three-speed Rudge to the lawyer's

office to find out how she was supposed to manage the rest of her life. Alan had always told her that he would take care of things. If what Woody said on the telephone was true, Alan had lied.

After spending the morning, like all mornings, in a sorrowful, lonely heap under the covers, she had finally pulled herself together into an old green sweater, tan corduroy pants worn to a shine at the knees and seat, a black oilskin jacket, and duck boots with orange laces over sockless feet because all her socks were in the laundry basket. Except for a few loose strands that whipped across her rimless glasses, her long red hair was stuffed into a tweed woolen cap.

It was an easy glide downhill and over the bridge past baskets of apples burnished by the pale November sun. Maggie squinted against the light and turned onto a dirt road, splashing through sodden leaves where the brook and road ran parallel. It was uphill for another mile, then down again, over a narrow, waving lane where a drooping harvest figure, turned soggy by chill rains, slouched against a tree trunk. Its pumpkin head was shrunken and collapsed, and the trace of a grotesque grimace lingered on its face. Leaves and straw poked out of the ragged, checkered shirt and the split seams of its pants. There seemed something indecent about its neglected chaff.

Maggie leaned her bicycle against the trunk of a maple, then shoved the figure beneath a mound of leaves. She had once made a harvest figure for Kristen, a green felt Big Bird with a Hermes scarf, a gift from Sybil, wound about its neck. Alan, who could reckon his family's community ties through six unpretentious Yankee generations, was angry when he saw the figure propped up on the porch glider with a wing around a cider jug. "You've got to stop being so competitive," he said. "Folks will think you're trying to outdo them." The next day someone had pulled out its stuffing, and Big Bird lay sprawled on the glider like a drunk.

When Maggie telephoned Sybil to complain that she

was still viewed as summer people even in her own house, her mother, who considered Vermont a rustic gulag, was no help. Sybil didn't believe in keeping a troubled marriage alive, but maintained a strict policy of pulling the plug when it was over. She advised Maggie to take Kristen and return to New York, and Maggie, who had seen three husbands go down the drain, including her own father, knew that Sybil practiced what she preached.

Maggie's recollections were interrupted by the mud-and-pebble spray from a speeding Chevy Nova with the red light of a volunteer fireman on its roof and a doe's head hanging out of its open trunk. Her glasses began to slip down her nose. She pushed them up with a spattered woolen fingertip and swallowed hard, while tears streamed down her face, then kicked the pumpkin head still showing beneath the leaves, astonished at how easily it fell apart and how good it felt to smash it with the toe of her boot.

Woody Pringle's law office, like most of the offices and shops in the village, was set inside a pale gray, mid-nineteenth-century turreted Victorian house that had a high-peaked roof and board-and-batten siding. By the time Maggie set her bicycle against the filigreed front porch and walked up the stone steps, her sockless feet were numb.

Woody wore an argyle sweater with a misplaced diamond in its weave that Maggie guessed his wife, Drew, had made. In his early forties, Woody's receding hairline fanned back over his forehead in a *V* to resemble the formations of Canadian geese that were honking their way south.

"You're late, Maggie," he said. "Why didn't you drive your car?" She started to tell him that she was out of antifreeze, but he kept on talking, telling her that Alan was too young to go. Then he straightened his bow tie, snapped a paper file together, and indicated for her to sit beside him on the sofa. "We were away that month," he added to explain why he hadn't been at the funeral.

"It's all right," she replied.

He patted her knee. "I knew you'd understand," he said. "I heard that Lester Perkins laid him out so lifelike he looked like he was sleeping." Then he advised her of a stronger need to economize, sprinkling caution with the aspergillum of his pen. "Are you listening, Maggie? I mean, you have to really dig in." Alan's estate, as he explained before, included a mortgaged house, a modest term-insurance policy, some money in trust for Kristen's education, social security benefits, and benefits for Kristen until the age of twenty-two, as long as she remained a full-time student. As Maggie also knew, Alan left to his brother, Owen, his half of the Morgan horse which they jointly owned, and left to his mother, Letitia, the cider press that Alan's grandfather had given to them when they were first married, since Maggie never seemed to have any interest in it.

She took off her cap and shook out her hair while he continued to explain that in his capacity as executor, he had been obliged to pay off certain outstanding debts other than the mortgage. The bottom line was that now she and Kristen would have slightly less than one quarter of Alan's former income to live on.

Maggie's idea of money was something that came and went but was always there, like electricity in a socket. Her attitude was formed by early experiences when her mother, Sybil, had been alternately lavish and strapped, depending on the wealth of her present husband. Birthday parties could range from hiring a troop of spangled acrobats who smelled of Ben Gay, to a subway ride to the zoo with a friend of her choice. After Maggie married, Alan, who reasoned that Sybil's cavalier attitude had left its mark, decided what they could and could not afford, and engaged the hospital bookkeeper to balance their personal checkbook. Maggie did not mind. It let her off a hook of debits and credits, one of the more tedious aspects of becoming a wife.

"Did he really write that?" she asked. "About the cider press?"

Woody ignored the question and began to address her in slow, measured syllables and dependent clauses, as he did anyone who was not getting the message. She needed to assess her expenditures, then draw up a budget. She had to realize that entertainment, except for an occasional movie, was beyond her means. Things like lift tickets, trips of any significance, and country club memberships were out of the question. And if she hadn't already done so, she would have to sell one car in order to reduce her insurance payments.

"I know one thing," she said. "I'm not selling the house. No matter what."

He smiled, as he would at a child. She might be able to keep it with certain privations and the strictest budgeting, but he advised against it. He tried to imagine her red hair spread out over a pillow; she, grateful but not demanding. Then he blinked his eyes as if to erase the thought. He had seen clients suckered by pity into a go-nowhere relationship. If he had any inclination towards an extra monthly mortgage payment, it would be for a twenty-five-year-old in another county, not for a woman close to forty and to home. "The bottom line," he said again, "is that you and Kristen can get by, it's done all the time, but you have to economize." He rested his chin in his hands. "This seems to come as a surprise, Maggie. Didn't you and Alan discuss eventualities?"

They had talked about a lot of things in the bathroom while she was showering and he was shaving, in the bedroom under the Lone Star quilt, and in the M.G. on their rides to New York to visit Sybil. They discussed how far Kristen had gone with Ranger; Sybil's newest husband, a furrier from Manhasset who specialized in lining raincoats with his clients' outmoded minks; a chain saw that Alan wanted; the chipmunks eating all the grass seed; Alan's chances for a faculty appointment; and the dirt in the carburetor that was causing the M.G. to stall. Nobody ever mentioned anything about anybody dying.

Maggie shook her head.

"Maybe you ought to think about getting a job," he said. "Nothing fancy. Just something to give you spending money."

Doing what? she wondered. They lived in a small village, surrounded by other small villages, where most businesses were shoestring and family-run, which limited employment to selling lift tickets, or, if one was perky and aggressive, to hustling real estate. Maggie had never worked. Despite a weekly lecture in chapel about Smith students leaving to marry before obtaining a degree and taking the places of those with a serious commitment, she had married Alan in her junior year while he was a first-year resident at Yale-New Haven. When they returned to Vermont, Alan made it clear that he did not want her to work. None of the wives of his friends worked, except for Pam Daley, and that was only because her husband owned the inn, which meant that Pam's basic role of helpmate had not been altered.

"Like what?" she asked.

"Have you thought about selling Avon or Tupperware? I know a gal who does real well with Tupperware. Especially after they came out with snap-on lids."

Maggie wanted to unravel his sweater. She shook her head and stuffed her hair back into her woolen hat.

"I have another idea," he said. "The city folks next door to us are looking for a house sitter. Someone to take care of their plants, feed their dog, check the house for leaks. With Kristen away, it might be just the thing. Of course, it's only three or four times a year."

"I have my own house to look after," she said, pulling on her oilskin jacket.

He drummed his fingers and then pushed back from the desk. "Don't close your mind off, Maggie. I'm trying to help you. Your best bet is Tupperware. Check it out." He closed the file and Maggie stood to leave. "By the way, was Alan playing singles or doubles?"

"He was tying his sneakers."

Woody opened the double oak doors. "Time will heal, Maggie," he said.

I can't wait, she thought as she left. It hurts too much now. His last question had pulled off the lid from a memory that she had bottled, of standing outside the cubicle in the emergency room, trying to get up the courage to push aside the curtain until Anne's husband, Peter, took her elbow and led her in. She saw Alan still in his tennis clothes, his left side streaked with crumbled clay, his left knee scraped, his skin still warm. Of rubbing his leg as if it were tarnished and calling his name, and hearing Peter say, "He's gone, Maggie. He was gone when we brought him in."

She remembered, too, wondering who would fix the tattered canopy hanging over their four-poster bed that they had jarred loose that morning with their lovemaking, then suddenly shivering in an icy coldness in which there was no feeling at all.

When Maggie picked up her bike, she was angry at Woody for his condescension. She had been an art history major, for God's sake. She had memorized over two thousand slides and still remembered most of them, including the one that everyone else had thought was the Parthenon but what was really Hephaestus Temple. The difference was in the number of columns, which she was the only one to notice. She was angry at Alan for leaving her with no warning, no advice, no cushion, and much too soon. How could you? she thought.

The Chevy Nova with the red light on its roof was parked on the side of the Mobil station. Dried blood spattered the Massachusetts plate. A middle-aged man with his hair brushed straight back and his teenage son, who looked just like his father except for a leaner, bonier face, stood talking to the station owner. The older man was saying that the year before he had taken a buck weighing two hundred and twenty pounds. "Belly full of corn," he said. "I dressed him myself."

The station owner, whose name was Schuyler, pulled a tick from the hide of the doe with a tweezers. "Did you mount the head?" he asked.

"No, but I sold the rack to some guy for a hundred dollars."

Maggie pulled a bottle of antifreeze from the rack and put it in the basket of her bicycle, then turned to the father and son. "You splashed me with mud," she said, her voice trembling. "Why don't you watch where you're going?"

The three men glanced at one another in a fleeting exchange, a wingbeat of shared understanding that women often behaved in ways which could not be accounted for. "You have the wrong person, ma'am," said the older man. "I never would have splashed a pretty lady."

"It was you, all right. I recognize your trunk."

Schuyler dropped the tick into a specimen jar and wiped the tweezers on his overalls. He spoke gently. "They're not from around here, Maggie. Might be they got lost coming out of the woods, and weren't paying particular attention."

Maggie handed him a credit card. He handed it back apologetically. "I can't take this."

"Why not?" she asked.

"It's in Alan's name. The company won't honor it anymore. It's policy, Maggie. There's nothing I can do."

Maggie reached in the pocket of her oilskin jacket and handed him crumpled dollar bills. "I don't know why you're weighing that little thing anyway. I'd be ashamed to report it." She wiped her eyes with the back of her woolen glove, resettled her glasses, and pedaled away.

It was dusk when she reached the shortcut past the old, neglected cottage that had fallen into its cellar. The foundation and the remains of a chimney were covered over with berry bushes. Kristen had fallen through the untended hedge when she was five, the year Maggie taught her to ice skate by dragging her around the pond with a broom handle. It was also when she taught Kristen to make snow angels by falling backward into soft, spongy drifts, to cut open an apple and find a star, to slide in rainy weather down the ironing board. Kristen thought Maggie knew everything then. Maggie had called the owner of the property to upbraid him for his carelessness. Alan's mother, Letitia, in turn called to upbraid her. "Nathan would have been glad to fence it off for you, Margaret, but not the way you asked. You can't demand things in Vermont. I thought you understood by now how to deal with our people."

Maggie wheeled her bicycle to the garage, through drooping sunflower stalks that some woodchuck had eaten the tops off weeks ago, and picked up the mail. There were a few bills, a postcard that announced that the Jazzercise class would be held in the basement of the Episcopal church, letters of condolence (she was surprised that they were still coming in and that some had dropped the Mrs. from her name), Peter Bouchard's business card with a note scribbled in the corner that he would be by in a few days, medical journals addressed to Alan, nothing from Kristen, and a manila envelope.

She bolted into the center hall colonial with the old, uneven split-log floorboards, and slammed the door behind her, seeking sanctuary beneath the hand-hewn ceiling beams and refuge beside the French military prints hanging on the blue-stained, knotted pine wall.

Before she opened the manila envelope, she stacked Alan's medical journals on a cherry desk that they had bought at auction the year before. The envelope contained a summons from the sheriff's office for jury duty, notifying her to appear at the Superior Court. She had ten days in which to respond.

Maggie considered jury service an act of a good citizen like voting or paying taxes but not now, not when she had to drag herself out of bed wrapped naked in the Lone Star like an Indian, when she still cried at the drop of a hat. Her sister-in-law, Jenna, who understood the proprieties of any situation, would know what to do.

Maggie placed the summons in a cubbyhole of the desk and sat down to write a hasty, angry letter to Kristen about not receiving any mail or phone calls, and about pulling away just when Maggie needed her the most. Kristen would most likely respond with the annoyance she reserved for the cloying. Except for an occasional lapse, she was like Alan in that regard, clear-sighted, collected, and unemotional. Maggie put the stamped letter beneath the summons.

If Woody was right, things were much worse than she had thought. Maggie wondered if that was the only reason she felt so angry. Resentment was a handicap, like trying to swim in ski boots. Grief was all she could handle, not that she was doing so well in that department. For some reason, she felt especially resentful toward Sybil. Every time they spoke on the telephone, Maggie found herself recounting Sybil's sins, going as far back as kindergarten when Maggie, hobbled in snowsuit and mittens, had sat through endless afternoons waiting to be picked up. As far as Maggie was concerned, Sybil was still committing misdemeanors, like the other day when she had thoughtlessly compared Alan to her own husbands, especially to the most recent, whose oversupply of raincoats had threatened his cash flow. "At least you could always count on Alan," Sybil had said. "Alan was dependable."

He left me without a note, thought Maggie. That's not dependable. She ran upstairs to sprawl like a starfish under the asylum of the broken canopy and to cry into her lumpy down pillow, which was still sodden from the morning.

CHAPTER 2

Voir Dire

PETER STOPPED ON HIS way home from his office as he had said he would. When he showed up carrying his toolbox, Maggie was in the kitchen wearing her dingy chenille robe faded from a navy to an iron, machinist blue, painstakingly cleaning the filter of Alan's aquarium with Q-Tips the way he used to do. She was trying to decide whether a fish that looked pregnant should be screened off or strained out.

He reached a hand out to rumple her hair. "How's it going, Mag?"

Maggie pulled up the corners of her mouth the way she had learned to do in the past few months, as if tightening a drawstring. "I'm okay," she replied.

Peter had not been fooled. "You don't look okay."

He and Anne had done so much, especially in the first few weeks when Maggie had wandered like a dreamer through her doorways, finding herself suddenly in the center hall, or the summer kitchen, or even kneeling in the unfinished rock garden that she and Alan had started that spring. They had installed extra locks on her doors and a timer to control the yard lights. They brought brandy into the sanctum of her darkened widow's bedroom, answered telephone calls, filled her refrigerator with casseroles and Jell-O molds, and helped her search for the mound of bankbooks, deeds, car titles, tax returns, W-2 forms, social security cards, military-discharge papers, insurance policies, birth certificates, and death certificate that had to be collected before even a modest estate was settled.

"Can you give me a job?" she asked.

"Be serious, Mag." Then he insisted, with his characteristic crooked smile, that there must be something in the house that needed fixing. He was right. Everything needed repair, including a leaky kitchen faucet, fluorescent kitchen bulbs that flickered, a washing machine that would not go into the spin cycle, and Alan's twenty-year-old M.G. that continued to drip oil all over the garage.

Maggie said the toolbox wasn't necessary, and that, except for his clothes, Alan's things were intact, just as he left them. Peter said something cryptic. "I'm counting on that, Maggie." Then he went directly to the faucet, on his way brushing against her breasts. The aisle was narrow. Maggie assumed the brush was accidental.

Peter adjusted the faucet with the cool efficiency of a builder skilled in the crafts of his subcontractors: a turn here, a twist there, a quick look at fittings, a well-considered "that ought to do it." Then suddenly, with no warning, he put down his toolbox, wiped his hands on his jeans, and grabbed her, pressing her tightly against the sink, and slipped his hands inside her robe with the same sureness he worked the Allen wrench.

Maggie had been immobilized, feeling his fingertips circle her nipples in suspended detachment, as if the assault were happening to someone else, or even more removed, as if it were not an assault at all but something to be gotten over with, like a clinical palpation with a uniformed nurse standing by to insure neutrality. In twenty years of marriage, except for Woody Pringle's older brother's antiquated dips and the half-intentioned now-you-see-em, now-you-don't banter of the safely married, no one had ever come on to her, other than a tourist from Quebec who was looking for a bed-and-breakfast, nor had she ever made moves in the other direction. She was as astonished by his ardent blitzkrieg as she had been at the age of ten when she happened on Sybil lolling in bed in reckless, maraboued abandon with some leggy, skinny man who hovered above her like a praying mantis.

"Lighten up," he said, burying his face in her neck, "you're as stiff as a board." He cupped her buttocks in his hands as if weighing them. "Nice," he said. "Very nice." When he pushed his knee between her legs and whispered, "Come on, Maggie, I've been getting your message for weeks, don't change your mind now," she struggled to wriggle loose, causing her hair, which had been twisted in a careless knot, to come tumbling down and her glasses to fall to the slate floor. It was not so much his actions that jarred her into rebellion as his patter. Alan seldom spoke when making love.

"Are you crazy?" she asked, scrambling on her knees for her glasses. "I hope my glasses aren't broken."

"You'll learn," he said coolly, with the tone of one who had been deeply offended, "that you can't come on to guys and then back off. That might have been okay when you were a teeny-bopper but not any more. Not today. The odds have changed. There are hundreds like you and no takers. You're going to find that out soon enough. I was here to help, Maggie. In every way. As a friend. Remember that." Then he turned to leave. Maggie ran after him with his toolbox, clutching her open robe together with her other hand. He took the toolbox and stalked off in self-righteous indignation.

"What about the timer?" she asked. He didn't reply.

The lemon-scented courtroom was paneled in linenfold. Shafts of silver light came in through the window. Outside, a freezing rain coated the twigs and alder tassels, and caused the maples to shine like satin. Maggie sat in the empty courtroom, clutching the jury summons while she reviewed the events of the night before step by step, like advancing slides on a carousel, trying to figure out what she had done wrong.

She looked with dismay at the spindled summons in her hand. She hadn't meant to roll it and now she tried to press it flat against her gray flannel skirt. Her sister-in-law, Jenna, assured her that Judge Atwill would dismiss her from jury duty. All she had to say was that she was still in mourning and she would be automatically excused. Maggie was relieved. Decisions like whether to throw out the toaster or to have it repaired, much less those affecting the life of another human being, seemed overwhelming without Alan's advice.

Maggie turned to glance at the clock on the wall and at the second hand that staggered around its face. It was almost nine. After she was excused from jury duty, she would call Jenna and tell her what happened in the kitchen with Peter. Maybe she could sort it out. Then Maggie thought of her forthright sister-in-law and decided against it. Jenna would insist that she tell Anne. Jenna also would say that if Maggie had sold the house, as she and Owen had urged, Maggie would be living rent-free in an apartment over Letitia's garage, and none of this would have happened. It was difficult for no-nonsense Jenna to understand that the house, where she still heard Alan's key in the lock and his footsteps at the door, was Maggie's anchor.

The wood-paneled chamber began to fill rapidly with prospective jurors in mackinaws and down-filled jackets who scurried from the corridor. A few looked familiar. Maggie's heart beat faster. She wished that she were home, this minute enveloped in Alan's old green plaid flannel shirt that still bore his smell, the only piece of his clothing that she hadn't given away.

The prosecutor briskly entered the courtroom carrying a cordovan briefcase which had been buffed by use to a deep maroon. Maggie had seen him a few times at the club. She didn't know very much about him except they said that he carried old, worn golf clubs scripted with names like niblick and mashie that had belonged to his grandfather, and that he had no waggle when he swung, which Alan said proved the man was not only a tightwad but tight-assed as well. He opened his briefcase on a table next to the jury box, took out a yellow legal pad, then turned to give Maggie a steady, measured gaze, which was less a look of recognition than of assessment. With shining steel-threaded hair and gleaming white collar slick with starch, he seemed packaged in cellophane, as glossy as his briefcase. Maggie's cheeks flame-stitched from the unwanted attention. She looked away, hoping he would do the same.

The fault last night had been hers. Even though Peter had seen her often in sloppy dishabille, it was different now. She wasn't Alan's wife, she was his widow. Somehow, without meaning to, with her glasses on and no makeup, in her ratty, faded chenille robe, she had given Peter a message. Forget that she was forty and the widow of his best friend, the signal was as clear as crossing her legs too high, or leaving too many buttons opened on a blouse.

Satisfied with her conclusion, Maggie pulled into herself, trying to put thoughts of last night out of her mind and planning what she was going to say to the judge. She had forgotten to bring Alan's death certificate. What if the judge didn't believe her? People began to whisper behind her in a susurrus of speculation that rustled to the ceiling beams. Someone said they heard from the guard in the hall that it was a murder trial. Someone else said the trial might take weeks, perhaps months. They might even have to stay overnight.

The whispering stopped as if someone had caught it in a bag. Maggie looked up. A rumpled man who seemed to be the defense attorney, as disheveled as an unmade bed with his tie flipped back over his collar, led a young girl by the elbow to a seat at a table on the other side of the judge's bench. Maggie judged the girl to be in her early teens. Somebody's child. What was she doing there? The girl was dressed inappropriately for November in a cotton dress with an uneven hem, a cardigan sweater that was sizes too big, gladiator sandals over hot pink socks, and her long blonde hair pulled into a ponytail and cradled in a banana comb. She sat down and folded her small, dimpled hands on the table. Her face was heart-shaped, tender, with plump, shiny cheeks and a softly rounded chin. When the defense attorney sat down beside her and rested his hand lightly on her shoulder, someone muttered that he could talk the handle off a pump.

Maggie thought of Kristen and felt the old tug. She supposed she would always feel it. It was visceral. Where? Heartstrings? No such place. A romantic idea. Phantom sensations at the site of the old umbilical attachment? The cord had been severed. She had seen it herself, lying like an old telephone cable, yet she felt as connected. Kristen did not suffer from any such impediment of bondage. Maggie and Kristen had argued over the telephone the night before. Kristen acknowledged receipt of Maggie's forlorn letter and complained that her mother was piling on guilt unfairly. Then she said that she needed a car and that Alan would have wanted her to have the M.G. When Maggie said that they couldn't afford to keep it, primarily because of the insurance, Kristen announced that she didn't intend to have an accident and that she knew someone who could repair it for practically nothing. The conversation ended badly: Maggie waiting for her daughter to tell her that she was homesick, while Kristen, mumbling first to someone with her hand over the receiver, said she had to run.

A court officer, wearing her eyeglasses slung on a ribbon, banged the gavel and instructed everyone to rise as the black-robed judge mounted the steps to her bench. Then Judge Janet Atwill, assigned to one of the few homicides on the docket, addressed the panel in the concerned but friendly tones of a high school principal. She told them that the defendant, Melody Jessica Bean, had been charged with murder in the first degree of her mother, Joyce Hibbert Bean. She said this with gravity yet with detachment, as if she were announcing that the junior boys, because of their carelessness, were no longer allowed access to the basketball court. There was a collective intake of breath. She added that although Melody was fifteen, it was the judgment of the court that the protection of the community was best served by trying her in a court of criminal jurisdiction. Maggie looked at the girl fixing her banana comb and wondered how it was possible that she could have hurt a puppy, much less her own mother. She looked cherubic, her pouting lips reminiscent of a baby's.

The defense lawyer whispered something to his client. Melody Jessica Bean spat her chewing gum into her fingers and looked up at the ceiling. When she thought no one was looking, she stuck the wad of chewing gum under the table.

Judge Atwill went on to explain about challenges for cause, and peremptory challenges, forcing eye contact when she thought a panelist was not paying attention, as if to say, This is going to be on the test. "We are about to begin a criminal trial," she said, "in which the prosecutor or defense lawyer may object to the seating of a potential juror. If you are excused, you should not take it personally. It only means that for one reason or another, you were not considered right for this particular trial." She called for excuses and a microphone on a long cord was brought to the balustrade.

Several people stood, including Maggie, some with doctors' notes in their hands. A woman who said she was the prosecutor's second cousin once removed on his mother's side was excused, but a man who identified himself as a ski instructor was not. "This is the beginning of my season," he said with petulance and then added lamely, "The mountain has two feet of snow." The judge replied that there were enough ski instructors to meet the needs of the slopes. A man wearing an intricately cabled sweater, whom Maggie recognized as an auctioneer named Hobart Straw, known for getting flatlanders to bid against themselves, announced that he had been the victim of a crime. His request for dismissal was denied when the judge, who asked the nature of his crime, learned that a vandal had scored his station wagon with a key.

Maggie's knees trembled. She had put her hair up. Now it wisped, defeated, about her face. She tried to tuck a few strands behind her ears. The judge seemed impatient. "Speak up," she said.

Maggie wondered if she could get electrocuted holding a microphone with sweating hands. She wiped them on the sides of her woolen skirt, then cleared her throat, hoping she wouldn't make a fool of herself. "I'm recently widowed." It came out as a bleat.

The judge leaned back in her chair and stared at the ceiling like a visionary. Little lines cornered her eyes like quotation marks. "How recently?"

"Four months."

"Do you believe that your loss would make you unable to render a fair verdict?"

Maggie had not anticipated questions. Jenna said it would be easy, her dismissal perfunctory. "I want to do my duty, Your Honor, but I don't think I could do a good job." Her voice started to crack. Why now did she have to fall apart, in front of all these strangers, when for weeks she had kept a stiff upper lip and her shoulders squared, when she had been a good scout?

"Does your grief keep you from normal function?" Judge Atwill persisted, as one used to getting to the bottom of things.

All eyes were on Maggie. No one she knew would ask such a question, much less expect her to answer it. Maggie thought about her reply. She couldn't think straight or concentrate: she was afraid to go out, and she still reached for Alan in the middle of the night. Was that grief? More important, was it normal? "I don't know how to answer that, Your Honor."

"I'll try to be more specific." Judge Atwill sat upright and leaned forward. Maggie saw that she wore a plum-colored lipstick. "Do you go about in your community? Do you keep abreast of current events?"

Last week Maggie had found herself huddled in the doorway of the post office. Yes, she went out, but she was not connected. That was the problem. Alan had been her connection. Marriage had been her connection. But both had been severed. She learned current events through the capillary action of gossip: who had been arrested for drunk driving, who was getting dotty and had to be watched, the real reason the town decided not to open the skating rink, or that the six-couple Potluck Supper Club was going to drop her from its membership.

"I'm in touch, Your Honor."

Judge Atwill made a tent of her hands. "I sympathize with your loss," she said. "If it had been a matter of a few weeks, I certainly would have excused you. But I'm of the opinion that after four months, it's time to join the living. Your community needs you. Please take your seat."

Maggie looked in alarm from face to face—the clerk, the judge, the attorneys, the defendant still fixing her banana comb—waiting for someone to say that a mistake had been made, that she wasn't supposed to be standing in front of all these people, that she was supposed to be home, where she could breathe her grief in privacy. Under the scrutiny of both attorneys, she filed into the jury box between a black electronic technician from IBM and a woman she recognized as a teller from the bank, remembering that she had forgotten to strain out Alan's pregnant guppy, and that Letitia was coming over that afternoon to look at the cider press.

The judge asked if anyone was related to the defendant. Had they formed an opinion about the defendant's guilt or innocence? Were they members of any law-enforcement agency? A man in a down jacket who identified himself as a fire warden was asked to stand down. A curly haired journeyman carpenter, who answered to his number as if he had won at bingo, was put in the warden's place.

The prosecutor stood. Maggie saw that his light blue tie matched his eyes and wondered if he had selected it for that reason. He identified himself as Jim McKeen, the state's attorney, scanned the jury one by one, then read off a list of those who might testify or be mentioned in the course of the trial. A garage mechanic seated in the back row of the jury box said that his brother's name was on the list. The mechanic was excused and a retired army colonel put in his place.

McKeen was very polite, almost diffident. Armed with facts on every member of the panel, he questioned the jurors at random, looking for any bias or predisposition of personality that might prejudice them toward his case. A woman who described herself as a potter was asked if she had read or heard anything prior to coming to court. When she acknowledged that she had, he asked if what she had heard or read would influence her decision. She said she didn't know.

The judge interrupted, leaning over to scrutinize this panelist as far as her bench would allow. "Do you mean to say that if I instruct you to decide this case solely on the evidence, you wouldn't be able to follow my instructions?" The potter said she guessed so.

The prosecutor questioned a photographer by first asserting that it was the state's belief that society needed protection from Melody Jessica Bean—to whom he pointed—just as it did from her adult counterpart. Then he asked the photographer, a man with unsmiling eyes, whether the defendant's age would make him unable to reach a verdict which might carry a life sentence. The photographer said he wouldn't let the defendant's age influence him one way or another.

Already aware that Maggie was a doctor's widow with a seventeen-year-old daughter, he asked if she had children at home. She told him that she had a daughter who was a freshman at Smith. He asked if her late husband was the sort of man that valued law and order.

Alan might have valued it, she thought, but he did not contribute to it, leaving glass rings and dropping socks like spoor all over the house. She said he was. He said he imagined she shared her late husband's views, then asked if she felt that people should be accountable for their actions. She said she did.

"Mrs. Hatch," he said, "I have the impression that you are a private person, one that I might call even reticent." Maggie did not like the tone of reticence. It sounded wimpy. There was no point in arguing. She nodded. "Do you believe that you can try this case without fear of criticism by friends who may disagree with the verdict?"

Maggie thought of the constant scrutiny she had lived under since she married Alan, a subtle community monitoring that had shaped her actions and the actions of everyone she knew, except for town crazies like Indian Eddy, who hung out at the bus stop giving out arrows. It was a simple barter. The town exacted proscribed behavior in exchange for acceptance and, for families who settled prior to Andrew Jackson's defeat of John Quincy Adams, unqualified inclusion. With Alan gone, her motive for compliance seemed diminished. She answered yes.

His voice became low, supportive. "Do you feel sufficiently confident to stand by your opinion based solely on logic and not be swayed by your own feelings of sympathy?"

He was giving her a subtle message: I like you, I want you on the jury, but first you have to give me some assurances. He was coaching her like the tennis pro—I will put you on the B team, Maggie, if you promise to come close to the net and stand your ground. "Yes," she replied.

"Juror number two passed for cause."

As the clerk tossed the cardboard and pizza crust debris of their box lunches into a green plastic bag, the defense attorney stood, riffling through the pages of his legal pad like a dog pawing after a bone. He was not satisfied with his preparation. He never was. There was always the niggling, unanswered, embarrassing question, the loose end, the opened gate, the unzipped pants, ready to undo the most carefully laid defense. He had known the prosecutor long enough to know that McKeen tolerated certain crimes but hated others. Abusing a dead body was one of the latter. The prosecutor had initially agreed to a plea bargain in a package deal in which they would settle three cases at once, but changed his mind when the coroner's office told him that they had evidence that someone had jumped up and down on the body of the murder victim. The defense attorney's hand remained on the shoulder of the girl.

"Ladies and gentlemen of this prospective jury, my name is Dan Giotti, and this is my client, Melody Jessica Bean, who I will be defending in this trial. My first duty to Miss Bean is to select the most impartial jury possible, one that will presume her innocence. To do that, I need to find out more about you."

Melody Jessica Bean peeled off her fingernail polish. She did it methodically, carefully, pushing slowly from the cuticle until it came off in sparkling purple petals. She arranged these in a semicircle while her attorney interviewed the bank teller with questions that glossed over such tedium of her life as her job description. Then, slipping deeper beneath the surface, he said he understood that on occasion her mother received instructions in the form of revelations. He treated this disclosure with respectful gravity and asked if these instructions ever conflicted with her usual habits. She said never.

He moved in closer. "Do you agree with the standard in criminal law that in order to convict someone of a crime a person must be determined guilty beyond a reasonable doubt?" Of course, she said. He asked that if the state could not prove their case beyond a reasonable doubt and her mother received a message that told her that his client was guilty, which would she believe? It would be no conflict, she replied. They had been instructed not to discuss the trial with anyone. She took that to include her mother.

Giotti turned to the ski instructor and asked if he believed someone could be provoked to commit a violent act. The ski instructor said no. Then Giotti smiled over his shoulder at a retired librarian with cheeks as soft as dough, and asked if she believed there were circumstances under which people commit acts for which they should not be held accountable. Hannah Watson paused before answering yes. He turned like a dancer and stepped closer to the balustrade, speaking as he walked.

"Do you feel, Miss Watson, that a person is responsible for a crime even though, due to his or her mental condition, he or she could not meaningfully or maturely reflect upon his act?"

No, she replied. It was Maggie's turn. Giotti sympathized with her loss, then decided that this was as good a place as any to prepare the jury for the testimony of the girl's boyfriend, who had turned state's evidence. "Mrs. Hatch," he said, looking directly into her eyes, "do you understand the meaning of the word 'accomplice'?" She said yes. "The testimony of an accomplice is regarded in law as testimony from a tainted source. Do you promise to scrutinize any such evidence with caution?" She said she would.

"Speak up, Mrs. Hatch," said the judge. "None of this is adversarial. We're all here for the same purpose and we have to be able to hear you."

Giotti checked his pad. "If you were to find that you were one of a minority, or the only juror who believed that the prosecution had not established every element of its case beyond a reasonable doubt, would you change your vote because you were in the minority?"

Maggie was already in a minority. She was a widow. "No."

The questioning reminded her of a consciousness-raising group she had gone to at Smith with another student named Lila, who wore homespun ponchos. Lila tearfully confessed to needing a man's approval. That satisfied the group, which took turns rocking her in its collective khaki bosom, until they moved in on Maggie, accusing her of wearing a badge of bondage in the circle pin which she wore on her white Macmullen blouse. Maggie had wanted to run out, as she did now, afraid of her answers, afraid of their questions. She never went back. Nothing changed except she put her circle pin in the keepsake box in the attic, along with a ticket stub to see Peter, Paul, and Mary at the Yale Bowl, and a picture of her father leaning against the rigging of a forty-foot Bertram.

"The prosecution will bring in witnesses who will testify against my client, Melody Jessica Bean. Have you ever thought you recognized someone and later found out you were mistaken?"

"Yes." The week before she had chased a man down the detergent aisle of the supermarket because he had looked like Alan from the back, had even moved like him, executing a nimble dive into the meat counter for a package of ground round. When he turned around, she saw that he looked nothing like Alan. She ran out, leaving her groceries still in the cart.

He dropped his voice to a sympathetic whisper. "What was the cause of your late husband's death?"

"Cerebral aneurysm." Like a blowout on a tire was the explanation of his associate. No one could have predicted it.

Giotti came within inches of her face. She could smell his toothpaste, and thought it was the kind with gel in the middle. "Do you believe you could be fundamentally fair to my client?"

She had tried so desperately to get out of jury duty, now suddenly, perversely, she wanted to be selected, to prove that she had not been blown out by an aneurysm along with anyone else. She wanted to be legitimized by a man who couldn't keep his tie straight. "Yes," she replied.

Giotti made a rapid evaluation. Women as a rule were

more sympathetic on a jury, usually because criminal defendants were most often male. This woman's widowhood might make her even more so. Yet the fact that she was the mother of a seventeen-year-old girl might prejudice her against his client. It was a calculated risk. He decided he would rather have her on the jury than the retired army colonel. He turned on his heel, causing his tie to flip back onto his shirt. "This juror is acceptable," he said.

Both attorneys faced the jury box, alternately excusing jurors for no reason that Maggie could detect other than there was something about the juror's appearance that they didn't like. The prosecutor excused the student, who went flying out of the box, leaving her book behind her on the seat. The defense attorney excused the ski instructor. The prosecutor excused the bartender. The defense attorney excused the insurance agent. The prosecutor excused the potter. The defense attorney excused the retired army colonel. It was a chess game. They were pulling off each other's pieces. Maggie resettled her glasses over her ears.

Replacements were made, alternates selected, and it was over. The jurors were given an oath in which they solemnly swore to well and truly try, and true deliverance make, between the state of Vermont and the prisoner at the bar. For one forgetful moment Maggie wondered what Alan would say when she told him that she had been selected for jury duty.

The defense attorney guided his client out of the courtroom. From somewhere she had gotten more gum. Maggie watched her button her cardigan sweater over her thin cotton dress. She had no hat or coat, no gloves. Melody Jessica, she thought, did you do in the one person who would have told you to dress warmly?

When Maggie returned home it was late afternoon. Bare branches etched against the pewter sky. Mike, the handyman, was in the driveway hammering in red snow markers at the corners of the driveway to guide the snowplow. His sandy hair bristled over his shiny scalp.

"I hear you're on a jury," he said. "Is it the kid who killed her mother?"

"I can't discuss the trial," she said.

Chastened, defiant, he smiled and leaned on his shovel. "The chipmunks have been at your bulbs again."

That had seemed so important in the spring. They wasted all May discussing whether to sprinkle dried blood on the soil to discourage the rodents from eating the grass seed, and spent all June sprinkling. Despite four ten-pound sacks of dessicated cow blood, the chipmunks thrived. Alan accepted defeat. "It's a fact of life, Mag," he had said. "This is their territory as much as ours." She had been annoyed at his indifference. Now it didn't matter. She choked back her tears.

Mike seemed mollified by her puddled eyes. "The hardware store has a plastic owl," he said. "Real lifelike. Chipmunks are afraid of owls. I could hammer it up."

"I don't think so," she said. It was time to tell him. "I can't pay you anymore."

He continued to pound a stake with the back of his shovel. "I thought maybe with the doc's insurance and all . . ."

"It's not enough," she said. "I can't afford a yardman. Maybe from time to time. But not steady, I'm sorry."

"I'll finish posting your driveway all the same."

"I appreciate that," she said. She was at the door to the summer kitchen. "Mike, do you know how to set a timer?"

"Don't know right off, probably tells you right on the box."

"I don't have the box," she said.

"That's too bad," he replied. "You always need to save the box."

Maggie yanked open the door. It usually worked hard, but this time it opened easily. She must have left it unlocked. "Some guy was here with your brother-in-law," he called. "The fellow carried a briefcase."

She stepped into the summer kitchen, where the boards had been the most uneven, making the narrow room seem like a listing ship, and pulled off her boots. Owen, now working in the mail-order division of a fly-rod company, must have brought an appraiser, even though she told him not to. That was typical of Owen, who considered her a tenant in his younger brother's house.

"You have to conserve your assets," he had said, speaking with Letitia's clamped lips. "The carrying costs will eat you up."

Maggie, who had spent the last two days huddled in a wing chair with a calculator, disagreed. "I don't have to sell the house, Owen," she said. "I figured out that I can manage the mortgage payments if I cut down on the maintenance."

Owen spoke bluntly. "It isn't just the mortgage and the taxes or even the maintenance," he replied. "It's the size. Face facts, Maggie. You don't need that kind of space anymore."

She would have known without Mike's disclosure that Owen had brought someone in, the way anyone knows when a stranger has entered the house: a chair angled the wrong way, a rug curled at its corner, the smell of unfamiliar nostrums invading the privy nooks and crannies where one keeps shopping lists and string.

Maggie straightened the hooked rug with its faded, worn scene of an ice skater on double-edged skates. She also ignored the canvas she had found in a tag sale a week before Alan died, an early, primitive piece of a young boy with a rooster by an artist with a poor regard for perspective. She had been filling in the gouges with paint laid by knife edge like a trowel, a technique of restoration she had learned at Smith from a graduate student who worked at the art museum. Maggie usually lost interest after the first few minutes, and the painting became something she alternately picked up and set down, like the phone bill or a toothbrush, or anything in the house that she didn't have the energy to complete.

She went to change the charcoal of the fish tank filter, a task that required little skill. The house seemed large and empty. She wondered how much it was worth. The fish that had been pregnant was sleek and swimming, its pendulous belly emptied while the other fish darted about, gobbling babies the size of commas. She picked up the tiny net that hung over the rim of the tank and tried to catch the few that remained, but they were too small and her glasses were smudged. Maggie sadly put down the net. The fish were Alan's. She had let him down.

"As long as you were here, Owen," she said, "you might have fished out the babies."

Maggie thought about calling Anne to tell her she was on jury duty, then decided it was too close to the time Peter would be home and she had no interest in speaking to him. She took off her clothes and dropped them on the way upstairs—a recent habit—then went into the bathroom with the old clawfoot tub to take Alan's flannel shirt from the hook.

She and Alan were going to tile the bathroom themselves. They had gotten as far as buying the mastic, bringing home a color chart, and then they had squabbled over the color. Alan wanted mint green. Maggie said they had to choose colonial colors. Alan said it didn't matter since the colonists didn't tile their baths. She lost the argument. Alan usually had the final word, primarily because they both were in agreement that his was the sensible word.

Maggie now began to cry, suddenly, without warning. She grabbed the sink. Why did you leave me? she sobbed. Why? Why? The scab was off again. It would never heal.

When she picked up her head, the person that looked back from the mirror had a red nose, swollen eyes, and a face streaked with tears. Maggie looked hardest at her body. When she had been first married, nothing moved. After twenty years she had softened up, like butter left too long on the counter. If this kept up, she would melt.

"Margaret, are you upstairs?"

Letitia. She had forgotten all about her. Maggie buttoned the flannel shirt, pulled on the pair of jeans that hung over the doorknob, and ran out. "I'll be right down," she shouted.

Maggie found her mother-in-law squaring off Alan's medical journals with the palms of her hands. They faced each other warily, as adversaries who had never stepped into the ring, but who had railed against each other for the press.

"Owen was here," said Maggie.

"I know," said Letitia. "I hear you've been picked for jury duty. Didn't you explain your circumstances?"

"Yes," said Maggie.

"You must not have explained it well enough. It's time we talked, Margaret." She moved toward the cabbage-rose-printed sofa.

Maggie stood where she was. The bad news, criticism, or whatever it was on Letitia's mind, would be dispatched more quickly if they didn't sit. Letitia turned to face her head-on. "It's probably as good a time as any to tell you that a few years before he died, Alan borrowed money from me."

"How much money?"

"A goodly sum. Thirty thousand dollars, to be exact. To make some repairs on the house, to finish his office."

Maggie's heart began to hammer in her chest. "He never told me about borrowing money."

"Most men don't discuss those things with their wives."

"Why didn't I find any papers about it?"

Letitia's face crusted. The question corroborated her evaluation of her daughter-in-law's ancestral stock, which included the double helix of an investment banker father who traded on inside information and a mother who changed husbands the way other women changed slipcovers. "There are no papers between mother and son. It was a verbal arrangement. The situation is simply that I need the money. There is only one way for me to recover it."

The implication that the house had to be sold was clear. "I don't know," said Maggie. "I never thought about it before."

"I'm not here to throw you into a tizzy. Actually, I'm here to take a look at the cider press. But I thought it's time you knew."

They stepped sideways down the narrow cellar stairs into a furnace room with a cement floor, then through a door and down another shorter flight of steps. Maggie pulled a string and an old bulb flickered. "It's down here somewhere," she said.

A fetid smell billowed from the vegetable cellar with its dirt floor and rows of shelves where Alan kept the cider press and jugs of apple cider he had made the year before. Ceiling and shelves were bathed in a pale amber, strong-smelling, sour mash brew, while corks that had ricocheted off the old adzed beams lay in trembling suspension on the muddy floor. A cork popped in a final sally, an afterthought, a thumb at the nose. Letitia's eyelid jerked and Maggie chuckled.

"I don't know what's so funny," said Letitia. "The place smells like a brewery."

Maggie began to laugh. It boiled up from somewhere in her chest and spilled over in rolling stomach spasms that made her sit on the cellar steps to catch her breath, as her mother-in-law felt her way upstairs. "I'll come back when you're feeling better," Letitia said.

The need to talk to someone was strong. Jenna would not do because she would switch the topic, alternating its volume and frequency like a sound engineer, and they would end up talking about selling the house. Sybil would absolutely not do, and Kristen didn't care to do. Anne was the only one she could talk to, would want to talk to, in the murmuring, crooning, scolding, giggling, consoling, sometimes contentious way of close friends who spoke their own code of half sentences and obscure references. She wanted to talk about Letitia's visit and the murder trial she wasn't allowed to discuss, about Owen bringing an appraiser when she told him not to, about missing Alan, about selling the house, about the ache.

The Jazzercise class had moved to the basement of the Episcopal church. Anne, a faithful votary, would almost certainly be there. It was Maggie's first time back since Alan died. She took a deep breath and went in.

The walls of the basement were covered with drawings made by the Sunday school class. Boxes of nativity scenery, including plastic palm fronds and a shepherd's crook that had been donated by a retired sheep farmer, were stacked against a wall opposite a pile of exercise mats.

Maybeth Chase was the first to greet her. Chunkier than the others, Maybeth wore an apple-green golf skirt wrapped around her leotards. She thought it concealed her bulges. Actually, everyone knew not only her exact weight, but its distribution (bad in her thighs, hips, back, worse in her buttocks), how many times she had tried to lose it, and that the one time she had tried to do it with the help of pills, she had repainted her living room three times.

Maybeth embraced Maggie tenderly, then took her aside. "About the potluck supper club. You'd be uncomfortable, dear. Everyone is paired off." She squeezed Maggie's arm and added with a knowing whisper, "Everything happens for a reason."

Pam Daley, who followed close behind Maybeth, told Maggie that she was smart to keep in shape since she was young enough to marry again, adding that the inn might need help at the front desk on the weekends. "It's hard to get started with Tupperware," she said, with the twisted face of understanding, "especially in the winter."

Win Dyer's wife, Hope, whose great-grandfather had installed electricity in the Statue of Liberty, snapped to the small cluster like an atom. She said that she was sorry that she had only been to visit once since Maggie lost her husband in a tone which implied that Maggie had somehow misplaced Alan on the Long Trail. Having offered their condolences, they seemed uncomfortable and began to debate whether maple syrup pie was better with Macintosh or Cortland apples, then they switched to a whispered feeding frenzy of gossip about Justin Herrick's widow friend who had been seen off the green with the golf pro, all the while looking at Maggie strangely in quick smiles when she caught their eye, and in anxious frowns when they thought she was not looking.

Anne was easy to find. She lay on a mat in the front row, touching her elbows to the floor in side-to-side stretches, her blonde hair pulled back with a pink grosgrain bow that matched her leg warmers. Maggie smiled when she saw her closest friend. There need never be any mention of last night. As far as Maggie was concerned, it was done with and forgotten. Anne was the one who kept insisting that she get out with other people. She would be glad to see her.

Maggie dragged a mat beside her best friend, squeezing into a narrow space with the ease of one who assumes her welcome. "Hi," she said. "I was hoping I'd find you here." The other women looked first at one and then the other, like spectators at a tennis match.

Anne continued her stretches. "Hello, Maggie." Her tone was polite but cold. She made no move to adjust her mat to accommodate Maggie's. Instead she put a sweatband on her forehead and stood while the instructor, a spirited anorexic with hips like knobs, turned on the tape and clapped her hands over her head. There was an awkward moment before Maggie, bewildered, a strange clutch in her solar plexus, moved her mat to the back of the room. She rationalized that when they spoke later she would find that there was a perfectly good reason for Anne's preoccupation and that it had nothing to do with her.

Maggie was hopelessly out of shape, barely adequate through the lunging twists and bicep swings, but rapidly falling apart during the plié presses. By the time the others were on the mats doing leg lifts, she sat muscle-cramped and out of breath, with her arms wrapped around her knees, and wondering if it were possible that Peter had said anything about the night before. She thought it unlikely that he would confess his actions. In any case, even if he had, Anne would be angry with him and not with Maggie.

When class was over, Anne left the church basement with her head up, her eyes forward in studied indifference, surrounded by a phalanx of women in leotards and leg warmers. Maggie picked up her things and put her mat away, anxious to find out what it was that had caused this sudden coolness. She hoped, with a sinking heart, that it had nothing to do with the night before. Maybeth came to Maggie's side. "She knows," she said.

"She knows what?"

"Anne knows you invited Peter into your house and came on to him. In your kitchen."

"But that's not true. That's not what happened." Maggie hurried to the door. "I have to tell her."

"I'd leave well enough alone," called Maybeth.

The church basement was locked with bangs and slams. Maggie hugged her duffel bag to her chest and came out into a light snow in which everything was hushed and muted. She sat in her car waiting for the others to leave, then buckled her seat belt and turned the key in the ignition, wondering when she was going to get a chance to explain, or how she was going to do it. The beam from her headlights caught a doe and two yearlings at the edge of the woods behind the church. They appeared like phantom creatures with flicking white flags and wide-staring eyes, the plumes of their breath strung out on the frosty air. Suddenly they were gone, vanished into the snowfall, and Maggie was alone with the shush-shush of her wipers, wondering if there were any way she could somehow manage to keep the M.G. for Kristen.

CHAPTER 3

Twelve Good and True

MAGGIE FOLLOWED BEHIND THE early morning cinder truck as soft, wet snowflakes melted on the windshield of the Subaru. The road ahead shone with a dull gleam where the lintlike snow cover had been blown away like feathers, revealing a slick but manageable ribbon of ice. She drove with her gloved hands clutching the wheel, trying to keep from sliding off the road, and to ignore the pickup truck that was edging up behind her, hoping the other drivers saw the red streamer tied to her antennae. From time to time she flexed the fingers of one hand like a pianist preparing for an arpeggio, or a starfish in its last, pumping gasp on the sand.

The part of her mind that was on automatic continued to sift through her options in an endless rumination begun in a sleepless night of searching for a way to reconcile the misunderstanding with Anne. Maggie first had to ask Anne what was wrong. She did not think she could pull that one off, since it suggested that she knew nothing. A second and even less desirable course of action was to ask Peter what he had told Anne, a confrontation she did not want to enter into since it meant seeing him alone. The third option was to discuss with the two of them exactly what happened, and to do so in a rational and friendly manner, preferably over a kitchen table stirring mulled wine with swizzle sticks of cinnamon. It was the memory of Peter's rude, insistent knee between her thighs that jarred her to the grim conclusion that the best she could hope for was that the situation would blow over and be forgotten. The question that continued to nag, even during a mild skid—a breathless slide over twenty yards of highway—was why Peter had said anything about the incident at all. His was an abortive attempt, nothing more, no more serious than that of a dozen guys from high school and college who had cornered her in parking lots, cars, dorms, locker rooms, laundry rooms, dance floors, elevators, closets, toilets, telephone booths, loop-the-loops, and once, in the library stacks. He could have predicted the rift that it was bound to cause. What was clear was that he had covered his tracks in a preemptive strike before Maggie took the initiative and accused him first, which led to an equally grave question of how he could be both friend and foe.

The Subaru swerved. Maggie began to sweat beneath her layers of clothing. She tried to negotiate the slippery road by keeping one wheel on the hem of cinders and gravel at the edge as an approaching car fishtailed in a wide arc. Her rearview mirror confirmed that the pickup was right on her tail, a Ford Motors gumshoe, coupled to her bumper like a freight car. "Pass me, you idiot," she said into the mirror. If it had been Alan behind the wheel, this couldn't have happened. No one could have gotten within ten car lengths of Alan, a talent, like his skill in repairing a knee through an arthroscope with a diameter of less than half a centimeter, of which he was very proud. By the time she began her descent down the icy hill, she was driving with almost no traction, peppering the brakes with pumping strokes and shielding her eyes from the glare created by the morning sun.

Maggie pulled with relief into the parking lot of the courthouse and realized that Anne's hurt could never be made right. What had happened happened. There was nothing any of them could do to undo it. Like certain things that Sybil had done that she could never forget, such as not telling her about her father's letters until Maggie found the packet of envelopes embossed with the seal of Marriott, a patrimonial cache, hidden at the bottom of a lingerie drawer.

She creaked over the parking lot, the imprint of her boots stamping a trail of giant paramecia on its crusty glaze. If Alan had been around, Peter wouldn't have said anything. It was because Peter had nothing to fear from Maggie, and therefore nothing to lose, that he had protected himself at her expense. But then, if Alan had been alive, Peter wouldn't have tried anything in the first place.

The assembly room crackled with jurors shedding the husks of their outer clothing and staking out their territory, claiming a chair with a sweater, a section of a sofa with a book, a part of the closet with boots and parkas. They set mugs on a worm-eaten maple sideboard, ran the water taps, flushed the toilets, then piled on every available surface and in every corner of the room, photographs, magazines, chess sets, jigsaw puzzles, knitting, stationery, address books, customer lists, hampers filled with meat loaf sandwiches and brownies, and overnight bags with Nitro-Dur Patches, Inderal, Lithium, Zantac, Lomotil, Valium, aspirin, razors, lipsticks, socks, pantyhose, maxipads, and hair dryers, and key rings hung with flexible pink monkeys.

Many of them knew one another. If they did not, they knew a brother, or a neighbor, or a distant cousin with the same chin, the same hearing loss, or the same excess of pride. Some of their parents and grandparents had almost married one another instead of the spouses they ultimately chose, and the near miss of such alliances made them relatives of a sort. At the very least, they knew one anothers' villages and the shortcuts between them.

Hannah Watson, the retired librarian, acknowledged Maggie's arrival with a smile that stippled her cheeks. "You're the one who brought in the book lists. Know your mother-in-law. Went to school with Letitia. She was a real cutup."

Maggie found the image of Letitia as anything but grim-lipped as unbelievable as the theory advanced to her by Alan that the same atoms had been used over and over again since the beginning of time. She was wondering if there was any way to get thirty thousand dollars without selling the house when the clerk yanked on her glasses and announced that it would be awhile before they were called into the courtroom. The attorneys were speaking privately to the judge. About what, she did not know. Someone said they were arguing motions, probably having to do with evidence.

Everyone was impatient to get on with the trial, eager to hear about murder firsthand. No one spoke about it. Instead, Maggie opened her purse and removed a square of needlepoint stamped with the picture of a medieval woman with a high conical hat and long, flowing veil, a gift from Jenna, who said she would need something to do with her hands. The auctioneer and a beekeeper known for his dandelion spring honey sat down to a game of chess. A farmer's wife, with gray hair cut like Hans Brinker, went to the telephone to call her married daughters with urgent instructions on the care of their father's meals and laundry; her conversation was punctuated by soft questions about babies and husbands. Hannah Watson opened a giant jigsaw puzzle on a card table, the photographer sat with his eyes closed, his chair tilted back against the wall and his boots perched precariously on a rung, and the journeyman carpenter poured himself coffee from a steaming pot. Pursued by both a girlfriend who had decided that they would marry in the spring and an innkeeper named Daley from whom he had accepted a deposit on pantry shelves he hadn't begun, due to the hunting season, which had made serious inroads on his time, the carpenter filled his mug like a man who just escaped with his life.

The antiques dealer threaded her way through a lineup

of boots to introduce herself to Maggie. "I'm Trish Robidoux," the woman said in a strong, resonant voice. "We're in the same boat." Trish Robidoux was somewhere in her mid-fifties with blue-black hair, black eyebrows plucked to thin, vaulting arches, and a mouth fixed in a perpetual smile. Maggie had heard about her. She was from somewhere in Connecticut, known for importing armoires which she converted into mirrored, fluorescent-lit bars complete with dry sinks and glass racks. Maggie asked, "How so?" although she guessed that Trish Robidoux was probably widowed, too.

"I lost my husband, same as you." Trish Robidoux spun her bracelets. "Did you have any advance notice?"

"I'm not sure what you mean," Maggie replied, threading a needle with a skein of mauve wool, and thinking that no one had sent out flyers.

"His passing. Was it sudden or were you expecting it? I was expecting Tom's heart attack. I was the one who sat with him on the sofa all night long. He couldn't breathe when he lay down. He used to have to sleep in a chair at night. Sitting straight up. It was the only way he could breathe."

Their bereavement should have created an instant bond, but it did not. Maggie felt nothing in common with a woman who had the benefit of advance notice and an armful of gold bracelets, that hinted, like the tip of an iceberg, of a lot more where they came from.

"It was sudden," she said, remembering Alan's tennis friends standing clustered awkwardly in the driveway, like a herd of sheep crowding into its center, a fallen soufflé of whites, and wondering what they were doing there.

Trish Robidoux masked a fleeting envy with a sigh and a benign halfway smile that said, We're not happy here, just sympathetic. "Sometimes that's a blessing, at least it is for the one who goes. Does your mother live nearby?"

Maggie pushed her glasses up over her nose and adjusted the frames behind her ears. "No. My mother lives in Manhattan."

"That's too bad. She could be a big help to you. A real comfort. Mine was. When a husband passes, it's your mother you want again; that is, of course, if you're young enough to have one. Most widows can't claim that luxury. Their mothers are usually gone, same as the husbands."

Sybil, a one-time musical comedy star who spent more time cataloging her faded clippings than her household accounts, was a liability, not an asset, certainly not a luxury. When it came to family matters, she was a wash-out. Maggie could not remember any advice from Sybil that made sense. Once she even suggested that Maggie have another child in order to break what Sybil called the Kristen/Alan deadlock. Maggie didn't want to get into any of it, which was just as well since Trish Robidoux, having decided that she was drawing blanks, was off in a clink of bracelets to talk to the journeyman carpenter.

Maggie studied the veil on the canvas, trying to figure out what was wrong with it when something began to annoy her, like a label at the back of the neck. She realized it was the photographer, the way he set himself apart from the others, peering at her through slitted eyes and forming silent judgment like a laboratory technician scrutinizing the contents of a petri dish. She didn't like his dark, drooping mustache or the way his plaid shirt opened at the neck, revealing a white undershirt with black, renegade hairs curling over the edge. She decided not to look in his direction if she could help it and bent over her needlepoint with new intensity.

His voice was disembodied, a ventriloquist's thrust which he tossed like a javelin. "It's better to downshift when you're on ice," he said. "Pumping your brakes is the best way I know to go into a skid."

"Were you speaking to me?" She sounded silly and she knew it. They were the only two on that side of the room.

He leaned forward and opened his eyes. She saw that they were a soft, amber brown, like the skin of a sweet potato. "You drive a yellow Subaru. I was right behind you."

The pickup. She hadn't been able to see its driver, but she pictured him with eyes bouncing around their sockets like pinballs. This man, even if he did not know how to keep his shirt buttoned, seemed normal enough. He had no excuse. "Didn't anyone ever tell you that tailgating was dangerous?"

"You drive too skittish," he said. "That's a lot more dangerous. If ice has you so spooked, you ought to get chains."

"How I drive," she said, "is none of your concern."

"Lighten up, lady. I was trying to help." He held up his hands and leaned back against the wall.

"I don't have to lighten up and I don't need your help." Her throat began to constrict. A few heads turned toward them in quick swivels, like figures on a cuckoo clock. She jabbed through the scrim. When she looked up, his eyes had closed once more to slits. Oh no, you don't, she thought, you don't get away that fast. She put down her needlepoint. "You think it's easy to put chains on a car?"

"It's a piece of cake."

"That's what you think."

"My mom thinks so, too."

"I seriously doubt that. Not if she had to drag them out of the garage." Her voice rose, climbing on its anger— "And before that move a four-hundred-pound refrigerator that's standing in front of them,"—and cracked in tinny slivers. "And after that move an old M.G. with a dead something or other, and cement blocks in front of its wheels."

Maggie decided she had said enough, that she couldn't say anymore even if she knew exactly what it was she wanted to say to this man. Her heart beating from the unexpected assault, she left to pour a cup of coffee, then join the knot of jurors crowded around the card table, poking through the puzzle pieces for shades of blue.

Hannah Watson held a piece of a cumulus cloud. "We're

on the sky," she said to Maggie, sifting for its match like a ferret. "That man you've been talking to is Amos Stringer. He's a bad apple. Gave his daddy a mite of trouble few years back."

Bill Hogan, the electronics engineer from IBM, looked up from the card table. He was a big man with sad, surprising pale gray eyes, the only man in the room wearing a suit. He spoke softly. "He didn't give his father any more trouble than he gave himself. In any case, I understand that was over fifteen years ago. It's all been squared away and forgotten."

"Maybe squared away, but not forgotten, at least not by everyone," said Hannah Watson. "Ask my sister Edna if she forgot. See what answer you get." Her softened chin, drooping like an overripe peach, began to quiver. "I'm surprised he's on a jury."

"He didn't lose his citizenship," said Hogan.

"I better not speak more on the subject. We have to work together. You've got the rest of this cloud right there in your hand."

Hogan turned to Maggie. "Was there any decaf?" he asked.

"I'm sorry," she replied, "I didn't notice." She wondered, as did the few uninformed at the table, what it was that had been squared away and forgotten. But unlike the others who were unwilling to ask the question, only because to do so would be considered a breach of good manners, Maggie was determined not to show any interest in a man who wore an undershirt that could be seen.

It was early afternoon by the time the puzzle people noticed that a chunk of sky was missing, the beekeeper and the auctioneer exchanged bishops, and the journeyman carpenter pocketed a deposit from Trish Robidoux for the installation of six armoires. The clerk announced that the judge decided that since it was so late in the day and another storm was expected, there was no point in beginning until the next morning. They were dismissed.

Maggie picked up her needlepoint, making a great effort to avoid the eyes of Amos Stringer. The morning was wasted. She walked out beside Trish Robidoux. "Why couldn't they tell us earlier?" she said. "I don't have all day to sit around and wait."

Trish Robidoux wound a gold-threaded scarf about her neck and chin. "What else do you have to do with your time?" she asked. "I have a business to run. Lucky you, you're free as a bird."

Jenna and Owen lived in a converted barn on the property of a retired sheep farmer. Their home was immaculately clean, smelling at all times of Mrs. Murphy's oil soap. It had two bedrooms: a master bedroom where Owen and Jenna's flint-faced ancestors stared from the walls in custodial vigilance, and a second, smaller, unused bedroom with a white iron bed where Jenna kept her sewing.

Jenna and Owen were childless, a mystery they never sought to unravel, accepting their lot as they did the fact that Owen had not been gifted with the intellect, status, or the earning power of his handsome younger brother. To offset the deficit of offspring, they took a city child into their home to live in their pristine, white iron bedroom for two weeks every summer.

"You're losing weight" was the first thing Jenna said when Maggie dropped by on her way home from the courthouse. "You're probably not eating right."

"Probably," conceded Maggie, pulling off her hat and shaking her red hair free as she watched her sister-in-law lay out a size-sixteen dress pattern on a bolt of printed polyester. "I'm on a jury," she added. "Nothing's happened yet."

"I heard about it," said Jenna. "The girl from the junction who killed her mother. Letitia told me. So did a neighbor of Trish Robidoux. Can't stand the woman." Jenna pinned a tissue-paper collar to the fabric. "I also heard about you and Peter. This is a small town, Maggie."

Maggie felt sick in the pit of her stomach, a core place

that registered despair somewhere in the coil of her intestine, a visceral Geiger counter with the kick of a mule. Everyone knew. She was glad Kristen was away at school. "It wasn't my doing, Jenna," she said. "Peter made the move."

Jenna spoke with pins in her mouth. She looked like a giant catfish. "It's the woman who has control of those things, every time. Don't ever let anyone ever tell you different."

"You don't understand. It happened so fast."

Jenna had no conflict. Speed was not an issue in what was a straightforward matter of duty. "You should have gone straight to his house and told his wife. Anne had a right to know."

"I couldn't do that. And I don't think I'd want anyone else telling me that kind of thing about Alan, either. I'd rather not have known."

Jenna began to snip around the yoke. "It's easy for you to say that now when he's gone and it doesn't make any difference. I hate to say this to you with all you've been through, but you brought it on yourself, Maggie. You'd have to figure that Peter would say something. He'd be stupid not to and take a chance you'd say something first." Jenna paused. "If you had sold your house and been living over Letitia's garage like we all begged you to do, none of this would have happened."

A phenomenon of memory let Maggie believe she had played this scene before. "What should I do?" she asked. "All I can think of is that I want to make it right. But I don't know how."

"There's nothing to do," said Jenna. "The ball is in Anne's court. She has to make the next move."

"She might never make it. I miss her, Jenna. Terribly. I need her to talk to. It's just not fair," said Maggie.

"You have more important things to worry about," said Jenna. "Like how you're going to get thirty thousand dollars. Now, there is your priority."

Maggie was not surprised that Jenna knew about the

money. If in a rural precinct there were few secrets from the town, there were none from the family.

"There's good news, though," said Jenna. "Owen heard from the appraiser. About your house."

"What did he say?"

"He said you could get eighty, maybe ninety thousand being as it's small and needs repair and that the floor is uneven. Think what you could do with the money. Your worries would be over."

Maggie knew of nothing to do with that amount of money except to put it in the bank. "I wonder if that's a good price?"

"Sounds like it to me. You'd better ask Owen, though. He knows more about it than I do. Owen could advise you." Jenna lifted her tissue-pattern pieces attached by pins to printed shadows, polyester dopplegangers lining their flip sides, and put them in a box.

"I don't want to sell the house, Jenna," said Maggie. "I hope I don't have to. It's as if Alan is there somewhere. All the things he ever said to me still echoing against the walls, only the ripples are so faint, I can't hear them anymore. If I sold the house, I'd be selling Alan."

"You're talking out of your head, Maggie. I've never known you to do that. Get sensible. We can't always get to do what we want to do. You should know that by now."

That's true, thought Maggie. I wanted to stay married to Alan forever. "By the way," she said, "do you know anyone named Stringer?"

"Stringer," said Jenna. "There's a Stringer family near the depot. Father's a grain salesman. If I remember right, one of their boys ran off to Canada. Why do you ask?"

Maggie reached her house in the late afternoon. It seemed to be waiting, as it always did, with a promise of haven where she could retreat into cabbage-rose-printed depths or hide under the four-poster, staring up at the mattress forever.

She picked up her mail, remembering the winter before when she had looked through the frosted windows of the summer kitchen to see Alan standing near the mailbox, his pale green surgical pants stuffed into his boots, holding up the toboggan like a trophy. She had been waiting for a telephone call. From whom? She didn't remember. Kristen, on the other hand, dropped everything, her calculus homework, a tape of Twisted Sister, even her boyfriend, Ranger, whom she left sitting in the living room staring helplessly at logarithms. It would have helped if there had been a notation somewhere, a card of some kind, a coded message scribbled on cigarette paper, graffiti on a wall, even a sign, like a picture that suddenly falls out of its frame, or a black cat crisscrossing the road, some warning that said you have six months left with this man and you'd better enjoy it while you can. Maggie wiped the tears from her eyes with the back of her gloved hand.

She reached her front door to find that Anne had made the next move. Next to the iron boot scraper were two flowered porcelain casserole dishes and a travel iron. Where's my curling iron? wondered Maggie. As long as you were cleaning house, you could have returned my curling iron and my soup ladle. And my navy wool evening skirt. Now the ball was back in Maggie's court.

Once inside, she saw immediately that Anne hadn't been the only visitor. Someone had dripped snow on the floor and it lay pooled on the wood like a jellyfish. Don't make me go upstairs to find you, she thought. And don't jump out at me from the closet. If you're here, show yourself now. Maggie went through the dining room. One of the French military prints above the wainscot hung at an angle, as if someone had brushed against it. She heard footsteps coming down the stairs. Letitia? They were too sprightly for Letitia. Owen with another appraiser? An intruder? Alan?

"I know what you're going to say, but before you say it and get us both worked up, I can't find the instant hot chocolate. Hi, Mom."

Kristen, her hair the color of lemon sherbet, stood wearing Alan's plaid woolen shirt over her panties. Maggie felt a rush of love, a heady, heavy, sweet maternal syrup that made her eyes swim. Her daughter had come home to be with her, to console her, confess her remorse over her lack of letters, phone calls, and filial concern for a widowed mother who was really having a bad time of it. If she was just homesick, that was all right too. Maggie would make it right for Kristen, magically overnight, like a miracle face cream that pumped up laugh lines while you slept. She would send her back to school in the morning, or in a couple of days, if that's what Kristen needed.

"Krissie, what are you doing here? How did you get home?"

Kristen allowed herself to be hugged. She patted Maggie's back, but her body was unyielding. "I took the bus. The guy at the Mobil station drove me the rest of the way."

Maggie set down the travel iron. "How long have you been here?"

"All afternoon. And I'm starved. You don't have anything to eat in the house except apricot yogurt and vanilla ice cream. And where are the rest of Daddy's clothes? This shirt is all I could find."

"Why are you home, Krissie? I didn't expect you for three more weeks."

"You might as well hear it now. Straight."

Here it is, thought Maggie, the pie in the face.

"I left Smith. I can't stand it there anymore."

"Honey, you can't leave just like that. You can't just walk away and come home whenever you feel like it."

"Sure I can. You did."

"That was different. That was a different time. I left to get married. But we're not talking about me. We're talking about you. You're missing classes. You must have papers to write. Aren't you worried about your grades? And finals, they must be coming up soon. Krissie, this is nonsense."

"That's what I thought, so here I am." Kristen slung her long legs over the arm of the sofa and stretched out.

The telephone interrupted their silence. Maggie went to answer it, get rid of whoever it was as politely and as quickly as possible.

"Maggie Hatch?" It was an unfamiliar voice.

"Yes," she said. "This is she."

"I'm Justin Herrick. You don't know me."

"Does this have anything to do with my brother-in-law, Owen? Are you the appraiser? If you are, I'm not really interested. It was Owen's idea to bring you here, not mine. And my floors aren't uneven. They're very, very old. They're the original floors. I'm rather busy now, Mr. Merrick—"

"Herrick. I'm a friend of Woody Pringle's."

"Then you must be the person who needs a house sitter. I'm not interested in that either."

"House sitter?" He laughed while Kristen pouted with her arms folded beneath the French military prints that hung in the dining room. "No, Woody told me, asked me to call. Look, Mrs. Hatch— Maggie—I know you lost your husband last summer. I'm very sorry, and maybe this isn't the time to plan anything, but I'd like to meet you. Take you out."

The idea was puzzling, remote, out of context, a thatched hut on an iceberg. "I don't know," she said.

"Think about it. It doesn't have to be soon. Next week or the week after. I'll call again."

"Are you going to be much longer?" asked Kristen. "I have to call Ranger."

Maggie suddenly wanted to smack her. The only other time that she had felt so strongly compelled had been when Kristen was seven and told Maggie not to come to P.T.A. because she sounded like a flatlander. "You don't have to call again," Maggie said to the voice on the line. "Soon will be fine."

"Are you sure? I don't want you to feel rushed."

"I'm sure."

"How soon?"

* * *

They were upstairs unpacking Kristen's suitcase in relative silence, the kind that gets broken only with absolute essentials. Kristen's clothes were soiled, wrinkled, and ripped. She seemed defiant, waiting for Maggie to complain about their condition. But Maggie said nothing.

"I'm having the rest shipped." Maggie continued to sort. "Who was that," Kristen asked, "on the phone?"

"A man," replied Maggie. "This skirt isn't yours."

"Lisa and I exchanged things. What did he want?"

"A date."

"You're kidding."

It was the red cashmere sweater, shrunken to doll size, that did it. "I have to tell you that I don't approve of what you're doing," said Maggie. "I think it's impulsive, something you didn't consider very carefully, not like you at all, I think it's not facing up to things. Maybe it has something to do with Daddy. If it does, I'd like to help you. Maybe we could arrange for a leave of absence. A time to think things over. Under the circumstances, they'd understand. I'll call tomorrow morning. From the courthouse."

"Circumstances are for people to hide behind. That's not why I'm here. I don't have to hide behind anything. And I am facing up to things. There's no point in calling. I've already spoken to the dean. We've talked all about it and she knows that Smith has nothing for me. It's over. Face it. I did. What about the M.G.? I need wheels one way or another."

Maggie was tired. She wanted Alan's shirt back. She could have handled this better in his shirt. But how do you take your husband's shirt off your daughter's back? There was no point in any further discussion. They would talk about it later. Kids did this kind of thing all the time. Professors gave incompletes. It was not too late. Like Lazarus, the semester could be resurrected. "You can do the rest," she said, leaving Kristen with a jumble of sweat socks and bras stained a mottled pink while she went to answer the phone.

It was Sybil, calling to offer one of her rare apologies. She had been neglectful. She wanted to make it up. Maggie must come to New York. What better way to pick up the pieces of her life than to go where the possibilities for life were limitless? These included an opening night gala for the ballet with a Balanchine piece that hadn't been done in years, a photographic exhibition of the works of Jean Cocteau, Kabuki theater about young Samurais and fox spirits, even—a special concession—Sting in *The Threepenny Opera*. Maggie declined, explaining that she was in the beginning of a jury trial. Sybil upped the ante. If Maggie could not come to New York, she'd just have to come to Vermont.

Shoving that eventuality from her mind, Maggie ran downstairs to the writing desk and took out a piece of paper and an envelope which she addressed to Anne Bouchard. "Dear Anne," she wrote, her lower lip sliding out again. "The two casseroles and the travel iron are in my possession. Please note that you still have my curling iron, my soup ladle, and my navy wool evening skirt. I would appreciate the return of all of these as soon as possible." She signed it, Maggie, then as an afterthought, added Hatch. It gave the note formality, distance; it gave topspin to the lob. The ball was out of reach, dazzling in the sun. How do you like them apples?

CHAPTER 4

Opening Arguments

"NO ONE WEARS GLASSES anymore," said Kristen. "Why are you so afraid of contact lens?" Her lips were set like Letitia's: firm, patrician, closed.

"Because," said Maggie, shoving an English muffin into the toaster slot, "they pop out. And you need glasses to find them. That's why."

"It doesn't matter to me," said Kristen. "I just thought you'd like to know what's available. If you want to look like an owl, that's your business."

Maggie tucked her anger out of sight, like pinning a bra strap to a shoulder pad. Kristen was only seventeen and her father was dead, reasons enough for misdirected hostility which Maggie refused to return. Even so, Maggie conceded, she sure knows what buttons to push.

"I don't know what you're going to do all day," said Maggie. "I don't suppose you want to come to the courthouse?"

"What for?"

"To watch the trial. We can discuss it when it's over. It might be interesting for you."

"I can see all the trials I want on television."

"This one is real," said Maggie.

"So are the ones on television. Admit it. You only want me there so you can keep an eye on me."

Maggie had forgotten that the days of hidden agendas were over. There was one more card to play. "I won't be home until at least five. Maybe later."

"No problem. I need to kick back."

"Why can't you kick back over Christmas vacation?" Maggie faced her daughter squarely, as if trying to force reason through Kristen's frontal lobes. "This is silly. Let's pack you up so you can finish the semester. Two or three days won't make any difference, and then we can talk about whether or not Smith is right for you." Maggie watched Kristen pull out an eyelash, then squint at it, as if she was surprised to see it. "If you don't finish," continued Maggie, "we're out a lot of money. In fact, unless you're reinstated in some way, I doubt very much if we'll see any of it. Money is very, very tight right now. You understand?" Maggie decided to not to get into the business about losing Kristen's social security benefits, fearful that it might confound the issue.

"That has nothing to do with me. Not really. I mean, if you wanted to send me to college, you took a risk. What if I was killed in a car crash?"

Smoke drifted from the English muffin in a curling charcoal spiral. Maggie unplugged the toaster and stuck in a fork. "I don't need to hear that kind of talk right now."

"Sorry. About the car crash. Look, I've been thinking about this, I knew you'd be on my case, and I figured out it has to do with the kind of life you picked."

Maggie turned the toaster upside down and whacked it. Crumbs and dried shards fell out. "What do you mean?"

"If I spell it out, you'll get upset."

"I'm already upset. See, crumbs all over my sweater." Maggie banged the toaster against the counter. "A toaster that won't give me back my muffin. Believe me, it's already happened. Anyhow, Socrates said an unexamined life is not worth living. I'd like to hear about the kind of life I picked."

"For someone who spends a lot of time in the kitchen,

you're sure all thumbs. O.K. Here it is. *Number one torpedo, ready*. You don't earn money. If you did, you wouldn't be so frantic about all this. You'd be able to handle it."

"I don't see you handling things so well. You had one responsibility, taking classes and getting decent grades, and you ran away. It's not even that you're homesick." Maggie brushed the crumbs off her sweater. "And if I don't work, Krissie, it's because your father didn't want me to."

"I don't believe that. Daddy wouldn't have stood in your way if that's what you really wanted to do. We always talked careers."

"Where was I during those discussions?" asked Maggie, seeing incestuous shadows, feeling the pinch of jealousy which she was trying to restrain with reason.

"We didn't include you because Daddy didn't want to hurt your feelings. You couldn't join in. So we talked about it when we were alone together."

Kristen's disclosure unscrewed the lid, provided the license. Now Maggie could let loose her anger and not feel guilty. "That's cozy. The two of you shielding dumb old Mom from life."

"I knew you'd be defensive. Why don't you open the trap? That's what it's for."

"Because the muffin is jammed in the grid." Maggie inserted an ice pick. "This may not count for much, but I was too busy raising you to think about a job."

"That's a cop-out. Nobody says that anymore because nobody buys it. A lot of mothers work. Lisa's mother is a dentist. Anyhow, you still have other ways to go if money is a problem."

"That does it. I've had it with this stupid thing." Maggie pitched the toaster into the garbage can. "Such as? I'm waiting."

"Such as selling this old house and moving into the apartment over Gran's garage."

"Doesn't that bother you? It bothers me. I thought you loved this house. You grew up in it. Did Letitia tell you to say that?"

"Yes, no. I like it a lot. But it meant more when there were three of us and we were a total family."

The pain was as keen to Maggie as if Kristen had grabbed the ice pick and slid it between her ribs. "What are we now?" she asked.

"I don't know. Kind of like a package with its string cut. Face it. I won't be living here much longer. If you're keeping the house for me, forget it. You do what's right for you. I'll do what's right for me."

Maggie did not like the way that sounded. It spoke of separation, distance. It spoke of being childless. There wasn't even a word for it. An orphan had no parents. What did one call a mother without a child? She pulled on her woolen hat. "Don't you have any doubts at all? About what you're doing?"

"That's neurotic. There's a girl on our floor, Kelly. She does that all the time. Should I, shouldn't I, back and forth. It's like listening to a seesaw. Boring. All because she's going with this guy, Rog, who's bi. You know what that means?"

"I knew a few." Actually Maggie only knew one, a florist with bright pink cheeks whom Sybil had used as an escort between husbands.

"Anyhow, she really wants to make it with him. Rog has it all: he listens when you talk, intense, like he understands, and he's got great attitude, he stands with his thumbs hooked into his belt loops and stares at you with his eyes all narrowed. But Kelly's not sure. She's afraid he might have already caught the AIDS virus, even though he swears he never took it in the butt. She's trying to figure out his risk factor. Lisa's helping her. Lisa's good with stats."

Maggie drew on her boots. "There are other ways to get it than the way you say."

"Not with Rog. He says he talks them off."

"How does he do that?"

"With words. Rog is good with words. He's a walking thesaurus. He said he'd do it for me if I wanted, but I wouldn't do that to Kelly."

"Do what? It's all talk. There's nothing to do."

"To your way of thinking, but if you're into friendships with women, you don't do that kind of thing. Get off with their guy."

"What exactly does he say?"

"It depends. Rog finds out a person's fantasy, and he describes it in their ear, step by step, in the tiniest detail, until they get off."

Melting snow plopped from the trees and sparkled in the sun like iridescent cotton. "Kristen. Let's not get side-tracked. The issue is you. How are you so sure what you're doing is right for you? Tell me. I want to understand your thinking on this."

"That's easy. It feels right."

Maggie wound her scarf around her neck. Feeling right. For the second time since Alan died, Maggie had woken from a dream aroused, legs shifting uneasily, hips squirming and lifting, her fingers sliding in and out of moist, slippery folds as slick as satin. She did not stop herself as she had the night after the funeral. Instead, she drove on and on, rubbing the sweet congestion harder and harder until it exploded in little spasms of relief that went on and on like ripples in a pond, until she felt very right, until she got off, until the need returned and she did it again in the shower, this time in soapy, steamy comfort.

"There's nothing for you to eat. I would have food-shopped if I knew you were coming home."

"That's all right. Gran is bringing stuff."

"When did you talk to Letitia?"

"This morning. While you were in the shower. I called her. You haven't taken very good care of Daddy's fish. The tank looks all scummy. Don't you ever clean it?"

"I try. It gets away from me."

"You don't have all that much to do, Mom. God almighty. You need the algae tablets. I looked all over for them. What about the toaster? You going to leave it there?"

"It's history."

"You're really wired this morning. You know that?"

Maggie made a second decision not to get angry. This time it was with a sense of vested interest she felt, as when switching from a sensational mini-series to an educational program on the frogs of Caledonia. Maggie searched for her juror's pin while Kristen followed her to the door in relentless pursuit. "How come Mike didn't shovel the steps?"

"I let him go. Because of what I was trying to tell you. The money." The pin was on the windowsill next to her gloves.

"Then why didn't you shovel them yourself? Gran does, and she's sixty-nine."

Maggie jabbed herself in the chest. The pain was precise, satisfying. "Because the shovels are in the garage. And the garage doors are plastered shut with snow and I can't open them."

Kristen seemed pleased. "You're supposed to put shovels where you can get them in the winter. God almighty, that's fundamental."

Maggie concluded that Kristen had borrowed "God Almighty" from Lisa along with the skirt. "What are her chances?" she asked.

"Whose?"

"Your friend Kelly. What odds did Lisa give her?"

Kristen was suspicious. She looked at Maggie sideways, under lids lowered like awnings, the way Alan used to do when Maggie said things like *I did something interesting with the chicken. I think you're going to love it— My mother called— Of course I get the oil checked when I fill the tank.* "Do you mean that in a good or a bad way?"

"The best, believe me."

"One in fifty-four. I don't think it was Socrates that wrote about an unexamined life. It was Plato."

Icicles hung like daggers from the windows of the summer kitchen. Maggie ducked beneath them as cold air bit into her nostrils.

Judge Atwill had had her hair done, evident by its freshly tinted, dyed-brown uniformity and its shape, a brittle, oval helmet that framed her face like a pecan shell. She waited while the prosecutor and his assistants carried in labeled exhibits which they arranged in front of her bench like tribute. Then she instructed the jury that the state had the burden of proof beyond a reasonable doubt and that the purpose of the trial was to determine whether the state had met this burden. Although both parties would have an opportunity to make an opening statement, what was said in the opening statements was not evidence. It was only after the opening statements were made that the state would introduce evidence to support its charge.

Maggie listened carefully while she sat in the jury box, feeling the salubrious effects of its collective containment, just one of an aggregate, protected, indistinguishable, an egg in a carton, a card in a deck, a grape in a cluster, a single cell in a judicial battery, instead of a widow with as many problems as horseflies in summer, listening to the judge's instruction that their verdict had to be unanimous.

How was it possible, wondered Maggie, to get twelve strangers to agree on anything? She thought for an instant of the contention in an ordinary family, like the argument she had had that morning with Kristen, then was startled to find Judge Atwill staring at her. Maggie made a tent of her hands to demonstrate her consecration, while the judge cautioned the jury not to form an opinion one way or another until they heard all the evidence.

As they waited for the prosecutor to set up an easel, LaDonna Dyer, the dairy farmer's wife, leaned over the shoulder of a juror with center-parted hair to whisper to Maggie that her sweater was inside out. The juror over whom the information had been exchanged, a naturalized Polish concert pianist, shook her curtains of hair as if airing out bed linen and touched her finger to her lips.

Jim McKeen had begun to speak. He spoke softly, politely, aware of the natural resistance of the jury to accept the guilt of the ill-clad young defendant and of his need not to incur their indignation. He might have been describing a trip to the Grand Tetons as he charged that Melody Jessica Bean planned and executed the murder of her mother, Joyce Hibbert Bean, introducing an odorless white powder—mercuric chloride, a known poison—into a tube of dental adhesive, subjecting the decedent to its cumulative lethal effects.

Jim McKeen continued, this time with his voice pitched even lower, like someone visiting the bedside of the gravely ill. "I will prove to you," he said, "that in Joyce Hibbert Bean's painful dying moments, the defendant"—he stopped to point to the accused, his arm as rigid as a signpost—"with reckless disregard for her mother's weakened, rapidly deteriorating condition, drove her mother from her home, not to the hospital, not to a doctor's office or his home, not even to the home of a neighbor, but to the quarry, where she caused the confused and weakened victim to plunge sixty feet to her death."

The jury breathed in unison, a collective intake of breath that sounded like a bellows, then turned to glance in morbid fascination at the girl whose bangs had been slicked backed into her ponytail, giving her the smooth, broad forehead of a Renaissance madonna. She seemed to be listening with minimal interest. Once she turned to smile, her cheeks curved into plums, at the journeyman carpenter as he leaned forward, grinning.

McKeen engaged each of the jurors in direct eye contact, like an engineer coupling one train car to another, as he told them that any case was a jigsaw puzzle just like the one that the clerk said they were putting together in the jury room. He would give them the pieces which they would put together in the courtroom so that by the end of the trial, the entire picture would be clear. Then, while the judge turned to fix a steady gaze on the journeyman carpenter, the prosecutor rested his folded hands on the balustrade, only a few feet away from Maggie, and told them that his sworn oath as prosecutor was to do justice, and that justice in this case demanded a conviction of murder in the first degree. He said that when they heard the testimony of the medical examiner and others, they would understand why there was no other possible conclusion. If they still had doubts, these would be dispelled by an eyewitness, from whom they would learn that the defendant was a cold-blooded killer who had conceived and carried out an elaborate plan that led to the death of her mother. And that having done so, she carried out an equally elaborate plan to cover up her disappearance.

He asked them to listen with an open mind to the evidence, and to interpret the evidence with their common sense, then left them with a serious charge that made it clear to each juror that he meant business, that there could be no waffling, no hedging of bets. He told them that if the facts established the guilt of Melody Jessica Bean beyond a reasonable doubt, the state expected them to return a verdict of guilty of murder in the first degree.

McKeen had woven suspicion about the courtroom like a net. By noon recess, everyone was caught in it, including Maggie, who ran to the telephone to call Owen to ask him what the appraiser said the house was worth, while she wondered what elaborate plan the sweet-faced girl in the courtroom had possibly concocted.

"I can't discuss it with you now, Maggie," Owen replied in the distracted manner of someone with better things to do. "We've got trout flies to box. I'll have to get back to you later."

It was hard to hear him. LaDonna Dyer had the nearby phone and was trying to explain something to her husband. Ever since the federal government had bought out their dairy herd, she had been worried about him, especially after the day before when she had come home to find him trying to turn onion skins into a frozen compost pile, and her voice was shrill.

Behind Maggie, Willard Peterson was arguing with Bill Hogan in a steady monotone that sounded like the drone of swarming bees. Maggie guessed that they were discussing Amos Stringer, who sat, as he did every day, tilted against the wall at the far side of the room.

Maggie cupped a hand over her other ear. "I don't see what there is to explain, Owen. Just give me a number. I'll figure it out for myself. And speak louder."

"Now, Maggie, you know you don't have a head for figures," he said, giddy with the power of withholding information.

"I can't stay on the phone either, Owen. Stop playing games. What did he say?"

"Ninety, Maggie, but that won't mean anything to you because it's not the bottom line."

Maggie hung up. She heard the beekeeper tell Hogan that he couldn't see a hole through a ladder, and did he really think what Stringer did was right, not to mention moral, that it was anything but the act of a jellyfish?

Bill Hogan was all jointed arms and legs, like a grasshopper. "Here's what I think," he replied. "I was on burial detail in Korea. In Chon was a junkyard, hundreds of bodies lying around like scrap. Some just parts. An arm, a leg. We buried the parts all the same, just as if they were attached to the rest of the poor bastards they came from. You see that many dead men, you get your fill for a lifetime. And you realize that war is no solution."

"Well," said the beekeeper, "I guess you're entitled to your opinion, it's a free country and all, but he better not try to shake my hand." They split apart like a forking road. The beekeeper hooked a thumb under his upper dentures, clicked them into place, and went to resume his chess game with the auctioneer, while Bill Hogan turned to get his decaffeinated coffee, his long legs creaking as he strode. Maggie gathered up her courage and followed him to the maple sideboard.

"If this has anything to do with the Stringer fellow," he warned, "I've said all I'm going to say on the subject."

"No," she said, sorry that she had made the move. "It's just that I know you work for IBM, so you're probably good with numbers."

"I'm better with some numbers than with others." He smiled, making her feel as if all the shots were hers to call. Maggie saw that his teeth were yellowed, like ivory keys on an old piano.

"I have a hypothetical problem. Actually, it's a friend who has this hypothetical problem. This friend has a house he might want to sell. What this friend wants to know is, how does he figure out the bottom line?"

"That depends. Houses aren't exactly my field, although I've bought a few in my time. If you mean how much money he clears, he has to subtract his remaining mortgage, and unless he buys another property for more money, he has to pay taxes on any appreciation that he has realized. Of course," he said, "there's the broker's fees. That is, if the house isn't sold privately. I don't know if I've been much help to your friend."

"You've been a lot of help. I'll tell him what you said."

"You do that. If he has any other questions, I'd be glad to tell him what I know. Which isn't a lot."

Maggie took her needlework and found a seat beside the concert pianist, where she made a quick calculation. The mortgage was around forty thousand, thirty thousand to Letitia, which left twenty thousand, upon which she would have to pay taxes and probably a broker's fee. That was assuming she sold the house at appraisal value. It did not leave very much.

The woman beside her shook her curtains of hair and emerged from behind their concealment like an odalisque. "My grandmother used to work like that," she said. "With a needle. I did not know women in the United States still did that."

It could have been a compliment or an attack. Maggie looked sideways at the woman.

"I myself," said the woman, retreating into her hair. "I would not be bothered with needlework. For me it would be a waste of time. Of course, I cannot speak for anyone else."

* * *

The afternoon sun pierced the courtroom in shafts of silver. A few jurors, including Hannah Watson and Hobart Straw, had difficulty staying awake. Their heads snapped back and forth like whips as the defense attorney and the prosecutor stood huddled at the side bar conferring with the judge, with the court reporter between them, punching out the diphthongs of their speech. The defense attorney had just moved to suppress fingerprint evidence, claiming that his client's fingerprinting was the result of her being illegally taken into custody. The prosecutor argued that the order for the fingerprints had been signed by the judge of the juvenile court. Judge Atwill denied the motion.

Dan Giotti had not really expected the motion to be granted. Looking as if he had just been hustled out of bed with his knotted tie barely covering the opened buttonhole at the neck of his shirt, he moved that since the prosecutor's statement did not include necessary facts to prove the state's case beyond a reasonable doubt, a directed verdict be entered for his client. He did not expect this motion to be granted either. His stage-whispered objection was meant for the jury.

"Motion denied," said the judge, who understood Giotti's improper bid for the jury's sympathy. "If you try anything like that again, Mr. Giotti, I will hold you in contempt. You may proceed if you intend to make an opening statement."

Nonplussed, Dan Giotti stood beside Melody Bean, put a hand on her rounded shoulder, smiled at the jury, and told them that this was a difficult position for him to be in. A woman was dead, and his client, Melody Jessica Bean, was charged with her murder, probably the most serious crime which could be tried in that court.

Melody Bean shrugged off his hand. He slapped it against his trouser leg, as if it were an errant member he needed to keep close to his side, then told the jury that the most careful scrutiny they had to give was to the testimony supplied by the witness described by Mr. McKeen as a participant. "Ladies and gentlemen," he argued, "Kevin Clapp is no participant. There is no legal category of participant. Kevin Clapp is an accomplice who has turned state's witness. As a matter of fact, Kevin Clapp was involved in this murder every step of the way—"

"Objection," said McKeen, on his feet. "Kevin Clapp is not on trial."

"Sustained," said the judge, with a definitive lilt she might have used to announce that the hall monitors turn in their badges by four o'clock. "Change your line, counselor."

Giotti suggested that the jury would have to judge for themselves the testimony of an accomplice, and ask themselves his motive. He smiled gently when he said that this was a unique case. "I'm sure," he said, "that you have a natural curiosity about what kind of young girl would get herself into such a spot. Her grandfather, who sits at the rear of this courtroom, probably wonders the same thing."

Maggie turned, as did everyone else, to a handful of spectators seated at the rear, and found an old man sitting in the last row, his face as crumpled as an apple left on a windowsill, while Giotti said that he was not going to cast a smoke screen, that all he was doing was to allow this young, vulnerable girl her day in court. He promised to show that even though his client was involved in the acts that led to her mother's death, they could not be charged to her.

Giotti was prepared for the jurors' disbelief. "How can that be, you ask? Because she was the dupe of Kevin Clapp, under the dominion of an aggressive boy who had a plan. We will show that because of predisposing life experiences, she fell completely under his sway as if it were the most natural thing to do in the world, her complicity that of someone with diminished capacity, unable to form the mental states of intent, malice, premeditation, and deliberation, necessary to a conviction of murder."

Maggie resisted his premise as if it were a taste she didn't like, and watched as Melody Bean leaned back in her chair, stuck her legs out under the table as far as they would go, and folded her arms across her chest, refusing to face in the direction of her attorney. Then deliberately, and as slowly as she could, she opened her red plastic purse and removed a stick of chewing gum, which she unwrapped, folded, and placed like a host on her waiting tongue.

Satisfied that his client's behavior was fueling his opening statement, Giotti moved along the jury box, first looking into the sleepy, heavy-lidded eyes of Hannah Watson. "The prosecutor has given you his version of the facts. The defense disputes that version and contends that there are two sides to every question." Then he looked directly at Maggie. "The question you will ask yourself is whether Melody's immaturity, her limited ability, are reason enough for sending her to prison for the rest of her life, for depriving her of husband and children. You have heard that where there is smoke, there is fire. In this case, you have not yet seen any smoke. That is not to say you will not see smoke during the course of this trial. You may see smoke, but it is up to you to decide whether you also saw fire, and if you did not, your verdict must be not guilty."

Maggie stepped carefully through the frozen mud of the parking lot. Reeling from opposing information, her mind was spinning between the two faces of persuasion like a coin. She waved to the farmer's wife and to Hobart Straw, who had remembered when she and Alan bid on the cherry desk and confided that they overpaid, and that they could have gotten it cheaper if they had not appeared so eager.

Amos Stringer bent beneath the hood of his pickup, attempting to start it without success. He seemed vulnerable, as if caught in the jaws of a giant fish.

Maggie guessed that he had probably heard the things the beekeeper had said about him. "What's the trouble?" she asked.

"Battery's dead. You don't have jumper cables by any chance?"

"What do they look like?"

"Jesus. Forget it." He unscrewed the battery from its mount.

"Your truck's not going to start for sure if you do that."

"No kidding." He slammed down the hood and tucked his hands under his arms to restore their warmth.

The parking lot was deserted. Maggie opened the door of her car. "You need a ride?"

He nodded, not surprised that she couldn't get the toggles on her coat to match up. "The nearest gas station will be fine." He carried the battery on his lap. At first they drove in awkward silence, both staring straight ahead. For some reason she tried to mask her breathing; its sound was too intimate, and she held it in, exhaling silently and inhaling in shallow sips, like a connoisseur of wine.

"There's a Chevron station about a quarter of a mile on the right."

"That's where I'm heading," she said. He smelled of woodsmoke. It was on his jacket, his hair. "What was it like, in Canada?" She asked the question in a rush, then regretted that she had said anything.

"You eat potato chips with vinegar. Anything else you curious to know?"

"I'm sorry," she replied. "I shouldn't have asked that."

"It's common knowledge," he said. "Up for grabs. Thanks for the ride." He pointed to the lone toggle dangling from her jacket. "Next time start from the bottom and work your way up."

Maggie found Letitia and Kristen in Kristen's bedroom. Alan's toolbox and tools were strewn over Kristen's sleigh bed. Letitia, in a man's shirt and pants, was on her knees behind the pink-washed wardrobe that Maggie had painted with garlands and swags, inserting a wire through a newly drilled hole.

"Gran is wiring my stereo into the armoire. It makes more sense. We went to Daddy's grave," said Kristen. She was smiling, Maggie noticed, for the first time since she had come home, not with teeth exposed, but beatific, like someone with a vision. "You've been busy. Anything else?"

"We watched *General Hospital*, and Gran fixed the toaster. Did she do it?"

"I can't discuss the trial," said Maggie, still puzzling over how the girl could have killed her own mother on the say-so of someone else, over Giotti's assertion that he did not have to present any proof, that the burden was on the state.

"When was the last time you were at Alan's grave?" asked Letitia.

Maggie thought of the lonely, rocky cemetery where Alan lay buried next to his father. Many of the stones dated back over two hundred years, some with winged angels with truncated, timeworn noses. "I don't know," she replied. "Why?"

"I should think that you would want to visit Alan's resting place."

"He's not there," said Maggie. *He's not anywhere.* She missed him badly. Instead of getting better, the pain was getting worse, expanding, like a black hole, into a giant void.

"Jenna has told me where you think he is, although I can't believe you're serious." Letitia reached for the needle-nosed pliers at her side, making it obvious that she was not going to say any more on the subject of ghostly echoes.

"Where?" asked Kristen. "Tell me."

"Kristen tells me you've got a date with some man," said Letitia, changing the subject.

Maggie was at first so annoyed with Jenna for divulging her confidence that for a moment she forgot the telephone call of the night before. When she remembered the conversation with Herrick, she got angry at Kristen for her betrayal. "He's a friend of Woody Pringle's."

"Don't you think it's a little soon?" asked Letitia.

"That's what I thought, Gran."

"It's almost four months," said Maggie.

"It's been three months and three days," said Letitia. "Would you rather I waited?"

"That's not for me to say," said Letitia.

"But you are saying it. It's the first thing you asked me. Look, this man means nothing to me one way or another. The important issue is that Kristen belongs in school. Why haven't you said anything about that? It seems to me that that's a little more pressing."

"Because," said Letitia, "Kristen and I are in accord."

"What does that mean?"

"I support her in this choice."

Maggie looked at the two of them, accomplices, conspirators. A lump rose in her throat. Jealousy?

"Since when?"

"Since she called me two weeks ago."

"I don't believe this," said Maggie. "Krissie, you told Gran two weeks ago and you didn't tell me?"

"Just because of the way you're acting now. I knew you wouldn't understand."

"Kristen wants to go to school in Vermont," said Letitia, "that is, if she's sure she wants to go to college at all. It's not necessarily for everyone. Plenty of men and women never go to college and wind up making significant contributions. Plenty of men and women go to college and do nothing with their education."

Tired from a long day of paying attention, of blocking thoughts that crept in uninvited, of trying to remember all that she had heard, Maggie was in no mood for conspiracy. "Why didn't she decide this before I sent six thousand dollars to the registrar? Most of which I probably won't recover."

"Tuition money should not be the means by which Kristen is forced to attend something she feels is without value."

"That's OK for you to say, Letitia. I'm the one who can't afford to lose it. I'm the one who has to pay back thirty thousand dollars that I didn't borrow in the first place." Maggie waited for some reaction from Letitia. There was none. She turned to Kristen. "Then what is it you *do* want to do, Krissie? Because you have to do something. That's where I draw the line."

Letitia leaned on her side to stretch along the length of the baseboard like a tree that had been felled. "She wants to work with acid rain. And I think it's an important pursuit."

"Doing what? Who's going to hire her? And what about kicking back, Krissie? You told me this morning that that's what you needed to do."

"Actually," said Kristen, "it works out. I only have to collect water samples from the lake two days a week. The rest of the time I'm off."

"Everything is frozen, or didn't you notice?"

"Not at the edges," said Kristen, "or didn't you notice? Besides, you get an auger to cut through the ice. God Almighty."

"We didn't really expect you to understand, Margaret. You have to realize that Kristen has a feeling for the environment that is quite natural for someone born and raised here."

"Raised, maybe, but not born. She was born in Massachusetts General."

"The point is, that you've never developed that feeling, despite Alan, and all of us. Naturally, I am gratified to see that Kristen shares it."

Maggie turned on her heels. Tears were coming fast. "Do me a favor, Krissie, send 'God Almighty' back to Lisa along with her skirt." She withdrew the square of needlepoint from the bag that hung from her shoulder. "And while you're at it, take this to your Aunt Jenna when you see her. Tell her that it's wrong. That actually, those sleeves were not worn at the time of the wimple. Tell her to finish it herself."

CHAPTER 5

Recess

MAGGIE'S DATE WITH JUSTIN Herrick loomed like an execution. Maggie had accepted out of pique, impulse. Reluctant to ask Woody Pringle for Herrick's telephone number, and lacking a vigorous excuse—a headache or the willies would not cut it—there was no easy way to call him back and cancel. She decided to get through the evening the way she regarded a dental appointment: as quickly and as painlessly as possible.

Maggie moved aside Kristen's rapidly growing collection of milky water samples that lined the bathroom sink to reach her eyeshadows. It had been months since she had done anything with makeup, other than a touch of gloss to keep her lips from cracking. A lifetime ago. Alan said she didn't need it, but Sybil encouraged it, especially when women began to plant themselves in Alan's path like signposts, the time when most of their group came to the realization that marriage was as good as it was going to get. When Alan told her he preferred the unvarnished look, Maggie replied that Medici ladies put belladonna in their eyes to dilate their pupils and that in comparison, plum-tinted eyeliner was nothing. It was one of the rare times she listened to anything Sybil had to say.

Maggie's application of green and brown shadows resulted in eyelids with a peculiar iridescence like the carapace of a beetle. She wiped it off and started over, choosing instead to combine rust and rose, accidentally knocking over two of Kristen's jars, and trying to imagine the person that she had spoken to so hurriedly on the telephone. Justin Herrick was a friend of Woody's. That was all she knew. She pictured him balding like Woody, rounding in the middle like an apple, in his forties or maybe fifties, who carried a package of Tums that he popped like peanuts into his dyspeptic mouth. He said he was a widower. Maybe he was even older. He probably walked with a stoop like Mr. Purdy, the retired postmaster who crept bent through the village as if from the weight of some congratulatory hand.

The actual Justin Herrick, who arrived promptly at seven-thirty with the bong of the grandfather clock in the hall, was a surprise. Tall and straight, he had the craggy, Cro-Magnon good looks of an anchorman, a senator, a pictograph hurled into the universe on a space probe, with prerequisite chin and nose, and all his steel-gray hair. She judged him to be in his middle to late forties. It was hard to reconcile the man who stood smiling in the doorway with the image she had conjured.

"Maggie?" Herrick waited in the doorway.

She put out her hand. His was big and warm, a take-charge hand, like Alan's. She allowed hers to be cradled briefly in its warmth, for an eyeblink, a breath caught, a freeze frame of time, before she pulled it free, feeling guilty, feeling safe. It reminded her of the time Alan had taken her hands, rubbing them between his own when they had gone camping on the mountain and she had been cold, and Alan had made a fire with ribbons of birch-bark and a handful of evergreen twigs, using the opened flap of his mackinaw as a barricade against the wind. Maggie, whose idea of a vacation included a lobby, endured fingertips grown numb, and shivering that never stopped because such discomforts came with a package which included safety, reliability, Alan.

Herrick followed her into the living room, which smelled

of Murphy's oil soap and patchouli, studying her as if ticking off some personal scale of credits and debits, and dipping when he walked, like a man with a wooden leg. "Your floor needs to be leveled," he said, pulling off his down jacket and revealing an elbow-patched tweed jacket.

Bent on keeping the engagement uneventful, she endured his comment and poked her glasses back onto the bridge of her nose. "Would you like a drink?" she asked.

He offered to make martinis. She told him that she preferred an apricot sour, that the sour mix was hidden beneath the bartender's guide, and that she would give him a towel in which to bang the ice cubes because she did not know where the crusher was. His commission gave her a chance to fish out the dead guppies before they polluted the tank, and to refill Kristen's empty specimen jars that she had spilled at the bathroom sink, thereby eliminating two counts of guilt in a creative solution in which one problem would serve the other.

When she returned, Justin had seated himself with a drink in hand in Alan's wing chair and was settling his shoulder blades into its high back, as if trying to erase the imprint of its former occupant.

His chiseled face registered enlightened concern. "Would you rather I didn't sit in this chair?" he asked.

"It doesn't make any difference," she replied.

Justin had the knowing look of a man who could read minds. "It's all over your face. I'll get up." He sprang to his feet, smoothing the seat cushion as if glossing over ruffled feathers, giving it a final pat, then with no wasted motion, handed Maggie her drink and sat beside her on the sofa, a proper body width apart. She was glad he recognized such Letitia-like conventions that in other circumstances she usually ignored. It would make the evening bearable.

There was an awkward moment when they swirled ice cubes in silence. She thought of Amos Stringer, of driving him to get his battery fixed, and wondered if he had ever gotten his truck repaired. She couldn't imagine him drinking anything with an ice cube. "I think I told you on the phone," she said, "that this is my first time out with another man."

"I would have known it. Any man with experience would have known it. You didn't have to say a word."

The idea of being transparent was not a comfortable one. It left nowhere to hide. "How?" she asked. "How would you know?"

Justin crossed his long legs in an elaborate swing that promised a lengthy and considered discourse. She saw that his socks did not cover his shins. Alan's socks always came up over his calves so that you never saw skin between his shoes and his trouser cuff. It was a small chink, but a chink nonetheless. Maggie relaxed.

"I've found that widows are not completely at ease," he said. "It depends on how long they've been widowed, of course. For the two or three that I've gone out with, dating again is a completely new experience. The ground rules are different. They're not as comfortable as women who've been divorced. Of course, the ones I've met are older than you."

"How do you know how old I am?"

"Woody told me."

Civility was becoming a burden. "Why would he do that?"

"I asked him."

"What else did you ask him?"

He reached over to pat her hand. "Maggie, stop being so defensive. Relax. You might learn something about yourself. Actually, to their credit, widows are very, very active ladies, all of them. In sports, various organizations, clubs. The problem with most widows, and I hope you will not take this personally—"

She interrupted. It was something she rarely did. She usually suppressed what she felt. Now it just bubbled up out of some puckish spring. It felt strangely brave, like plunging into the lake in May. "How can I learn something about myself if I'm not supposed to take this personally?"

He leaned away from her, as if she were contagious. "What you're doing now is an example of what I'm talking about. You make yourselves unapproachable. You twist our words around or you back off into conversation that's safe, like your golf game. And you're all very uptight about romance."

Maggie sat upright, alerted. "I'm not much of a golfer," she said. "I know what clubs to use, and I know how to address the ball, but I was never any good. The pro says I lack commitment. Alan was a scratch golfer. Without even trying."

"You all do that, too," he said. "It's something you have to watch."

"Do what? Lack commitment?"

"Eulogize your husbands. I think it has something to do with guilt."

The staircase began to quake. It was Kristen, clumping down the steps in her ski boots, making the kind of angry racket that Maggie felt like making. "This is my daughter, Kristen. Krissie, this is Justin Herrick."

Ever since their argument that morning over the ownership of Alan's flannel shirt, ending in what Kristen designated as Maggie's imperialistic appropriation, Kristen was sullen. She appraised her mother's date with the same leaden judgment that Melody Jessica Bean had given the day before to the hunter who came upon the body.

Bits and pieces of Friday's proceedings floated up like bubbles in a soda. The witness, a plumber who liked to hunt, had been nervous under questioning, his Adam's apple riding his neck like an elevator. When asked what he had found in the quarry, he swallowed hard, as if he were trying to choke down a peach pit. The body of a woman, he replied. When Maggie squinted at the photograph—the jury's first tangible piece of evidence—she thought the object in the center looked like a lonely pile of rags. Willard Peterson said it looked deader than hay.

Later during lunchbreak, Amos had said the picture was shot with a wide-angle lens, and that the body was not as far from the edge of the quarry as it seemed to be.

"Maybe you ought to tell that to someone," she said.

"It's their show," he replied, and she had regarded him with pity, wondering if he knew that a button was missing from his shirt.

"Mom, are you listening? I asked you where you put my red cashmere sweater. I can't find it anywhere."

Maggie felt as if her mind had caught on a doorknob. She matched her petulant daughter with a petulance of her own. "You shrunk it, remember?"

Kristen stomped out of the room and called from the door, asking to see her for a minute. The request meant an angry, hurried conference full of hoarse accusations, with no satisfaction possible for either party.

Maggie sighed and excused herself. They stood in the dining room beneath the French military prints. Maggie decided to take the offensive. "Why are you still in your ski boots?"

Kristen parried. "He's doing a number on you."

"Were you listening to our conversation?" asked Maggie. "I don't like eavesdropping, and Letitia likes it even less."

"Why do you have to bring Granny into this? I wasn't listening on purpose. He's as loud as Woody Pringle. You can hear him all over the house. Mucho middle-aged macho. You can't be so wimpy with him. You have to assert yourself."

"Thanks," said Maggie, "I'll try to remember that."

"Another thing. What's going on with you and the Bouchards?"

"Why?" Maggie glanced into the living room, where Justin continued to swirl his ice cubes.

"Because when I saw Annie Laura at the mall, she acted funny. I asked her what was wrong and she said, 'Ask your mom.' "

"Some other time, Kristen. This isn't the moment."

"Well, when?"

"Tonight, when I come home."

"Another thing." There was no limit. "Where are the keys to the car?"

"Can't you ask me in another way? 'May I have the keys to the car?' would be better. I'll even accept 'can.' The answer is I'd rather you didn't drive. The roads are pretty bad. Can't Ranger come here?"

"Why would you think I'd want to be with Ranger?"

"Because he's been part of the woodwork for the last three years. Because he's a nice kid. Because he's the only one brave enough to chase Nathan's bull from the front lawn." Because when the roads are dry and he can get around on his dirt bike, he stops by from time to time to see if I'm okay.

"Ranger's a creep. If I have to stay home, I'm liable to get seriously depressed, you know?"

They sized each other up, like generals on opposing hillocks, overlooking the plain between them. Maggie looked into Kristen's silver-blue eyes. Was she kidding? Kristen, in turn, looked steadfast through her mother's eyeglasses. Did she buy it? "You're giving me two bad choices," said Maggie.

"I know how to drive."

Maggie kissed her on the cheek for the memory of the imperious two-year-old spooning apple sauce onto her chin. "Be careful."

"Because I'm all you have?"

"I didn't say that," Maggie called over her shoulder. "And I don't know why you had to."

"You were going to."

Maggie spun as if on skates. "I won't take the blame for something that you think I was going to say. That's conjecture. Incidentally, if you're on ice, shift down. It's safer than pumping your brakes."

"Who told you to do that? You never used to do that."

The day before Hannah Watson had remarked what a comfort Kristen must be, a frequent refrain from people without adolescent children. Kristen would never have asked Alan for the car keys the way she just had. Her request would have been softer, amiable, coquettish. Alan had been the buffer. Without him they rasped against each other like sandpaper.

"Don't worry about it," said Justin when Maggie returned. "All kids are like that. Mine were the same way. They have to show that they don't approve. Loyalty to the other parent. Let's not talk about kids. I hear you've pulled jury duty."

Maggie listened for the bang of the front door. "We can't discuss the case."

"I'm not asking you to discuss the case, Maggie. Just trying to make conversation."

"Sorry." Somehow she was at fault. "It's just that we were cautioned in a very definite way."

"You're really taking it very seriously, aren't you?"

"Wouldn't you?" Maggie did not remember Kristen wearing gloves. She listened to the Subaru squeal out of the driveway.

"Jury duty is something I've managed to avoid." He glanced at his watch. "We'd better get going if we want to keep our reservation. Have you been to the Valley Inn?"

Alan had taken her there on her birthday in early spring, when everything was plastered with mud and getting about was like plodding through mocha batter. He seemed distant then, but intent on pleasing. He bought her a garnet pendant in a box lined with velour. It was the wrong birthstone. She told him she loved it and let him clasp it behind her neck.

Sybil had been appalled when Maggie described her birthday gift on the telephone. "The man is a successful orthopedist and you're grateful for a pendant on cotton? You have to be kidding." They did not speak for several months. The next time was when Maggie called in tears to say that Alan had died.

Justin performed courtly services that Alan had deemed unnecessary and, in fact, harmful for a healthy woman who was about to step over the threshold of middle age. He held open her car door, helped fasten her seat belt, held out her chair, pointed out the items on the menu to give special attention to, and gave the waitress the order for both of them, saying, "The lady will have . . ."

Forced to sit face to face, just inches apart, Maggie played with her silverware and pressed the tablecloth with her fingertips while Justin inspected her mouth with his eyes.

"You have a lovely malocclusion," he said.

He was moving too fast and in the wrong direction. It was like wearing a dress inside out and backward. "Look," she said. "I'm feeling kind of funny about all of this. Maybe we should stay away from personal stuff and stick to something like current events."

He acceded with a hand wave and a tilt of his chair, wondering why some of them always made it a game. "Fine with me. I understand your judge is being considered for the senate."

"I didn't hear anything about that."

"I did. In fact, I know some of the people that might back her. Believe it or not, the fact that she is married is a drawback, which is interesting, because for a male in politics, marriage is a decided advantage."

This sounded like the time to tell him straight out. "I want you to know, Justin, that I'm not interested in getting married."

He laughed. "You made a big leap from congressional nomination to marriage. By the way, that's something else you all say. About not wanting to get married. Every single one of you. Don't you check with each other?"

He told her that he was a lobbyist for outside developers and that his wife had died of breast cancer. He said he was the first to feel the lump.

"How many others were involved?" she asked.

"I'm sure you didn't mean that the way it sounded," he said. She apologized.

Like pedaling her Rudge uphill, it was hard to get

conversation started again once it had stopped. And once it stopped, it was hard to keep out the trial and the little girl accused of poisoning her mother. Would McKeen make such an allegation if it were not so? Maggie pulled herself up short. She was not supposed to think in those terms. The girl was innocent until proven guilty. The real question was, Did it make you more or less of an orphan to kill your own mother?

With no inclination to manufacture small talk, Maggie glanced around the honeycomb of small dining rooms connected to one another by low, wide doorways fashioned when the women of a shorter population wore crinolines. She recognized a few people, among them the high school principal with a group she did not know, Trish Robidoux in a corner with another woman, dividing the check with quivering flights of her eyebrows, and in the fern-hung garden room beyond, a table of eight, including Woody Pringle and his wife, Drew, Maybeth Chase and her husband, Emory, Lester Perkins, the funeral director (Maggie could not see who sat beside him, but imagined it was his wife, Edna Louise, reportedly five years his senior), Anne, and half of Peter. Her heart began to hammer against her breastbone. She turned back, wondering how old she was going to have to be before she got control of her own body.

Justin had recovered and was giving it another try. It was a variation on the same theme. She was in good hands. All she needed to do was relax, give herself permission to have a good time, and realize that she was in competition with a lot of other women.

The waitress set asparagus vinaigrette before Maggie. It was what Justin had decided she would like. She wanted to poke him in the eye with a stalk. She relished the image while he continued.

"Widows have told me," he said, "that a woman without a man is nothing. A woman I'm seeing now is a case in point. Married twice, from what I can gather is well fixed, is invited everywhere. And she says, 'I don't want to feel like a third wheel.' It's gotten to a point, with the situation what it is today, including a hygienically dangerous single scene which we needn't go into, that what is uppermost in the minds of a lot of these widows and divorcees is to get married again."

"Count me out," said Maggie, shaking an asparagus stalk in her hand. "I already made it clear how I feel about that."

He smiled benevolently, wiping vinaigrette dressing from his tie. "And so you did. But even if you didn't, it's normal for a woman. Nothing to be ashamed of. The old story." He leaned forward and touched her other hand, a light stroke across the knuckles, and engaged her eyes. "Maybe you're one of those women who would just like to know that they have someone they can count on. Someone who will take them out, someone they can cook for, fuss over. In exchange for loving attention." He was explaining the deal.

Maggie needed a place to hide. When she had been small and Sybil too cloying, she hid, under beds, in closets. Once, for an entire afternoon she hid behind the sofa with a glass of strawberry Kool-Aid and a banana, despite frantic telephone calls to the police which she could hear, along with an anguished Puerto Rican janitor who swore the child had absolutely not been in the basement, contrary to the eyewitness report of the laundress from 3-G.

She glanced into the garden room with its hanging ferns and table of eight. A few months ago, she would have been sitting there with Alan, probably next to Lester Perkins, who, other than an occasional request for butter or salt, was never demanding. One could be relaxed beside Lester, at least before he came to be associated with death and loneliness, and not have to search out light and lovely comments that Anne and Drew were able to fire off like rockets.

Peter said something crooked-grinned and funny, causing everyone to laugh and Anne to lean her head with proprietary affection on his arm. It was not fair, thought Maggie, that they could be so happy, so connected, while she was as wilted and as truncated as a carrot stalk.

Drew Pringle was the first to spot Maggie and Justin. They all turned to look. Woody made a circle with his thumb and forefinger, Maybeth whispered something to her husband, then gave the forced smile of an aging, though still enthusiastic, cheerleader, while Anne and Peter turned away.

"How about that?" said Justin. "There's old Woody. Great guy." He waved in return.

"If you want to go over and say hello," she said, "go ahead."

"And leave you? Certainly not." He poured wine into her glass. "If you want to get back in the swim of things, Maggie, try to follow the lead of the divorcee."

Maggie sneaked a peek at her watch under the table. Talk about beating a dead horse.

"Never look back. You know why?"

"You turn to salt."

He smiled indulgently. "I don't mean not to keep fond memories, but invariably, when I take out a widow, I find a picture of the husband sitting on the mantelpiece, or worse, staring at me from a bureau. With a widow, I feel that I'm always being compared. The divorcée, on the other hand, tosses her photographs along with her ex."

"What about you, Justin? Do you have any pictures?"

Maggie did not wait to hear his reply. When Anne stood up and made her way to the ladies' room, Maggie crumpled her napkin, threw it on the table, and followed. She caught up with her in a tiny cubicle that smelled of cedar, then stood with her back to the door, clutching the knob closed with all her strength. "We have to talk," she said.

Anne had unclasped her bow and was smoothing her long blonde hair. She never took her eyes from the mirror. "I'm not a heartless person, Maggie. I have been, and will probably always be, very fond of you. You should know that. We've known one another long enough. You were lonely and you reached out, and Peter was there. I understand. Really, I do. Finish. End. I'm not mad anymore."

Maggie was angry with herself for not being able to let it go. It would be so easy. Why did she have to drag it under a light? "But that's not what happened. You never asked me what happened."

"I don't have to. There's no point."

"It doesn't mean anything when you tell me you're not angry anymore. That implies that you have reason to be angry. If you knew how it was, none of this would have happened. We've been best friends since our kids were babies. We told each other everything. Why won't you let me tell you this?"

"Why didn't you tell me how it was when it happened? Why did you wait? That suggests all sorts of reasons to me. None of them good. This is hard for me too, Maggie."

"Then why don't you believe me?" Someone knocked at the door. Maggie held it closed.

"Because I believe my husband."

"He's lying."

The pounding increased. "I don't mean to be pushy," shouted a voice from the other side of the door, "but aren't you guys ever going to come out?" It was Drew.

Anne snapped the bow closed over the knot of her hair. "I don't have to listen to this." She strode out as Woody's wife came in. "I hope someone ordered my soufflé," she said to Drew. Then she turned to Maggie. "By the way," she said, "you never gave me your navy evening skirt. Someone else must have it. Check with Hope Dyer. You may have lent it to her when she went to Dartmouth for Win's twenty-fifth."

Drew cranked a quick smile at Anne. She wore no makeup. With watery-blue eyes, dry, flaky, vanilla skin, and graying platinum blonde hair, she looked like rice paper. "What do you think of him, Maggie?"

"I think he's a liar."

"Not Peter," whispered Drew. "Justin."

"He might be a liar, too. It's too soon to tell."

"Don't become one of these bitter widows, Maggie. Try to think positively. You're a lucky gal. A lot of women would give their eyeteeth to get a date with Justin Herrick."

Maggie took out a deep rust lipstick and applied it with defiant slashes. "I'm getting tired of people who are not widows handing me a code of widow behavior."

Drew put her hand on Maggie's shoulder. "Something's happened to you. I hate to see it. You used to be one of the sweetest gals I know. Shy, reserved. It was part of your charm. Especially because you came from New York. It was a rarity. It told me here was someone special. Here was someone I wanted for a friend. She's a New Yorker, we all said to one another, but you'll really like her in spite of it. By the way, my Uncle Willard is on the jury. He tells us that it's real exciting. He says you had to look at some grisly pictures. How could you stand that, Maggie? I don't know if I could look at anybody who was dead." When she realized what she said, her mouth formed into a commiserative *O*.

"I can't talk about the trial."

Drew smiled sweetly. "I don't really need you to. Uncle Willard tells us everything."

Maggie fought back tears of anger on her way to the table. They spilled onto the bow of her ivory silk blouse.

"What happened?" Justin inquired as he stood holding out her chair. "I was worried about you."

"Please don't worry about me. I'm perfectly fine."

"Are you?"

He looked so kindly, so safe, she wanted to curl up in the shelter of his tweedy arms right there in the dining room of the Valley Inn.

It happened instead in the car before he put the key in the ignition. She clung to his down jacket, smothering her face in its quilted depths, and cried on his shoulder. He asked no questions. "I know. I understand. You're with Justin," he said.

On the way home she agreed to another date to go cross-country skiing. Justin said he had given up downhill after he dislocated his shoulder. You need to get in shape, he said. Try knee squats. If you work up to fifty a day, you'll do fine. She told him that she didn't have real wool knickers. He said he liked her sense of humor, then kissed her good night, darting in like a hummingbird before she knew what had happened. Maggie was so depressed she didn't care. "You're clenching your teeth," he admonished.

"That's because I'm shivering."

"Is there something the matter? Do I repulse you?"

"No."

"Then relax," he said, pulling her chin toward him. "You're allowed to do this. I just want to show you how lovely I think you are."

By separating her teeth. Maggie let her mouth go slack. He pushed in a tongue sweetened by Tic-Tacs and scoured her gingiva. "There," he said. "Was that so bad?"

Like a trip to the dentist.

Kristen was upstairs, sitting on her bed and swinging her legs over the side like a threshing machine. "I stayed home," she said, "because I knew you really didn't want me to go out. I got depressed."

Look what you made me do. Maggie was so happy to see her she forgave her the game. "I'm sorry, baby. That you're feeling down. I am, too."

"Tell me about the Bouchards," said Kristen. "Maybe it will cheer me up."

"I doubt it, Krissie. It's not that kind of story. But you have a right to hear it."

Maggie sat beside her daughter and told her what had happened in the kitchen, leaving out no detail. She waited for Kristen's contempt.

"That creep," said Kristen.

"You don't think it was my fault?" asked Maggie. She

pushed a wisp of hair from Kristen's forehead. Kristen knocked her hand away.

"That's blaming the victim. No way. You told him no, didn't you?"

"Not exactly."

"That's where you went wrong. Next time, say no. Don't equivocate."

Maggie kissed her. "Thank you, Krissie. Where did you learn 'equivocate'?"

"I've been using it since the tenth grade. What was going on in the car? The windows were all steamed."

"Nothing much. Just a good-night kiss."

"Yuck. Did you want to?"

"No."

"God Almighty, you're like a little kid. No wonder Daddy was so worried about you."

"He was," said Maggie, "wasn't he? Worried about me. I never heard him worry about you, though. He was so proud of you. Speaking of Daddy, I need another picture of him."

"There's one next to your bed."

"I want another one for the living room. I packed them away, but I forgot where I put them."

"There's a whole lot of pictures and stuff in Daddy's study. In the closet behind all his journals. How much longer are they going to keep coming?"

"I don't know. I guess I can't bring myself to cancel them."

"What's the point? I don't read them, do you?"

"No. But they mattered to him, Krissie. They're like his fish tank."

"No, they're not. The fish are alive. Or were the last time I looked. The journals are only paper. You're inconsistent, you know that? You go out with some guy right after Daddy dies, you don't even wait six months like Granny says you're supposed to, but you won't cancel his subscriptions."

Maggie sighed. The object of child rearing, as she understood it, was to make one's child as independent as possible. The problem was, independence created contrary opinions and, if the child was as bright as Kristen, articulation to match. How much longer was this going to keep up? Maggie was ready to call a moratorium. Maybe they could negotiate.

She dug through the boxes in Alan's study closet like a ferret. There were old X rays dating back to his residency, letters, posters, a record of Jean-Luc Ponty playing the music of Frank Zappa, the *Whole Earth Catalogue,* unframed photos, framed photos, and Christmas decorations—tree ornaments, wreaths, tinsel, lights, a white felt snow blanket for the base of the tree, streamers, and arrangements of berries and elves tucked into sleighs. Alan had always taken charge of Christmas, contriving the photograph for their yearly card, cutting down a spruce from his mother's property, decorating the interior of the house (he wouldn't string lights in the yard, that was showboating), and stashing presents along the ceiling beams. Maggie crouched on her knees, wondering how she was going to get through Christmas. Thanksgiving at Letitia's house with Jenna and Owen was bad enough. Maggie took out a picture of Alan in ski goggles, poised on top of Suicide Run, then threw everything back. One unopened box contained a papier mâché replica of an eighteenth-century angel with blonde hair coiffed in a pouf that could be seen through a cellophane window. On the outside of the box someone had scribbled, *Just call me angel of the morning, angel. AAA*

Maggie drove to the airport the next morning to pick up Sybil. The Subaru still smelled of woodsmoke. The odor was a mystery until Maggie remembered Amos Stringer and the acrid scent that clung to his garments. She wondered how he was spending the weekend, decided it was probably under his truck, and then wondered if he too was having to fend off nosy people who wanted to discuss the trial. She concluded that if he were under his truck, he couldn't be reached.

Sybil stepped off the concourse with her old zip. She looked terrific, her blonde hair coiffed in a shining sweep from her forehead, and her tight, trim body in a Donna Karan jumpsuit. If you didn't look at her hands, she looked no older than Maggie. She's had another tuck, thought Maggie, who knew that Sybil worked on her face like a tailor.

They embraced, Sybil smelled of Shalimar. "When did you have the lift?" asked Maggie. "You didn't tell me you were going to do it again."

"Actually," said Sybil, "it's a peel. You like it?"

Maggie examined her mother's shining, tight face. "It's startling. How do they do it?"

"They paint acid on your face. Then cover it with tape. You sip through a straw for a week. It's very good for weight control."

"Does it hurt?"

"Only when they rip off the tape. Then it just itches."

"My God, Mother, acid. Weren't you afraid?"

"Everything is a risk, dear. Having you was a risk. But look at my reward. Naturally I had the tiniest reservation, but my resolve was firm and I just put it out of my mind. The main thing is, you have to have confidence in your doctor, and I went to the best." She took out a packet from her Louis Vuitton traveling case. "Here it is. My ad, and the responses."

"What ad?"

"I put a personal ad in *New York* magazine."

When Sybil went to stand guard at the conveyor belt, Maggie ripped opened the packet. In it was a piece of newsprint on which a small box had been red-lined. The copy read: *Age cannot wither, nor custom stale, this lovely woman's infinite variety. Unretouched photos sent on request.* Inside also were a dozen envelopes, some ripped open, some sealed shut. "Aren't you still married?"

"A minor point," replied Sybil, hefting her luggage with a practiced arm. "I want you to help me evaluate the replies. Some of them look promising."

"You didn't come to Vermont for a point scale."

"You're right. I didn't." Sybil searched her daughter's face. "How are you?"

"I'm fine. Let me take that. The car's out in front."

"You haven't sounded fine."

"I'm all right, Mother. Really."

Sybil seemed to have trouble keeping up. "I'll feel happier when I know that for sure."

"What have you got in here?" asked Maggie, whose real question was, How long do you plan to stay?

Maggie had not seen her mother since the funeral, when Sybil had shown up wearing an enormous haute couture jacket with exaggerated shoulders that made her look like a linebacker. Maggie regarded her warily as she had all her life, with the familiar push/pull of distrust and fascination, manageable only with an angled perspective that gave one distance. "Kristen is home."

"So soon? I thought she wasn't coming home for Thanksgiving."

"She's dropped out."

"It's her life," said Sybil. "She's entitled to screw it up exactly as she pleases, like anybody else."

"You think I screwed up my life?"

"Maggie, don't take everything I say as a personal attack."

Sybil and Kristen did not enjoy a grandparent relationship. Sybil's occasional, erratic visits were as brief and hurried as snow flurries, with as much substance, melting as soon as they touched the ground. Kristen's idea of a grandmother included constancy and wrinkles you could count. Their connection was marginal, surface, and agreeable to both. They each gave the other a cordial but perfunctory hug.

"You look younger than you did at the funeral," said Kristen. "Is it going to fall?"

"I don't think so," said Sybil.

Kristen put toast on a plate. "That would be awful," she said. "If all of a sudden, it fell. And you didn't know it." She left carrying the plate, an opened jar of currant jelly, and a glass of milk upstairs.

Maggie held her breath until her daughter was safely at the top. "I would really like her to go back to school," she said. "I don't know what to do."

"It's her problem," said Sybil, slipping out of her shoes. They had gotten tight, she said, from sitting on the plane. Sybil always had slender legs and feet. Maggie was surprised to see her ankles so puffy.

"You say that so unfeelingly. Did you think that about me? When I told you I wanted to leave Smith to marry Alan. Is that what you thought?"

"I thought you loved Alan more than you loved art history, although I found him a bit stony myself. You said you wanted to get married. You were over eighteen. So I planned a wedding. We advertised for your father, you know. In the *Wall Street Journal*. You were so sweet, and no trouble at all. You wanted a traditional wedding. Thank God for that. Some of my friends were following their children into diving bells. I remember Letitia being an absolute pill. Alan's father, on the other hand, was very agreeable. Now, there was a good-looking man."

"I think he really liked me," said Maggie, drawing frost pictures on the kitchen window.

"Why shouldn't he?"

"You know that Letitia has never liked me very much."

"One's a man and one's a woman."

"That's not always the reason people dislike one another."

Sybil smiled. "You and Alan were so young. You kept tripping in your heels."

"That's because you took away my glasses. I couldn't see." Maggie had drawn little circles separated by two lines. She studied them absently.

"Isn't that too many for tic-tac-toe?" asked Sybil.

"You're right," said Maggie. "It's a jury box," she said, surprised.

"Jenna and Owen looked like a pair of ducks that somehow wandered in through the revolving door. Waddling about together, so out of place. I remember trying to talk to you before the ceremony. 'I know everything there is to know,' you told me. 'I'm not a virgin.' "

Maggie felt close to Sybil at that minute, experiencing a memory trace of riding sleepily in a car and laying her head on Sybil's perfumed fur collar. "And you said that's good, there won't be any surprises."

"I guessed that you had slept with Alan. I just wanted to assure you that it would get better."

Maggie never was comfortable talking about sex with her mother. "What do you mean?"

"Those early gropings usually aren't very good, for either one. Sex is like caviar. You acquire a taste. You also acquire the knack for taking just the right amount. Speaking of which—"

"No," said Maggie, rising from the table. "There's no 'speaking of which.' "

"Maggie, you can talk to me. I understand these things. And contrary to what you might think, I am still very much involved. You've been widowed almost four months. You're young."

"Not so very."

"So very. If you don't use it, you lose it."

"God Almighty," said Maggie.

"When did you start saying God Almighty? I don't remember you ever saying that."

"Since Kristen went to college."

Kristen came downstairs, dressed. "What about me and college? I've made up my mind, so don't anyone try to change it."

"We wouldn't dream of it," said Sybil.

"Do you want me to take you around town, Grandmother?" she asked. "There's a tag sale going on at Ruiter's."

"I can't think of anything more terrible. I want to talk to your mother. Privately. Why don't you busy yourself with something? Don't you have a boyfriend? If you don't you ought to get one. They're absolutely essential for carrying things."

Kristen, looking hurt, drifted out of the room on light feet, as if blown out by a wind.

"She moves like you," said Maggie. "Isn't that strange? She spends so little time with you. I wouldn't have thought you could pick something like that up so easily."

"Why does she call me grandmother?" asked Sybil. "It sounds evil, like something out of Grimm's fairy tales. What's wrong with gammie, or nana, or even Sybil?"

"Don't knock it," said Maggie. "It's a step up from referring to you as my mother. Now what's going on? With you and . . . what's his name, I forgot his name."

"Sidney. Your stepfather's name is Sidney. And there's nothing going on, except an enlarged prostate. I can only see trouble ahead."

CHAPTER 6

Physical Evidence

"WHY?" ASKED MAGGIE, JUGGLING a plastic bag crammed with clothing on her knee. "Why can't you just give these things to Mr. Giotti, or to the judge, or to Melody Jessica? Nobody has to know who gave them to you. Say that you found them."

"I'm quite sure that it's against regulations," said the clerk, twisting each word into a knot with a sanctimonious purse of her lips.

Maggie yanked open the drawstring, revealing a red cashmere sweater, skirts, sneakers, boots, socks, the sleeve of a blue corduroy jacket, and a plaid jumper that Kristen refused to wear. "Look. It's all stuff she can use right now. What if someone were to mail it to the courthouse anonymously? What's the difference?"

"Because you're a juror, Mrs. Hatch. That's the difference. The young lady you want to give them to is on trial for murder. It's just not possible."

"One thing has nothing to do with another," said Maggie. "The girl is cold. I have winter clothes I don't need."

"No can do."

"You've seen her sitting there. She's dressed for summer."

"Miss Bean is being tried as an adult. We also must presume she can dress herself."

"No, we can't," said Maggie. "And you know it."

The clerk left to consult with the judge, then returned to announce that if a third party were to make a donation of clothing to the county, and that if the prosecutor raised no objections, the clothing might get to Melody Jessica, but nobody was making any promises.

That morning marked the first appearance of spectators in the courtroom other than Melody Jessica's grandfather. Among them was the carpenter's girlfriend, a beautician with short spiky bangs, a reporter from the local newspaper who carried a beeper clipped to his pants pocket, and an elderly woman in a hat with earflaps who attended Judge Atwill's trials with the fealty of a groupie.

Melody Jessica, wearing a cheerleader's skirt and a sweater with an *A*, had a cold. She sniffed and snuffled, once wiping her nose with her knuckle until her grandfather passed forward a folded white handkerchief. The morning's proceedings, which began with Dan Giotti's cross-examination of the hunter who had come upon the body and who claimed to have seen a teenage couple run from the scene, were punctuated with her sneezes.

When Nathan Hook returned to the witness chair, it was with considerably less enthusiasm than was evident before the weekend. Friday's testimony had been a chance for center stage, excitement, attention, a chance to be somebody. Monday was a sink he had promised to install. Monday was money lost. Monday was Giotti. His Adam's apple bobbed as it had done the Friday before, only more so.

Giotti began affably, politely, slipping his belt buckle into a looser notch as he asked the witness if he had discussed the case with anyone.

"Yes, sir," replied the plumber.

"Who with?"

Hook jerked his chin. "McKeen over there."

"What did the prosecutor tell you?"

"He told me not to be afraid of you."

The journeyman carpenter barked once, a short yelp

like a dog that has been cuffed into silence. His girlfriend giggled in solidarity until the judge flashed them both a warning look.

Giotti continued, squinting his eyes as if searching for some inner vision. "In your testimony on Friday, you said you recognized Melody Jessica and Kevin Clapp. Were you able to see their faces?"

"No, but it was them."

"How do you know that?"

"It was a pair of teenage kids, all right."

"If you couldn't see their faces, how are you so sure who it was, or for that matter, their ages?"

"The way they ran when they saw me. Lickety-split."

"How fast is lickety-split?"

"Like a jack rabbit."

Giotti turned to smile at the jury. His expression was conspiratorial, companionate. "How do you know they weren't jackrabbits?"

"They were wearing sneakers."

Giotti grinned to show that tomfoolery was all right with him and glanced at his notes. "Mr. Hook, a court officer walked into this courtroom a few minutes ago and brought in some papers. He stood perhaps twenty feet from where you now sit. Can you describe him?"

McKeen jumped to his feet with an objection, his jacket open, his hands on his herringboned hips. Judge Atwill's decision to sustain was no surprise to Maggie, who was beginning to anticipate the pulse of the court, and who had expected it, probably because she couldn't remember the court officer either. Neither could most of the other jurors, who turned to Giotti, shaking his head as if in disbelief.

Deputy Sheriff Will Webberly was next to testify. Tall and angular with sunken cheeks, Webberly described how he had secured the crime scene, marking the perimeter with yellow tape, then made a rough sketch of the scene on the back of a McDonald's bag. McKeen passed the paper bag to both Giotti and the jury. It was returned, numbered by the court reporter, entered as evidence, and pinned to a bulletin board.

The interchange between prosecutor and his witness was rythmic, seamless: McKeen was low-key, respectful; Webberly was decisive, confident. McKeen's questioning established evidence in the form of tire prints found on the bluff consistent with those associated with an older-model Plymouth sedan. In addition, there were no footprints found near the body other than those belonging to Nathan Hook, from which was concluded, since there had been no freeze, that the body had been thrown off the bluff. Webberly also testified that he had found a plastic hair clip on the ridge near the tire tracks.

McKeen gingerly lifted a clear plastic bag from his table with a lime-green object inside on which there were visible whorls of fingerprints, and held it in front of him. "Is this the hair clip?" he asked. Webberly acknowledged that it was. When the box was passed to Giotti, he dismissed the need to see it with a casual wave of his hand.

By the time the jury recessed, their seats had become hard, unyielding, and they crept, crabby and stiff, to the assembly room to stretch, to sink groaning into cushioned armchairs, and to interpret the proceedings for one another over lukewarm cups of oil-slicked coffee. Hobart Straw and the beekeeper, Willard Peterson, argued over Judge Atwill's instruction to disregard Hook's remark about the position of the victim's skirt. Straw maintained that the reason they were asked to ignore the remark was because it was indecent, especially because the woman was dead. Peterson disagreed, insisting that it was stricken from the record because it was irrelevant. Straw then said he did not know how he was supposed to forget a statement once he heard it.

The wife of a snowplow man wondered why Giotti didn't want to see the hair clip. Maybe the hair clip wasn't important, suggested a commercial home canner, a former account executive from Albany who smelled from rum and apples.

"Might be," said Bill Hogan, emptying a packet of sugar into his coffee, "that Giotti just wants us to think it isn't important." No one knew the canner. They all turned to nod gravely, respectfully toward Hogan, as if he had said something sage. The only black man in his township, Hogan was used to excessive courtesies.

The home canner was beginning to feel the weightlessness of the ignored. "How can they keep us together all day long sharing the identical experience, and then tell us not to talk about it?" he asked. No one responded. It was as if he had spoken into the wind. "It's weird, you know?"

He repeated his question to Maggie, who only nodded absently. She was more concerned with questions of her own, principally how Kristen and Sybil were making out since neither cooked and neither showed any particular interest in the other, only the polite inquiries that strangers make of one another. They were both so bent on maintaining distance that each kept separate piles of toilet articles on the rim of the bathtub, a bad augury for a long day indoors.

While the last trial sessions had created subtle shifting of alliances that broke away and reformed like hillocks of blowing sand, there were attitudes on which the jury was still in agreement. Ignoring the comments of the home canner was one, and disliking Amos Stringer was another. They were uncomfortable with Maggie, who was contagious with mortality and plain bad luck, yet they were bewitched with the émigré pianist, Katerina Lodz. Nobody could pronounce her last name, but they whispered about her when she stood at the window, flexing her fingers. She was the closest thing to a celebrity in their ranks, and they relished the affiliation, however limited. Trish Robidoux privately acknowledged having had kielbasa at Katerina's house.

* * *

LaDonna Dyer had withdrawn from the others into the shelter of an old wing chair, lines circling her mouth like parentheses, her ankles crossed over opaque, pumpkin-colored hose darned for reinforcement at the heels. The trial was only an incidental part of her life. More important was trying to figure out what to do with a dairy farmer husband who had made a promise to the government not to produce milk for five years. Shy and reticent, LaDonna was also one of the few people on the jury with whom Maggie felt comfortable, primarily because she didn't cluck.

Maggie sat beside her and offered Godiva chocolates shaped like walnuts that Sybil had brought on the plane. "They used to give me zits," said Maggie. "Now they make me fat."

LaDonna took one, remarking how true to life they looked, and said, "You don't look very fat to me. In fact, before I found out you were a widow, I thought you were sickly. And skinny, like they had to shake the sheets to find you."

Maggie said the only one shaking the sheets was her.

Then LaDonna whispered that she might be out of line saying what she was going to say, but it must be nice with no one to answer to. Maggie answered that it was awful. "I thought it got better with time," said LaDonna, "being a widow."

No, said Maggie. Now she just felt numb, a minus feeling, the kind you get just before frostbite.

"I know that feeling," said LaDonna. "I felt it when I left the house this morning."

Maggie didn't tell LaDonna—in fact, there was no one she could tell—that the minus feeling sometimes got so bad she had had an urge a few weeks back, while in a vacant, empty state like a house that had just been cleared of all its furnishings, to dig him up.

LaDonna confided to Maggie that her husband was not talking again that morning. "He needs privacy for his figuring," she said, even when they went to cut stove wood before breakfast, she had to stand by silently shivering with her hands like ice, while he fiddled with an old, rusty chain saw. "There's no room for mistakes or bad luck on a farm," she said.

"Why did you have to stand there with him?"

"We do everything together," replied LaDonna.

As the jurors filed back into the courtroom, Maggie tried to tally the things that she and Alan had done together. Going to his mother's house for dinner didn't count. Neither did skiing, since they skied not only separate runs but separate slopes. She liked to work with her hands, he with his whole body. When Maggie applied the question to the house and realized that Alan liked to work outside, and she inside, Trish Robidoux caught up to tell her that she had seen her Saturday night at the Valley Inn. "Grass doesn't grow under your feet," she said. "Frankly I was surprised to see you dating so soon."

Maggie was struck dumb as she usually was by an unexpected onslaught, her mind racing like a blank tape, searching for a claw hammer of words to lay this woman flat.

When Amos Stringer remarked that the days were over when widows were expected to fling themselves on their husbands' funeral pyres Trish Robidoux flashed her vaulted eyebrows, making her face look like it was taking off. "My comments were intended for Mrs. Hatch."

"Then you'd better spend some time at the target range," he replied. "And stay away from buckshot. That one missed its mark by a mile and peppered everyone in the jury room."

"What would *you* know about marksmanship?" she asked.

Melody Jessica's cold was worse. Maggie could see it in the defendant's swollen, heavy-lidded eyes. The clerk brought a waste can to the defense table into which Giotti, when he was not behind the lectern, tossed crumpled wads of tissue that his client had dropped.

Webberly became a hostile witness, grinding his teeth

during his cross-examination so that the outlines of his mandibles could be seen flashing beneath his skin. Giotti asked him the length of time he had been on the force. Ten years, he answered, which did not count a two-year leave of absence to work in his ailing father-in-law's gravel pit.

"Deputy Webberly," said Giotti. "You testified that you obtained a plaster of paris cast of the tire track. Is that correct?"

"Yes sir," replied the deputy sheriff.

"Is it possible," asked Giotti, "to add cuts and marks to a cast to make it conform to a tire track, to change it from a Camaro, for example, to a Plymouth sedan?"

Judge Atwill leaned over the bench as McKeen rose to his feet. "This court is interested in facts, Mr. Giotti, not hypothesis."

Giotti became suddenly humble, contrite, willing to concede the deputy's expertise, and thanked him, then Webberly stood, about to leave the stand, and Giotti whirled around as if he had just remembered something. "Just one more question, if you don't mind." Webberly sat down again, the knuckles of his hands showing white as he gripped the arms of his chair while Giotti held up the McDonald's bag. "Deputy Webberly, from this paper bag, on which are printed two prominent arches, are we to infer distance as well as position?"

"I don't get your drift."

"There are no scale dimensions indicated. For example, some notation that says half an inch equals one foot. Without scale dimensions, how is anyone to read this with accuracy?"

"I'm no artist."

McKeen looked angry. He twirled a pencil between his hands. The jury knew he was angry. So were they. Giotti seemed to be badgering the witness, and they felt Webberly's discomfort as keenly as if it had been they who were under fire.

"No further questions," said Giotti, who had seen the

jury's pendulum swing in his disfavor, and decided to save his attack on the deputy's credibility for when it would do the most good.

On the way out of the court room to collect their belongings, Hobart Straw said that he heard that Giotti was originally from New Jersey. "That explains it," said Hannah Watson.

Hogan's overcoat had slipped off its hanger. He bent with difficulty to retrieve it, his knees stiff with arthritic changes produced by old college basketball injuries. When Maggie stooped beside him to pick up his coat, he straightened with little snapping sounds and asked if her friend had sold her house.

"Not yet," she replied.

"Just as well," he said. "This isn't the best time to sell a house from what I hear."

"When is?"

"In the spring. The end of the school year. Most people want to relocate before their kids have to go back to school."

Owen had called twice that week about a couple, a man and his wife who expressed an interest in the house. He wanted to know when he could bring them through. Not this week, she told him, or the next. Not while Sybil and Kristen were left alone to trash the house as they pleased, and she was not there to clean up after them.

Owen was persistent. "Buyers don't come along every day."

But they would come along in the spring. Maggie would tell that to her brother-in-law. It would get him off her back.

The bundle of Kristen's cast-off clothing was still in the jury room. Maggie made a quick reckoning. The clerk had said a third party, which excluded anyone on the jury. The reporter would not do, since he might consider it a human-interest story. The carpenter's girlfriend looked too angry, and Melody Jessica's grandfather looked too forbidding. That left the old woman. Maggie caught up with her as the woman crossed her woolen scarf over her bird-like chest, smoothing it flat like hands on a mummy.

Amos Stringer asked Maggie to drive him home. His pickup was in the Chevron station, waiting for a distributor cap. Maggie said she thought the problem was his battery. He said he had thought so, too. They rode in a miasma of woodsmoke and smothered false starts of conversation. From time to time he held the wheel while Maggie wiped her glasses on her scarf.

"You really blasted Mrs. Robidoux," she said.

"She asked for it. She's got no business sniping at you."

"You didn't have to do that. I could've taken care of myself."

"Not from where I sat."

"I was working on it. In my mind."

"You have to move faster than that."

"Anyone can say in-your-hat. Witty comebacks have to be figured out. I would have had one if you hadn't interfered."

"Like what? You looked pretty stumped to me. Even for a plain in-your-hat."

"I wasn't stumped. Just surprised."

"Let's drop it," he said. "I probably should've stayed out of it in the first place."

They passed a car that had skidded off the road to point up-ended in a gully like a missile. Maggie shifted into low. "We're not supposed to talk about the trial."

"That's what they say."

"Not even with each other."

"But you want to."

"Maybe. I'd like to hash it over with someone. My daughter and my mother are both out."

"And that leaves me."

"I guess you could say that."

He wondered if all widows were this cautious and if she was a real redhead. His friend Toby claimed you could tell without taking their clothes off. It's their skin, Toby had said, it smells like cinnamon. Amos pushed his knitted cap back from his forehead. "Go to it."

"What was all that about? When Mr. Giotti asked the plumber to describe the courtroom clerk."

"He was trying to make him look foolish, so that his testimony wouldn't count."

"That's what I thought."

"Then why did you ask?"

"I wanted to make sure I was right."

He turned to face her. "What if I'm the one that's wrong, Maggie?"

It was the first time he had called her by her name. She liked the way it sounded.

He lived in a converted silo that he rented from a tax attorney from Hartford who spent the summers in the nearby farmhouse. It stood a few yards from the highway, a cylindrical apartment painted a worn and rusty red. "It must be like living in a Snow Crop can," she said.

"Not once you're inside. Thanks for the ride." He slammed the car door and crunched through the snow.

Maggie rolled down the window to call after him. It was an impulsive act, almost as rash as wanting to dig up Alan. "Can I come in for a minute? I'd like to see what you've done with it."

"Suit yourself." While it was not exactly an invitation, Maggie accepted, following behind him as he put his shoulder to the front door and shoved.

The interior of the silo was heavy with the biting tang of woodsmoke. A skylight veined with the silhouettes of elm branches filtered in star shine. Amos switched on a lamp made from an old wrought-iron water pump. Its light illuminated a vintage mahogany library ladder installed on a track which led to a loft, a small refrigerator stacked high with yellowing proofs, a chipped enamel sink, a humpbacked Victorian sofa covered in frayed claret velvet which sagged like a dowager, a slip-covered easy chair, an

Indian rug, an end table made from a butter churn, a pie-shaped wedge of wallboard which set off a combination bathroom/darkroom, and black-and-white glossies of carbine-carrying Central Americans in fatigues and checkered headbands tacked to the walls.

Amos knelt to rekindle the fire that had been smoldering in the stove. A black-and-white cat uncoiled itself from the copper tub, where it had been sleeping on a pile of twigs, logs, and long sticks of punk, and came to rub against his leg while he nudged the embers into flames.

How easy it was, she thought. No particular interest in what she did or how she felt. The inattention felt salutary, warming, like sun on her neck. Maggie thought how it would be to sink into the easy chair and decided it was time to leave. She went for the door. "You're right," she said, tugging at the front door. "It's nothing like a soup can." The door rasped open, letting in a rush of frigid air which stung her nostrils.

He looked up suddenly from the stove as if he had just then realized that she was there. "You hungry? I'll make us something to eat if you are."

"I don't know," she said.

He shook his head. "It's not a big deal. Yes or no. You're letting in the cold air."

"If it's not too much trouble."

Maggie looked for something to read while Amos threw spaghetti and corn into a pot. Finding no magazines, books, newspapers, not even junk mail, she sat on the sofa rearranging her legs—cross, uncross, or tuck under—her hands, in her hair toying with a curl or folded—her arms, hugging herself or hanging over the back of the sofa, at the same time making inane conversation about everyone thinking she probably plowed into a snowdrift, and how lucky he was with no one to answer to. When he handed her a plate, a mug of Almaden wine, and a piece of paper toweling, then dropped to sit cross-legged on the rug just inches from her feet, she locked her body into position like a card table.

"It's all starch," she said. "Not that I care, but you really should have something green."

He rolled his corn across the butter. "My mom's only four miles away," he said. "I don't need another one."

Maggie picked corn silk out of the butter, wishing she had kept her mouth shut. They ate together in silence while the cat crept onto her lap and draped itself limply across her knees. Maggie pulled her plate closer to her stomach and realized what was different. Amos had not assaulted her with furtive darts, from breasts down to belly, up to face to zero in on mouth, down to buttocks, sideways to thighs. Instead he focused on her eyes as if they were lenses.

"I should be home," she said. "My mother's visiting."

He put down his fork. "Bag it," he said. "Stop playing perfect widow. Perfect lady. 'If it's not too much trouble.' 'I should be home.' Lighten up."

Maggie shoved the cat off her lap. It retreated, wounded, to the copper tub. "Tell me how I'm supposed to lighten up. I'd really like to hear this."

"For one thing, stop patting your mouth with your napkin. I know you're neat and clean. It's prissy. You probably have a roll of toilet paper waiting under a little crochet hat. Relax."

"That does it." Maggie put aside her plate.

"Don't tell me you want to hear something when you really don't."

"It should have been obvious the way I said it. The way I said it was dripping with sarcasm." She stood. "I'm really tired of people telling me what to do."

"Maggie, you act like a little kid that's lost in a mall. Maybe if you seemed more tightly wrapped, more . . . on top of things, everyone would leave you alone."

She reached for her coat. "As far as everyone is concerned, I stopped being on top of things when Alan died."

He pulled his mustache. "Competent was a bad choice. In control was what I meant. I guess I'm being a pain in the butt. Come on. Sit down. You haven't finished your supper."

Maggie lowered herself onto the couch.

"Was that your husband's name, Alan?"

She nodded, fighting tears.

"Take it easy," he said.

"In case you don't know," she said, "it's impossible to take it easy when someone tells you to. It's like saying stop thinking hippopotamus."

"Have some wine," he said.

Alan would have dumped it down the sink without even bothering to smell the cork. Maggie slugged it down. "I knew someone who went to Canada," she said. "He was going with a friend of mine when he got drafted. You don't talk about it. Was it so bad?"

"It was all right."

"I wouldn't exactly call you forthcoming. You tell me to loosen up. What about you?"

"You may not want to hear this. It might bring back some bad memories for you."

"It's okay. Most of them haven't left yet."

He leaned his back against the sofa. "Birthdays and Christmas were bad. That's when families glue themselves together if they see one another at all. You know?"

Maggie nodded her head. She knew.

"I managed to sneak over the border from time to time. When I did, some of the family wouldn't talk to me. The worst was when my grandfather died and I couldn't come to the funeral. I loved that old man. He bought me my first box camera. A Kodak. He got it at a flea market and made me a new shutter out of cardboard. Anyway, when they were waiting for him to die, my dad called to tell me that the feds were watching the house. They're smart that way. That's when most guys tried to get back. So I had to stay put. I went to his grave later. But it wasn't the same. Unless you see them toss him in, you're never really sure who's down there anyway. You might as well be talking to the dirt."

The sudden intimate revelation was too cumbersome to hold along with the plate on her lap. Maggie set down her supper on the butter urn. It was time to try out his name. "Amos, are you sorry? That you went, I mean."

"I'm sorry for ten years that dropped down the tube. I can't get those back. You have a whole history, Maggie, that I don't share." He reached over to pour more wine.

"You weren't in Timbuktu," she said. "You were just over the border. You read newspapers. You must have watched television."

"News isn't the same as culture. There's jokes that people tell each other, even if they travel clear across the country, they seem to stop at the border. Language changes. The shortcuts of slang, they come and go. I'm still using some of the old shortcuts. I have a kid brother who thinks I talk funny. It's everything, Maggie. The way you dress, the way you date. Women are different. Music is different. Rock is angrier than when I left. I'm the one who should be angry. What happened to Cat Stevens and Wishbone Ash? And the Mothers of Invention. I want them back."

"You didn't miss much," she said. "Except mood rings and pet rocks, and maybe *General Hospital*." Maggie searched for a connection. "I was an activist. In my sophomore year."

"I wasn't, except once and that was just for kicks. I just didn't want to come back in a zippered bag."

Maggie noticed that his voice was as mellow and as golden as his sweet-potato eyes, and his deep-toned resonances vibrated in her body. Women's voices didn't do that, she thought, only certain men, with certain timbre, their bass rumbling inside the caverns of one's interior, bouncing off bones, scuttling around sinew, ferreting out the secret places with an invasive percussion.

Maggie called home to clear her body of his voice. As she expected, Kristen was miffed because she was stuck in the house with Sybil, whom she referred to as "your mother," and who kept the bathtub steaming with long soaks in honeysuckle oil. Maggie chuckled. The sound was unexpected, like a trickle of water suddenly gurgling down a faucet.

"I don't see what's so funny," said Kristen. "If you don't stop laughing at me, I won't give you your messages." Maggie apologized, trying to clear her head of the giddiness that lay in wait in the corner of her mind.

"Try to get along with Sybil," she said. "I know it isn't easy."

"No kidding," replied Kristen, mollified enough to add that Justin Herrick called, Letitia called to find out what Maggie intended to contribute to Thanksgiving supper, and to ask if Sybil would attend, Owen called to say his buyer was getting cold, and somebody named Madonna Dyer called. She did not say what it was about. Kristen then announced that some of her water samples had had to be discarded because the people at the collection station said they were contaminated. She demanded to know who had been messing with her samples. Sybil could be heard in the background saying, "Don't look at me. I just got here."

Maggie said she would come home as soon as she could, then hung up and dialed LaDonna's number. The telephone rang a long time. When LaDonna answered, her voice was faint, as if she were inside a blanket roll. She seemed embarrassed when she recognized Maggie's voice.

"I don't know why I bothered you, Maggie. Everything's all right now."

Maggie pressed. "You called me for a reason. Tell me what it is."

LaDonna confessed that her husband had tried to kill himself. "I didn't know who else to call," she said. She hadn't told her daughters. "They'll say it was my fault," she said. "They'll say I should have stayed at home with him."

"I don't see that you had a choice," said Maggie. "You're on jury duty. Where is he now?"

LaDonna whispered that her husband, Freeman, was in the hospital for observation.

"Maybe they'll excuse you from jury duty," said Maggie.

"I wouldn't want that," said LaDonna.

"You wouldn't be asking for something that wasn't your right," said Maggie.

"It's not that."

"Then what is it?"

"Being home. With him. I'll go under, same as him."

Amos turned from the sink. "What's wrong?"

"It's LaDonna," replied Maggie, the dead phone still cradled on her shoulder. "Her husband tried to commit suicide."

"How?"

"I forgot to ask."

"How could you forget to ask how he did it? It's the whole point."

"I didn't, all right? Besides, it's not the whole point. The point is, he tried to end his life."

"You can tell by the way he tried to do it how serious he was. I mean, if he jumped off the barn, all he was looking for was a broken leg. Is he all right?"

"They've got him on a suicide watch or something. I think I'd better get over there. She must feel pretty desperate to call me. We hardly know each other."

"Do you want me to go with you?"

"What for?"

The farmhouse was built sideways, parts of the house added over time, connected by overhangs and tunnels, so that it looked like a clapboard train. Maggie knocked on the door while Amos waited on the shoveled walk.

LaDonna opened it a crack. She stood silhouetted in a sliver of light. "Go home, Maggie," she said. "I appreciate it, but it's all right now. Honest."

A man's voice called from inside. "He's back," she whispered. "He called our oldest girl. My son-in-law brought him home."

"Will I see you tomorrow?" asked Maggie.

The voice called again, petulant, demanding. "I've got to go." LaDonna closed the door.

Amos and Maggie picked their way in the darkness back to the Subaru. Neither spoke. Amos had a flashlight. He pointed its beam at the snow, revealing tiny, lacy footprints etched in flashlight and shadow, showing the drag marks of a long, slender tail. "It's a deer mouse," he said. "See, it springs like a rubber ball, its hind tracks register ahead of the smaller front ones. They're tree climbers. My guess is that it's got relatives in that abandoned bird's nest just over your head."

He illuminated a nest on a low branch that seemed to shiver in the cold.

"My glasses are getting foggy," she said. "It's hard to keep looking up."

"You don't care much for wildlife, do you?"

"I hope you're not going to turn out to be one of these nature lovers who think they cornered the market. I have one at home who's practically in mourning over a tank of fish that are still alive. At least they were when I left."

"You sure are one touchy woman." He took her mittened hand. "I'm not making a move on you," he said, "I just don't want to have to pick you up out of the snow." Maggie turned back and thought she saw LaDonna's face in the window. When she turned again and stumbled into the branches of a yew, she concluded that as far as safety was concerned, Amos was no better than she was.

"Some guide," she said.

Maggie came home to a detente. Sybil and Kristen were not speaking. The upstairs smelled of honeysuckle and the downstairs smelled of dead fish floating belly up in the fish tank. Kirsten was making the most of it. She languished on the living room sofa with her father's framed picture pressed to her chest.

"All you had to do was clean it. But you didn't care, and now they're dead."

"That was fast," said Maggie. "As of this morning, they weren't even very sick."

"It wasn't fast. They haven't been swimming right since I got home. Daddy loved his fish. He even gave them names. He had them as long as I can remember and now they're dead."

"They're not the same ones," said Maggie. "Fish died for him too. And he replaced them."

"Not all at once. And not from unnatural causes."

"I'm sorry, Krissie," said Maggie. "But you're the one who's been at home. You could have cleaned the tank."

Kristen wept anew. "You're the one with the car. I kept telling you to buy charcoal tablets. Daddy loved his fish. He said they mellowed him out. And now they're dead."

Sybil, wrapped in a plaid blanket over a chenille robe, suggested that Maggie run Kristen to the cemetery early in the morning before she had to go to trial, so they could bury the dead fish alongside Alan's grave.

"You're gross," said Kristen. "You know that, Grandmother? You really are gross."

Sybil, who was hearing "grandmother" for the first time, seemed hurt. She pulled the blanket tighter about her shoulders. "Well, maybe not all the fish," she said. "Maybe just the angel fish, as a token."

Maggie began to laugh in hiccups, like the week before in the cellar with Letitia when the corks of the wine bottles had popped. "I'm sorry, baby," she said between chuckles. "It's got nothing to do with you or the fish. I really am sorry."

"You're losing it too," said Kristen. "I can't live in this house with two weird relatives."

Maggie resisted the impulse to suggest that she return to the dormitory and glanced instead at her mother, recalling with surprise how much fun Sybil could be.

Yet Kristen began to cry again in great, gulping sobs: for the fish, for Daddy, for her roommate, for someone named Rudy. Her blonde, sodden hair fell over her face.

Maggie felt a wave of pity and knelt beside her to cradle her in her arms, then started to giggle again.

Kristen jerked away. "Leave me alone," she said. "Just leave me alone. You smell like you've been in a fire."

"It's probably woodsmoke," said Maggie.

"Where were you?" asked Kristen. "I didn't know where you were."

"Were you worried, sweetheart?"

"No," said Kristen, pumping her chin like Letitia. "Just curious."

"With a friend."

"Which one?"

"You don't know this one."

"And where are all my clothes? My red cashmere sweater is gone."

"You shrunk it, remember?"

"I stretched it out again. I could have worn it."

"No, you couldn't, Krissie. Trust me."

"And my blue corduroy jacket. It used to be in the downstairs closet."

"You said you hated that jacket."

"That was last year."

Maggie sighed. The giddy feeling was gone. "I did what I always do with your outgrown clothes. I gave them away,"

"To who?"

"Nobody you know. Just someone who could use some clothes."

"God Almighty, you're full of information. You go out all night with someone I never even heard of and then you gave my clothes away to some stranger. For all I know, they're the same person. Anyway, you should have asked me."

"She's right," said Sybil. "On the first part, not the second. You should have asked her before you got rid of anything that belonged to her."

"You're a funny one to talk," said Maggie. "You got rid of my father."

It came from left field. Even Maggie was surprised. Sybil responded softly. "I didn't give him away. He left all by himself."

Maggie regretted her remark. "Stay out of it, Mother," she said.

Maggie went upstairs to talk to Alan and suddenly stopped on the top step, startled. Alan was gone. Alan was dead. She wondered how memory lets up, for only a moment, to let in madness. This time the tears were only a flash flood, an eyewash that she brushed away with her sleeve.

Sybil called from below to ask if there were any extra pillows. She slept better sitting up. From the top of the steps, she looked frail, like a woman close to seventy. "Did you have a good time, dear?" she asked.

CHAPTER 7

Expert Witness

"WHITE MEAT OR DARK, Margaret?"

"She's been like that since Tuesday," said Kristen.

Maggie roused herself from recollections of the medical examiner's testimony of two days before, to the white point duchesse lace tablecloth in her mother-in-law's dining room, around which Letitia, Sybil, Owen, Jenna, and Kristen, sat in tentative, sober federation, helping themselves to cranberry sauce and sweet potato pie as if suspended from their necks on meat hooks.

Letitia, who had dressed for the occasion in a dark green woolen dress with pearl-and-diamond earrings, the latter which had been handed down like chromosomes from her maternal forbears, held out a blue-and-white mintonware platter. An age crack striated from its lip like a road and came to rest beneath a drumstick.

Sybil had also dressed for the occasion in black suede. She spoke with maternal finality, while flicking wax from Letitia's silver candlestick with an oval fingernail. "Maggie likes white meat."

Maggie turned her head. Her red hair lay coiled in a French braid. "Actually," she said, adopting a mask of attentive cordiality, "I just want a little skin." She served herself, then slid back to the East Indian doctor with the clipped, melodic voice who had said that Joyce Hibbert

Bean's death had been caused by prolonged exposure to mercury poisoning, that although the decedent was found at the bottom of the quarry, death was not caused by her fall but by the failure of her kidneys. McKeen had played straight man and asked if mercuric salts were easily obtainable. When the medical examiner said that it was found in certain fungicides, the prosecutor showed Singh the tube of dental adhesive, then read the laboratory report which confirmed that its contents had been laced with mercury salts. Would this be enough to cause death? he asked. Most certainly, replied Dr. Singh, especially if the deceased put in her dentures every day.

Letitia's voice came through again, this time intrusive and insistent like the drone of a mosquito. "Margaret," she said, "we're all sadly missing Alan. His loss is a painful thing to bear. For every one of us. You simply must make an effort."

Maggie quickened from her clandestine reveries a second time, carrying remnants of the trial like trailing ribbons. The orange and magenta palette of the Thanksgiving table had been cleared by Letitia's sometime helper, Mrs. Swanlea. Kristen had been excused to make a telephone call. Maggie dabbed her moistened napkin on a cranberry stain, recalled for a moment doing the same thing in Lester Perkins's office the day they had planned the funeral, and wondered if it were possible to harbor enough hatred toward a mother to plan her murder and still be sane. If so, and if Melody Jessica was guilty, then Joyce Hibbert Bean must have done something awful, something unforgivable.

"Alan was Maggie's husband," said Sybil. "Considering that it's only been a few months since his death, I think my daughter is doing very well." The gloves were off.

Letitia parted her lips, then set them firmly in a narrow line, while Jenna placed a tray of steaming coffee on the sideboard. Jenna spoke quickly while she poured coffee, as if spooning the same sugar into the conversation she now spooned into her cup. "I'll bet Maggie is remembering last Thanksgiving, when Mother Hatch invited the Bouchards and Alan was growing that awful beard."

Last Thanksgiving seemed to Maggie lifetimes ago, an event in a dim tunnel of recall. A memory of someone else, of the four of them, planning a spring vacation—Anne and Alan campaigning for Cozumel, Peter defending white-water rafting in Colorado, and Maggie wanting whatever Alan wanted. Something was wrong. Maggie sharpened the focus. No, I didn't, she thought. I wanted to go to the Charleston Music Festival. I just didn't say anything about it. Alan—or was it Peter?—sat cross-legged on the floor with brochures spilling from his lap. It must have been Alan because a new beard bristled on his chin. Maggie and Anne were the only ones who liked it. The beard had given Alan, whose genetic drift had been blown by both an Algonquin brave and an eighteenth-century French cavalry officer from Quebec, an exotic, foreign look.

"Actually," said Maggie, "I was thinking that the minimal lethal dose of mercuric poisoning for a one-hundred-fifty-pound woman is five-hundred milligrams."

There was silence, then a clatter of silver against china, the activity of the discomfited who, not knowing what else to do, stuff food into their mouths.

"I invited the Bouchards again this year," said Letitia. "They declined, but said they would try to stop by for an after-dinner drink."

Was it possible, wondered Maggie, that Letitia did not know? Or worse, that she did know? "Why would you do that?" she asked.

"I don't understand your question," replied Letitia. "Peter was Alan's closest friend."

Owen glanced at Jenna, as if checking a clock, then turned to Maggie. "I guess you have to be in court tomorrow."

"Actually, I don't," replied Maggie. "Melody Jessica

has a fever—they think she has the flu—and since it's a holiday, the judge granted an adjournment until Monday."

"It's funny that you call her by her name. What is she like?" asked Kristen. "I've never seen a killer close up."

"I have," said Sybil. "I see them all the time."

"She's a fifteen-year-old girl," said Maggie.

"But what is she like? Does she have, like, a hard-nosed attitude?"

Maggie studied her daughter, whose hands had worked like shuttlecocks that morning to secure the closure of Maggie's curly red hair. "I honestly don't know, Krissie. I never get any closer to her than that sideboard."

Kristen pouted, as if her mother were witholding something that was rightfully hers. "I don't know why you can't at least tell me what she looks like."

"All right," said Maggie, making herself a second cup of Irish coffee which she pumped with Cool Whip. "She's like you."

"That's a terrible thing to say," said Letitia.

"Maggie is Kristen's mother," said Sybil. "A mother would never say anything to hurt her own child. Maggie had a reason to say what she did."

"What reason?" asked Kristen.

Maggie sipped her coffee. "I only meant that she's a young girl. And pretty. And likes gladiator sandals."

"She's a murderer," said Letitia.

"We don't know that," said Maggie.

Sybil was on a roll. "Maggie always has to have the facts," she said, "before she makes a judgment." Maggie turned to look at her mother in amazement. No one could accuse Sybil of shying away from hyperbole. They both knew that Maggie seldom had the facts on anything. She did most things in her life on impulse, including falling in love with a handsome medical student equipped with a life plan as detailed as a city map, and declaring that she planned to follow him home to Vermont. The truth was, Maggie would have followed Alan to the ends of the earth for the stability his blueprint implied and the sexual energy he promised. How easily Sybil lied for her, she thought, and how beautiful she looked in the candlelight: a full-blown, seasoned Kristen, with skin as shiny as wax paper and motivation a little more transparent.

Owen cleared his throat. "Travers and his wife really liked the house. Except for the floor. They said the house needs a lot of work, but they're willing to tackle it. They asked me to give you their bid."

"Now?" asked Maggie. "I haven't really put it on the market yet."

"Now's as good a time as any," he replied.

"Okay. What's the bid?"

"Ninety. But that's a no-dickering ninety, Maggie, since there's no broker's fee, and it's an all-cash deal."

"What does that mean?"

"It means they have cash to lay off," said Sybil.

"Not necessarily," said Letitia. "In Vermont it means that frugal people have saved their money and don't need a mortgage. It means Maggie doesn't have to wait to see if they qualify, and it means she doesn't have to take back a second mortgage, which is always, I can tell you, risky."

"I don't know," said Maggie. "Do I have to decide this minute?"

"I'd think about it seriously if I were you," said Owen. "You might not get another offer as good."

"Take your time," cautioned Sybil. "A few months won't make any difference."

"There are mitigating factors, Sybil," said Letitia, "that you may know nothing about."

"What mitigating factors? I don't know of any mitigating factors, and Maggie tells me everything."

"No, I don't, Mother," said Maggie. "Not everything. Just drop it."

Sybil complied. The corners of her mouth sagged like a jacket slipping from a hanger, while Jenna jumped into the breach as briskly and as purposefully as entering a horse stall to announce that she and Owen had sat at the same table with Justin Herrick at a church supper. She said he had been with a widow from Dorset who was a wonderful cook, as evidenced by the fact that the supper committee had used her recipe for venison and she wasn't even a member of the church. Jenna and Owen would have visited with Justin and his date a little longer, but they were not permitted to sit over a second cup of coffee because another seating was expected and the church people needed the table. Owen added a non sequitur by saying that Justin's saltbox house and barn were exceptionally well kept, as were their forty surrounding acres.

"What's so great about that?" asked Kristen, returning from a second telephone call.

"It means he's well fixed," said Sybil.

"What Owen means," said Letitia, "is that the man is responsible." She folded her napkin and placed it on the table, the signal to move into what used to be called the parlor. On the way in, Jenna asked if Maggie had heard from Justin. Maggie replied that Justin had called her twice, once when washing clothes, and the second time while washing her hair. She acknowledged that they were going cross-country skiing on Saturday.

"If you insist on dating," said Letitia, "it's just as well if you keep it outdoors."

"That's weird, Granny," said Kristen. "Why?"

"I'd like to know myself," said Maggie.

They were interrupted by the Bouchards, who, with their overweight daughter, Annie Laura, arrived like snow in a flurry of light, cold-lipped, airy kisses. Peter was bearing wine and cheese, Annie Laura was sullen, and Anne was as charming and as gracious as if nothing had ever happened. Kristen curled her lip as she had done when she discovered the dead fish, and went to make another telephone call. Maggie found herself suddenly and unexpectedly mobilized.

She cornered Peter in the chilly mudroom, where he had returned to stuff his gloves into the pocket of his storm coat, and closed the inner hallway door behind her.

He smiled his crooked, quirky smile. "I knew you'd change your mind. Sooner or later."

Maggie shoved him hard in the shoulder. The last time she had done that to anyone was in the fourth grade.

"What's wrong with you? You've gotten very hostile, Maggie, you know that? It's not a good sign for a widow. It means you're getting bitter."

"You want to know what's wrong with me? That's funny because I want to know what's wrong with you. You came on to me, the whole stupid thing was your doing, then you dumped it on me, and cost me my best friend. Nothing will ever make that right again. I even thought it was my fault. You know who set me straight? Kristen. My seventeen-year-old daughter. You know what else? I didn't look too great that night. In fact, I looked so awful that I figured out that you must do this kind of thing all the time. With everyone. No matter what. You must come on to women every chance you get. Does Anne know that? Does she?"

"You've had too much Irish coffee, Maggie." He opened the door to the hall and lowered his voice. "Hey, lady, you think Alan never played around?"

She felt herself trembling as pain slipped over her heart like an envelope. "Alan would never have done what you did." She did not want to ask the obvious question. Yet she stood with her hands at her side like a soldier waiting for orders.

"Enough said," he replied, with the snap of someone who knew he had said more than enough and regretted it. He walked out into the hall. "Where is everybody?" he called.

Everything outdoors was frozen over, glazed in the fading evening light in palest lavender, even the spruce boughs behind them piled against the foundation of the house. Cars whined, boughs snapped, and the ice on Letitia's pond cracked like whip snaps as it spread wider and deeper.

Maggie scraped the windshield of the Subaru with the bristles of Kristen's vent brush, then, content with stippled visibility, drove with her forehead pressed against the glass.

"Did he try anything?" asked Kristen from the backseat.

"No," said Maggie. She wondered about the awful thing that Peter had implied while Sybil smeared the windshield with her woolen scarf.

"Did who try anything?" asked Sybil. "You mean Owen with his high-pressured sales pitch?"

"It has nothing to do with Uncle Owen, Grandmother," said Kristen. "It's something private."

"That leaves Peter," said Sybil. "I wish you both would let me in on the big secret."

"I don't want to talk about it," said Maggie.

They rode in silence until Maggie turned slowly into the driveway. "Who left the light on in the garage?" she asked. "I know I didn't."

"I was going to tell you," said Kristen.

"All I can handle are muggers," said Sybil. "Don't ask me to fight off anyone with a chain saw."

"Tell me what?" demanded Maggie.

She stomped into the garage, with Kristen and Sybil following behind, carrying foil-wrapped leftovers. Maggie would have known that someone had recently opened the garage door even if the light had not been on, since the ice over the jamb had been chipped away. A space heater rattled in the corner. Bending over the M.G. was a tall, narrow-hipped boy with slender, graceful wrists and a needle-nosed pliers in his hands, wearing a down-filled vest and a single gold earring glinting on the lobe of one ear.

"Who are you?" demanded Maggie. "What are you doing here?"

Kristen stepped between them like a referee. "Rudy, this is my mom. Mom, this is Rudy."

"I'm Sybil."

Kristen turned in grudging admission. "This is my other

grandmother, from New York. She's going back on Tuesday."

Rudy, his translucent face made paler by the light, wiped his hands on his jeans.

"I didn't ask anyone to do anything with the M.G.," said Maggie. "Who sent you?"

"Rudy's doing it for nothing," said Kristen.

"Doing what?"

"Rudy is going to get the M.G. to work."

"Do you live around here?" asked Maggie. "I don't remember seeing you before. What's the matter? Why doesn't he talk?"

"You're making him nervous," said Kristen. "Back off. He'll talk, won't you, Rudy?" Rudy looked distant, aloof, a profile on an ancient coin. "Rudy is staying with us awhile."

Maggie whirled around. "Who said?"

"He's already been invited. Just until the car is fixed. I thought you'd be glad." There was a chip at the edge of Kristen's voice. Maggie had never heard it before.

"I haven't sold this house yet, Kristen. I like to be told who's been asked to visit it."

Kristen was in tears. "You can't send him home. He lives in Pennsylvania."

"What does he need to get there, a visa?"

Rudy turned scornful pale blue eyes on Kristen. "Didn't you tell her?" he asked. "You said you were going to lay everything out."

"Let him stay," said Sybil, with a hand on Maggie's arm. "It's worth it to you even if all he does is fix that old thing. It won't do you any good rusting in the garage."

"Lay what out?" asked Maggie. "I can take it. Try me."

"I don't need this," said Rudy, fastening the toggles of his vest. "You didn't tell me your mom was so sarcastic."

"Let me get this straight," said Maggie, needling home a point of clarification like Giotti. "If you knew I was sarcastic, you wouldn't have come?"

"Relax, she doesn't mean any of this," said Kristen.

"I don't think I'm going back on Tuesday," said Sybil.

Rudy put down the needle-nosed pliers. "I don't have to take this," he said.

Kristen tried a tactical diversion. "Rudy goes to Hampshire College."

"Used to," said Rudy.

"As of how long ago?"

"Two weeks."

"I see a connection," said Sybil.

Maggie turned to Kristen. "It was bullshit. All of it. Leaving college had nothing to do with Daddy, or needing time out. It was him. He left, so you left. I thought you had a goal of your own, Kristen. That was your strong suit. That was what you had going for you. I never had the hand to play. You threw it away."

Kristen clutched at Rudy's flannel shirtsleeve as he headed for the door. "She's on a jury."

The house was in chaos. Not only were Kristen's and Sybil's belongings scattered and piled on every surface, including the antique ladies' desk and the dining room table, but there were duffel bags, skis, poles, ski boots, western boots, jackets, hats, blanket rolls, and boxes of books lining the entrance hall and stacked beneath the French military prints. In addition, two hanging plants had been secured into the ceiling beams and trailed down into the living room like question marks.

Maggie ran upstairs to take a hot bath. Her urgency had something to do with the remedy of steam, which would cause everything unpleasant to rise up with it and vanish in a vaporous puff.

Kristen knocked on the door of the bathroom. "Well," she asked through the door, "can he stay?"

Maggie filled the tub with sweet-smelling honeysuckle suds and lay soaking to her neck. "Why ask me now? You've already decided that you don't need my permission. In fact, it looks like he's taken over. You win. Do whatever you like. I don't care. Except for the ceiling beams. Tell him to take down his plants."

It was all going wrong, she thought. All of it. She remembered whispering to Alan that she could not live without him. And I can't, she thought. It was not just something said in the heat of passion. It was plain and simply true. She noticed idly that Alan's shirt was missing from the hook.

What had Peter been insinuating? Was it a cheap parting shot to hurt her? Or had Alan actually cheated on her? With whom? When? He was always so busy, so wrapped up in his surgery, his car, his skiing, his tennis, his daughter. Most especially, where? The village was so small. So was the county. Someone would have told her.

Maggie had a strong need to get out of the house. But not to see anyone from the village and have to wonder if whoever she went to visit knew something she didn't. Since LaDonna had her hands full, that left only one person. He was no great shakes, but he made no demands. He even cooked.

A hand snaked in the door. It was Kristen's, with Alan's shirt hanging from her outstretched fingertips. "I meant to get this back to you," she said.

"That's OK, keep it." Maggie stepped out of the tub and toweled herself with brisk, energizing rubs, then oiled herself with Sybil's body-firming lotion. She looked in the mirror. Not bad, she decided, if you moved quickly. She knotted the towel over her breasts, and, with Kristen at her heels, went into her bedroom and pulled out jeans and a sweater.

"You can't run around in a towel anymore," said Kristen. "You have to put a robe on." Maggie made no reply. Kristen stepped in front of her, holding Alan's shirt like a silver spike. "And don't try to live your life through me."

"I'm not."

"Then why did you say that I have something that you didn't?" Maggie fluffed out her hair and slicked cherry lip gloss on her lips. "Where are you going?" asked Kristen.

"To see a friend." Maggie smiled. The jeans fit better than when she had bought them two years before.

"I thought you'd like to know that Rudy is sleeping in his blanket roll. He'll be in my room but not in my bed."

"Do what you like."

"Don't you care? You're my mother. You're supposed to care. How come you don't want to discuss birth control?"

"You want to talk about birth control?"

"Not especially."

"Neither do I."

"I thought you'd be pleased that he's sleeping in his blanket roll."

"Don't observe conventions just for me. You're mixing me up with your father."

"That's a terrible thing to say about Daddy."

"You want to be up front, Kristen. Be up front."

Kristen locked her slender arms over her head. "This is some kind of guilt trip you're laying on me, isn't it?"

"Believe it or not, Krissie, this has nothing to do with you."

Maggie took the leftover stuffing and turkey from the refrigerator, found the foil-wrapped sweet potato pie in Kristen's room beneath Rudy's vest and part of his foot, located the Frank Zappa record she had seen in the study next to the Christmas angel with the cryptic AAA on the box, and left. Sybil was at the top of the stairs. "No one you know," said Maggie.

"I didn't ask."

Amos opened the door, his stereo blasting behind him, his hands smelling of darkroom solution. "Maggie." He wiped his hair from his eyes with his thumb. "What are you doing here?"

"I brought you turkey, stuffing, and sweet potato pie."

"You didn't have to do that. I already had Thanksgiving dinner. With my folks."

"Then heat this up tomorrow. You mentioned Zappa.

Here." She handed him the album and the foil-wrapped package, then unbuttoned her coat.

He took the packages and the album from her hands. "It's after eleven," he said.

"I'm wearing a watch. You have some kind of curfew?"

Amos pulled his upper lip. His soft brown eyes were shining in the light. "No. I don't have any curfew. Are you making some kind of statement?"

"Why do you ask that?"

"Because I don't think you know the ground rules."

"You said you didn't know them anymore either. That makes us even as far as I'm concerned." She took off her parka and threw it on the sofa.

"You want to talk?" he asked, wiping his hands on his jeans.

"Not especially. I just need to be with a friend."

He reached to the stack of proofs piled on top of the refrigerator and pulled one out. "After you left the other night, I found this." He showed her a black-and-white photograph of an old man whittling in a rocking chair. The man was as gnarled and as scored as the wood of the porch around him. "That's my grandpa."

"It's very good. You've captured a motif of grooves and lines that give it the feel of a woodcut." She brought it under the light. "You caught something else. The decisive moment of an event at its peak." It all came back, dredged up from art history and a twenty-year-old lecture on Cartier-Bresson.

"You see all that?" he asked.

"Sure. Look, it's here, in the visual organization. And here." She pointed at the old man's hands.

"I don't think I was looking for, whatever you called it."

"Decisive moment."

He smiled and poured wine into coffee mugs. "Decisive moment. I didn't worry about things like that. I just wanted a shot of my grandpa doing what he liked best. I was concerned with stuff like shutter opening and light direction, and keeping him from remembering that I was standing there watching. What's the matter?" he asked. "Did the wine go bad?"

"No," she replied. "I got sidetracked. I guess I was thinking about the light in the quarry."

"I don't think that's so important. You should be asking yourself, Why go through the trouble of poison? According to the autopsy, it had to be continuous and three weeks' worth. There are other ways that are a lot faster. And much less trouble."

"Like what?"

"Stabbing. Shooting. Smothering."

The answer slid out for Maggie like the bottom drawer of a cash register. It seemed so simple. "They're all hands-on. You have to be really involved with someone to do it the ways you mention. Poison is impersonal."

He frowned, then reached over to tousle her hair, holding high a handful, then letting it drift down about her face. "If there's no fire left in the grate, Maggie, it's because it's all in your hair."

Maggie listened to the sound of a cinder truck swishing ashes on the highway and concluded that there was something the matter with her, something unnatural to make her wonder what it was like to kiss a man with a mustache when she was still getting condolence cards.

She stood up and told him that her house was being turned inside out by her daughter, her daughter's boyfriend, and her mother. "I have to get home and see what's happening."

"No one's stopping you."

"And I'd like to set the record straight. I'm not into games."

"I believe you."

"Where's my hat? I can't find my hat."

He held out her parka. "You stuffed it in your sleeve."

"You probably think I'm not playing with a full deck, don't you?" she asked.

"Get going while you can still get behind that cinder truck."

Maggie came downstairs for breakfast from a restless night of tossing like a fox tail to find Sybil already dressed and Kristen removing bran muffins from the oven.

"Where were you last night?" asked Kristen. "You weren't at the Bouchards and you weren't at Granny's. I know because I called both places, and you weren't with that guy Herrick because he called here."

"I was visiting a friend."

"I know all your other friends."

Maggie dropped into the seat beside her mother and yawned, grateful that Rudy was nowhere in sight. "Not all."

The truth erupted on Kristen like measles. "Were you with another guy?"

"That's my business," replied Maggie.

Kristen said she hoped it was not true, especially in light of the facts that her father had just died, that it was Thanksgiving, and that Maggie was forty.

Sybil spooned orange marmalade over her muffin half. "I think I'll address the last point," she said. "I see it as a grandmother's duty."

"Don't," said Maggie. "Please, Mother, don't."

"Don't what?" asked Sybil.

"Just don't complicate things."

"I was just introducing a little levity. I think it's needed."

Maggie turned. "You're close to seventy. You're supposed to set an example."

"I wish you hadn't said that. There's no need to actually spell it out."

Maggie dragged herself to the sink to wash muffin tins and mixing bowls, thinking of Amos and the sleepless night before and responses that she thought she had buried with Alan, when Rudy burst into the kitchen with red, frostbitten fingers which he stuck under his armpits. He reported to Sybil, whom he reckoned as an ally, that the M.G. needed points, plugs, and other parts that could only be gotten from a dealer who specialized in old-model sports cars. Sybil said she would see what she could do, but not to hold out much hope.

"Rudy's parents know that he's here, in case you're wondering," said Kristen.

"It's the furthest thing from my mind," replied Maggie.

"They want me to spend some time at their house, but Rudy and I prefer Vermont."

"Don't be selfish, Krissie. You've got to share."

"I think she's being sarcastic again," said Rudy.

Maggie poured a capful of Lemon Joy into the sink, unaware that Rudy, Sybil, and Kristen watched her from the kitchen table. Her legs trembled and she leaned against the sink. Why was that? she wondered. Why did longing make women weak and men strong? Maybe it was programmed into the human species that women were supposed to fall down and wait to be serviced. You couldn't have sex with a strong, running woman.

"She looks like she's doing calculus in her head," whispered Kristen. "You're her mother. Why is she acting this way?"

"I think it means that she's upset," replied Sybil.

Rudy spooned cranberry mold into a coffee cup. "Did she do it a lot?" he asked. A psych major, he was looking for a pattern.

"On and off," said Sybil. "She was angry with me most of the time."

"Why?" asked Kristen. "Were you always on her back?"

"I'm not sure. I didn't think so at the time. I thought we were having fun."

"When was the last time she did this?" asked Rudy.

"Right before she left school to marry Kristen's father."

"You have a good memory," said Kristen.

"Long-term memory," said Rudy. "It's the last to go. It's short-term memory your grandmother has to worry about."

"As if I didn't have enough problems," said Sybil.

* * *

The decision to go ice fishing was made an hour later. Amos called to tell Maggie that he was on assignment for a newspaper and that she could come along if she wanted to. If it was an invitation, it was a heavily qualified one. "I don't know if you'd like it," he said. "All it is is men sitting around drinking and throwing cigarette butts into ice holes."

It sounded barbaric, like a truck stop that she and Alan had once pulled into, with stopped-up toilets and men with three-day beards and hostile eyes. But staying home sounded worse. Maggie left Rudy banked with envelopes, helping Sybil rank order her responses, and Kristen curled up in the wing chair, watching Vanna White open a car door.

"I'm going to the lake," she said. "You want me to collect water samples for you, Krissie?"

Kristen kept her eyes on the screen and answered in her I-hope-you're-satisfied voice: "They won't take my samples anymore."

Several hard freezes had turned the water into a plain of ice where square plywood fishing shacks beckoned from the perimeter. They picked their way onto the frozen lake, the bitter cold making their eyes tear and their throats sting when they tried to talk. Amos had taken off his lens cap and began to shoot as they walked, while Maggie waited for him to mention something of the night before to corroborate her recollection that some line might have been crossed, to say that he too had felt something, which they would both then agree was precipitous. Instead he told her that the fishing shacks were all exactly the same size, eight feet long and forty-six inches wide, to fit, he explained, on the bed of a pickup truck, and that inside of a month, when the ice had thickened, the boxlike constructions would be moved toward the middle of the freezing lake.

Amos found his father's shack, somehow picking it out

of several others that all looked exactly alike. They ducked into the low doorway into an interior of cardboard, like the inside of a shoebox, warm and smoky from a fire burning in a small wood stove. Fish hooks and a penciled list of Stringer's fishing hours hung from the cardboard walls. Around the ice hole were two stools, a bucket filled with tackle and bait, coffee cups, and a deck of cards on an upturned barrel. Jig sticks with little flags bobbed up and down in the greenish water. Amos said they were called tip-ups, and that his dad was somewhere around, probably visiting another shack.

A Skidoo snarled on the ice. Amos said it was the game warden checking fishing licenses. "I want to get started while the light's still good. Why don't you try your hand at fishing? It's warmer in the shack."

"There's no room in that little hole for any more lines," she said. "I'll just sit and think about the trial. There are things I need to sort out, like why the kid doesn't seem to get it. What I mean is, even if she managed to block out her mother's death, it should matter to her that she's on trial for murder."

He checked his equipment, disinterested for the moment in Melody Jessica Bean, his attention on his shoot. "You don't care if I leave you here?"

"I don't mind waiting, if that's what you mean."

"Suit yourself." He took her chin in his hand. "I'm not the answer, Maggie. I'm not even the answer for myself." He bent his head and kissed her, taking some kind of measure, a surface probe with his lips, wondering if death left a taste and thinking that it would be a lot easier if she was still married and running around on her old man.

They were both unaware that his father had stooped into the shack. Maggie pulled away first while Enoch Stringer kept his eyes on his tip-ups. "This is Maggie Hatch," said Amos. "I told her she could stay in here with you where it's warm."

Stringer nodded to Maggie, then turned to his son. "You here to take them pictures?"

"That's the plan."

"How long you fixing to be gone?"

"Twenty minutes. Max." Amos dipped his way out, then paused at the opening. "Maybe you could make her some coffee."

Maggie had to wait for the fog on her glasses to dissipate before she could see his father clearly. He was a bitter, lean-faced man, missing teeth and hair, a sorrowful, older Amos, with a wattle at his neck. This was the man that Amos said had written him a Dear John letter when he was in exile, calling him a coward, telling him that the family was ashamed to hold its head up, and getting all the members to sign, including his mother and his seven-year-old kid brother, who could only print his name. "You're the bone doc's widow," he said.

"Yes," she replied.

"What do you want with Amos?"

She was startled by the question. "He's a friend," she replied. "We're on a jury together." It was safer to change the subject. "Do you catch a lot of fish out here?"

"Seven years ago," he said, "I got fifty trout. About half legal. One eight-pounder. Nowhere near as many fish now as when I was a boy. Most of the fish we catch now are stock fish. Native fish have nice white fins. You never see any."

She sat on a stool, watching the jig sticks bobbing in the hole, waiting for the flags to signal fish, trying to recall his kiss, to dust for trace of memory, and thinking what a stupid thing she had done. She was better off at home. If there was hostility there, at least the house was bigger, which brought up another problem. She had to sell it. Letitia had asked her again for the money and said she did not want to have to go to Woody Pringle for redress. Maggie felt a stab of anger toward Alan. He was supposed to solve her life, not screw it up.

"My wife never has been out here," said Stringer.

What was that supposed to mean? Where was Amos,

and how long did it take to get a bunch of pictures of ice shanties and men spitting into holes?

"Had a fellow once," said Stringer, "told me to pour kerosene in the hole so it wouldn't freeze over. Takes all kinds."

"I'm not going to make any stupid suggestions if that's what you're worried about."

"I learned a long time ago that worry gets you nowhere faster than a flea hopping on a dog." He rubbed the bristles on the side of his face. "Used to get a lot of nice pickerel."

Maggie poked her head out the door. Sleet stung her face and peppered the ice. She sighed and came inside again, thinking that she should be home solving problems that hung like buttons from a thread. Sybil needed something from her, she did not need anything from Sybil; Kristen needed nothing from her, she needed Kristen. Rudy was another matter that had to be settled. And soon.

After what seemed like an eternity, Amos crawled into the shack. "Any luck?" he asked.

His father gave him a curious glance. "You know nothing happens when people come out."

Amos shrugged. "I got what I need," he said to Maggie. "You ready?"

"How do you stand him?" asked Maggie when they were safely outside. "Why do you bother?"

"He's my old man. I don't have another one."

Maggie thought that said it all, the curious attachment of family that required neither merit nor effort to sustain its legitimacy.

He seemed distant, remote, almost like the first days of the trial when he sat leaning against the wall of the jury room. They were almost off the ice when she slipped and twisted her ankle. He caught her before she fell. "Can you walk?"

"I think so." She leaned on him for support and limped to the pickup, trading pain for guilt somewhere deep down in the iceberg of her subconscious. It was an easy barter, made easier by the Charleston Music Festival that she had never gotten to see, and the question raised by Peter.

How did it happen, she wondered, that a short while ago Amos was just another stranger, a face in a window, an obnoxious guy who wore an undershirt, who happened to sit with her on a jury, now suddenly becoming someone she needed to talk to, needed to see? "I have a date to go cross-country skiing tomorrow afternoon," she said. "Although it looks like we'll have to think of something else to do."

He seemed uncomfortable. "That's your business."

"The point is, I can probably see you tomorrow night."

"I'm sorry, Maggie," he replied. "I've got something else to do."

The twinge of jealousy was unexpected, like a hunger pang when one has forgotten to eat. It's different now, she thought. I've got to learn the rules.

By Saturday morning, her swollen ankle had dimpled, the way Sybil's did at night, blown out of proportion like the news that she had been out on the ice with Amos Stringer. She heard this from Letitia, who phoned in her disappointment and surprise. "It is disrespectful to Alan's memory," she said, "to be seen in the company of a deserter."

"Amos was a resister," she said. "Besides, that was twenty years ago."

"I can see," said Letitia, "that there is no talking sense to you."

"Are you in trouble?" asked Kristen when Maggie hung up.

"I guess so," said Maggie.

Justin Herrick presented himself Saturday morning even though Maggie had called the night before to tell him that she could not go cross-country skiing. He arrived as Kristen was bringing her mother a bucket of ice, and Maggie, on the telephone with AAA, was told that AAA never had a promotion involving Christmas tree angels.

Justin walked past Alan's prominently displayed picture, making a studied effort to keep it out of his line of sight, handed Kristen a complimentary ski-lift ticket, and kissed Maggie on the cheek. "You needed to put ice on it when it first happened, Maggie. Ice does you absolutely no good once the swelling has begun."

"My dad was an orthopedist," said Kristen. "My mom knows all that stuff."

Sybil drifted in wearing black cashmere warmups and her hair tied back with a black silk scarf. She looked like a tanned and shining spider.

Maggie introduced her mother to Justin. "It's hard to believe you're Maggie's mother," said Justin. "But then I guess you're used to people telling you that."

"You're being kind," said Sybil. "As a matter of fact, I did have Maggie when I was very young."

"That figures," he said while Maggie shook her head and thought that there was no end to her mother's duplicity.

"How young?" asked Rudy. "And where do you want this chart?"

"Who are you?" asked Justin.

"He's waiting for parts," said Maggie.

Justin took charge. He did it with forthright, benign, and fair-minded command. It was hard to oppose him. He announced in the car that he was taking her to an auction.

"Your hair smells like woodsmoke," he said, kissing her on the forehead. "Did you miss me? I don't mind telling you, I spent a great deal of time thinking about you. And you know what I decided?"

"What?"

He drew her closer beside him on the seat. "You're all right, Maggie. We're all right. And everything is going to be all right."

"You're hurting my ankle," she said.

He pulled away. "What were you doing on the ice in the first place?"

The auction was held at the grange hall. Hobart Straw, wearing a vest with a pocket watch, was laying down an incomprehensible patter. He nodded to Maggie and smiled.

"He gets a percentage of the take, you know," said Justin. "And even though he denies it, I have it on good authority that he uses shills to jack up the bids."

Maggie looked through the crowd of farmers and their wives. A few local tradespeople in open mackinaws and parkas had babies over their shoulders and hot dogs in their hands. Everyone looked honest and tired, hopeful of getting a bargain, willing to settle for a few hours of entertainment. She wondered which ones were the shills.

Hobart Straw was addressing a man on the aisle with easy familiarity. Maggie saw that it was Schuyler from the Mobil station. "Are you going to let a woman trim you for five dollars?" he asked. Schuyler shook his head.

Justin sat with his arm resting on the back of Maggie's folding chair, not proprietary so much as preemptory. "Here is where you learn a lot about human nature," explained Justin. "Some folks won't let the other fellow have it, no matter what the price is."

Straw moved in their direction and said to Justin just loud enough to be heard in the first three rows, "You got you a fine lady there, you should see her in the courtroom. Pays real good attention," then turned to the latecomers standing in the rear. "The terms of the auction in four letters is *cash*," he said. "The cashier is waiting back over at the coffee urn. If you don't have a number, get one. If two people claim the same bid on the same item, it goes to the smallest number." An assistant held up a bow-back chair. When Maggie leaned forward, Justin put a restraining hand on her arm. "That's not a Windsor," he said. "It's a reproduction."

According to Justin, Maggie knew nothing. She bid on

the wrong things, she bid too quickly, and what she did get she paid too much for, especially an old, mildewed hatbox filled with old, flower-garlanded Brussels lace. It cost ten dollars and he said it was the sort of junk that would only clutter up her closets. When very little was left, except knobless pot lids and lamps that needed to be rewired, Justin insisted on showing her his house.

It was a museum and he was its curator. Everything had a place, a niche, a description, and a history, including a cloisonne vase that had come from Woodrow Wilson's home, and a collection of tin soldiers arranged in regiments on lighted shelves that he said were worth, conservatively, two thousand dollars.

Holding her under the elbow, he led her into his bedroom to show her his closets, where suits and jackets hung precisely two inches apart, and where pairs of shoes, one inch apart, were lined up in neat, gleaming rows. Then he picked her up and carried her in his arms. She assumed he wanted to save her the trouble of walking, especially since his direction was out of the bedroom. Hence her surprise when he slung her on the sofa and jumped on top of her, kissing her wildly, rolling her about like someone flouring a lump of dough, and running his hands all over her as if checking for her wallet. Later she reasoned that it was the daylight and her limp that had lulled her into false security.

Maggie let out a yell and pushed him away. "Get off!" she shouted. "Get away from me!"

This aroused him even more and he tried to unbutton her blouse. Then Maggie really screamed, a bloodcurdling, atavistic shriek that made him sit up as if he had seen a ghost.

He said she was a tease. Why did you come into my bedroom, he asked, if you were not prepared to make love?

"You said you wanted to show me your closets."

"It was a euphemism."

"Then why did you show them to me? And why did you bring me out here?"

"That was my wife's bed, Maggie." He smoothed his hair. "Does it have something to do with the way you feel about yourself? Are you thinking that you're over the hill? If you are, let me assure you that you're not."

"Thanks," she said. "Jane Fonda is twelve years older than me. Why would I think that I'm over the hill?"

"I'm trying to be understanding. Look, most widows and divorcees had unsuccessful sex when they were married."

"Don't compare me to a divorcee. It's different."

"Different how?"

"I had a good marriage."

"All right. I won't compare you. The point is, if you will relax with me, trust me, I would like to show you how wonderful it can be. I like you, Maggie. Very much. You don't cry on my shoulder, you never asked me how much money I make. I feel as if we can develop a real relationship. But you can't get hung up on guilt."

He blew in her ear as if he were trying to fill it with air. Maggie knocked his hand away. "Why don't you get the message?" she asked, then stood up painfully and hobbled toward the door.

He followed after her. "It's obvious that you're not ready for an intimate relationship. What I resent," he said, "is a woman who's bad in bed because I try very hard to please."

"I wasn't bad in bed," she shouted. "I was bad on the couch."

"I'm not going to beg you, Maggie. I don't need to beg any woman. I have never had any complaints because I'm not selfish in bed. Do you understand what I'm saying?"

"My ankle has swollen up," she said. "I want to go home."

His instructions never ceased. On the way home, he said she might be frigid. He asked if she was frigid with Alan too. He repeated that he did not usually put up with this. He didn't have to, did she understand what he meant? It was only out of consideration for her ankle and because she was so waiflike, and he had a thing for waifs, that he even wanted to see her again. She felt like punching him in the shoulder, but restrained herself because she could not bring herself to touch him.

Justin spoke of the dangers of having Rudy in the house with Kristen home.

"Should I send her away?" she asked.

"There you go again, Maggie. You may think it's a put-down when you make those smart remarks, but from a man's point of view, let me tell you that it's a put-off, if you get my meaning."

He asked about Sybil. Was she well fixed? he wanted to know. She appeared as if she were.

Maggie told him her mother had been an actress when she was younger. What parts did she play? he asked. Maggie didn't know for sure. The only one she remembered was a musical called *Sweet Charity*, in which Sybil had been one of the dance hall girls.

"You must have been proud of her," he said.

"Not really. I was in high school at the time."

Maggie set down her mildewed hatbox after Justin drove away.

"What's in the box?" asked Kristen.

Maggie hugged her hard. "Laces," she replied.

Kristen wrinkled up her nose and said that Sybil was packing.

Maggie found her mother in the guest bedroom, creaming her face and throat. Garments lay folded on the easy chair. "Can't you stay a little longer?" she asked.

"I thought I was getting on your nerves."

"Not so much."

"You could have fooled me." Sybil wiped her hands on a tissue. "I don't like to be in the position of someone who is unwanted. Not ever. Not with a husband. Not even with my daughter."

Maggie thought about what Amos had said about his father. She could not bring herself to say such things to Sybil, principally because she was not even sure that she thought them. "I wish you could stay a little while longer. Especially with Rudy and Kristen in the house. At least till the trial's over."

Sybil acceded as Maggie had begun to wonder where Amos was going that evening and with whom.

"Justin isn't the one you went to see the other night," said Sybil.

"How do you know that?"

"I may not know a lot of things, but I do know about men."

"They why do you keep choosing the wrong ones?"

"That's a question I ask myself all the time," replied Sybil. She stepped closer to Maggie and inspected her daughter's face in the light. "Use this under your eyes," she said. "It plumps up the lines. Here. I'll do it for you."

Maggie sat dutifully on the edge of the bed and let her mother pat cream under her eyes. She was eight years old again, and Sybil was dabbing her chicken pox with calomine while two men with dollies came to take away the huge cartons containing her father's belongings.

Maggie suddenly rubbed the cream off with her fingertips. "I like expression lines," she said. "They give you character."

CHAPTER 8

Search Warrant

MELODY JESSICA'S COMPLETE RECOVERY was apparent to everyone, including the shuffling spectators who packed the last rows and speckled the first, and Jessica's grandfather, who sat in the rear, jammed between two strangers with coats in their laps, his arms folded across his chest, his immobile face carved into flinty resignation. She tripped into the courtroom, light-footed, lighthearted, wearing a tight red cashmere sweater and fishhook earrings that danced on her ear lobes like mayflies, then searched the jurors' box with bright, shining, pale blue, saucer eyes.

Dr. Singh was back on the witness stand. Thin, nervous, the color of caramel, his morning's meditation in a miasma of aromatic gum had been of little value in reducing his annoyance at having to return to the courtroom. He tapped the witness box with elegant, opalescent-tipped, impatient fingers.

With the weepy, rheumy eyes of a head cold, Dan Giotti faced the prosecution's witness, resolved to maintain a low-key, supportive tack, and asked if there were cases of mercury poisoning from certain diuretics or ointments used to lighten the skin. Singh replied there were, but that the occurrence was rare.

The deceased, for example, continued Giotti, was known to use an ointment for freckles. Could such a product be the cause of her death? McKeen, wearing a pale gray suit that made him look like a shaft of silver, stood to object. That fact had not been established.

Judge Atwill sustained the objection, her thoughts drifting toward her congressional campaign and the question of how deep a media probe to expect. McKeen sat down and scanned the jury. He noticed that the red-haired widow seemed distracted. He remembered seeing her at the club, owl-eyed, quiet, standing in her husband's shadow like a kid with a ticket to the wrong night. For some reason, the Bean girl had smiled at her. It happened from time to time. Someone on the jury had established eye contact with one of the principals. Although it might bear watching, it did not mean anything more than a momentary diversion, a game. McKeen's more immediate concern was the youngest member of the jury. He had been counting on a union man to make up a solid core majority that he would need for conviction. The carpenter seemed uninterested, bored, like the medical examiner, who was explaining the difference among mercury compounds, or the defendant, who pulled on her hair, making minute twists and spirals that trailed to her red cashmere shoulders. It was the sort of disinterest that might make him vote to acquit. McKeen resolved to arrest his attention while Giotti smiled a saintly, patient smile. He apologized for being only a country lawyer and asked Singh if his experience included the use of mercury in suicide.

Maggie tried to read LaDonna's reaction out of the corner of her eye while Singh replied that a person intent on suicide would more likely take a massive dose. His findings, on the other hand, revealed a chronic, cumulative poisoning. Singh folded his fingers. "Suicides do not slowly poison themselves to death."

Giotti shook his head, said that such medical lingo was beyond him, and held aloft a journal, ignoring his client, who bent to rub spit into her shiny black boots. He referred to an article about careless autopsy in which the authors complained that the chain of possession from one investigator to the next that must be noted and signed for was sometimes compromised.

When the prosecutor objected, saying that counsel was trotting out a red herring, Judge Atwill turned to Giotti. The movement was pro forma, programmed. She was somewhere else, dredging up recollections with the chain belt of her memory. "Where are you leading, counsel?"

"I am trying to show, Your Honor, that the data upon which Dr. Singh has based his findings may be inaccurate."

"Continue," said the judge, wondering if the media would research as far back as law school.

Giotti lifted a sheet of paper from his table, showed it to the prosecutor, then waved it at the jury. When Melody Jessica jumped up to peer over his shoulder, Giotti pushed her down into her seat, where she sat with a pout and a bang of her heels as Giotti moved toward the witness stand.

"There is a notation here of materials, tissue samples that were sent to you, sir, from the laboratory at Montpelier. Here is the signature of the sender, who I presume is the laboratory technician. Beneath her signature, the messenger has also signed his name. If these materials were sent to your office, where is your signature?"

"Objection," said McKeen. "Beyond the scope of direct examination."

"I will allow it," said Judge Atwill. It wasn't the takeover of moot court she was worried about. She had been only one of dozens of law students. It was the photograph taken when they leaned out of the windows to hang their sign.

Giotti blew his nose again. This time it was an explosive snort. "When Mr. McKeen questioned you on the witness stand last week, sir, you testified that you studied toxicology. Just how long was that period of study?"

"Four weeks," replied Dr. Singh.

"And how long was your residency?"

"Four years."

"I see. Four weeks out of four years. No further questions."

"You may step down," said Judge Atwill. To her best recollection, it was a small news photo, the size of a driver's license. No one could ever identify her from that picture, not even with a magnifying glass. She had looked so different then.

The jury, for the most part, despite the tedious morning's testimony, was collectively glad to be reconvened. If they had not had a surfeit of Thanksgiving and family, they had gained attention for their role in a case that everyone was talking about, and they enjoyed the notoriety.

Maggie, for one, was eager for the chance to get out of the house and the possibility of spending more time with Amos. The only juror who wished he were back on his job was Yancy Scruggs, the apprentice carpenter. At first he had relished the freedom from his mother, whose doors needed planing, his girlfriend, who expected him to take his last dime and buy her a ring, and his boss, who was making him learn dry walls and acoustical tiling. Now he was trapped in a dumb trial, forced to listen to picky bits of evidence, in a narrow jury box more confining than any crawl space. Worse, he was really beginning to hate Trish Robidoux, who could not be pleased, no matter what he did with her old, wormy chests. Holes were bored, holed were plugged up again with wood filler, braces were made to reinforce sagging corners, braces were ripped out, shelves were flimsy, shelves were warped, shelves were stained the wrong shade of cherry, and the lighting showed. According to this old woman, who did not understand that there was no place to put all those wires, he ruined every piece he touched. In addition, she had been coming on to him, he was sure of it, since he knew women about as well as he knew wood. About as well as he knew wood.

Most things were the same as the week before. The jigsaw-puzzle people were complaining that someone had taken the keystone of Waterloo Bridge, without which their puzzle could not be completed. Hannah Watson had already lined up two major suspects, Amos Stringer and the accountant-turned-canner, who that morning had brought in samples of zucchini relish for each member of the jury including the alternates, a finger of guilt, if she ever saw one pointed.

Katerina had performed over the weekend. She remained aloof and stellar, dispensing half smiles like dippers full of water behind her curtains of hair. Even though the jurors strained to understand what she said, she was theirs and they looked at her with pride. Heard you, Katerina, they said. Took the wife. You were real good. Willard Peterson said that if she needed someone to turn pages, he would be glad to volunteer.

While Katerina's stature had increased, LaDonna seemed shrunken, like an apple left too long on a sill. A violet and purple bruise petaled over her eye and cheek. She told Maggie she had gotten it when she slipped on the ice carrying vegetable peelings to the hens. Maggie asked if her husband was any better.

"Nothing I do is right," replied LaDonna. "I try to please him so he doesn't go and do it again, but it's hard. Because there's no pleasing that man. The girls don't believe that. They blame me. They say if I treated him right, he never would have gone and done what he did."

"That's ridiculous," said Maggie. "It's not your fault. Every dairy farmer in the state has the same problem. You had nothing to do with it."

"I know that. But knowing something and believing it are two different things."

"Does he say what it is he wants?"

"He wants to get back in dairying. He's sorry he ever signed with the government. He wishes he never took the first penny. He wants to buy a small herd, pull out the old vacuum line that's in the barn, and put in a milking parlor."

Maggie searched the room for Amos. "What's that?" she asked.

"You ever see a grease pit in a garage? It's the same

idea, only it's better lit. It's a pit where you can do the milking standing up. You push a button, in come the cows, marching single file. Eight stations on each side is his dream. Sixteen in all. He likes a herringbone parlor. That's where the cows stand on a bias, although you can have all kinds of shapes. A parlor we know of in Salisbury is round. The problem with that is that all you see are cows' rear ends. I've heard of a diamond shape. They say the cows move in and out of that one faster."

Maggie found Amos at the window. They exchanged the fleeting check of the covalent.

"You're seeing him, aren't you?" asked La Donna.

Maggie bent to examine her fingernails.

"Don't worry," said LaDonna. "I won't say anything. I'm real glad you stopped grieving."

Maggie had not exactly stopped, but there was no point in quibbling. It was more that grief had gone underground, paved over by other, newer feelings. She no longer kept a box of Kleenex beside her bed, and if she cried at night, she could always get it to stop. Did that mean that grief was over?

They were joined by Hobart Straw, holding a sweating can of Dr Pepper. He asked Maggie if she had noticed that he put in a good word for her with Justin Herrick. Then he teased her about her bid on the cardboard hatbox full of old laces and told her that she had to learn to pay attention to the real buys. Didn't she see the nifty Majolica pitcher with just a little chip on the spout that she could have had for less than what she paid for scraps? He tipped his head back and sipped, then narrowed his eyes.

"Herrick's wife," he said. "Now, that lady knew her cloisonné, upside down and sideways. A fine woman. Had a hard death. Cousin of my sister's husband is the charge nurse at Northside. Said she turned the color of a turkey gizzard." He left to talk to Willard Peterson. The beekeeper knew good stories and Straw, who got higher bids if he told a good story, was always on the lookout for new material.

Maggie engineered the move to Amos. She did it by moving from person to person, back and forth toward the window in twists and turns, like a garden hose snaking its way across the grass.

He smiled, asked about her ankle. She said it was fine. His amber-colored eyes were warm, glowing. "You're breaking out, Maggie," he said. "You used to dress like Wally Cleaver's mother: skirts, heels, blouses with bows at the neck, buttons at the wrist . . ."

Maggie had waited all Sunday for him to call, but she could not bring herself to tell him that. Instead she pushed her sweater to her elbows and said that it was easier to sit all day in baggy pants. His wood scent made her want to lean against him. When she caught herself swaying toward him, she stepped back, making the space between them the public space of strangers, an arm's length, close enough to hear, too far to touch.

"So far," he said, "McKeen hasn't introduced anything that isn't circumstantial."

"Like what?" she asked.

"Everything you've heard this morning. The fact that she was poisoned. That's what Giotti was getting at. He was trying to show that there might be other reasons for the medical examiner's evidence."

"I didn't hear that," she said. "I must have been thinking of something else." Maggie played idly with the ends of her hair. All motion in the room seemed suspended as if everyone waited to see what they would do next. She searched for something to say. "I have an offer on my house. I'm thinking of taking it."

"Where will you live?"

"I'll probably move in with my mother-in-law. At least until I get on my feet."

Amos stared out the window, then traced slow, random smudges on the frosted glass. "I got the idea that you didn't like her very much. What's the rush? Why don't you wait until after the trial? Some things have a way of turning around."

"I'm running out of money."

"I know the feeling." Motes of dust danced in a light beam. "You need any help with the move?"

"I don't think so," said Maggie. "I've got a houseful of people. One of them should be able to help me storm-proof the front door and chase the bats out of the attic." It was awkward and he wasn't helping. She turned away.

"Maggie." His voice was low, hoarse. She had to strain to hear him. "You're easy to be with."

Maggie felt her cheeks flush, the way her face radiated when she came in chapped from the cold. Heady with excess, she left Amos and sought the safety of LaDonna, but Trish Robidoux planted herself in Maggie's path like an oak.

"You're making a mistake," said Robidoux.

Maggie rode the wave of her exhilaration. "What are you talking about?"

"I think you understand me, dear. I just want you to know that you're not fooling anybody."

"I'm not trying to," said Maggie. "Why don't you say what you mean, Mrs. Robidoux? Straight out."

White roots showing at her center part made the antique dealer's black hair look like wings. "Very well. As jurors," she said, "we're obliged to behave with propriety and that includes avoiding even the suggestion of misconduct. Is that plain enough?"

Maggie focused on the white hair. It made the woman less threatening. "You need a touchup," she said.

During noon recess, the attorneys argued motions before the judge. Giotti, who had taken an antihistamine, sought to suppress the evidence of the deputy sheriff since it had been obtained on a search warrant from an anonymous source. Straining to stay awake, he argued that information furnished by an anonymous telephone caller was sufficient to establish probable cause only if the officer recognized the voice of the caller and could state that this same caller has furnished reliable information in the past. In this case, said Giotti, information was supplied by an informant whose reliability had not been established. What would have been more proper, he argued, was if the officer had used the information as an investigative lead, and then established probable cause for issuing the search warrant as a result of his investigation.

Judge Atwill denied his motion on the grounds that even though the informant was anonymous, the facts that were stated would cause an ordinary, prudent person to believe the information to be true. Giotti took this minor defeat with equanimity. If he lost the case, he would appeal it on this issue.

The first witness called in the afternoon was the chief of police. Mervil Hammer operated radar traps in the spring and caught nude swimmers in the summer. His advice to young people was to get off drugs and join the Masons. While McKeen held up the search warrant and asked Hammer if it contained his affidavit, Maggie took off her glasses to squint at the courtroom with narrowed eyes. Resolved to pay closer attention, straining to see was the best way she knew to insure that it would happen.

Hammer described the location of his search as a two-story red brick residence located on the south side of highway 37, also known as Rocky Hill Road. McKeen was polite when he asked what he found and unruffled when the witness replied a tube of Fasteeth.

Hammer then identified the partially squeezed tube inside the plastic bag which McKeen presented for his inspection, and it was entered into evidence, along with a laboratory report which listed among its contents two thousand milligrams of mercury salts.

"As a result of your investigation, Chief Hammer, did you have an occasion to make an arrest?"

"Yes, sir, I surely did." Giotti put a protective arm around his client.

"Is the person you arrested here in this court?"

"Yes, sir, she is."

"Would you point her out please?"

Hammer pointed to Melody Jessica. "Sitting right there. Like butter wouldn't melt in her mouth."

Giotti pushed himself to his feet. "Your Honor, please."

As Judge Atwill instructed the court reporter to strike the witness's last remark, Melody Jessica shrank back from the pointing finger and began to cry. She continued to weep as Hammer testified that the defendant had told him that maybe her mother's boyfriend had done it, then when they went to type her statement, changed her mind and said that on second thought, it was probably her own boyfriend who had murdered her mother.

Maggie knelt in the attic, reviewing the day's proceedings while she tacked up pieces of old screen across the opening in the eaves. Melody Jessica's prints on the tube of denture adhesive were easily explained. Kristen's prints were probably on everything Maggie owned. If Melody Jessica had been sent to the drugstore, or if Melody helped her mother clean the bathroom, either would account for it. The question was, How did they know what to look for? The poison could have been anywhere. In anything. Maybe it still was. Trish Robidoux's veiled threat was the more niggling issue. Maggie was trying to decide whether to mention it to Amos when she thought she heard fluttering from somewhere above. Jenna had once said that bats often tangled themselves in your hair. Maggie gripped the tennis racket, ready to swing, while trying to keep herself from running out of the attic and screaming, both of which she would have done when Alan was alive.

She had wanted to make the attic into a studio, with baskets, bulletin boards, and a harvest table with a drawer, so she could spread out her collection of laces and figure out what to do with them. Alan said no. He would agree to insulate the attic only if she first had a specific plan of action. How can I know what to do with them when I can't lay them out? Lay them out on the kitchen table, he had said. I can't do that, she replied. I have to study them. For days. He had an unpleasant way of withdrawing when he was crossed. She gave in. The laces remained moldering in their boxes. Twenty years of accommodation to make a marriage work. She wished she had back some of her compromises.

Rudy stood silhouetted in the light of the upper story, offering suggestions. "You're locking them in that way," he said. "Now they'll never get out."

A mild irritant at first, Rudy had taken over, like mildew. The M.G. was in bits and pieces, dismembered like the parts of a sentence. The laundry room was heaped with his dirty underwear, waiting for someone to wash it. Maggie guessed it was Kristen, but considered the possibility of Sybil. Not only did Kristen defer to him, but Sybil was beginning to seek his counsel. Sybil, reported to be an eyewitness, said he was a channeler. "There are people who can do this," she said. "You shouldn't close off your mind." The principle was similar to cutting taps into the bark of a maple tree. According to Sybil, Rudy tapped Jack Hawkins, who even as a spirit was unable to talk, and he tapped Hegel, who spoke of the blend of duality and unity in a heavy German accent. He even tapped Alan. When Maggie asked Sybil how she could take seriously the advice of an eighteen-year-old boy who still carried a retainer in his pocket, Sybil replied, "He's an old, old, soul."

"If he's such an old soul," said Maggie, "he should know that Bobby Kennedy didn't pitch for the Cardinals."

Actually, Rudy made it easier to accept the bid on the house. If nothing else, it was a way to get rid of him. Maggie closed the box of thumbtacks and slipped it into her pocket. "He doesn't want you to sell the house," said Rudy.

"Who?" asked Maggie.

"Your husband."

"This is very unhinging," said Maggie.

"It is to him too."

"Try not to say that to Krissie."

"Kristen already knows. I told her first."

Maggie swung down out of the attic. "I don't appreciate this, Rudy. I really don't. I don't mind telling you that you're wearing a little thin."

"Just say the word, I'm gone."

"Tell me what it is. I've tried every one I know."

Anger made her resolute. Maggie marched to her bedroom telephone and dialed Owen. Her brother-in-law said she had caught him clearing off the last batch of trout flies from the assembly table. "Tell them I accept," she said.

Owen's response was less enthusiastic than cautious. "You have to be out in five weeks," he said.

"I don't know if I can, Owen. I'm in trial."

"That was the deal, Maggie. They need the house, signed, sealed, and delivered by the first of the year."

She nailed down her wavering resolve in the way she tacked screen in the attic, and asked him to set it up with Woody Pringle. He said he would be glad to make the arrangements, then told her she better start thinking about what she wanted to do with her furniture. "You can't take it all to Mother," he said.

Kristen, with Rudy right behind her, was in a rage. She held a crumbling granola bar. "I can't believe you would sell the house to spite me," she protested.

"I'm doing no such thing," said Maggie. "And don't eat food upstairs. A few weeks ago you told me the house meant nothing to you. Now suddenly it does. What happened in the meantime?" She fixed her eyes on Rudy.

"I thought about it," replied Kristen. "It's where I grew up. It's all I remember. My father's dead. I deserve some stability."

Maggie pulled off her boots. "Who told you to say that? Stability isn't in your lexicon. The truth is, I can't afford to keep the house. I owe Letitia money."

"Why did you borrow money from Granny?"

"I didn't. She says your father did."

Kristen looked injured. She bit into the granola bar. "You called Daddy 'my father.' "

"Sorry. It was a slip."

"That was a really lousy thing to say," said Rudy.

Sybil knocked on the door, peeked in a shiny face, and sided with her granddaughter. Maggie had acted too hastily. She should have waited. She could always sell the house.

If Maggie was annoyed with Kristen and Rudy, she was suddenly furious with Sybil. Her voice became clipped and brittle. "You never waited for anything in your life," she said. "You did whatever you pleased as soon as you got the idea. I never knew what color your hair was going to be. You know what that means to a little kid? You changed husbands and fathers as often as you changed apartments, and if that wasn't bad enough, you were never home. You drifted in and out of my life like Glinda the Good, and now you have the nerve to tell me that I should wait. Stay out of this, please. I don't need your advice."

"You're carrying around a lot of baggage," said Rudy.

Maggie came close to punching him when the doorbell rang. She ran downstairs, grateful for the opportunity to get away. She was surprised to see Amos at the door, blowing on gloveless fingers. "What are you doing here?" she asked.

"I thought I'd help you fix your weather stripping, clear out the bats. Clean out your clogged-up gutters, unless they're too frozen."

Maggie did not tell him how glad she was to see him. Instead she led him through the living room, not caring that he did not bother to wipe his feet or that mud streaked after him on the rugs like cancelled checks.

Amos stopped to look at Alan's picture. "Is that him?" he asked. "He was a good-looking guy."

It seemed like an introduction. Maggie felt uncomfortable. When he left to fix the weather stripping, Kristen stood in the doorway, holding a knife and a box of laundry detergent.

"Who was that?" she asked.

"Amos Stringer is on the jury," replied Maggie. "And you don't need a knife to get that open. Just push the dotted line with your thumb."

"What's he doing here?"

"He came to help me fix up the house."

"Is he a handyman?"

"Actually, he's a photographer."

"He smells like a fire."

"That's woodsmoke."

"He's not very neat."

"Neither are you."

"That's different. He must be almost as old as you are."

Maggie was getting a headache. If she took two aspirin quickly, she would stop it before it started. "You can't apply rules selectively, Krissie. You have very rigid requirements for me that you don't seem to have for anyone else. If neatness is an issue with you, how about that skinny swami upstairs? He's been wearing the same shirt and the same earring since he got here."

Kristen jammed the knife in the box top. "Rudy's here to help us out. Did you forget that? He's got the M.G. almost working. I heard the motor turn over myself and so did your mother. And your mean remark about his earring just shows how out of touch you are."

"You're a snob, Krissie. You really are. Rudy is okay, but Amos is not."

"There's a difference. You just can't see it. Rudy is still young. That guy is old. He's supposed to have it together by now. You're lucky I'm here to point that out."

Maggie thought of the chain of her possession, from Sybil to Alan to Kristen. She pulled into herself as she did when she really got angry, balling up as if for a strike. "No way, Krissie, you're going to sign for me too."

"Sign what?"

Sybil came in quickly. Not running, but gliding fast, her shampooed hair wound in a towel turban. "There's a man dashing around the attic," she said.

"He's a friend."

"Which one?"

"You haven't met him."

Sybil kindled. "Oh," she said. "That one."

The light also dawned for Kristen, whose eyes darted like moths.

"Don't touch Daddy's picture," cautioned Maggie. "I have it turned exactly the way I want it, and I don't want to wipe off fingerprints again."

Amos ran downstairs gripping a bulging, dark green plastic bag. "They're still alive, Maggie, but I think I got them all."

Sybil appraised him with a critical, appreciative eye while he clutched tighter the squealing bag.

"This is my mother," said Maggie.

"Sybil," said Sybil, extending a graceful hand, the thin skin of which had been bleached free of age spots.

"And this is my daughter, Krissie."

"Kristen," said Kristen, hardening like taffy dipped in ice water.

"Would you like to throw that somewhere?" asked Sybil.

After Amos disposed of the bats, Maggie invited him to an awkward supper in which Rudy and Kristen rattled plates and utensils like sabers while they discussed the supernatural motifs of the silent films of the Weimar Republic, passing vampires and somnambulists across the table like rolls. When Sybil learned that Amos was a professional photographer, she asked if he could photograph her the way that Avedon had shot Marlene Dietrich. Amos, whose own mother hovered blurred and transient in the back of family photos like kitchen smoke, said it was the oldest trick in the book. After the dishes were cleared, he asked Maggie for an old pair of hose, which he slipped over the lens of his camera, then shot Sybil through a veil of Lycra, while Rudy described the hologram mounted in the front hall of his parents' home of his grandmother blowing kisses.

Sybil went down first. Sleep for her was hibernation, and she never took it lightly. Rudy and Kristen were more resistant. They sat in the living room watching MTV with Rudy's knobby arm around Kristen's elegant shoulder, as if maintaining a death vigil, the odium of their hostility settling like grit over everything including Amos, who knelt before the grate picking at the firewood.

"Who do you work for?" asked Rudy. "Who prints your pictures?"

Amos stood and wiped his hands on his jeans. "Whoever pays me." He turned to Maggie. "Someone's sold you a bunch of green wood."

"You do weddings, stuff like that?" Rudy smirked at Kristen. His tone implied that such pursuits were Mickey Mouse.

"Sometimes."

Rudy spun his earring. "You probably can't relate to this," he said. "I mean, rock has changed since your time."

Amos settled on the edge of a wing chair. "That's true."

"It's better now," said Kristen. "The old rock had a lot of fuzz and distortion. It didn't take much skill. All they had to do was put up the amps. It was slow, boring—"

"And sloppy," said Rudy. "Now it's blazing fast, clean, technically perfect."

"You're the expert," said Amos. "Not me."

Maggie grabbed the remote control from Kristen's hand and switched channels to a late-night movie while Kristen and Rudy exchanged glances.

"How come you want to watch this?" asked Kristen. "You never stay up this late."

"I do now," said Maggie.

Kristen lowered her voice. The pitch was deep, accusatory, her words dropping one by one, like marbles. "When Daddy was alive, you always went to bed first."

Maggie dropped her voice even lower. It came through her chest. "When Daddy was alive, you weren't rude to my guests."

The phone rang after Rudy and Kristen went upstairs in a huff. It was Justin, apologetic for the lateness of the call.

He couldn't sleep, she was on his mind. It must be her gamin quality. He was a sucker for dippy women. She needed him but didn't know it. That appealed. How was her ankle? She said she dipped, but it was better. How was the trial? He heard that the Bean woman had been poisoned. Maggie couldn't discuss it. That seemed to annoy him. He changed the subject and invited her to a dinner party as his date at the home of Maybeth Chase. He knew they were old friends and he thought she might enjoy it. She said she would let him know. He said she sounded sleepy. He loved sleepy women, with half-closed eyes. Sleepy women were uninhibited women. He asked if she was wearing pajamas. She said she had company and that they were watching the late show, and that she would call him back the next night.

Maggie settled down with Amos. She asked him if he wanted coffee. He said no. They talked a little about themselves, giving each other chary bits and pieces. She confided that she had never known her father. He told her that when he was in exile in Canada, he did road construction near Alberta, just below the Arctic Circle, that he worked from May till freeze-up in November, that it wasn't so bad, that a deserter he knew who worked on an Arctic oil rig had lost an arm. Then he told her that he had been married once. Maggie had thought of him as a single man, whose women were considered in the generic. The idea of any one woman with an exclusive prior claim was far more threatening. They had divorced, he said, after Nina had had an abortion without consulting him. Amos felt strongly about that.

"She should have asked me," he said.

Maggie's questions, if not germane, were specific. Where did Nina live and what did she look like? Neither answer was satisfying. Nina lived thirty miles away in Rutland. Nina was beautiful.

Kristen giggled from somewhere upstairs. "She's beautiful too, isn't she?" asked Maggie.

"I guess so."

"You don't say that with much conviction. Everyone thinks Krissie is great-looking."

"She's a snotty kid."

This could only be settled in silence. Maggie switched off the television set. "Krissie may have been out of line tonight, but she's still my daughter."

"Don't get bent out of shape, Maggie. You asked me a question. I just don't see her the way you do. To me, she's a snotty kid who's had it handed to her her whole life. I know the kind."

"Then you're also speaking about me. I've had a privileged life too, sort of."

"You could have fooled me. You don't act like it."

"Why not?"

"You seem more needy. Like you had to chain yourself to the deck just to stay on board."

"Where do you see that?"

He touched the corner of her lip. "Here. I bet if I said something mean enough I could get this to tremble." He pulled her down into the wing chair.

"Why would you want to do that?"

"Actually, I'd rather do this." He put his hand on the back of her neck and pulled her toward him. This kiss was different than the one in the ice shack. It was urgent, enveloping, demanding. Maggie was startled from the soft sound that came from her. She stiffened up, collected her feelings while the grandfather clock in the hall signaled the half hour.

"This morning Mrs. Robidoux implied something about us. She was pretty nasty. Do you think it means anything?"

Deciding that this was beginning to feel like work, somewhere between peeling vegetables and reading subtitles, which, when he left Canada, he swore he would never do again, Amos stood. "It means that if she tells the judge, or either of the lawyers, someone might want to declare a mistrial. Maybe not. For sure it means we should probably keep a low profile, not be seen out together. It also means I better go."

"Do you have to?"

"No, but there's another problem here, with us, Maggie, that has nothing to do with Trish Robidoux."

That was true. Maggie was unsure where Kristen was concerned. There was no precedent for this, no one to give advice, to offer a code of conduct. No one that she knew, other than her mother, had ever been in this situation, and Sybil never let men who weren't husbands sleep over. There was no precedent in Maggie's experience for kissing another man ten feet from a dead husband's picture.

"It's Krissie. She's only seventeen. I don't know that she'd understand."

He cupped her chin in his hand. "I think she would. Mothers lay this kind of thing out to their kids all the time."

"Do you know of any?"

"I might."

Maggie was jealous. She had not felt the feeling in a long time. How fierce it was and how painful, a quick slicing, like a paper cut across the heart. After the leaden weight of grief, she was surprised that she could feel anything that keen again.

"The problem isn't with your kid," he said. "It's with you. Maybe it's too soon."

"Maybe. Maybe it's because we're here, in my house."

"You don't have to explain, Maggie. It's okay."

When he left, she straightened up the room, feeling a need to clean, to open and close a window, to dust the furniture with her sleeves, to plump up pillows and stick her hand deep behind the cushions to get at the dirt behind them. She went for the Dustbuster, wondering what Nina looked like and if she had ever seen her. In the dusty crack of the sofa she found a dime and a matchbook. Maggie held them in her hand and examined the matchbook. Neither she nor Alan smoked. It was from an inn on the New Hampshire border. On the back of the cover, someone had scribbled, AAA. She recalled the Christmas angel.

Maggie went upstairs to bathe away Amos's traces, the reddened places where his beard had scraped, his wood scent. She wondered if the fingerprint expert who had been on the stand that morning would be able to lift Amos's fingerprints from the back of her neck as he had lifted Melody Jessica's prints form the tube of dental adhesive; if he could distinguish whorl patterns made by Amos from those made by Alan?

Immersed to her chin, she felt suddenly overwhelmed with remorse. I'm sorry, she cried. I'm really sorry. I didn't mean for this to happen. She dried herself and put on Alan's shirt, but its woolen consolation only made her feel worse. She should have waited. What was wrong with her that she could not have waited? Six months was the rule of thumb. A year was even better. Jenna said you had to get through all the seasons, all the birthdays. AAA. Whose matchbook cover was it? How did it get in the sofabed? AAA. There had to be a connection to the Christmas angel.

That night Maggie dreamed of Alan sleeping in the attic, hanging upside down like a bat beside Joyce Hibbert Bean, and AAA sending out a repair truck to get them down. She woke up shouting, her heart beating. AAA. A for Alan. It had something to do with Alan, she reasoned, with the clarity that comes when one is awake in the middle of a silent night with nothing to do but think. She listened to the beat of her heart, and the creak of shrinking floorboards, and considered what the other two A's stood for.

CHAPTER 9

Eyewitness

THE DECISION TO CONTINUE to see Justin was born of the need to continue to see Amos. It was a straightforward trade-off and Sybil's idea. She explained that it was done all the time. If Maggie was determined to have a relationship that was discountenanced, if not actually prohibited, then she needed a beard, a cover, the sort that Justin could provide. The logic was simple: being seen publicly with Justin would shift the focus from Amos. Maggie, who found herself needing Amos with the urgent, mindless, id-spawn, middle-of-the-night estrus that allows no way out, saw the virtue of Sybil's plan.

Even though he was fighting off a head cold, Justin was pleased with her call. His subdued enthusiasm was a buttoned-down gladdening, hobbled by personality and by Actifed. To celebrate her first real opening move, he invited her to a supper given by the preservation league of which he was a trustee. Held in the Victorian mansion that housed the library, it was as public as the auction ring at the grange. Anyone in the village with any civic claim was present.

Letitia presided, as upright as a pillar, selecting a deviled egg with Jenna and Owen, silent, polyester janissaries at her side.

While Indian Eddy, dressed as a Union soldier, carried

a tray of wineglasses through the crowd, Maggie checked her sleeves in a convex Empire mirror which was surmounted with a spread eagle, its tin coating tarnished in a blackened fretwork. Even though she had tacked on the lace in a hurry, the overall effect was good. No one would suspect that the delicate point d'espri covered moth holes the size of quarters.

Letitia greeted Justin with a practiced cordiality and the varnish of endowed gentility as thick as the stair treads; Jenna suggested to Maggie that she needed vitamins. Everyone needs them, she counseled, not just any old vitamins, the kind that get stored away on some drugstore shelf where they lose their potency, but fresh vitamins, compounded from natural products and laced with zinc. You would be surprised to know how much you need zinc, she said. Owen seemed more nervous and rabbity than usual. "Maggie doesn't want to hear about vitamins," he said.

Maggie appraised her brother-in-law, still offended that people said that he and Alan resembled one another. Their features might have been similar, but they weren't put together in the same way. While Alan's face had been crisply modeled, Owen's had a washed-over look, like a sand figure eroding from the tide.

Justin propelled her toward the Pot Luck Supper Club, who moved before them in fixed constellation from crudités to wet bar. Its members greeted them with glittering smiles as bright and as unsteady as neon. They stood back from Maggie as if it were she, not Justin, who was contagious and said she was looking well. Drew Pringle complimented her lace-trimmed sweater. What was the world coming to, asked Maybeth Chase, when kids took it upon themselves to murder their parents? Peter Bouchard, smiling his crooked, quirky smile, said it made no sense. There are a lot of people, he pontificated, myself included, that believe a piece of evidence is going to be found to show that this whole business was the work of some transient.

Maggie took a glass of wine from Indian Eddy's tray,

thinking that the unlikelihood of such a possibility could only be understood by someone closely following the trial. "I'm not supposed to discuss the case," she said. "I'm not even supposed to listen to you talk about it."

Her enjoinder, which implied that she was privy to something they were not, seemed to annoy them. They shrugged away its significance like horses twitching flies, while Justin put a protective hand on her shoulder. "Maggie is a real stickler," he said. "She should have been a schoolteacher."

Anne suddenly glared at Justin and fixed him with clear, blue enlightenment. "One thing has nothing to do with another. Maggie is simply obeying the law. You make it sound as if she's a persnickety old biddy." Her unexpected defense was a surprise to everyone. Even Peter turned.

Woody Pringle changed the subject to Hannah Watson's sister Edna, who had gone back to her car to get raffle tickets, slipped and fell, and had to be taken to the hospital for X rays. The orthopedic reference, however removed, caused Woody's wife, Drew, to poke him in the ribs, and made everyone else suddenly fall silent like pots with their lids clamped on. If Alan had been alive, it would have been his fingers that had palpated Edna's osteoporotic pelvis, and his car that would have taken her to the hospital.

They had been inseparable friends when Alan was alive. Now they were like scavengers, picking and darting away, dashing back to pick again. Maggie excused herself and fled into the crowd.

She recognized McKeen from the back. It was the gray suit and the shock of platinum hair. The prosecutor's civil duties included advising local government on such matters as zoning, and he was telling the owner of a gravel pit that the noise ordinance did not apply since he was in the county, and that it was unlikely that any suits drawn against him would be heard by the board.

Maggie ducked her head, trying to get around him

without attracting his attention, but he had already seen her.

They looked at each another just long enough for the gravel pit owner to down the rest of his wine. "I'm afraid to say anything to you," she said.

"It would be a whole lot easier in the city," he acknowledged. "The problem is, we country folk are too connected. Yellows and whites in the same eggshell. Would you like a glass of wine?"

"I've had four."

Justin suddenly appeared, dodging his way through the crowd like a halfback. When Maggie introduced them, Justin was proprietary, take-charge, as if he had come to collect his football.

"Are you supposed to be talking to one another?" he asked as they moved into the chilly, space-heated carriage house to dine at long, paper-covered trestles. Katerina Lodz kindly agreed to play the piano. Someone gave her the sheet music to a Civil War ballad about tenting on old campgrounds which she played like a mazurka. Justin confessed after the applause that he had dropped the two other women he had been going with. "Why did you do that?" asked Maggie, who felt a slipknot of panic at his revelation.

"A hunch," he replied with a broad grin.

While Justin filled her wineglass and everyone at their table spoke of the great snow on the mountain—a twenty-inch base and it wasn't even Christmas, and all trails operational except Suicide Run, which continued to be a sheet of ice—Maggie thought only of Amos. She wanted him next to her, now. There was nothing special she had to say to him. She was too drunk to make clever conversation. She just wanted him beside her. Why not Alan? she wondered. Pincers of guilt wrested the question, and caused tears to pool and shiver in her eyes. Why wasn't it Alan's thigh she wanted to press against, Alan's hand to plunder beneath the cover of the table? The answer was simple, although her hold on it was weak. Alan, who had become responsibility in life, had become grief in death. The graft could not be removed from the host. Amos, on the other hand, was unfettered with domestic adhesions. Amos was still only peeled-back feeling. She squirmed in her seat, hoping that Justin didn't notice her preoccupation, as she recalled the night before, dialing every hour and letting the phone ring into the lonely night. When he finally answered, he was distant, aloof. She excused him. She told herself she was imagining things, but could not dismiss the sick feeling percolating up from the pit of her stomach.

Justin played with her hand as he talked about his house. He told her he did everything: cleaning, food shopping, interior decorating, everything. He even kept a special file for supermarket coupons.

Maggie told him that she was thinking of selling her house.

Justin made a quick assay, then looked at her as if in sudden recognition. "I hope you find a place that's bigger than mine." He said this quietly and levelly, and with what he hoped was a maximum of dispassion.

Maggie jerked her hand away. "Don't worry. Moving in with you never entered my mind."

Her expression caused Justin to back off. He refilled her wineglass while beating an attentive, if not hasty, retreat. "I didn't mean that the way it sounded," he said. "It's just that after twenty-seven years of marriage, I love the freedom of being a bachelor. I can basically do what I want all the time. No daily negotiations. Lots of spur-of-the-moment activity. No accounting for my time or money. I can decide not to shave, or leave a dull party as soon as I get there." He lowered his voice to a whisper. "We don't have to wait for dessert."

His warm, caressing whispers tickled her ear, and she bent her head to rub it on her shoulder. That did it. No longer revving up, Justin turned on. It was apparent in the flare of his nostrils and the sweat that beaded beneath his hairline.

Just then Maggie spotted Hope Dyer wearing Maggie's navy wool evening skirt. Maggie knew it was hers by the embossed gold buttons on the pocket and the gold chain link belt. It was one of the few gifts Sybil had ever given her that she liked. She rose unsteadily, not bothering to excuse herself, and wended between the seated diners in the sedate and careful manner of the stoned.

She cornered her quarry next to a tray stand. "I want it back," she said. "That skirt you're wearing is mine."

Hope looked surprised. "Sorry, Maggie. I didn't know it was yours. I borrowed it from Anne. Naturally, I thought it was hers."

"I want it. Now."

Hope fingered the silver heart suspended from her neck as if it were an amulet. "I told you I would give it back. I'll drop it by next week. I promise."

A liter of Paul Masson robbed Maggie of any compassion she had left. "Take it off," she said.

"Here? Now? What am I supposed to wear?"

"The skirt I'm wearing."

"It doesn't even match. Are you crazy? You know, Maggie, we all feel sorry for you with Alan gone and all, but you've really become unhinged. Everything they say about you is true." Her voice dropped to a hiss, like steam escaping from a loosened valve. "And I'm not even sorry that you have to sell your house."

They undressed in the mansion's old pantry, which was a sterile, white and steel-trimmed corridor, bounded on both sides by floor-to-ceiling tea sets, dishes, platters, pitchers, goblets, and salt cellars behind glass cupboard doors, with drawers of linens and flatware beneath. Maggie enjoyed the drama. It tempered the fact that she was with Justin and not Amos, and that Alan was nowhere to tell her that everything would be all right. The skirt hung loosely on her hips. Jenna was right; she had lost weight.

Hope left without another word, her head held high, her nose and chin pointing up to the stenciled ceiling, not even bothering to speak to Anne, who brushed in beside her.

Anne smiled. "After all these years, Maggie, you're still pushing your way into a subway."

Flushed with victory, Maggie was in no mood for good humored gibes. "It was your responsibility to get the skirt back. You were the one I lent it to."

"They're all talking about it. What you just did. You're a blast of fresh air, Maggie, and you're smashed."

"I'm perfect."

Anne bent down. "You're smashed and your skirt is crooked." She twisted the garment so that the pocket showed in the front where it belonged. "How are things?" she asked. "Are you managing all right?"

Maggie held her cards to her chest. "They're up in the air," she replied.

"I hear you're going to sell the house. That you were offered $90,000 for it."

"This town's got a world-class grapevine."

"You'll have a lot of packing to do. A lot of sorting through old stuff. I'd be glad to help."

Letitia came in stony-faced. "Is what I have just heard true?" she asked.

Anne's serene, pacific brow conveyed an integrity of the untroubled. "I don't know what you heard, Letitia, but Maggie did Hope a favor. Something spilled on the skirt Hope was wearing. Since Maggie was not on the committee, she offered to make an exchange. Wasn't that sweet of her?"

Letitia had her doubts. They lay concealed beneath half-closed lids. "I don't see any spills."

"That's because the skirt is navy," said Maggie, leaning an elbow on the ancient white birch counter. "You can't see spills on navy." They were weaving a maypole, she and Anne, one lie upon another. Maggie danced in with her ribbon.

Enid Mulcahey smoothed her glen plaid suit skirt over her knees while Jim McKeen entered into evidence a handful of cancelled checks.

The jury was attentive, as yet unaffected by noontime hunger and the tedium of listening to details in drips and drabs. Maggie, hungover, was in her usual seat, her cheeks whipped pink by the cold and her head like a sponge. Driving home the night before, Justin had suggested a nightcap at his house. He told her it was like jumping in the lake. She had to take the plunge sooner or later. He knew she wasn't easy. She had already made that point the last time she was at his house. Why waste more time? She could have told him that she had a headache, which she did. Instead she said she had to be at the courthouse by nine.

The document examiner scrutinized the checks slowly, reshuffled them, then stacked them in order with a sharp rap on the rail before her. She explained that there was a difference between the checks made out in July and August, such as the deposit for cheerleader camp, and those made out in September and October. The latter, she pointed out, demonstrated what was called the tremor of forgery, a shaky writing caused by a laborious, often painstaking tracing over the original signature.

McKeen next entered into evidence absence excuses which he passed first to Giotti for inspection and then to the jury. He glanced once at Maggie, then moved on to the next juror as if Maggie were just a word on a page. "Do you believe these to have been written by the decedent?"

"I believe them to have been signed by the decedent, but the contents were written by someone else."

"On what do you base your conclusion?"

"The handwriting is labored, slow. In addition, the contents are feathered at the fold in the paper. Feather-edging is always seen when wet ink is folded over. In this case the signature, which also appears in the fold, has no feathering. The signature and the contents were written on different occasions."

McKeen's third exhibit was a handful of postcards postmarked from Daytona Beach, Florida. Mulcahey testified that the handwriting on the postcards, which told of having fun at the dune races and of plans to stay a long time, was the same loopy scrawl as that of the absence notes. She added that the contents, specifically the grammatical usage, made her suspect that they were not written by an adult. The most condemning aspect was their close. It was not customary for a parent to sign "yours very truly."

"Objection," said Giotti. "Beyond the witness's competence."

"Your Honor," protested McKeen, "these postcards, which we will show were displayed to friends and neighbors of the decedent, directly bear on the state of the defendant's mind."

"The fact of their dissemination has not been established," declared the judge. "Sustained." Judge Atwill was trying hard to concentrate. She ironed her forehead with her fingers while McKeen introduced the final document, a composition written by the defendant in tenth-grade English. He asked the witness if she had seen the handwriting before. When she replied that she had, both in the body of the absence notes and in the postcards, Maggie watched the defendant staring out the window and wondered how anyone who behaved as if she were in detention hall could be capable of forgery, much less involved in a carefully planned murder.

Maggie popped two aspirins. Her head was still vibrating in a hangover's low oscillation. She watched Amos grab his coat and bolt from the jury room, and thought that if she hurried she could catch up with him. Then she checked herself against village standards of propriety, which did not include chasing after some guy while you were supposed to be in mourning.

While Hannah Watson was explaining about the pin the doctors had put in her sister's hip, Maggie opened her lunch beside LaDonna. Her friend's purple-tinged eyes were sunken and ringed like those of a barn owl. She said that her husband spent all evening sitting at the kitchen table polishing and cleaning his guns.

"I can't stand the smell from the oil rags," LaDonna said. "It's in everything. Especially now that the windows are shut tight. I go out into the freezing cold in my nightgown just to breathe fresh air." Maggie unscrewed her thermos and poured hot chocolate into LaDonna's cup. "The girls set such a store in how he is, worrying is he eating, is he sleeping, tiptoeing around the house, shushing their own little ones, did he try anything again? They never ask me about me."

"He's their father."

"He was never much of one."

Maggie considered the bond between Kristen and Alan that set them in tandem like two wheels on a single bicycle, then that of her own father, the strange link forged by absence and a random collection of disconnected memories, bits and pieces of paternity, a rebus of Vaseline hair tonic, white Bermuda shorts and white knee socks, and a puzzled, handsome colossus handing down a raincoated Barbie doll and asking what it was doing in the living room. "I guess a man doesn't have to be much of a father. It seems enough that he is one." LaDonna seemed to be slipping down some drain. Maggie reached for her. "Why don't you just sell and move away?"

"That farm is everything in the world to him. The land it's on was settled by his family in 1839. It's been in his family for five generations. Freeman has slept in that bedroom for forty-nine years. He was born in that room."

"Then why don't you leave him?"

LaDonna shrugged. "Where would I go?"

"Your own folks, the girls."

"You can only do that when he's dead. Not when he's alive. At least not farm folks. It's like you're born with one coat. All along the way, everyone pulls off a thread. They think they're helping you. Finally it's threadbare. But you wear it, because it's all you have."

"It's the out-of-staters," said Willard Peterson, standing behind them in a red vest. "They pay so much money for real estate, it's drove up the assessments."

Violet Mobeley was excessively fat. The rims of her glasses slid into her cheeks like tires in mud as she testified that she lived off the road behind the Bean house. "You can't see it too good in the spring and summer on account of the leaves."

McKeen asked if she knew Joyce Hibbert Bean. Mobeley replied that she had known her more than thirty years, that they had been in grade school together, and that she knew everyone in the family, including both grandmothers. Then she identified the decedent's father, Renfrew Hibbert, sitting in the back of the courtroom.

At the mention of his name, Hibbert slipped deeper into his coat so that his face was hidden by his collar. Only his callused hands were exposed, folded in his lap. Maggie watched him, thinking that he was probably the age of her own father. The man she only faintly remembered had had weekly manicures and a smooth pink face. If his middle years had been excised by distance, surgically removed like the ten years that Amos spent in Canada, would he still have aged like Hibbert?

McKeen rested his elbow on the lectern, as if he had all the time in the world. "How would you describe the descedent?"

"Joyce was a quiet person, stayed to herself. Not gossipy like some. Kept herself and her house clean. She had in mind to go to beauty school, but she never could get the money to do that. Then she found this correspondence course in beauty. She always had a knack for hair. Did mine regular and never charged me a cent. She married Dacey Bean right out of high school. Dacey drove the school bus and ran the snowplow. Had a bad accident at the snowplow maybe eight, ten winters ago. She did the best she could after that. She lived some off the insurance, some doing folks' hair out of her house. If Joyce did your hair, it lasted all week. It was a talent."

McKeen asked how well she knew the defendant. Mobeley pointed to the girl sitting cross-legged on the chair beside Giotti, then said she had known Melody Jessica since the day she was born. She dropped her voice and said that Joyce had had her hands full on account of Melody was running wild with Kevin Clapp. Her youngest son saw them under the high school bleachers rolling around in the trash, soda cans and all.

"Objection," said Giotti with a pencil in the air. "Hearsay."

"Sustained."

"Move to strike," said Giotti.

The judge instructed the jury to disregard the witness's last remark and Maggie wondered how. *Forget what I said. I didn't mean it* never worked. Asking people to forget something called attention to the thing they were asking you to forget. If anything, it ensured the engram.

McKeen asked Violet Mobeley if Joyce Hibbert Bean had told her anything prior to her disappearance.

"Yes, she did," she replied. "She said she was real sick, her ankles were all swollen. She had these headaches real bad, her hands were so shaky she didn't think she could do anybody's hair." Violet Mobeley paused and shifted her bulk. "And she couldn't pee."

"Where is this leading?" asked the judge.

"I'm trying to establish, Your Honor," explained McKeen, "that the decedent's symptoms were consistent with the findings of the medical examiner."

"The witness may continue." Judge Atwill was discouraged. Despite all the reading she had done on municipal affairs, there were a few questions following her talk at the Chamber luncheon for which she had not been prepared. It was hard to be on top of everything. She turned her attention to the witness.

". . . said she thought someone put a spell on her. I asked how do you know, and she said, I have a bad taste in my mouth all the time, it's like I'm being poisoned."

"Objection," said Giotti. "Hearsay and irrelevant."

The judge sustained the objection and once more Giotti moved to strike. Jurors were supposed to forget words they had clearly heard. The accumulation was getting harder to expunge and it was building, like sludge in a septic tank.

"Mrs. Mobeley," continued McKeen. "Did you see anything unusual on the night of July 17th?"

Mobeley replied that she had been laying rocks on the garbage can lids so the raccoons wouldn't get in, then saw Melody Jessica and the Clapp boy haul a body into the trunk of her mother's Plymouth. They were pushing and tugging until the boy lifted his foot and kicked it the rest of the way.

McKeen asked when she had last seen Joyce Bean, and Mobeley replied that she never saw her again after that. When he asked what she thought had happened to Joyce Bean, Mobeley said that she thought her neighbor had gone to Florida. Though she wondered why anybody would go to Florida in the middle of the summer.

It was Giotti's turn to cross-examine. Slowly, deferentially, he left his table to approach the witness box. His voice was low and somber. "This is a terrible crime, isn't it, Mrs. Mobeley?"

"Terrible."

"You would like to see someone pay for this crime."

"Yes sir, I would."

"Anyone."

"Objection. Counsel is badgering the witness."

"Your Honor," protested Giotti, "this goes directly to credibility."

Judge Atwill sustained McKeen's objection.

"Mrs. Mobeley, anyone can make an honest mistake. How far were you from the persons you think you saw?"

"Forty, maybe fifty yards. I'd know that girl anywhere, and I know they were stuffing a body into her mother's car."

"From the distance of half a playing field? Through

foliage so dense it's difficult to make out the outlines of a neighboring house? Mrs. Mobeley, which do you believe is more important, to make an identification or to make an accurate identification?"

"I don't understand the difference? You're mixing me up."

"I withdraw the question. I have no further questions." The point had been made. Giotti resumed his seat and laid his hand to rest on the back of his client's chair while the witness, her body shuddering in its girth, was helped out of the box by the clerk.

It was still daylight. Biting cold sucked the breath from the mouths of the jurors and dried their eyeballs. They scurried through the parking lot, their thoughts spun with strands of forgery and teenage malfeasance from the prosecutor's spindle. Maggie covered her face with her woolen scarf and caught up to Amos at his truck. She wanted to spell it out and tell him how she felt. Instead she asked who he supposed sent back the postcards if it wasn't the Bean woman.

He pulled her up into the cab of his truck and ran the motor. "It's too cold to stand out there and talk about postcards."

Maggie let her scarf fall to her shoulders. "Why haven't you called me?" *There. Straight out.*

His lips were cracked with cold. When he smiled, his lower lip bled. "Things came up. I've been sidetracked." He put his knuckle to his lip to wipe away the blood, then pulled her down on the seat, and slipped his hand inside her parka, rummaging under her sweater to caress her breasts with mittened fingers.

"I thought you'd like a new sensation," he whispered.

"How do you know it's new?"

"I'd bet money on it." He kissed her neck and throat. "Do you like it?"

"I don't know. It's scratchy."

"That's the idea."

"I like it, but I think it's kinky."

"Not on a scale from one to ten." He withdrew his hand and buttoned her parka. "I've got to go."

"Now?" She seemed surprised, hurt.

Amos's mother had said it in the same way when Amos, slung with duffel and backpack and armed with a street map of Toronto, had told her that he had to go. She had been bent over the soapstone sink in a habitual stance, doubled over like a meathook, and she scraped her knuckle.

"Now?" she had asked, stanching the fresh blood with a kitchen towel. "This very minute?"

"I better get going," he replied. She made no move to straighten up while his father silently opened the screen door as if he were letting out a fly.

"Sorry, Mag." He lifted her chin. "You're not primed for any of this, are you?"

"You mean the trial?"

"I mean you didn't plan on being a widow. You expected to be a doctor's wife until the day you died. Now you're a fish out of water. You're in worse shape than I was after amnesty. I might have been on the edge of things, but you got locked into a place in time that goes back over twenty years. Boy, this is hard. Look, Mag, you didn't go through any changes. This, between us, would be a lot easier if you had slept around."

"I did once, a long time ago, and it was a mistake." That was all she remembered about the event—it had taken place in the docent's office of the art museum. She didn't even remember the name of the graduate student who earned his tuition with restorations, only his long, soft hair that covered both their faces, and the paint from his hands that smeared the backs of her legs.

"It's really not my business anyway. All I'm trying to say is that it might have helped. That's all."

"You mean if I had had casual sex I would have been able to deal with casual sex?"

"You don't know what casual sex is, Mag. Casual sex is

if I made it with you in the cab of my pickup, dropped you off, and forgot your name."

They heard the crunch of feet. Maggie slunk down.

"You think all this is like punching a commuter ticket, where so many punches earns you the conductor. You're still back there with the Supremes. You're still humming 'Baby Love.' "

Was he right? They were the same age, more or less, yet he had gone one way, she another. It was as if the seismic sixties had opened up a fissure. Some stayed where they were, others made it to the other side. Her roommate used to make fun of her. So did the whole dormitory when they learned that Maggie's DMZ began at her navel. She didn't care. She didn't want to be like Sybil. Not being like Sybil was more important than any peer approval to be gained from going all the way.

"Mag, I don't go around chasing bats out of attics for everyone, and if this thing goes anywhere you'll never see me jackknife out of bed. That ought to tell you something."

"It tells me you probably don't heat your loft."

"Listen, I'm still trying to piece myself together. I need to be able to see you without strings to trip over and without worrying if I'm doing something to your head. I wish it could be that way for you. But if it's not, there's nothing I can do about it. I'd like an assignment to Central America. There was a kid in Nicaragua, couldn't have been more than two, bald-headed, his eyes haunt me. I still see them. He used to follow me around. The other kids teased him, slapped him on top of his head. No one could tell me anything about him. I'd like to go back. Find out what happened to him. Nobody's making any moves to send me back. I either live with that fact or I don't."

It was his eyes, like melting caramel, that softened her.

"I wish you'd let me help. Maybe you just need more exposure. My mother knows a lot of art dealers, gallery people. She could probably get you a show."

He drew her close, burying his face in her neck. "You smell like cinnamon."

"Does that mean you don't want to talk about it?"

"Not like cinnamon. More like maple sugar." She kissed him first, matching lip to lip, corner to corner, like sealing an envelope.

He pulled away. "Pump your brakes, Mag. The road looks pretty slick."

"As long as we're giving advice, here's one for you," she countered. "Forget trying to put yourself together. You're missing too many pieces."

"Why do you want to drive all the way to the other side of the mountain just to see where his ex-wife lives?"

"I don't know," said Maggie. "I guess you think I'm peculiar."

"I'll take you," said LaDonna. "But I sure don't know what you think you're going to see. By the time we get there, it'll be almost dark."

They found the address in the phone book at the gas station. LaDonna said she thought she knew the street. It was where her son-in-law's grandfather lived. The snow had been heavy. Giant pyramids of snowbanks, erected by a crisscrossing snowplow, narrowed the intersections. LaDonna drove with her neck craned over the steering wheel and her forehead bumping against the windshield. She said she was beginning to believe that the Bean kid did it. Some kids, she said, were trouble from the day they're born, and there's nothing you can do about it. Maggie, whose education had been weighted heavily on the side of environmental issues, said that she couldn't believe any baby was born bad. Things happen to children to make them the way they were. What about Mobeley's testimony that Joyce Bean had pinched her baby's nose shut when she cried?

"I think that's it over there," said LaDonna. Maggie adjusted her glasses. They passed by the frame house once. A light was on in the front window with a shade drawn halfway, making it look like a winking eye. Maggie thought she saw someone inside.

"Turn around and pass by again, slowly."

"What do you think you'll see this time that you didn't see before?" asked LaDonna.

"I don't know," said Maggie. "I just don't want to miss anything." She ducked down.

"Did you see enough?" asked LaDonna.

Maggie nodded, and LaDonna backed up the station wagon. Its rear wheels whined as they spun treadlessly in the snow. LaDonna wasted no time. She jumped out, took the jack out of the rear to raise the axle, and sent Maggie to search the floorboards for an old scatter rug to spread on the snow for traction.

The front door of the frame house opened. A woman stepped outside and trained a flashlight on them. "Need any help?" she called. She was tall and thin, wearing a woven poncho about her narrow shoulders and her blonde hair in a long braid that trailed down her back. She was very pretty, almost beautiful, with the deadly serious expression of someone who doesn't get the point.

"No, thanks," shouted LaDonna. The woman reached around the front door and pulled a sled up by its ropes to lean against the steps.

"We might as well have set off cherry bombs," said LaDonna.

"Do you think she saw me?"

It was the first time that Maggie ever had seen LaDonna smile. "No one could miss all that red hair, Maggie. Even at dusk."

"Did you see the sled?", asked Maggie.

"I saw it."

"It means a child," said Maggie.

"Most times. Sometimes people use them just to carry things. But it usually means a child."

Maggie was depressed. The feeling had sifted down into the cracks of her life like a fog, smothered in her own connective tissues of guilt, self-doubt, and jealousy. Letitia's car was in the driveway and inside the front hall there was a note on the boot box. Sybil, Rudy, and Kristen had gone to the bus stop. Good news. Rudy was going home.

Maggie found her mother-in-law in Alan's study. Letitia seemed drooped and wrinkled, like an overcoat trailing from a hook. "Margaret. I didn't hear you come in."

At the sound of her full name, Maggie girded herself for combat. It was instinctive, a quick tensing of chest and stomach muscles, an internal cuirass coded in ancestral memory as preparation for fight or flight. "I didn't know you were coming." Then Maggie turned to the timid woman beside her. "This is my friend, LaDonna Dyer. She sits on the jury with me. This is Letitia Hatch, my mother-in-law."

LaDonna pumped Letitia's extended hand with her mittened fingers as if she were priming a well.

"You must be related to Win Dyer," said Letitia.

"He's a cousin to my husband. I don't know him too well. Only saw him two, three times." LaDonna turned to Maggie. "I can look at the lace some other time."

"No time like the present," Maggie said. "Come on upstairs." She dumped the contents of a few baskets over her bed. Lace spilled out and floated onto the quilt like ancient whispers. "Help yourself."

LaDonna fingered the remnants. "I don't need this any more than a pig needs a wallet, but it sure is pretty."

"There's lots more, boxes and boxes. I don't know where I'm going to put it all when I move. Take what you want."

LaDonna offered to store the lot, then hesitantly selected a narrow band with which she planned to trim a baby cap.

"She seems a nice enough woman," Letitia said when LaDonna left. "Although to be honest with you, I don't see what you have in common. When jury duty is over, you'll find that you'll not have much to say to her."

"I thought you said farm people are the salt of the earth."

"I meant what I said. Every word."

"But not *these* farm people. You mean the kind that ride their horses, not the kind that hitch them."

"Your manners are dreadful as always," said Letitia. "Although under the circumstances, I suppose you can't be blamed. Let's not argue. I thought it might be useful if I went over your furnishings. I'll tell you exactly what I can and cannot accommodate."

"I'm too tired to even think of it now."

Letitia shook her head. "I'm being less than truthful. I feel the need sometimes," she confessed, "just to touch his things."

Maggie was jolted by this intimate revelation. It was a rare glimpse at the flip side of Letitia, the soft and vulnerable underbelly. Letitia continued. "Do you ever think of Alan?" she asked.

It was a strange question, hurtful and accusatory. Alan had become an absence, a space, a black hole of grief, some sort of force field that had pulled everything about him into its inky oblivion. Even the sound of his voice was getting fainter.

"I think of Alan all the time," she replied, tugging off her parka and throwing it on the sofa. Maggie amended her comment. "Most of the time. No one thinks of anyone all of the time. You couldn't go on living if you did that. You wouldn't have space in your mind to remember to eat."

"I guess it surprises me that you think of Alan at all."

"Does this have anything to do with the preservation league supper? With Justin Herrick?"

"Actually, Margaret, it doesn't. That's the strange part." Letitia straightened, seeming to plump herself up like a pillow. "It has to do with the trial. You are very caught up in it. Everyone is talking about how self-righteous you have become about your part in it, however small it may be. I'm not the only one to whom it occurs that you're giving more thought to a murder case than to Alan's memory. You were married for almost twenty years, yet you never talk about him. I never see you grieving. You don't even carry a handkerchief in your pocket." Letitia stroked the spines of Alan's books, tapping an occasional errant volume into line. "There isn't a minute that I don't think of him. You never expect that you will outlive a child. In times past, you had six to see two grow into maturity. There are places in the graveyard where you can see a row of tiny headstones, whole families of children struck down at the same time, usually diphtheria, or some other awful thing. All those mothers. How did they stand it?"

Maggie made a move toward Letitia, but felt her mother-in-law fold closed at her approach like the wings of a moth.

Maggie had struck a match to another balled-up newspaper when an icy blast of cold air funneled in from the front door, whipped up the ashes in the fireplace, and scattered them over her lap. Then there was the sound of stamping feet in the mud room, followed by Sybil, Kristen, Rudy and a man Maggie had only seen once before.

Black smoke curled into the living room, "No wonder Daddy always made the fire," said Kristen. "I bet you forgot to open the flue." Kristen flipped up the latch.

"You remember Sidney," said Sybil.

Sybil's present husband was hale and hearty, exuding bonhomie and the bristling good humor of a furrier in winter. In his youth he had had other aspirations which included dress designing, but these didn't pan out and his brother staked him to skins. The last time Maggie had seen him was with Alan the previous spring on a week-end in New York. She and Alan had gone to see a Red Grooms retrospective. Alan was bored with everything, even when Sybil and Sidney took them to a party in someone's penthouse furnished with satin Chesterfield sofas and Miro doors and introduced them to Beverly Sills.

Maggie wiped her hands on her pants and stood, ready

to extend her hand. Instead he slammed her against his chest and belly, enveloping her in a powerful, ursine, embrace. It was like rolling with a barrel. "You'd be dynamite in nutria," he said. Then he looked at Sybil. "Remind me."

Sidney railed against the bus in which he had been entombed for five hours with a stopped-up toilet that spilled into the aisle of the bus like a tributary and a seatmate who kept turning off the overhead light.

"He surprised me," said Sybil. "I had no idea he was coming."

"Keep 'em guessing," said Sidney.

Maggie could not keep disappointment from her face. It had nothing to do with Sidney. It had to do with Rudy, who had not gone home and who was fanning plumes of smoke with the *New England Journal of Medicine*.

Sybil and Sidney went upstairs to unpack, providing the usual drawer slamming of houseguests settling themselves into new surroundings. In the kitchen below, Rudy sat on a stool as Kristen, bending to squint at her line of sight, shaped his new flat top with shears and a level.

Maggie diced onions, thinking of the photograph of the murder victim, a closeup in a newspaper article that she wasn't supposed to read. While Kristen continued to feint from right to left, seeking the bubble in the level that would tell her she was on course, Maggie thought of the woman in the blurred picture. Cutting hair had been her life's ambition and she had been good at it.

"I'm trying to tell you something," said Kristen. The armory had a franchise show, she said, where they went while waiting for Sidney's bus. "There were these booths of franchise agents representing everything you could think of: foot massagers, vitamins, picture framing, coin laundries, African art, robotics, quail farms, you name it. Guess who was there? Jenna and Owen."

"What were they doing there?" asked Maggie. She had begun to think of Amos, of his wood scent and the feel of his hand inside her sweater.

"Collecting brochures," said Rudy, whose hair now looked like a shelf. "I saw them sign up for a course in natural vitamins."

Sidney, who had come in hopes of a reconciliation, had changed into country clothes, a sweater cross-stitched with a giant stag head, and new jeans that made him walk stiff-legged and bent forward, like a man in stilts. "I love roughing it," he said. "It's the only way to live."

Sidney was seven years younger than Sybil, a fact that didn't bother him since he figured that all women lied about their ages. Besides, she was an Episcopalian with class. He admired the way she laid her knife and fork on a plate, as deft as any surgeon, or the way she could get any waiter's attention just by lifting an eyelid. He didn't know how she did it. What mattered was that she was beautiful and exciting. She knew how to dress. She knew how to put herself together. She was an actress, with clippings. His brother Eddie thought he remembered seeing her in a musical forty years ago. He thought it was her, but he wasn't sure. He loved the way she let him do in bed whatever he wanted whenever he wanted to do it. She wore undergarments from Victoria's Secret, some with ruffled, pre-slit crotches that he ordered for her from the catalogue. More important, she was lively and interesting. He never tired of hearing details of intimacies with leading men she had known. Dan Dailey? He wore silk stockings to bed. Like this, he asked, did he wear it like this? Ezio Pinza? He liked to spring suddenly from a closet. Did that scare you? No? I'll do it again. This time don't look. What Sybil couldn't remember, she invented.

Maggie was drained. She was angry that this Nina person was anywhere around, especially with a sled leaning against her front door. She was angry that Letitia felt she could let herself in whenever she pleased, a habit which didn't bode well for their future cohabitation. She was angry with Rudy for still being there and shedding his hair all over her kitchen floor. She was angry at Kristen for defying her at every turn, even angry with Sidney, who thought a sweater stitched with antlers was roughing it, although of all of them, Sidney deserved her ire the least. He had been sweet, considerate, albeit clumsy, taking her aside while Kristen swept up Rudy's hair to ask if Maggie needed money.

"Look," he had said, "I'm a little rough around the edges, so if I don't say this right you'll understand. I'm in good shape. Even with my business in the shithouse. And I'd like to help you out."

Maggie insisted that she was fine, but he was not to be put off.

"Come on. Don't be embarrassed," he said. "Everybody gets tapped out once in his life. I've been there, believe me." He had reached in his wallet and peeled off some bills. "Take it."

"I can't," she said.

"Suit yourself. You know where to come if you need it."

Maggie seized on Sybil. "Can I talk to you?"

"Of course," said Sybil.

"Alone," said Maggie.

They stood in the chilly summer kitchen.

"There's something I want to know," said Maggie.

Sybil stroked Maggie's forehead. "He won't stay long. He has to be back in the shop by Monday. You look tired."

"Don't try to put me off." Maggie was wise to Sybil's tricks. She remembered them from the old days. The soft hand, the sweet, beguiling smile, the lovely perfume that filled her nose with roses. "Why did you hide my father's letters?"

"What makes you think I ever did such a thing?"

"Because I found them. When we lived at Beekham. I found them in a trunk. Hidden away."

"Oh God, Maggie. That must be thirty years ago. I don't remember. I'm chilly out here. Aren't you?"

"Stop avoiding the issue. I know you remember."

"All right. I must have been afraid the letters would only stir things up. You were so unhappy. You were just beginning to get over the separation. Like a little lost puppy."

Maggie persisted. "You hid my father's letters. You told me he went away. I asked you if he said anything about me and you said no. I believed you."

Sybil sat down on a wicker bench. "This can't be what's bothering you. It must be the photographer. Or the trial." Maggie's crossed arms told her otherwise. "There's got to be some kind of statute of limitation on this sort of thing. Why didn't you ask me then, when you found them?"

"I don't know why not. Probably because I was just a kid. I thought in some way I had made him mad and that's why he left. I didn't want to make you mad too. Why couldn't you have made an effort to get along with him? You shouldn't have made him leave. You should have tried to keep things the way they were. Why did you have to break up our family?"

Sybil raised her tired eyes. She fixed on Maggie for a long time. "I didn't send your father away, Maggie. He left."

"I don't believe you. Why would he leave? Just like that?"

"Why do people leave? They think there's something better. They get bored. Restless."

Sidney missed the step down into the summer kitchen, stumbled, and caught himself by slamming his hand against the wall. "This place is like a fun house. Hey, it's cold out here. Come back in the house."

"In a minute," said Maggie.

"You shouldn't let your mother shiver like that," he said. "You should take better care of her."

The thought was strange. Sybil was the mother, not she. "She's a mature woman," said Maggie, "she can take care of herself."

Sidney looked at Maggie with narrowed eyes and helped Sybil from the settee. "Don't be too sure," he said.

Sybil shot him a warning look and laid her hand on his arm.

Maggie's next act was impulsive. She found them in Kristen's bedroom, Kristen in her bra and jeans, Rudy holding a bottle of sesame oil in his hand. She ignored Rudy and the implication of the oil.

"I want you back in school. When the semester begins."

Maggie felt like a runaway ski—going downhill and picking up speed. Rudy started to speak. "You stay out of it," she said. "Just butt out. Pick a school, Krissie, in Vermont, and send for your transcripts, I don't care where you go. See who has a course in acid rain. But do it."

"Grandmother won't agree with you."

"Letitia's not your mother. I am."

"I don't like you like this," said Kristen. "It's unnatural."

"You're going back. Period. End of sentence."

Kristen pouted, like Melody Jessica, thought Maggie, only with a three-year edge on finesse.

"You're going to learn something," said Maggie. "You're going to graduate and get a job with a briefcase, and command some respect in this world. That's what you're going to do."

Maggie heard them whispering on her way out.

"Maybe it's PMS," said Rudy.

"Don't be stupid," said Kristen. "She'll be forty-one in March."

Maggie closed the door to her bedroom. Lace lay spilled on her bed. She brushed it to the floor and sat down. Her legs were trembling. What made it happen, this sudden failing of muscles and nerves? She looked about the lonely room where Alan was no more: the closet with empty hangers that swung and clattered against one another whenever she opened the door, and the dresser top that no longer held his keys and pocket change. She felt an aching emptiness in her belly, like hunger, only more settled in. Maggie pushed herself to her feet and found his shirt hanging in the bathroom where she had left it weeks before. When she tried to button it the second button pulled off and clattered to the bathroom floor. Maggie knew why Giotti blocked every piece of evidence and every witness. He *had* to keep it all back. One chink and it would all come rushing in, like tears.

She bent to retrieve the button and began to sob, keening into the shirt for Alan, whom she had betrayed. She cried also for herself because she had been betrayed by a father who had been bored, probably with her—it couldn't have been with Sybil.

CHAPTER 10

Accomplice Witness

THE ICE STORM THAT barreled in from the Great Lakes had wrapped everything in frigid, brittle, Midwestern transparencies, delaying the court reporter, half the jury, and the judge, who commuted daily from her home, fifty miles away. It was early afternoon, when the ice had taken on a post-meridiem, lavender glaze, before the prosecutor could present his star witness.

Kevin Clapp was a member of 4-H and just five merit badges shy of becoming an Eagle Scout. He sat in the witness stand, wearing a dark blue suit that his father wore to funerals. Someone had taken it in across the shoulders, but had not altered the sleeves and they stopped short of Kevin's wrists like skid marks. A tie that was knotted too short in the back and too long in the front cinched the collar of his starched white shirt. His dark blonde hair was slicked back except for a few strands which fell lank across his eye, and from time to time he switched his head to clear the hair from his face like a man without hands.

He would rather have worn his Dead Kennedys T-shirt that pictured Jesus crucified on a dollar-bill cross. The assistant principal made him wear it inside out. Kevin liked being offensive better than being frightened. He had to go to the can again. He licked his lower lip and folded his hands in his lap.

They told him it was a trade. It was called a plea bargain. I don't beg, he said. A plea bargain is not begging, Kevin, they said. It is a way to save time and money for the state and for you. McKeen assured him that they had enough evidence to get them both, him and Jessie. In exchange for his cooperation, however, he would be allowed to plead to a lesser charge, manslaughter, instead of first-degree murder. The prosecutor's recommended sentence, subject to approval by the court, meant that he would probably get only two years, probation and a suspended sentence if he was lucky. The alternative was life. That was the choice. You could die in there an old man, Kevin, older even than your grandfather. You know what they do to young guys in prison? You become someone's chicken. What was that? he asked. I'm not chicken. I'm not afraid of nothing. Someone's girlfriend, Kevin.

Kevin wasn't sure how it happened that his world had suddenly turned to pigshit. Everything had gone faster than a slasher. He wished he was back cruising in his cousin Robbie's 1977 red Camaro with its spoiler, five-hole Enkel mag wheels, playing 2 Live Crew and the Beastie Boys, riding with the windows cracked open and the car low to the ground so that it vibrated from the bass.

His mother and father sat watching him from the front row. They looked just as wasted as they had when his grandmother died. He turned his attention to the jury. Except for a guy who looked bored and maybe one or two others, they were all as old as his teachers. He recognized Giotti bending over a desk. He had seen him before at his deposition, when they asked him a lot of questions and took down what he said. He didn't like Giotti. The man was like the assistant principal, firing questions like rubber bands and looking at him in that smart-ass way like he could see into his forehead. Don't let that show on your face, McKeen had warned. He has a right to ask you questions. You may have feelings one way or another about somebody, but you can't let it show in court. Your testimony is the only thing that counts. Nothing else.

Kevin saw her as soon as Giotti moved aside. Her dandelion-colored hair was tied back with yarn in two bouquets. She looked small and pudgy, more like a ninth grader with baby fat, no shiny pink gloss on her lips, no dangling earrings dancing against her cheeks. It was the first time he had seen her since the day he was called out of homeroom to find the sheriff and the assistant principal pillaging his locker.

Kevin's Adam's apple slid up and down his neck like an elevator. The girl is the most important one of all, said McKeen. Look her straight in the eye. Don't smile. Look me straight in the eye. Don't switch your head around. Don't switch your hair around. Keep it locked up, Kevin. Keep it under control.

They had wanted to get married. He had saved almost eighty dollars. He did not want to marry her now. He did not even want to date her. She was trouble. She was bad news. She was him sweating in a smelly navy blue suit that belonged to his father. She used to be sweet and juicy, like a peach, with a shaft to ease the throbbing and make it go away, at least so he could think. Her arms wrapped around his neck made him feel like somebody. She used to look up at him through her eyelashes. It made him dizzy. It made him hard. He never got over the way she looked up at him through her eyelashes. Get over it, said his father. Get over it, said McKeen. He thought he loved her. His father said Kevin only had the hots for her.

Maggie watched McKeen begin, slow and easy, making no sudden moves, asking about 4-H, his voice a seductive drone, as if he were gentling a colt. The other night, Amos had spoken to her in the same way, before she had slipped off her glasses and put them on his butter churn, telling him that she was blind without them.

They had stepped together awkwardly, ardently, in an aroma of woodsmoke, fixer, and Lancome body-firming lotion. He brushed her lips with light, exploring kisses, then parted them with the tip of his tongue and held her close, one hand at the back of her neck. They swayed together, then climbed the ladder to his loft, Amos behind her, his hands over her hands as she grasped the rungs, while he pressed more tightly against her with each step.

A skylight let in the shadowed gunmetal of the night to illuminate a patch of shoulder, a curve of chin, a length of thigh, a strand of glinting coppery hair as Maggie and Amos gasped through half-filled promises, and selfish, driving urgency.

It should have been wonderful. Maggie assumed that somehow the misconnections had been her fault. He asked if she was thinking about her husband. She said no, sorry that he mentioned Alan. Then she had found him looking at her. He told her she looked vulnerable without her glasses.

Maggie heard the witness testify in a cracking, half-finished voice that Jessie was like a pit bull who never let up. Then McKeen asked as easily as if he were lacing up his shoes when the defendant had first told him of her plans to kill her mother.

Last May, Kevin replied. Jessie had wanted to go to cheerleader camp. "The whole squad was going," he said. "It cost five-hundred dollars. You learn some good moves, like elevators, pyramids, stuff like that. The school pays half. Jessie worked this car wash last spring to earn her half. She made it too. Then her mother said no. Just like that. Jessie cried and said, 'She is spoiling every chance I have to get ahead.' She said, 'I have to get me something to poison her with.' "

"What was your response?" asked McKeen.

"First I told her to forget the idea. But like I said, Jessie gets stubborn. I didn't really think she'd go through with it. I figured she just wanted to make her mom sick to her stomach to teach her a lesson. I thought of the stuff you use to kill root maggots. Calomel. A friend of mine over at 4-H, he said his uncle still has some stored in a shed. You can't taste it and you can't smell it. That's what I want, she said."

McKeen moved to neutralize the sting from Giotti's cross-examination by exposing Kevin's weak spots himself. He asked if Kevin felt he was doing something wrong when he supplied the defendant with calomel, a form of mercury salts.

Giotti rose to his feet, certain that McKeen was attempting to establish that it was remorse that led the witness to turn state's evidence. "Objection. How the witness feels is irrelevant."

"I will rephrase the question," said McKeen. "What did you think would happen, Kevin, when you supplied the defendant with poison?"

"I didn't think she would go through with it. Like I said, Jessie sometimes gets an idea, then drops it for something else. I thought she'd forget about it and quit bugging me."

When asked if they had plans for the future, Kevin said that Melody did. She said that as soon as they dumped the body they were going to party on her mother's bed.

"And did you?" asked McKeen.

"Yes, sir. Only I said we should take off the spread first, and fold it back."

Giotti tried to put aside the thought that at that moment his wife was having to deal with a plumbing system that had frozen over. The plumber, a cousin of Willard Peterson, said there was nothing he could do until there was a thaw, maybe sometime in March. Hoping this was not some sort of sign, Giotti faced the boy in the witness chair.

The kid was the most damaging witness the prosecution had, and it appeared as if McKeen had prepared him well. He certainly looked and acted differently than he had the day his deposition was taken. Giotti had to undo him. But he had to do it carefully, the way he hoped the plumber was disassembling his pipes. He began by asking about his grade-point average.

"I did all right," replied the witness.

"You're being modest, Kevin. I'd say you did more than all right. I'd say you were a 3.8. Almost a straight A. What were some of your subjects, Kevin?"

"American history. Algebra 2—"

"If I may interrupt for a moment . . . Algebra 2, is that also trigonometry? Radian measures, tangents, stuff like that?"

"Yes, sir."

Giotti thrust out his lower lip to suggest that he was impressed. "Kevin, you testified that you raise rabbits and sometimes even show them. Where do you show them?"

"Fairs, mostly."

"Any ribbons?"

"Yes, sir. Two blue, one yellow."

"Let's see." Giotti produced a newspaper from his pocket, displaying it to McKeen and then to Kevin. "Is this you at the fair, there on the left? Weren't you disqualified from competition because of certain suspicious circumstances, specifically, that after you were seen hanging around the hutch of a competitor, his rabbits were found dying with nicotine on their fur?"

Kevin looked as if he was getting ready to vault from the witness stand. His panic was not lost on the jury.

McKeen noticed that the doctor's widow—his barometer for jury attention—had stopped rummaging through her handbag and was watching Kevin Clapp closely. Even the draft evader, who had been watching the widow, now was intent on the kid. The prosecutor's anger was harnessed by his desire for a third term in office. It showed only in the narrowing of his slate-gray eyes. It was the same old crap. No matter how hard you tried to prepare them, there was always a loose end, an unexpected twist that could tie you up in knots. No matter how detailed the groundwork, an accomplice witness was as unpredictable as an irregular verb. Why hadn't the Clapp kid told him about the disqualification, especially since he had asked him over and over again, ad nauseum, if there was anything he should know that Giotti might bring up? If I know what's coming, he had said, I can tell you how to handle it. McKeen rose to his feet. "Improper impeachment, Your Honor. Its shock value greatly outweighs its probative effect."

"Sustained," said Judge Atwill. "Let's leave the newspapers out of this."

Giotti shrugged, as if it did not matter, and charged the witness box. "Kevin, what kind of deal did you cut with the prosecutor?"

Kevin Clapp looked down at his hands. "He said if I cooperated, he would let me take a walk."

" 'Take a walk.' I wonder what he meant."

"That I wouldn't get nearly as much time. He said that if I told the truth about what happened, I could get two years, maybe nothing, but he couldn't make any promises."

"We get the idea that the better you do in court, the better sentence you get. How many hours did you spend in preparation for your testimony today? Come on, Kevin, anyone who can ace Algebra 2 should be able to make an educated guess. Ten hours, twenty?"

"Maybe twenty."

"Did he tell you what to say or what to wear?"

"Sort of."

"Kevin, you testified that you provided my client with a lethal substance. Weren't you afraid of the consequences?"

"No, sir. Jessie don't always do what she says she wants to do. I figured she'd even forget where she put it."

Giotti tried not to smile. Kevin had just drawn Melody Jessica as scatterbrained and not too tightly wrapped. It was a freebie. He asked if his client was the only girl with whom he had sex.

Kevin Clapp replied no, shamefacedly. He had made out with another girl on the squad, and right before his arraignment had been halfway there with a third. Melody Jessica turned to face him head-on, the bunches of her golden hair trembling with her anger. Giotti scanned the jury, hoping they got the message, that love could not have been Kevin's motive since he was getting it on with other girls, that Kevin's involvement was caused by something else. "You seem to gravitate toward cheerleaders," said Giotti. "It is because they're more popular?"

"No, sir. They're just friskier than the others."

Maggie hoped she could get away without having to talk to Amos, without having to be reminded that the major difference between what had happened the night before in Amos's loft and lovemaking with Alan was that no one made a move to hang anything up.

Swaddled in guilt, Maggie wrote to cancel Alan's subscription to the *New England Journal of Medicine*. She found that her mournful retreat spiraled inward like a snail made it easier to concentrate. There were fewer distractions. It became clear to her while she licked the stamp that Kevin Clapp sold his friend down the river in exchange for leniency. It was equally clear that either Melody Jessica planned the murder herself or at the very least knew all about it. How did something like that happen? As angry as Maggie had ever been with Sybil, could she have poisoned her? Maggie remembered once thinking she would like to kill her, like the time at Smith when Sybil had come to visit, trailing a young boyfriend behind her like a life raft, jerking his moorings from time to time to straighten his silk pocket handkerchief with long lacquered fingernails. But killing Sybil had only been a fist-clenching thought, not a serious wish to end her mother's life. What subtle shift transfers such thoughts to action? What carcinogens of family interaction could produce the festering that leads to murder?

Hogan, whose wife, Eunice, had been in New Jersey visiting their oldest son, was dialing his home. Eunice was unhappy living in Vermont. They were the only blacks in their village, one of a handful in the township. It wasn't that everyone wasn't nice. They were polite and helpful in their reserved and democratic Yankee fashion. The people at IBM even went to bat for them and another black couple who had been refused a mortgage by threatening to withdraw corporate funds from the bank in question. The nitty-gritty truth of the matter was that Vermont was like living, she told Hogan, inside a loaf of white bread. She was lonely for her friends and family. Most of all, she was lonely for her church. Even though she considered herself a modern, educated woman, with none of the old-timey holdovers that kept so many of her friends from the mainstream, she liked to rock when she sang gospel. They didn't rock in Vermont. They never even heard of "Didn't My Lord Deliver a Daniel?" When they sang hymns, they stood immobile, as rigid and as stony as their stiles.

Hogan checked his watch. She should have been back by now. He let the telephone ring as the other jurors wound their necks with scarves, pulled hats down over their ears and gloves over their hands, and hurried home, most beginning to divine, through one offhand remark or another, where each other stood on the matter of Melody Jessica Bean's innocence.

Maggie waited for Hogan to put down the receiver. "Is something wrong?" she asked.

"I'm not sure," he replied. "I was going to ask you the same thing."

"I guess it was the boy's testimony," she said. "It shook me up more than I expected it would. Maybe it's because it was so matter-of-fact, like a spelling bee."

"Maybe," he said. Or maybe, he thought to himself, it was the first time she had come face to face with murder and realized that by comparison, death was white bread.

Amos found Maggie alone in the coatroom. She was moving slowly as if through pudding. "I guess you didn't see the Clapp kid's father go after Giotti," he said. "You missed all the action. McKeen and the court officer tackled him at the railing. It was a dumb thing to do. The guy was all over Giotti, had him by the tie, looked like he was getting ready to climb on top of him."

Maggie looked away, realizing that she could not consider him without guilt. "I guess any parent would feel that way about someone who had just demolished his kid."

"He did, didn't he? Totally destroyed his testimony. Clapp was lying through his teeth."

"I don't think that at all," she said.

"That's probably because you haven't been following everything. You have to give it your best shot, Mag. Forget about selling your house and all that. You've got to pay attention."

"I was paying attention." But she knew she had not, not the whole time. That was why she was trying to piece together Giotti's cross-examination. She had been thinking of Amos, trying to reconcile desire with guilt.

"He didn't help his kid any. By the way, I have the proofs of your mother, Mag. Some of them look pretty good. You want to come by later and pick them up?"

"I don't think so," she replied. Maggie put on her earmuffs, then realized Amos was waiting for another answer. "Why don't you bring them in tomorrow?"

He glanced in the direction of a few scraggling jurors. "That's not a good idea."

"Then mail them."

Amos pulled his collar up and studied Maggie as if he were checking an f-stop. Older women weren't supposed to come unglued. They were supposed to help you out, not the other way around, like the chemist who had taken him in when Nina left and asked for nothing other than to fold his laundry. Maggie seemed to be going backward, acting like she was at the beginning of the trial when she was still wearing silk blouses with bows. Only at this moment she was more like a little kid trying to stiffen a trembling lip, trying to show him that he didn't count. "I know you went to check out Nina," he said. "She told me about these women who got stuck in front of her house. I figured it was you and LaDonna." He put a tentative hand on her coat sleeve. She shrugged it away.

"I owe her. She followed me to Canada. Stuck by me almost the whole time."

"It's your business," she said, walking away. "Not mine." She did not ask him about the child. Nor did he volunteer.

She had followed Alan. Did Alan ever feel he owed her? Not that she knew. What was the difference? Maggie factored all the possibilities. The answer that made the most sense was that Amos thought he was taking Nina from good to bad. Alan, on the other hand, had thought he was delivering Maggie to higher ground.

Maggie shoved her way into Sybil's bedroom, and found Sidney and her mother on the bed locked in a clothed embrace. Sidney, a horn-rimmed incubus still in his ski sweater, was pushing up her mother's dress with his free hand. What was it about her house, wondered Maggie, that spawned all this activity?

"Maggie," said Sybil, "knock, for heaven's sake."

Sidney jumped up and smoothed his hair while Sybil provided a catalogue of the day's events. Rudy had gotten the M.G. to work. It was still in the garage, although purring like a kitten. Not to worry, Sidney made him crack open a window to let out the carbon monoxide. They watched *General Hospital*. Grant got blood poisoning after Anna stabbed him in the hand with a fork. Kristen had gone to Letitia to complain about Maggie. Letitia picked her up. Justin called. Oh, yes. The people who had a deposit on the house stopped by with a tape measure and an architect by the name of Peter Bouchard. Sybil didn't know what else to do, so she let them in but not before Sidney made them show identification. Travers Ormsbee was a dentist, although not a very good one if his wife's horsey, Chiclet-sized caps were any indication of his work. They said the house had wonderful possibilities. He was going to check the zoning ordinance to see if he could turn the summer kitchen into an office.

Maggie felt suddenly protective of the dwelling that had sheltered her family and kept its secrets, just as it had kept generations of family secrets safe within its steadfast, colonial walls. "I think this house is wonderful just as it is."

"That's how people talk when they're buying someone else's home," said Sybil. "It doesn't mean anything. It means they think they have great taste and you don't."

"The floors could stand some work," said Sidney.

Maggie ignored her stepfather. She faced Sybil and moved in as she had seen Giotti do. The sudden switch. The unexpected attack. "You didn't try very hard to get him to the wedding," she said.

"What is she talking about?" asked Sidney in the worried, conspiratorial hush of someone inquiring of the incompetent.

"She's talking about Sterling."

"Oh," said Sidney, "that bum. Sorry, Maggie. I forgot."

"Actually, Maggie," said Sybil, with a restraining hand on her current husband's sleeve, "your father called two days after the ad in the *Wall Street Journal* appeared. It sounded like he was calling from the airport. He said he was genuinely sorry to miss the wedding. He sounded sincere, Maggie, and I believed him. He was on his way to the French Riviera to join his new wife at the Hotel du Cap, but he sent Cincinatti water works bonds to defray the costs of the wedding." Sybil turned to face her husband. "Sterling was never actually indicted. There's no need to vilify him."

Maggie sat on the bed and hugged her middle. Her father had remarried. She hadn't even gotten an announcement, much less an invitation. And he hadn't even wanted to delay his trip long enough to come to her wedding. She felt like trash sliding down a chute. "Did you cash them?"

"Of course."

She had been at the Hotel du Cap with Sybil when she was fifteen. There were riots in Paris and they had had to connect from Amsterdam. She hated it. The three-story white mansion was designed for display. From the beach club mats overlooking the Mediterranean to the glass-enclosed elevator in the lobby, the hotel was a parade ground, a pageant, an exposition of the tanned and beautiful, and superbly confident. While Sybil bought briefer and briefer bikinis every day, Maggie hid in the cabana and would not come out, even to meet Johnny Carson, who had the cabana next door. She thought of her father rubbing suntan oil onto the sleek, bronzed back of a faceless second wife, and realized that she could not imagine his face either. She could envision him only as a phantom in white bermudas.

"I'm sorry," said Sybil. "I never intended to tell you, and I wouldn't have, except that you kept pushing. I'm afraid your mother's getting too tired to fight you."

Icicles tinkled and slid from the eaves, then splintered on the branches of the snow-covered hawthornes as Maggie fled into the trial and thoughts of a murder victim also too tired to fight, and of Kevin's testimony that Melody Jessica said that her mother was spoiling her chance to get ahead because she wouldn't let her go to cheerleading camp.

"You weren't much of a mother," said Maggie.

Sybil sat up. "You weren't much of a child. Your nose was always dripping and you were afraid of your own shadow, like a little owl. The only thing attractive about you was your hair. I never understood what made you so timid. You certainly didn't get it from me. And you were so awkward. Once I had you brought backstage at the Shubert. Do you remember? You were eleven. The wardrobe mistress thought there was something wrong with your feet. You tripped over everything, you knocked down the scenery, somehow you sent the backdrop into the flies, and you stepped on the understudy's gown. It was awful."

"I couldn't see. You took away my glasses like you did at my wedding."

"What was the play?" asked Sidney.

"*The School for Scandal*. I was Lady Teazle." He seemed disappointed. "It closed after sixty performances."

"I'm not surprised," he said. "I never heard of it."

Maggie regarded her stepfather with a disdainful flick of her eyelids, then turned her attention to her mother. "You were always selfish," she said. "That story proves it. You never gave one thought to how miserable I might have been. Your only concern was that I embarrassed you. You thought of yourself first and me second."

"That's not true," said Sybil. "I gave up the role of Bianca for you. I could have given you up instead of *Kiss Me Kate*, had a baby later, or never, like lots of my friends." Sybil sighed, the sound of snow sloughing from a bough. "I was the best mother I could be, Maggie. Just like you're the best mother you can be. I don't have any apologies."

"I don't think so," said Maggie. "I don't think I'm the best I can be." She turned to Sidney. What had he meant last night in the summer kitchen when he said, "Don't be too sure"?

"Ask your mother."

Maggie faced her mother. "What is he talking about?"

"Nothing," replied Sybil. "Sidney's a worrywart." Sidney sat like the Clapp boy, looking down at his hands.

"I don't believe you."

"Maggie," said Sybil, "you've been saying that to me since you could talk."

Maggie looked at the woman who had led her on a roller coaster for the first nineteen years of her life, and from whom she fled the first opportunity she had. Her beautiful face was smooth, unlined, as if sealed with a creamy impasto. "There had been times when I was really angry with you, she said. I mean really angry."

"I figured it out."

She looked frail and transparent, old. Maggie reached across the bed and hugged her, amazed at the delicate and mortal feel of her mother's body. Was anything wrong with her that could not be fixed? Could you intuit the knowledge, gather it in some way through an embrace? Was the hint of the finite palpable in tissues and bones, could one touch some clue of conclusion, like the ending of a book that has spelled itself through its plot?

Maggie sorted her belongings into the night and thought of Amos and how she was denying herself in order to be strong. She reasoned that even Alan would have admired her strength of will just as Letitia would admire her propriety. Surrounded by cartons and boxes which she had pulled down from the attic, where they had been stored for years against some eventuality of need, she collected string, Scotch tape, and colored labels, and began with the summer kitchen. Except for the splintering icicles, the ticking grandfather clock in the hall, and an occasional creaking footstep from Sybil's room, the house was quiet. The only constant sounds were the beat of Maggie's heart and the blood pumping in her ears.

She organized everything into five categories: take, store, Salvation Army, tag sale, and questionable stuff, like a pair of chipped whale oil lamps, a tin of hand-forged, square-shanked nails, the blemished painting of the boy with the rooster and a Barbie beauty salon. Baskets of lace were tagged for LaDonna. Old cracked boots and broken umbrellas with spines that stuck out like knitting needles were flung into the Salvation Army box. A collection of figurines was divided between the tag-sale container and storage, the latter judgment borne of guilt. Maggie had never liked the figurines. They were romantic, ornate, fluted permutations of the baroque that Alan had bought as birthday gifts. When she told him as gently as she could that her tastes in art ran to late Gothic, he bought her a bisque Rapunzel with a gilt-edged collar.

Sidney appeared on slippered feet. "Organization is my strong suit," he said, offering to help.

They filled the tag-sale boxes with glass bottles, butter molds, molasses jugs, copper kettles, bowls, a mezzotint of an ice-boat race on Lake Champlain, and a tall, black Remington typewriter that belonged to Alan's grandfather.

"I've been married before," he said. "The first time we had kids together and made a home. Like you."

Maggie reached for a pair of 1964 Herbert Hoover Centennial coffee mugs which she found the year before at someone else's tag sale. Alan had said they were pure junk.

"With your mother," said Sidney, "there's nothing to tie us together—no kids, no mortgage, no parents hanging over our shoulders, telling us to stick it out like they did no matter what."

"My mother never told me that," said Maggie. "She told me just the opposite."

He laughed. "That sounds like her. You know, I wake up in the morning and watch her face. I wait for her to wake up. To give me the program for the day. What I'm trying to say is this—I never thought such a thing could happen to me. I wish it for you. You're young yet. You'll meet someone else, believe me."

Maggie told Sidney that it was late and that she would do the rest herself. "I know you mean well but I'm just not ready to think in those terms."

His face took on a sober look. If it wasn't for his sweater, he could have been one of Letitia's ancestors. "I'm anxious to get your mother back to New York," he said.

"She can leave anytime she likes."

"That's the problem, Maggie. She won't go back unless she thinks you're making out all right."

"What do you want me to do about it?" she asked.

"Maybe once in a while you could let her see you having fun."

Maggie pulled her hair into a rubber band. "This isn't fun, Sidney. I thought you noticed."

"Then how about faking it for your mother's sake?"

Nobody had asked Sybil to come, neither did anyone ask her to stay. Annoyed that Sidney had put this on her, yet chilled by his parting words, Maggie slapped labels on a coat stand, a reed rocker, and Kristen's old swing cradle for which Alan had insisted on securing the ropes himself. Maggie had held onto these things the way a glacier holds stones. Now she sorted and tossed them without a backward glance, all except the swing cradle and Rapunzel, which she shoved against the wall.

Alan's library would go to Letitia, all except *Merck's* manual, which might come in handy. Maggie began to pull books from the shelves. At first she attempted to stack them efficiently, shape matched to shape, size to size, and some packed sideways so that there was no wasted space. With fatigue she grew careless and wound up tossing them into the cartons. A snapshot fluttered out of an old anatomy textbook. Alan and Anne in shiny black wetsuits, holding sailboards with sails like butterflies in front of what looked like Lake St. Catherine. They were smiling in the delirium of love. She had forgotten how handsome he was. Someone had taken it. They must have asked a stranger. Surprisingly, it did not hurt to look at it. It was like the night before, when the draft of icy air had funneled its way from the front door to the fireplace to poke its frigid fingers down her lungs. She gasped, but she could still breathe.

AAA: Alan and Anne. Always? How long? While she and Anne had canned tubs of apple butter for the junior league sale as they exchanged good-natured husband complaints. She remembered telling Anne how she always had to wait for Alan in bed as he stood in the bathroom with a flossing string hanging from his mouth. Had Anne repeated this to Alan? Had Alan disclosed their tentative, Yankee incursions into the variances of love? I don't think I want to tie you up, Maggie. It suggests you're not a willing partner. All right, she countered. Not with the kind of knot you made for Kristen's swing. A silken knot, from scarves, she saw it in a movie, the kind that slips when I really want to get out. Had he told that to Anne? Even if he hadn't, he must have compared them. She had to come up short. What woman would not come up short matched against Anne? That's what Peter had meant that evening in the foyer of Letitia's house. That fake. Those fakes. Both of them. All of them. Fake, her father included. Like the cheap electric-blue shaggy stuff attached to key chains. Fake, except Sybil. Sybil, despite her shining, collagen-pumped face, was real. Sybil was exactly what she said she was, no more, no less.

Maggie drew herself to her knees. The town knew, as they knew everything. As Schuyler at the gas station had once said, they knew everything, they only read the newspaper to see who got caught at it. They all knew. And not one person had told her.

The tears were hot. Maggie clenched her teeth. I'm not going to cry, she said to herself. Not this time. I'm not. I'm not. The ring slid off easily as it always did in cold weather. She slipped it into the pocket of her jeans. I'm not a widow anymore, she thought. A widow is someone still married to a memory. An attachment to the past. An attachment to a memory. I'm not a memory and I'm not still married to one either. I'm alive. And I'm unattached.

She carried the damaged oil into the kitchen to look for paper plates. Absorbent and disposable, they made a good palette. Later, when she was not so tired, she would begin by filling in the gouges, then the cracks, and much later, when the topography of the painting was seamless and the trial over, she might tackle the color.

CHAPTER 11

Weekend

THE IDEA TO RENT a stall at the indoor flea market was LaDonna's. Her scheme blossomed, as most notions do, from disconnected strips: the baskets of filmy spiderwebs of lace that Maggie brought for storage, the need for ready cash, a concept of self-reliance bred in her bones from early settlers whose cross-stitched motto of Root, Hog, or Die hung on her bedroom wall, and from her new friend's peculiar set of chin. LaDonna, alert to signs of depression, saw them surface in Maggie. They were different than those of grief. Grief was active. This was quiet resignation. This was withdrawal. LaDonna didn't like it.

LaDonna engineered the entire effort, pushing and pulling a reluctant Maggie in and out of thrift shops to sort through jars of odd buttons, strips of beading that had been cut from shredding, antiquated gown, rolled and bound with rubber bands, scarves, and tightly knit, unstained sweaters which they could wash and cut. Armed with shopping bags full of cotton batting, foam rubber, and goosedown still in its mildewed pillow casings, they sewed at LaDonna's house Thursday night, Friday night, and Saturday morning on a foot-pedaled sewing machine. While Maggie was less than enthusiastic, she was glad to get away from her own house after she learned that the buyers were returning with their architect to take additional measurements. She especially did not want to be there when Peter opened the envelope that she left for him marked personal, and found the photograph of Alan and Anne with a note that read, "I wasn't there either."

LaDonna's specialty was baby caps, little circles of antique silk grenadine and cotton batiste gathered at the crown, trimmed at the edges with satin rosettes, ruchings of Dutch linen lace and Irish needlepoint, and finished with streamers of ribbons. Maggie's long suit included lace-trimmed sweaters and pillows inserted with fine, close Valenciennes lace and rose point joined by gossamer ligatures so delicate as to be almost invisible.

They were interrupted twice. The first intruder was LaDonna's husband, Freeman, who wandered into the low-ceilinged sewing room. Lean, thin, and accusatory, cast only from bones and sinew, he stood in the doorway like a reminder.

"You the doc's widow," he asked. Maggie nodded, her mouth full of pins. "He fixed my hand a year ago October. Mashed it in a baler."

Maggie pulled out the pins and stuck them in a cushion she wore on her wrist, wondering what to say to someone who had attempted suicide. "It seems fine," she said, hoping that it was.

"Couldn't bend my thumb more'n this far at first," he said. "Now I can bend it all the way. Guess he did okay. I don't use it much for anything, anyway, so I don't see what difference it makes." He stretched his hands over his head and grabbed the lintel of the door as if he were trying to lift up the room, then he turned to his wife. "You done yet with that jury trial?"

"Not yet," replied LaDonna, an unfinished, pink crepe bonnet resting on her fist.

He rocked into the room, still clutching the top of the doorway. "Janine called. The baby is sick. She wants you to sit."

"She'll just have to stay home with her, Freeman. We have to finish all this by Sunday."

"What's so important about Sunday?"

"Sunday is the flea market. Me and Maggie took a booth. We need to get ready."

He slapped his hands down at his sides. Maggie, who had been tacking a rose point collar to a sweater, stuck herself with the needle. "Who do you think is going to buy all this junk?" he asked.

LaDonna pulled the concentric circles of gathers and the bonnet shaped itself into a tiny, convex crown. "I fixed a bean casserole," she said. "You want me to heat it up?"

He seemed ready for something, edgy, like a sprint runner digging a toehold. "I'm not hungry." Both women held their breath. "Seems to me they just call up a jury without a by-your-leave, bust up their lives, just for one juvenile delinquent who's as guilty as sin."

"We don't know that for sure," said LaDonna, averting her eyes as if directing her response to the window.

"Guilty as sin," he asserted. "Always a puzzle to me why the judge can't decide. What are you going to tell him that he doesn't know better in the first place?"

Maggie bent to look for the goose down. When she picked up her head he was gone.

"Don't mind him," said LaDonna. "He didn't used to be like this. Believe it or not, me and Freeman had good times."

"I believe it."

"This business with the buy-back has really got him going."

"I know." Maggie lifted a sweater from the sweater bag and noticed the stains. Neither she nor LaDonna had seen them before. The sweater had cost three dollars. Maggie frowned, reluctant to call the investment a loss.

"Seems to me you're not feeling too chipper yourself."

"I'm okay," said Maggie.

"Did something happen?"

"Nothing happened."

"Don't get like him, Maggie. That's what he tells me and you can see for yourself it isn't so." Not wanting to pry any further, LaDonna changed the subject. "I don't know about you, Maggie, but with Christmas coming I can really use the money."

The mention of the season brought a pang. Maggie braced herself, absorbing it like a body blow. She had not allowed herself to think about Christmas, deliberately refusing it entry into her consciousness despite the signs that were everywhere: the fir trees nailed by the volunteer fire department onto wooden stands, the elms draped with strings of colored lights, the crèche in front of the Episcopal church, and the gift-wrapping stand near the checkout counter at the supermarket. The music was the worst of all. It sang of family and memories. Maggie choked it off. "How much do you think we can make?"

"Egg money. If we're real lucky, maybe a little more."

Maggie plunged a hand into the goose down and stuffed a neck roll. She had been dreading the first Christmas without Alan. That was before she found out about Alan and Anne. Would it make a difference? Would knowing about them make it less than awful to be without him? Pin feathers drifted about the sewing room like snow and reminded her of Kristen, not in winter but in summer, when she was eight years old. Kristen was standing in a field of whirling, floating dandelion puff, twirling dandelions until the thistles floated about her head like a veil. The child was so beautiful, so precious, that she could not get enough of her then, especially since it was becoming clear that Maggie was in competition with Alan. She thought, too, of Sybil and of her mother's absences on the road, in rehearsal, during tryouts and fittings, but then Maggie had been nothing like Kristen.

Maggie was also nothing like Anne. Alan had loved Anne. Anne had given him something; Maggie had not and now he was dead. Maggie checked her tears with her sleeve while she closed the end of the neck roll with tiny blanket stitches taught to her by someone, she couldn't remember whom, it clearly wasn't her mother. Whatever had happened, she still had her life while Alan had lost his. Could she forgive him? She tried to marshal all the reasons why she would not harbor hurt, angry feelings that soured a person like lemons. The most comfortable rationale was that it had been a mistake. He hadn't planned to do it. It just happened, like hitting his thumb with a hammer. The question was, could she really make herself believe that everyone was entitled to a mistake—if it was a mistake? Maybe, Maggie considered, she had been the mistake in his life. She must have been a disappointment to him. When did this become apparent to him? she wondered. Had the qualities he found so endearing at twenty become tedious by forty? Maybe it was noting as logical as that. Maybe it happened when she refused to have anything to do with the Morgan horse, or the cider press, or after she stripped the gears on the M.G. None of that mattered. More important was that maybe Peter didn't know anything for sure, but only had a hunch. Maggie would keep her husband's secrets. "I need to use your phone," she said.

She found it on the kitchen wall over the old, dented copper hot water tank that stood next to the stove. Sidney answered.

"Did they come?" she asked.

"They're in the shanty."

"That's the summer kitchen."

"Whatever. That's where they are. They're talking about turning it into a waiting room."

"Did you give Peter Bouchard the envelope?"

"Maggie, they just got here."

"Don't give it to them."

Convinced that his neurotic stepdaughter's problems would be solved by a good man, Sidney promised he wouldn't and as an afterthought mentioned that some guy named Amos called.

Maggie saw it as soon as she returned to the table where LaDonna was working. It's strange, she thought, how solutions appear when you turn onto something else. The problem was solved when she pulled an old floral scarf from the basket, draped it over the stains, snipped off the flowers, puffed them out with cotton batting, then stitched them into place. The finished sweater had a mosaic, Gothic look, like stained glass.

"That's beautiful," LaDonna said. "How did you think to do that?"

"I don't know," replied Maggie. The set of her jaw had softened. LaDonna decided that the change was not so much in Maggie's jaw as in her lips, now parted in a fever of discovery. They worked through the night.

Amos appeared Saturday morning while Freeman sat hunched in the dilapidated backhouse adjoining the kitchen, swabbing the barrel of his rifle with oil. As Maggie and LaDonna, their eyes red-rimmed and hollow from lack of sleep, pinned price tags to their collection with tiny gold safety pins, Maggie recognized his pickup in the driveway. How did he know I'd be here? she whispered. LaDonna took the offensive. Her tone was firm as she went to let him in. He called and asked if I knew where you were. He sounded so lonely that I couldn't lie to him. You could have told me, said Maggie. That's so, replied LaDonna as she opened the door.

Amos's eyes were bright with cold. He whipped his woolen cap from his head, ran his fingers through his dark, thick hair, flicked ice from his mustache, and grinned his wary, cautious smile. LaDonna asked if he wanted to see their project.

He trod heavily as he followed them through the connected buildings strung sideways like a row of blocks, from the big house to the kitchen. Maggie looked away. How dare he show up uninvited, making the floors vibrate with his footsteps, bursting with his particular brand of renegade vitality, percussing her body with the resonances of his voice. Maggie tried to ignore him, regarding him as only a nuisance, an acquaintance who had overstepped, unaware that their intimacy had already been stamped upon them, so that even a casual observer could have seen it in the way they watched each other out of the corner of their eyes, or from the careful way they avoided one another's touch.

"It looks like a lot of work," he said. "Who did what?"

"More than half belongs to Maggie," said LaDonna.

He offered to help load their stuff. Maggie said no thanks. LaDonna said yes, thanks, excused them both, and took Maggie aside. Don't look a gift horse in the mouth, she advised. Freeman was not about to help and it was a long trudge to the car.

Amos helped them carry everything to LaDonna's station wagon, which was parked behind the sugar house. The snow looked like icing on a cake. Amos shielded his eyes from the glare and said there comes a day when the sun doesn't glance off the snow but soaks through the crust to get the waters running and start the flow of sap in the maples. He had a shot of that particular moment, taken when the light was just right, when he hadn't had to tent his subject, or sidelight it with a lantern. The sky had been overcast, the light diffused, creating early morning shadows that outlined every ripple.

Maggie turned him out. She was remembering how Alan held four-year-old Kristen over a trough that emptied from the gathering tank, her little tongue lapping the cold, trickling sap, with the steam rolling from the roof vents of Alan's grandfather's sugar house behind them. Alan had picked up Maggie under his other arm, and dipped her over the sap trough. The ends of her hair had been sticky with syrup. Later that night, she had dried it before the fire, and Alan had curled around her on the rug like a pledge, confiding that he would like to be on the teaching faculty of the medical school. "Not just a clinical appointment," he said, "a real one, with pay and tenure."

When LaDonna crawled inside the backseat of her wagon to adjust the shopping bags, Amos mentioned that if Maggie wasn't busy that night he wanted to take her to his sister's home. She was having some people over to watch the playoffs. Nothing fancy, just family and neighbors bringing chips and dip, six packs of beer, and trays of soggy lasagna. He was thinking that maybe they ought to get out together. This was a way to do it and not be seen by someone connected with the trial. Maggie declined. She already had a date with Justin.

Originally the beard, Justin now had merit of his own. There was status and acceptance in being with him, a guaranteed inclusion to events that restricted membership, other than public affairs like church or Rotary, to the coupled. Everyone knew Justin, liked him, admired him. Justin was a take-charge person, and if the sight of him didn't turn her on, as it did with Amos, that was to be regarded as a plus. Leg-trembling desire made you vulnerable. Maggie was vulnerable enough. She didn't need to add to it.

Light snow began to fall around them. Amos rapped beneath a woodpecker hole dug in the stub of a decayed elm. A gray, furry squirrel with liquid-dark, bulging eyes poked out its head. Its movements were quick, darting. The squirrel leaped to an adjoining branch. Amos turned back to Maggie. "Tell me flat out, Mag. Should I quit trying?"

"Maybe. I don't know."

Maggie was the first to see Freeman run out of the backhouse, crunching through the crusty ice. Despite the cold, he wore only a quilted hunting vest over his woolen shirt. When he reached them he halted, like someone who had forgotten why he was there in the first place. The three stood waiting. His scrutiny was for Amos.

"You the one ran to Canada?" he asked.

Amos stuffed his hands in his pockets. "That's me," he replied.

Freeman shook his head from side to side as if he were swinging a lantern. "I'm glad there's someone here that wasn't a fool."

"Honey, you warm enough?" asked LaDonna.

He ignored her and continued to address Amos. "On good sap days," he said, "had me a team of Clydesdales, they stood seventeen hands high, well matched in color, too, chestnut with cream manes. . . . Spunky devils. Had to change their bits to keep them from taking off downhill with a tankful of sap. Horses like sugaring. Much better for them to work every day than stand in the barn. You know what I mean?"

"I think so," replied Amos.

"I knew you would." Freeman turned on his heel and headed for the house, having said all that he had come to say.

"How is he?" asked Amos.

"He seems better," replied LaDonna. "At least he's not lying in bed with his face turned to the wall. He's up and about as you can see."

LaDonna dropped Maggie off at Letitia's house, where Kristen was waiting with the car. Maggie's plan was first to see to things in the apartment, then drive Kristen to Marlboro College for her interview. As Maggie climbed the narrow steps of Letitia's garage to the apartment above, she wondered if the chiming church bell in the nearby steeple was something one got used to.

It was cold in the apartment. The baseboard heat had not been turned on. Maggie flicked the switch. The system kicked in with a bang and a shudder, then began to chortle and buzz in a clatter of failing fittings.

Originally the servants' quarters in the attic of the carriage house, the apartment had been remodeled for Alan's grandfather after he could no longer be trusted to live without close surveillance. It contained a sitting room with a tiny kitchen, a bedroom, and bath. Boxes brought over by Kristen and Rudy stood stacked against a wall. The place was dreary and cramped. Here she would live, rent-free, between the racket of the steeple bell and the baseboard heater. She would pay off Alan's debt to Letitia, save a little, then somehow manage to afford a place of her own. It was the sensible thing to do. It was the only thing to do, other than to move in with Sybil, which would have been, by anyone's reckoning, much worse. Still, it was depressing.

Maggie sighed, angry with Alan again, and guilty about her anger. She looked around, for the first time, keenly. Two narrow dormer windows projected between the rafters, one in the bedroom hung with dust-laden curtains with a view of the neighboring house, and the other in the sitting room overlooking the driveway. A key-wound, eight-day schoolhouse clock sat on a badly scratched Queen Anne tea table. Hanging on the faded, lettuce-green wallpaper was a tintype of nineteenth-century patriarchs clutching swords and canes. Two Amish-blue wooden armchairs with rush seats leaned, chipped and broken, against one wall. Their insolent tilt reminded her of Amos. A stove had been fitted into the old brick range. Beside the brickwork walls were open kitchen shelves cluttered with broken cups and saucers, salt cellars, a green glass orange juice squeezer, rusted tins, and an assortment of wooden spoons. Maggie flushed the toilet and ran the tap water and wondered where in this dismal apartment she was going to put her corner cupboard, French military prints, cherry lady's desk, four-poster bed, and a favorite Aubusson carpet that was too big for either room.

She heard the firm, steady tread of Letitia on the creaking stairs. Alan's mother, wearing woolen slacks and a sweater over a turtleneck, appeared tall and exceedingly straight. It was typical of Letitia to run about without a heavy jacket, no different from LaDonna's husband. Both were defying the elements with a kind of Vermont machismo. "I heard a car drive up. Was that the Dyer woman who brought you?" she asked.

"Her name is LaDonna," replied Maggie.

Letitia revealed her attitude toward LaDonna with an elegant lift of an eyebrow. "Did you get a good look around?"

"I didn't see a hookup for a washer and dryer."

"You can use mine," said Letitia, "every day but Sunday and Monday. Sundays I don't permit any machines running, and Monday is my own washday. Mrs. Swanlea would have a fit if she didn't get first call on the washer."

Now was as good a time as any. Maggie felt for the photograph in her pocket. She fished it out and handed it to her mother-in-law in the way McKeen handed evidence for marking to the clerk.

"What's this?" asked Letitia.

"Take a look at it."

"I don't have my glasses."

"I don't think you'll need them."

Letitia acted as if Maggie had tried to stick a tongue depressor down her throat. She held out the photograph to see it more clearly, then turned to Maggie looking as stone-faced as the figures on Easter Island.

"Did you know?" asked Maggie.

Letitia took a long time before she answered. "Yes," she said.

"And you never told me."

"There was no reason to."

"I was his wife."

"It was an indiscretion, Margaret. Nothing to break up a marriage over."

"That was my call, not yours."

"What's the difference? He's dead. Alan's gone." Letitia's shoulders heaved, then settled back upon her frame. She put the photo on the eight-day clock. Maggie did not pick it up, but deliberately let it lie out in the open, a reminder, a Kodak print, one-day process accusation that could not be put aside.

Voices were heard from below, then two sets of footsteps, one heavy, one weary. Jenna and Owen showed up on the landing. "It needs a good sweeping," said Jenna. "The windows should be thrown open, and the place aired out. You'd be surprised what that will do."

"I sure would," replied Maggie.

"Now, Maggie," said Owen, "there's no call to be sarcastic to Jenna. She's only looking out for your welfare."

"What's this?" said Jenna, picking up the photograph.

"You tell me," said Maggie.

"Oh," said Jenna. She passed it to her husband.

"Oh," said Owen.

"You all knew," said Maggie. Owen turned to look out the window. Jenna took over.

"Maggie, we were between a rock and a hard place. Darned if we did and darned if we didn't. If we tell you, you feel bad, maybe do something you'll be sorry for later. If we don't tell you, there's no real harm done to you, and the less attention paid to that sort of thing, the quicker the thing has to burn itself out."

"Why did you tell me I had to say something to Anne? That it was my fault that I led Peter on."

"Because I believe that," said Jenna. "Just as I believed that Anne led Alan on. He never would have done such a thing if she didn't encourage him."

"You didn't give me that courtesy when you thought something was going on between me and Peter."

Jenna claimed irrelevance. "That was different," she said. "You were newly widowed. One is cheating, fooling around. The other is quite another matter."

"The way I see it," said Maggie, "in one the spouse is alive, in the other the spouse is dead."

"Try to see it this way," said Jenna patiently. "In the first instance, people look the other way. The other is something folks find hard to tolerate."

"You've lost me," said Maggie.

"Please," said Letitia. "Let's just drop it."

Maggie turned to Owen. "How are things at the fly factory? You must be boxing like crazy."

"Owen quit his job," said Letitia.

"Right before Christmas? Why would Owen quit his job now?"

"Owen's thinking of getting into something else," replied Jenna.

"Like what?" Maggie faced Owen head-on, unwilling to believe that her drone of a brother-in-law had any interest save early retirement.

"I don't know yet. I just know that I've worked for someone else long enough."

"It's his turn now," said Jenna.

Letitia rapped on the window to open it, then leaned her head out. "We're up here," she called to someone below. Within moments Kristen bounded up the stairs like a spring and cornered her mother at the Queen Anne tea table. "What have you been so busy with these past two days?" she asked Maggie.

"Helping out a friend who needs Christmas money. We're taking a booth at the flea market."

Letitia's dismay was immediate. "Margaret, no," she said. "Why on earth would you want to do such a thing?"

"Which friend?" asked Kristen.

"LaDonna Dyer."

"Oh, her. Why do your new friends have to be so grungy? You and Daddy didn't have grungy friends."

Maggie's anger was sharply focused and she alternately faced Letitia and Kristen like a spotlight. "I never taught you to be a snob, Krissie. Why is LaDonna Dyer wrong and Win Dyer right?"

It was then that Kristen noticed the photograph lying forgotten on the key-wound clock. "Where was this picture of Daddy and Anne Bouchard taken?"

Maggie quickly buckled the mantle of maternal protection that she had worn for seventeen years, determined that Kristen would not feel as if she, too, had been dropped down a laundry chute. "Lake St. Catherine," she replied.

"How do you know?"

"I took it."

"You were there? I didn't think you liked ice sailing."

"Of course I was there. How else do you think I took the picture?"

"They look really happy."

"Daddy just told a joke."

Kristen glanced quizzically at her mother. "Daddy never told jokes, he played jokes, but he never told them."

Letitia looked at Maggie if not warmly, then with kindled regard, as Kristen lost interest and dropped the photograph. "If you like, Margaret, we can arrange with Mr. Peterson to have your own washer and dryer installed."

"That would help," said Maggie.

The yellow Subaru waved a little red flag that would stay fastened to its antenna until mud season, when the deep drifts of winter snow were no longer a threat. They drove to Brattleboro, a crossroads nestled in rolling hills that bordered the Connecticut River, on their way to Marlboro College, where they had an appointment at the admissions office. It had snowed light, powdery crystals during the last three hours and spindrift flew in the whipping wind.

Kristen catalogued Vermont colleges for her mother. She had investigated, according to her report, all of them and liked Marlboro best. Maggie couldn't figure out why.

They drove behind a cinder truck. Maggie's eyes were locked to the road. "What is it you like about it?" she asked.

"They do rock and ice climbing, and every year they have this five-day paddle down the St. John River in Maine."

"What else?" asked Maggie. "There must be something else you like about it."

"Of course there is. They have independent study. Mt. Snow is only fifteen miles away and Hogback is only five miles away."

"Lift tickets are expensive, Krissie."

"Mt. Snow gives you discounts. Look, this is your idea, not mine. I'm picking one that I think I can live with."

Maggie decided on a positive approach. "I like the fact that you're only an hour and a half away."

"That's the part that I like least."

"I knew you'd say that, Krissie."

"I hate when you say you knew I'd say something."

It was like a war. Everything was strategy. Maggie protected her flank. "What's wrong with UVM?"

"Too big."

"Vermont College in Montpelier?"

"They're all med-techs and nurses. That's not what I want to do."

"What do you want to do?"

"I don't know, but I know it's not that."

"Johnson?"

"Teachers. Same for Green Mountain and Windham. Norwich, business and engineering. Marlboro doesn't train you to be anything."

They drove in silence, past a winter carnival on both sides of the road, where people in down jackets and ski hats, some working with propane torches, were building elaborate snow sculptures made slick by washings of water which turned quickly to ice. One sculpture was a trio of ice figures mooning the passing drivers; another in front of a Wendy's was a hamburger on skis.

"You hate Rudy, don't you?"

"I don't hate Rudy," replied Maggie, searching for the road to Marlboro. "Anyhow, what I think about him is moot at this point. He'll have to go home soon."

"No, he won't. If I get into Marlboro, he's going to get a job in Brattleboro."

The car went into a skid. "Go with it!" yelled Kristen. They stopped, and started again.

"I hope you don't mean what you just said about Rudy. What about his parents? What do they say? They must want him back in school."

"His dad says he can do what he wants as long as he doesn't have to pay for it. Rudy hasn't asked him for a nickel."

"But he's asking me, Krissie. Don't you see that? His food and lodging, it's coming from me. Someone's paying for it and it's not Rudy. Anyhow, that's beside the point. How do you expect to concentrate on your work with him around?"

The admissions officer wore woolen argyle knee socks and earth shoes. Her graying brown hair was parted in the middle and gathered loosely at the neck with a tortoise-shell barette. She took them into her office, putting Kristen across from her desk in a chair and Maggie on a sofa on the far wall. There were posters of Garfield the Cat and Greenpeace, a sign that said "THINK SNOW," trailing plants, and an Indian rug. Maggie was nervous and had to fold her hands to keep them still in her lap. Kristen, on the other hand, was confident and poised. She seemed almost bored as she raked her long hair with her fingers.

Marlboro liked transfer students. It was clear that the admissions officer liked Kristen. "Selfishly," the admissions officer said, "it's always nice to get one of our own back to the state. I see that you were one of thirty-eight students from Vermont admitted to Smith, Kristen. How were your grades?"

"I didn't take the finals, so I don't know for sure."

The admissions officer was used to dealing with equivocation. "Students generally have an idea of how they're doing."

"Not too good," admitted Kristen.

"And yet you made very good grades in high school, good enough so that you were an early decision." The statement begged a reason.

Maggie supplied it. "Her father died," she said.

The admissions officer and Kristen exchanged glances. "What courses did you take?" asked the admissions officer. Maggie had asked the same question herself, but had not received much of an answer. She was eager to hear Kristen's response.

"Peace and War Studies, Cross-Cultural Construction of Gender, Ritual and Myth, Plants and Human Welfare, and math."

The admissions officer picked dead leaves from her plant and dropped them in the wastebasket. "We welcome transfer students to Marlboro. In fact, we urge our four-year students to take a term elsewhere. I guess I'd like to know why you want to transfer from Smith."

"I didn't like it."

"No? Why not?"

"I went to Smith," said Maggie. "I think I can answer that."

"Please don't take this the wrong way, Mrs. Hatch, but you went to Smith a long time ago. I'd rather hear what Kristen has to say about it."

Maggie understood for the first time what it felt like to want to punch out someone's lights. She bit the inside of her cheek instead.

"They're a bunch of spoiled preppies. Everyone is super career-minded, it's very high pressure. All they think about is doing something big in the world."

"And you don't?"

"I don't know yet. Right now I just like to hang out and look around. Isn't that all right?"

The admissions officer spun in her chair. "It should be. Is that why you haven't done very well?"

Kristen's silver-blue eyes opened in honest, widened opalescence. "I don't have any excuse. And it doesn't have anything to do with my dad dying and all. I just goofed off." Maggie was astonished at her daughter's simple candor.

"Why did you choose us?" asked the admissions officer, who, not being the parent, was not obliged to make judgment.

"You're small, there's no pressure, a lot of independent study, and you don't have to be in the theater program to try out. At least that's what it says in the brochure."

It was an alliance on sight. The rest was pro forma.

"Motivation is a strong factor here," said the officer. "We understand about hanging out and looking around, but you'd be expected to make a commitment to whatever you decide to study. I think you're at a crossroads, Kristen, and I also think Marlboro is the right road to take."

When Kristen graciously nodded, the admissions officer moved into hard sell. She talked about the music center with its year-round program, about the local movie theaters and discos, co-ed dorms of no more than thirteen to twenty-eight people, even the eventual possibility of a quiet, secluded cottage in the woods, although these were not available to entering students. Her voice became conspiratorial when she described the college legislative assembly held in the form of a town meeting. Kristen liked that. She leaned forward and rested both elbows on the woman's desk. The admissions officer began to embellish. The town meeting had the power to vote down with a two-thirds majority even faculty decisions. She made a gratuitous turn to Maggie to announce that each student was assigned to one week of dining hall crew each semester in order to keep room and board to reasonable limits. She swiveled her chair back to Kristen on the excellent faculty–student ratio, and then, spinning in both directions, she said when Kristen graduated she would have the ability to define a problem, set limits on its area of inquiry, analyze the data, and arrive at a reasonable if not creative solution.

Having discharged her arsenal and certain that she had fired home, she turned her attention to Maggie. "What do you do, Mrs. Hatch?"

"She's on a jury," said Kristen.

The admissions officer was not about to accept Maggie as a career juror. Her tone was condescending. "That must be exciting for you. What stage of the trial are you in?" she asked.

Maggie realized that although her hands were folded, she was clenching her toes. "Analyzing the data, but I don't think we're allowed a creative solution."

The frigid air bit like pincers into their lungs.

"You didn't have to be sarcastic."

Maggie stabbed the key into the ignition. "Oh yes, I did."

"You were really hostile. Sometimes it's hard to know which one of us is the parent."

"Read my lips. I am," said Maggie, losing traction on a slick patch of highway and skidding lazily from one lane to the other. "You never told me you had an interest in theater," she said when the car stopped its slide. "When did that happen?"

"Since Sybil came."

Maggie made no move to correct the appellation. "Sybil," although not "grandmother," was a step up from "your mother." They drove through town. On both sides of the street the winter carnival was in full late-afternoon swing. Maggie turned her eye back to the road. "Maybe mothers and daughters aren't meant to get along with one another," she said. "You don't seem to have problems with Letitia. I guess it has to skip a generation. The pressure's off or something."

"Just because you have problems with someone doesn't mean you don't love them. You're not as tightly wrapped as Granny, but you're still my mom."

The unsolicited acknowledgment, although coupled with a slam, kindled a glow that lapped the edges of Maggie's heart. "I never really liked my mother," she confided. "I wonder if it's possible for any daughter to like her mother."

"Of course it is." Kristen rolled down her frosted window to shout a greeting at a girl in a black woolen cape dressing a snow figure as Darth Vader.

Maggie waited for Kristen to roll up the window. "How long do you think that takes?"

"Not long. As soon as daughters are sure they're not like their mothers. You and I, we're not anything like."

"Are you sure, Krissie?"

"Of course I'm sure. Your hair is red, mine is blonde. You can't light a fire. I can. And I drive better than you any day in the week. You're all over the road. Maybe it's those mittens. If you took them off and gripped the wheel with your hands, you'd get better traction."

They parked behind the Bonny Peter Motel. Skiers returning from the mountain were unclamping their skis from their racks. Behind the motel stood the stone wall of the cemetery, protected only by bronze griffins with white snow bonnets, and an honor guard of iced, denuded elm trees planted by Alan's great-grandfather. Without the soft, green drapery of spring and summer, it was a lonely, solitary place, where single, dessicated leaves shivered in the wind.

Maggie and Kristen stomped their way through snow that lay on the ground like a quilt. Dates and sentiments were buried beneath the drifts and only the tops of the headstones showed.

When they reached Alan's grave, Kristen's head drooped like a sunflower. She began to cry, then checked it, holding her lips tight and spread, the way Letitia did. "It's not fair," she said.

"No," said Maggie. "It's not."

"What do you suppose he'd say to us now?"

"Get home before the roads freeze over."

"He'd say that to you," said Kristen. "Not to me."

Maggie pulled her daughter into the cradle of one arm. Her tousled hair, falling from beneath her knitted cap, covered Kristen's face like a brassy veil. "Your dad had a lot of confidence in you. I'm going to try very hard to show that I have it, too."

"Do you think he knows you have a date tonight?"

Maggie was startled. Kristen sure picked her time and place. "I don't think dead people care about those kinds of things, Krissie. Besides, your father was a doctor. He was on the side of life."

Kristen balked at fashioning Maggie's hair in a French braid on two counts. Her mother's hair was too curly for a style that was supposed to be sleek, and it was only going to come down again. It was only after Sybil assured her that her mother was going out with Justin Herrick that Kristen agreed.

Maggie left in a giddy excitement that had nothing to do with her hairdo or what she was going to do once she got to Drew and Woody Pringle's tree-trimming party. It had to do with the appearance one hour earlier of Ranger, taller if possible, broader in the shoulders and in the neck, transmogrified by anabolic steroids, military presses, and the sight of Kristen into a grinning rhinoceros rampant. It was not the gifts he brought (body oil for Kristen and a power screwdriver for Maggie) or his insistence on showing Maggie how the battery-charged screwdriver would change her life. It was the certainty that he would give spindly Rudy a run for his money.

The mood at Woody Pringle's house was festive. Candlelit from a hundred grinning tapers and smelling of pine, the interior of the gable-roofed Cape Cod was draped and garlanded by evergreen boughs pinned with pink bows and threaded with gilt-flecked pine cones. An eleven-foot tree stood waiting on a carpet of cotton batting. Everyone was dressed: the men for the most part in ties with ducks, and plaid vests, pants, or jackets, except for Woody, who wore a kilt in the colors of his grandfather's clan, and Justin, who wore a cable-knit sweater; and the women in occasion dresses, sipping nutmeg-sprinkled eggnogs while they helped Drew and Woody and their three children hang Orrefors crystal snowflakes on the tree.

After the episode of the navy Chanel skirt, for which he took partial blame, Justin saw it as his responsibility to monitor not only Maggie's drinks but Maggie herself. His solicitude, which Maggie tolerated, was not without benefit. As long as she was under Justin's aegis, the guild of the married treated her with almost the same favor she had been accorded when Alan was alive. In exchange for his protection, she remained at his side as if they shared a common abdominal wall while Justin, always gallant, guided her by her elbow.

Someone laughed about the dentist who was buying Maggie's house. He had seen him in the village wearing rubbers over his shoes. Someone else had seen him lose a ski down the slope. The man was earmarked. Maybeth, who had never gone to college and so had never recognized the need to lose her syntax, said the man was clearly as stupid as a bag of hammers.

Someone asked Maggie if she had made Justin's sweater.

When Justin changed the subject, Maggie guessed that the anonymous knitter had been his other widow. Maggie was on a jury, Justin said. She was too busy to do any knitting.

The mention of the trial prompted a discussion of Judge Atwill's political aspirations. Woody said he wasn't backing her because her opponent promised to deliver a Japanese industrial plant, which meant a lot of jobs. Plus she had no war chest, she was not docket conscious, and when she spoke at a bar association dinner you couldn't hear her over the clatter of the dishes.

"That wasn't her fault," said Maggie. "That was the fault of the waiters."

"It has to do with picking your time and place and making yourself heard," said Woody, who then began to lecture on what he understood to be the recent testimony of Kevin Clapp. He said the boy had admitted that he had purchased a rowing machine, a stereo, and made a down payment on a Camaro, a transaction never legally completed, because Giotto had shown during cross-examination that the signature of Kevin's father had been forged.

Woody's forehead glistened in the candlelight. He winked at Emory Chase. "You better not listen any more, Maggie. I'm going to give my opinion on where he got the money for all those goodies and how those kids arranged to get postcards mailed to them from Florida."

Justin smiled in resolute good fellowship and led Maggie across the room, where Peter Bouchard was describing to Lester Perkins the changes that the new owners wanted to make to her house. Lester bent to kiss her on the cheek, but Maggie ducked and offered the side of her head instead. It had been that way ever since Alan's funeral. It didn't matter that Lester most likely washed his hands daily. What was done was done.

Anne greeted Maggie warmly and asked how her packing was coming. When Maggie replied that she had it knocked, Peter said she sounded just like that fellow

Sidney, who had made him show his driver's license before he let him in.

"Sidney is my stepfather," said Maggie in a sudden burst of loyalty.

Dudley Daley asked Maggie to find out from her fellow juror Yancy Scruggs why he could not build pantry shelves for the inn over the weekends. Dudley said to make it clear that he did not want his deposit back. He wanted the shelves. His wife, Pam, reminded Maggie that they needed help at the front desk in case she was interested.

Maggie took a deep breath and announced that she had rented a booth for Sunday's flea market. Why? she was asked. To make some money, she replied. Everyone recoiled as if from a miasma of gnats. Selling wares at a flea market was as odious as wearing a fur parka on the slopes. While the phylum of the privileged Yankee held tag sales, charitable or otherwise, they did not take booths at flea markets.

"I'm doing it with your cousin," she said to Win Dyer.

Win looked puzzled.

"You know, LaDonna."

"We're cousins only through marriage," he replied. "Actually, Freeman Dyer is only my second cousin once removed."

"Why would you want to do that?" asked Hope. "I thought you were going to have a garage sale."

"I am. This is different."

"It's a lark," said Justin. "And I think it's grand."

"No, it's not," said Maggie, putting a strain on their common abdominal wall with the kind of impunity that comes from zeal. "It's not a lark. LaDonna and I have been sewing for days. We're selling things trimmed with lace—pillows, sweaters, baby caps, stuff like that. We even have a name for our booth. We're calling it Nostalgia." No one was listening. Their attention was elsewhere.

The feeling was back. Maggie was miserable, floating sideways with a sickened stabilizer, like Alan's dead fish. It had nothing to do with Christmas or losing Alan or even

Amos, whom she had managed, for the most part, to put out of her mind. It had to do with her feelings toward everyone at the party, a stockpile of frustration, impatience, annoyance, mostly anger. Were they always this silly, skirting over the tops of things like tablecloths? And would she forever be the outsider? Now was the time to do it. She had almost forgotten the box left beneath her jacket in the other room. Maggie excused herself and went to get it.

Justin watched after her in fond propriety. "Can I help?" he asked. "I'll do it myself," she replied, jerking away like a dog on a lead. Then, slipping off her pumps, she stood on a chair and fastened the angel high on a bough, arranging its wings so that it looked as if it were in benign and saintly flight. When she stepped down, she looked directly at Anne, who was anxiously fingering the pearls around her neck. The look said, *I know and I'm letting you off the hook.* Maggie's feelings toward Anne were knotted and congealed like spaghetti that's turned cold: a strand of rage because Anne had been duplicitous and unfairly judgmental, another of pity, because Anne had loved Alan and now was stuck with Peter.

Justin was tender and considerate the rest of the evening. "That meant a great deal to you, didn't it?" he asked. Maggie realized he was talking about the Christmas angel. "I think it was a selfless, generous gesture to give an ornament to Woody and Drew that obviously holds sentimental value for you. I admire you for it."

He told her of his plans to take her to Aruba as soon as the trial was over. He would bear all costs, with the exception of hairdressers, souvenirs, and long-distance telephone calls. Having decided that she was not frigid but inhibited, he offered her a glass of wine and a toast to getting away. The act saddened her. He was trying. The plain truth was that nothing he did could change reception to response. Still, she appreciated his efforts and was grateful to him for the security he offered, and she lifted her glass in return.

* * *

It was near the sheer, ice-slicked rock face at the edge of the road that Maggie slid into a rut with her tires grinding and squealing in tractionless spin. Why am I doing this, she asked herself. It served her right if she got stuck and had to have a state trooper get her out. She should have left well enough alone, left things where they were instead of asking for trouble worse than getting stuck on a wintry highway at night. Maggie stepped out, deciding that she must be crazy, and reached in the rear for a bucket of sand. Oh God, she thought, lugging out the bucket, this was so stupid. She poured sand into the rut, then got back behind the wheel and rocked the car back and forth until she finally jerked forward onto the highway, thinking that it was too bad Kristen was not there to see that she had managed that rather well.

By the time she got to the silo, the wind had picked up with a keen-edged fury and she had to bang on the door. Amos smiled when he saw her.

"How was your sister's tree trimming?" she asked.

"You could have asked me on the phone," he replied, "and saved a trip. I just got back. An hour ago." He slammed the door shut behind her.

"Does she live far from here?"

Amos replied that she lived in a mobile home right off the interstate. Maggie asked if she and her husband traveled a lot. They don't go anyplace, he replied. It's up on cinder blocks, hooked up to water and electric and anything else they need. They even had this pull-down porch they used in the summer.

"Then what's the point?"

"A trailer's cheap, Maggie. That's the point. It doesn't cost as much as a house."

"How many people can you get into one of those things?"

"I don't know. I never counted." He unwrapped the scarf from her neck, then drew it around her waist and pulled her to him. "I'm glad to see you, all pink-faced with the cold. At first I was kind of mystified. Couldn't understand what happened. But I figured it out. After me and my sister mulled it over."

"You mulled me over with your sister?"

"Not everything about you, just the snags."

"What kind of snags?"

"She said you were punishing yourself. If that's what you were doing, I'm here to tell you to quit, Mag. There's enough around in life just waiting to do it for you. You don't need to add to it." He took her hand and led her to the ladder. They climbed to the loft, where they undressed quickly, flinging their clothes like banners about the room. Familiarity made it a little easier than the first time. They sprawled on the bed like starfish, wriggling toward each other while Amos turned her this way and that in the moonlight, then switched on a lamp to see her better.

"You have fine skin," he murmured. "It's like marble. No, it's shinier than marble. More like sheet metal." He ran his fingertips over her body, brushing lightly at first, then prodding and pressing rudely as if he were trying to mold her. She was quickly ready for him, the instant arousal she had felt long ago with Alan when they were still in school, and Alan, unencumbered with attachments of mother, village, and patients, was only sex.

Amos whispered her name, never any declaration, just "Maggie." It would have to do. She told him what pleased her, he told her the same, they whispered in the dark like conspirators. This time it was lavish and wonderful, for Maggie a release of little firings that never seemed to stop.

They talked the way lovers speak when both are vulnerable and naked. She confided that she had never known her father and that she would never forgive her mother for sending him away. He told her his sister was the linchpin between him and his family, that she had come by bus to visit him in Canada. He told her he would love to photograph her skin.

Then Maggie made a tactical error. She asked him what he thought of her. Amos locked his hands behind his head and stared at the skylight like someone pissed off that what he had offered had somehow not been enough. "I'm here with you, Maggie. I want to be here with you. That's the best I can do."

CHAPTER 12

Fleas

MOVING LIKE ACOLYTES AT an altar, the silent couple in the booth next to Maggie's unloaded fifty years of marriage: bibelots of glass and china, composition Kewpie dolls, Coca-Cola trays, Bing Crosby records, a satin pillow embroidered "I LOVE YOU, MOM," salt-and-pepper sets of matching corns, a set of demitasse spoons from the 1957 Schenectady Fair, Mayo cut plug tins, and a carefully lettered sign that read "DO NOT TOUCH." On the other side of their booth stood a man with sideburns that ran along his jaw like hockey sticks, selling bootleg tools wrapped in plastic cases, each tool set neatly into its own clear pocket. Across the aisle, a young man with the earnest face of an evangelist, getting ready to sell miracle tarnish remover, tucked polishing rags into his belt and smiled sincerely at no one in particular, like a musician tuning up.

It was early. While dealers combed the aisles, offering to take merchandise off one another's hands, Maggie and LaDonna rearranged their display, trading worries like bundles. LaDonna told Maggie that even though Freeman seemed better, he was still not himself, rather some other fretful stranger who rattled doors and banged on the arms of chairs. Maggie confided, as she checked a price tag, that there was something wrong with her mother, but no one would say what it was. She added that Sidney had made veiled references which Sybil drew blinds on and she wished they'd come out with it.

The woman selling Coca-Cola trays warned them to watch out for shoplifters. "They'll steal you blind," she said, telling them to be especially careful when they made change. "That's when they're the worst." She also whispered that the tool man's merchandise had fallen off a truck and not to buy anything from him. When they appeared not to understand, she looked at them with the purse-mouthed pity reserved for the feebleminded and added, "It's hot."

The morning was slow. Business did not pick up until noon, when the aisle suddenly swelled with townspeople and winter tourists dropping the cold from their red, frostbitten faces and crackling hair like aluminum wrapping. They stuffed gloves into their pockets as they swarmed among the booths, some shoppers with infants in backpacks, a few still clumping in their ski boots. Maggie felt like a bear in a zoo. "Maybe we were dumb to do this," she said after the first wave of onlookers had passed them by, looking them over as critically as they did their merchandise.

"I'll tell you the same thing I tell Freeman," said LaDonna. "Never look back. Once you set you a course of action, you're supposed to go at it like a bull at the gate."

Maggie was not reassured. It was not until the sale of their first item, a peach chiffon baby cap for seven dollars, that she brightened up. When her headcold pillow with side pockets for handkerchiefs and a box of cherry Luden's tucked prominently into place went just minutes later for twenty-four dollars, LaDonna suggested that they may have underpriced.

Standers and lookers attracted other standers and lookers, and it was their combined press like alpha particles bombarded with radium that created a chain reaction of buying. What began as a listless picking over, in the way of invalids' hands on bedsheets, escalated into competitive plunder. They couldn't keep up. Maggie thought she gave one person too much change from Kristen's old lunchbox with the Snoopy decal and another not enough. LaDonna said not to worry, that as long as it evened out, the Lord didn't care.

Every now and then someone they knew passed through the sifter of their activity. LaDonna's oldest daughter, peevish and tired, showed up with her husband and baby, only to leave when it was clear that her distracted mother not only had no interest in taking the baby so she could look around, but called her by her sister's name. Mostly they caught glimpses, snatches of familiarity snagged in a blink of an eye: Yancy Scruggs with his girlfriend bobbing through the crush like a duck in a shooting gallery; Schuyler from the Mobil station, who asked if they knew where the model railroad man set up his booth; Lester Perkins's wife, Edna Louise, who bought one of Maggie's sweaters; and the prosecuting attorney.

Maggie first recognized Jim McKeen's platinum head as it inclined toward a frail, elderly woman who tottered like static from booth to booth. He nodded in their direction. They nodded to his nod. LaDonna plumped a pillow, tucked her chin to her chest, and spoke under her breath: "Tomorrow the Bean girl is going on the stand. At least that's what Willard Peterson said."

Maggie kept the gleaming prosecuting attorney in the corner of her eye, the place where you pull out stray lashes, and wondered what he was going to ask Melody Jessica. More important, how? The girl's mother was dead. Even if Melody Jessica had been talked into her mother's murder, an unwitting dupe, she had to be feeling remorse, guilt, confusion, something. She had to be grieving, despite her dancing mayfly earrings, even though her sorrow might have been only the tissue-packed variety that Maggie was now experiencing, still there, but folded out of sight.

McKeen's style up to now had been easy. There was nothing to suggest he would be otherwise. Still, how do you ask a kid if she's killed her mother? "I hope he's not too hard on her," she whispered. "She's only fifteen."

"Don't be fooled by his fair-spoken ways," said LaDonna. "He'll probably go after her like a dog after a bone."

Maggie felt him watching her. Sometimes during the trial he pinioned her with his eyes as if she alone were responsible for its outcome.

"Do you ever get the feeling that McKeen is speaking directly to you?" she asked.

"Well, of course, he's speaking to us," replied LaDonna.

"No," said Maggie. "I mean to you."

"If I do, I suppose it's because that's what he wants me to think so I'll pay attention."

Jim McKeen stood with his mother on his arm, trying to decide which of the two women discussing him behind the busy booth was likely to affect the other and how that might work for or against him. His guess was that the farmer's wife was stronger. Probably for him. He wondered if the Hatch woman was still seeing Justin Herrick, whom he considered a pompous ass, and if it were true that there was interest between her and Stringer. He hoped not. They were ideologically distant, so there was little likelihood of Stringer corrupting her opinion to his, which McKeen surmised would be on the side of the defendant. His objection to Stringer was that the guy was a loser. There had been other ways of avoiding the draft which did not include the stupidity of skipping to Canada. She was a fine-looking woman. Beautiful skin and hair and she didn't seem to know it. At least she didn't hold herself with the solemn ceremony of women who strutted their stuff in slow pivots. What he remembered of her husband was that he was an arrogant fellow, something like Herrick, who hotdogged when he skied. He was also reported to have been a ladies' man, if all the stories were true, with women chasing him in and out of the hospital like process servers.

McKeen's mother stroked a lace fichu. Her hands were small, bony, like the carcass of a bird. She addressed

LaDonna and Maggie in a thready voice. "Jim tells me that he can't speak to you because you're members of a jury. I'm not the prosecuting attorney, only his mother, so I can do what I please." She lifted the fichu with delicate metacarpals. "I had one exactly like this," she said in the plaintive, wistful manner of those whose recollections past and future are all behind them. "I might still have it, for all I know."

"How did you wear it?" asked Maggie. "We weren't sure."

McKeen's mother slowly placed it at Maggie's throat. "Like this. With a brooch." Her hands trembled as she laid it back. One eye was clouded with the fine opacity of a beginning cataract. "You're Letitia's daughter-in-law. When I was a girl, her grandfather's hosiery mill kept the whole county alive. Letitia wanted to run it after he died. Imagine that. Her mother said no. Letitia was barely twenty. She wasn't even married, although there were plenty around courting her. Letitia wouldn't take her mother's say-so. She went straight over her head to her grandfather's lawyer. Told him she was going to sue for control. He told her that her mother had the law on her side." She stopped abruptly, arrested by the flight of some idea and seemed to forget for a moment what she was about.

Maggie repinned a price tag. "What finally happened?"

"Where?"

"To the hosiery mill."

"Oh, that. Her mother was afraid that a girl who hadn't yet decided how to wear her hair would run a factory into the ground. She sold out while the getting was good." McKeen's mother braked herself, then selected another thought as if pulling a can of soup from the shelf. "I have yards of old lace. I would be glad to let you have it. I'm never going to use it."

Jim McKeen whispered in her ear.

"That's the stupidest thing I ever heard of," she muttered as he led her away, pointing out the tarnish man across the aisle, while Maggie thought about a twenty-year-old Letitia who had wanted to run a hosiery mill and could not.

By four o'clock LaDonna and Maggie had sold out. The take was $280.

"Maybe it's just the Christmas rush," said LaDonna cautiously.

"Maybe."

"Maybe we have a business."

They looked at each other, their eyes snapping together like fastenings on a work shirt. The realization of a potential livelihood and its implications, even if only a possibility, brought hope to LaDonna and strength to Maggie. Since LaDonna always had strength, and Maggie always had hope, it was a simple exchange.

Maggie found her home hushed, subdued, the way it had been right after Alan died, when even the refrigerator seemed to have stopped its humming. Sidney, with a Band-Aid over his eye, sat listening to Sybil tell about having drinks at Sardi's when she was on the line of *Pal Joey*. Who did you see there? he asked. Helen Hayes and Henry Fonda. Did they know you? Maggie interrupted. Where was everybody? Rudy and Ranger had worked it out, a kind of lopsided negotiation that sent Kristen and Ranger out for a pizza and a movie, and Rudy upstairs.

"Did you have fun?" asked Sybil absently.

Maggie told them that she cleared $140. Her mother, who spent that amount at Georgette Klinger getting her pores opened and closed, conceded that it was nice in the manner of someone who tells you they brought in the newspaper. Maggie asked what they had done all day. They had taken out the toboggan. At first Sybil was afraid of breaking anything, especially her hipbones, which would certainly need to be pinned, but Sidney convinced her the snow would act as a cushion and they slid down the hill behind the property three times. It was great fun until they hit a boulder and went out of control, running down Rudy, who had been coming out of the garage. The poor kid, who did not expect his girlfriend's grandmother and fourth husband to come barreling from out of nowhere, was upstairs brooding about his assault and about Ranger, who he had said couldn't take a hint even if it ran over him like a toboggan.

Sidney turned his attention back to Sybil and asked about Gene Kelly. What could she tell him that she alone knew? Sybil lowered her voice, speaking quickly, in breathy pauses, as she pushed a strand of hair from her placid brow.

She was beautiful, radiant. Kristen would look like that fifty years from now, sometime in the future when a weekend to Pluto would be no big deal, and when, even more unthinkable, Maggie would probably be dead and gone herself. Maggie looked hard at her mother. How do people die, especially cared-for people like Sybil? Rogue cells, like runaway elephants, attacking some organ, or a mechanical failure of the heart, a valve that stuck, a tubing choked with Crisco were the big two. "I want to know what's going on. Now."

Sybil exchanged glances with her husband, who had just heard something about Gene Kelly he found hard to believe, while Maggie zeroed in. "I'm tired of the tap dance."

Sybil recognized the resolution in Maggie's face. She had seen the look when Maggie's father said he was leaving, before and after she seduced him with his cuff links still in place.

"I'm waiting," said Maggie.

"I have a little heart thing," replied Sybil.

Maggie felt her insides sucked as if by a vacuum. "You should have told me before that you have a heart condition."

"It's not a condition. It's just a little blip on a chart."

"What are you doing for it? What does your doctor say?"

"Medication. Rest."

"Charging down a hill on a toboggan doesn't sound like rest to me. What are the symptoms?"

"Someone sitting on your chest. Not all the time. Just once in a while."

Maggie was somewhat relieved. Someone sitting on your chest didn't sound too bad. Besides, there were a million ways to fix the heart, if you got there in time. If you weren't on the tennis court. If it wasn't like a blowout of a tire.

There were other questions that she thought to ask, like how long did you know, or did you get a second opinion, but the slam of a car door interrupted their assembly.

"That can't be Krissie," said Maggie. "The movie hasn't even started yet."

Maggie recognized Owen's key grating in the lock. He had cut it himself and it had never worked properly. Owen let himself in with the sheepish expression of someone stealing a package of chewing gum. Behind him were Jenna, Peter in ski boots carrying a note pad and a tape measure, a man who wore a bow tie beneath his opened parka, whom Owen introduced as Dr. Travers Ormsbee, and Ormsbee's wife, smiling at no one in particular in quick, joyless flashes.

Sidney squeezed his eyes shut and sucked between his teeth.

"Did you know they were coming?" asked Maggie.

"I must be blocking," said Sidney.

"I'm equally to blame," said Sybil. "I guess we didn't realize where the time went."

Travers Ormsbee and his wife came for a final look-around, a last inspection of Maggie's house to ensure that it was really what they wanted, and to try, if it was possible, to knock down the price.

The encounter was adversarial from the moment they stepped inside. The Ormsbees liked nothing. Ormsbee said the window sashes had termites in addition to a few of the windows showing distortions. Maggie said there were no termites in Vermont, and that the wired bends he saw proved that the windows were the original glass. Ormsbee's wife wanted a recessed porch. Peter said such a porch belonged to the classical revival period and would not suit a center hall colonial unless he could install Doric columns.

"Then put them in," said Ormsbee's wife.

If Peter had problems with architectural protocol, he had lots of other suggestions, mostly destructive: tear this down, build this up, drop air ducts for heating and air conditioning under the floor, don't worry about the floor it has to be redone anyway, steam off the wallpaper, sink steel to shore up load-bearing walls, break through from this room to the next, rip the closet out of the mudroom, it doesn't belong there in the first place.

Maggie's problem was not so much with Peter as with Ormsbee's wife. She didn't like the way the woman touched the walls, running her fingers and her eyes over everything as if it were already hers. Travers Ormsbee, for his part, was polite, but generally ignored Maggie as if she were just another ceiling beam.

The worst was that no one asked her anything, such as is there a special way to get this stove to work (you had to turn on the right rear burner first), how do you get out of the summer kitchen in the winter when there's heavy snow (you don't), or what makes the ceiling beams creak (a ghost or heat diffusion, depending on whether you agreed with Maggie or Alan). It was as if the house was no longer hers, as if she were nonexistent along with her dead husband. It was a useless feeling, like the time she had gotten stuck in a rowboat without an oar and had spun in little eddies before Alan came and got her.

Maggie wanted them out, out. If she had a broom in her hands she would have chased them, the way she chased spiderwebs and mice. "The floor dips badly," she said. "You have to be careful where you step."

"We've noticed," said Travers Ormsbee, his bow tie bobbing up and down, as if he were continually surprised. "But we appreciate your honesty."

When Peter led them past the French military prints of the dining room, telling them how he could break through the ceiling into the bedroom (Kristen's) above to give them the twenty-foot-high library of their dreams, Maggie raised her voice. "Bats sometimes get in the attic."

Mrs. Ormsbee closed off Maggie as she might a pair of shutters. The bathrooms, she said to Peter, had to be gutted. She couldn't live with fixtures stained with green. While they discussed where to put a Roman tub, Jenna took Maggie's arm and pulled her into the kitchen. She said that she should have had bread baking in the oven, or at least potpourri simmering on the stove to make the house smell homey.

Maggie listened to suggestions from Jenna that she would have resisted from any other source, primarily because Jenna had been a friend from the very first. It had been Jenna who told her to leave her strappy high heels in the closet, to give her Louis Vuitton bag back to her mother, Jenna who bandaged her feet and carried Maggie's twenty-pound backpack in addition to her own when Maggie said she could not go another step on the Long Trail.

Maggie's response, therefore, was less vitriolic than with someone else. She said that she hadn't known the Ormsbees were coming, and even if she had simmering potpourri was the last thing she would have done.

Jenna tried to reason with her. "You ought to let them look around by themselves. Isn't there someplace you like to go?"

"Like where? It's ten degrees outside."

"Visit Letitia. She says you never come to see her now that Alan's gone. Look, Maggie, it kills the sale if the owner's home. I know that to be a fact."

"Maybe that's not a bad idea."

Sybil was less sanguine. "What do you want with this old house anyway? Get rid of it. Get on with your life."

Peter came running down from the bedrooms with Ormsbee and Owen behind him. "What's that kid doing upstairs?" he asked.

"He's talking about Rudy," said Sybil.

It was Peter's presumption of claim, an allodium even

more cocksure than Owen's, as if having been Alan's closest friend granted him the guardianship of his estate and all who resided therein, that became the final straw. "I know who he's talking about," said Maggie. She turned to Sidney. "Do you mind if I go out for a little while? This is really getting to me."

"Go ahead," he replied. "Everything's under control. They'll be gone soon. We're going upstairs to bed as soon as they leave." He leaned over to whisper. "Think of it this way. You're going to have the last laugh on this one."

Maggie was torn between duty and the unaccountability that Amos was coming to represent. "Maybe I should stay home with you."

What for? asked Sybil. Maggie didn't know. Maybe to steady her mother's heart in her own two hands, to squeeze out the blips with her fingers, maybe to wash the fingerprints of strangers off her walls.

The door to the silo was open. The living room was dark except for the firelight from the wood-burning stove. Maggie found him in the darkroom, bathed in a wash of garnet light, jiggling a tray of fixer that smelled like onions. "This won't take long," he said. "Your mom's prints are clipped to the clothesline."

She told him what she had earned that day while he dusted negatives with a brush. He said it was great. He knew people who spent all day at the flea market grubbing for peanuts. Then he said, in the same offhand manner, that he knew he was in trouble when all he could think of was the next time he would see her.

Maggie made no response, but held his admission to her chest like a present that she was afraid to unwrap. It was the closest thing to spoken intimacy he had ever shared. They went into the living room, where he turned on a light so Maggie could look more closely at her mother's photos.

The black-and-white glossies were all eyes and mouth. Sybil's face was flawless, lineless, yet somehow transparent, fragile, a going-somewhere look like a face seen through the window of a train. Amos had caught something else beside glamour, even through the Lycra. He had captured Sybil's certain mortality.

She could stay for just a little while. He had a half-eaten pizza and some Amstel Light. They sat side by side, comfortable together, speaking in floating clauses, bumps and pats of language, instead of the slick, artful patter of performing strangers who string their words like beads.

She told him that a dentist and his wife were rummaging through her house. She had to get away. He told her he was getting tired of free-lance work. He had to spend as much time promoting his photos to potential clients as he did shooting in the field. The paperwork was getting him down, with all the labeling of slides and coming up with captions. Why bother then? she asked. Pictures sold better with captions.

She asked if he would rather do portraits.

He shook his head. He really wanted to do documentary work, photojournalism, the kind of work that gets you sent to Central America or the Middle East. Those assignments were hard to come by. He had had one once, to Nicaragua, just before the country went into open revolt. It was a free-lance assignment where he had to pay his own fare. The best way to take pictures was to stay away from the international press, so he traveled with a local photographer. There was a lot of killing in the villages, especially at night. Bodies were left on the street on purpose. Why? she asked. To make people afraid. There were close calls all the time. The army attacked the guerrillas. The guerrillas attacked the army. Then the PR people took them out to the country in buses and put on a silly presentation to draw them away from the fighting. His stuff would have been in the center of the action, but he had come home after Nina's baby was born. Why did you leave? Maggie asked. I didn't like the guy she was living with. I came to watch over things.

"It's a catch-22. Editors want to know what I've done,

and I haven't had much of a chance to show them. Ice fishing and Memorial Day parades don't cut it."

She told him that maybe things would turn around, then decided that one of the reasons that being with Amos was so easy was not that he showed little interest in protecting her—other than a few lapses, like the time he had told her to pump her brakes—but that unlike Alan or Justin, Amos was not arrogant with success. Like Maggie, he wore his doubts openly, stuck on his shirtfront like their jury pin.

It was clear that he was beginning to see her as a person of his own size and weight when he said she was getting her shit together. I am, she thought. It was just like sweeping up crockery with a few shards left in the dust-pan. The rest, the smaller pieces, the glittery crumbs that adhered to everything they touched, she would have to stoop over for, search out in the dimly lit cracks and corners of her life.

Then he scanned her eyes as if reading cue cards and pulled her to him, his mouth and hands sealing them both in a laminate of desire. Maggie made a feverish effort to free herself, not from his locked embrace but from her clothes. Yes, he said, undress down here. I want to see how your skin shines in the light when you climb the ladder naked.

He was both tender and fierce, invested in her as she was in him, corroborating, in a never ending dialogue of moans and murmurs. With him she became aggressive, as demanding as he, and if Maggie had any notions that men and women were treated differently in her community, she knew for certain that bed was one place where both could be equal.

As they lay back beaded with each other's sweat, Maggie also realized that two weeks before Christmas, with the memory of Alan still twinging like a toothache, she was wild about a man who lived in a silo and who didn't use a top sheet.

She traced the pattern of his mustache and the hairs

that lay curled and damp on his chest. "Why are you so secretive?" she asked. "Why can't you just come out and say what you do when we're not together?"

He kissed her fingertips, then ran his tongue between her fingers, along the palm of her hand, tracing her life line to her wrist. He sighed and turned over on his back. "I don't know, Mag," he said. "It's probably a holdover from running."

Why was it always back to that? She never talked about losing Alan, about the awful loneliness, had kept it from him the way she might have hidden dark circles beneath her eyes. Why hadn't he felt the same obligation? "Can't you forget that? You've been home over ten years. Besides, I don't see where you had to run once you got to Canada."

"You ran every time you crossed the border. And if you had family, you crossed the border every chance you got."

She thought of him taking risks for his sullen father and wondered if the payoff had been worth the gamble.

He wanted her to stay, but only if she wanted to. She said she wanted to, but that her mother was leaving the next day. Besides, Giotti was putting on his case in the morning. They both needed to get some rest.

Maggie got home after midnight, with the stars glistening in the winter sky like the perspiration that had glistened on their bodies. Sybil tiptoed into her room, then sat at the edge of her bed and gave her the kind of rare attention for which Maggie at age six would have given up her entire Barbie doll collection. Sybil rubbed her back. "A masseuse once told me that she can always tell when a woman is having a great love affair. She has absolutely no sign of tension in her back. We're leaving," she said. "Sidney and I. We're going back to New York tomorrow. I'm going to give him another chance."

"What happened to your philosophy? About dumping a guy when it wasn't working out."

"Sometimes you have to trade one philosophy for another. You try them on like shoes and find one that fits you at that particular moment. There was a time when I would rather die than to walk out in any heel less than a four-inch spike." Sybil stroked back the hair that fell in her daughter's eyes. "You want to tell me about him?"

"There's not much to tell. He's probably all wrong for me."

"That's the best kind," said Sybil.

"I mean, he has no money, no job, he's not very well educated, we don't like to do any of the same things, we don't really have much in common."

"Yes, well, you can't have everything. He reminds me of my second husband. You remember Niccolo."

"I hated him."

"I knew you did. And I tried to make things right between you. But I couldn't help myself. I was wild about Niccolo, unreasoningly so. He was all wrong for me, too."

"I'll say. He was fifteen years younger than you."

"Twelve."

Maggie turned on her back and squinted at her mother's face. "Was he a head waiter or something?"

"Who told you that?"

"The janitor."

"No, actually, Niccolo demonstrated men's cologne, when he wasn't at the actor's studio. There is one like him in every woman's life, a man who doesn't quite fit, like a shoe that gives you blisters no matter how hard you try to stretch it. If she's lucky."

"I didn't see that you were that lucky. He used to bring his boyfriends home when you were on the road."

"I knew all about that."

"How?"

"The janitor." They laughed. "There is a time for comfort, you know. For stability."

"I had that."

"Yes, you had that. And you might have it again."

"Is that your way of saying that you think Amos is wrong for me?"

"It's my way of saying that nothing stays the same."

It was still dark when the phone rang. Maggie was jolted awake in an adrenaline rush that made her throat beat like her heart. It was LaDonna. Freeman had gone berserk and shot up a convenience store near the highway. It had happened earlier. She hadn't learned of it until an hour ago when they notified her that they were holding him without bail pending a hearing and a psychiatric evaluation, and told her that she might want to pack a small bag and bring it down. The girls were blaming her. They said it was her fault. Maybe it was. She had no one else to turn to.

Maggie said to stay where she was. She would meet her at the police station. Then Maggie wondered if she should wake Sybil up. She decided against it. Her mother needed her sleep and LaDonna needed a friend. She would leave a note. Sybil would understand. Sybil was always leaving notes. Sometimes it was just a sandwich-slapping maid's announcement: "your mother isn't," "your mother can't," "your mother said to be a good girl." But the notes were usually there even though Sybil wasn't.

CHAPTER 13

Case for the Defense

THEY SAT SIDE BY side and waited. It was a lonely time, the trough between night and morning when the day is still unlit and the isolation of dark and sleep has severed all connections to anyone or anything. LaDonna's knees were trembling. Maggie felt the shiver through her jeans in a frisson of polyester that quivered like a current. She realized that she had forgotten to brush her teeth.

LaDonna's eyes were fixed and glassy like those of a doll. "He was bluing his gun, Maggie, laying hot salt solution on the barrel with long, even strokes, it seemed to quiet him. I told him how much money I earned. 'That's nice, honey,' he said. The solution drying as fast as he applied it. Him taking steel wool and rubbing each time he applied the bluing—four, six times. I was so excited about what had happened to us, I guess I didn't realize. The barrel getting that steely blue. Him adjusting his sight. It's glass. He's proud of that sight, it's better than metal, costs more, but it's better. Leastways, that's what he says."

The chief of police spun away from his desk, rolled his chair with his feet to rest alongside the two women on the bench, and hooked both thumbs into his belt. Mervil Hammer looked different close up from the way he looked at the distance of the witness stand. At first Maggie could not figure out what it was. Then she realized that he didn't seem as testy as he had in the courtroom, but more at ease, like a person entertaining guests in his own living room. No, Freeman couldn't go home. He was over at the psychiatric hospital for evaluation. They would probably hold him awhile. "Can you afford a lawyer?" he asked. His voice was kindly, deep.

"That depends on how much they cost," replied LaDonna.

"I'll tell you what," said Hammer. "Go and get yourself a public defender. They're younger, and more gung-ho, and you don't have to pay a red cent. That'a a fact, LaDonna. I wouldn't steer you wrong."

LaDonna asked for details. No one had told her very much over the phone. Hammer offered to tell her all he knew. It had happened earlier in the evening. You know the time, he said, when the weekend is over and most people realize they've run out of just about everything. It was a mess. He could tell her that. People scrambling across the parking lot, Schuyler who ran the filling station, his wife used her body to shield their sixteen-month-old baby girl from the gunfire. A bullet ricocheted off the cinder bin, splintered, and ripped through her side. The butcher, Lomar Thomas—maybe she knew him?—rescued a bunch of panic-stricken shoppers through the back door. He was injured, shot in the legs. Freeman fired, as near as they could tell, an eight-shot burst of rapid rifle fire with an H & H 300. Was anyone else hurt? she asked. Someone—they didn't have an I.D. on him yet—trying to load injured people into a pickup was shot in the back. Freeman doesn't remember the shootings. All he would say was that everyone who worked at the food store talked about him all the time, how he wasn't farming anymore, calling him a homosexual, staring at his private parts. Did you know anything about that? asked Hammer. LaDonna shook her head.

"I didn't think there was anything to that," said Hammer. He spun around and shuffled back to his desk. "They probably won't let you sit on the jury," he added.

LaDonna clasped her hands tightly. Why not?

"Someone's bound to object—the judge, that Italian fellow, more likely Jim McKeen. Remember all those questions they asked before they put you on? They're very particular about who they let sit on a jury, and now you've got a husband in serious trouble with the law."

"You'll treat him right, won't you?" she asked, standing. Maggie stood beside her.

"We'll see he's taken care of. You can count on that. Freeman's a good fellow. He just wasn't fixed on retiring. This whole bad business could have been avoided if he had himself a hobby. That's what a fellow needs when he retires."

Maggie retrieved LaDonna's abandoned purse from the bench, and slipped its strap over her friend's shoulder. They turned to leave. "I hear you sold your house," he said to Maggie. "Get a good price for it?"

"Good enough," she replied.

He was determined that the redheaded widow understand the complexity of their mutual splicings. "Ranger is my oldest sister's husband's nephew. He gives you any trouble, you let me know about it."

He was like ants on a breadbox.

Maggie masked her annoyance for LaDonna's sake. "Ranger is no problem," she said. "I like Ranger just fine."

"Good to hear," he said. "I'll pass that along."

Maggie insisted on driving to the courthouse. LaDonna sat beside her with her head at half mast and spoke into her coat. "Being on that jury is what keeps me going," she said. "That and you. I don't know what I'd do without you to talk to, Maggie. I surely don't." Maggie felt the same. It was a full-up feeling, difficult to return when you were trying to stem an overflow. Maggie realized that their friendship, developed on its own with no prompting or encouragement from anyone else, was as different from what Maggie's friendship had been with Anne as flowers stuck willy-nilly in a bottle were different from an arrangement with putty and wire. She said nothing.

Chief Hammer had been right. After Judge Atwill heard the morning's motions, she summoned LaDonna into her chambers. Both attorneys were present, in conversation about a serious blizzard expected in three to four days. Giotti, still in residence at the inn, took the weather report with the equanimity of the irresponsible who considered snow removal someone else's problem.

LaDonna slipped in silently, like a wisp of smoke. Conversation stopped, halted abruptly by the reminder of an awkward, unexpected situation which made her its central issue.

The judge's hair color had changed over the weekend. No longer a reddish brown, it was now threaded with gray through a complicated process of reverse frosting at the insistence of one of her major backers, the Civil Service Employee's Association, that she maintain a natural look. Judge Atwill expressed sympathy for LaDonna's present predicament, but cautioned that she had very grave concerns about LaDonna remaining on the jury. This was a capital case, she explained. A young girl was on trial for the murder of her mother. Judge Atwill's concern was actually threefold: justice, the public eye which was surely upon her, and the fear of mistrial or judicial error that might cause reversal on appeal.

She tried to concentrate on the matter before her, attempting to forget her irritation over having to share a law clerk with another judge who continually cut into her time. It was bad enough that she had to read case law each day whether or not she was in trial, prepare judgments and orders, research points of law, and commute an hour and a half each way. Now there were other worries having to do with her campaign, such as how she was going to win the favor of the labor unions without losing her soul, or the pollster-analyst who had told her that she had no image, negative or positive. He said that vision was the key, and that unless she came to be associated with one or two big issues, she could pack it in.

Judge Atwill brushed these concerns from her mind, together with the argument she had had that morning with her husband, and asked LaDonna if she thought she could remain on the jury without prejudice. LaDonna said she could. Judge Atwill then asked if her husband's present difficulties would prevent her from rendering a fair and impartial verdict. LaDonna said no. What followed was an expectancy, as ready as a salver, in which the judge and both attorneys seemed to be waiting for something more, some assurance that would clinch the question.

LaDonna searched for ways to make her answer more acceptable, then told them she would put her husband's situation on hold, in its separate drawer, the way she kept her house, a place for everything so that nothing got mixed up. One thing had nothing to do with another. You didn't keep a sewing basket and a milk can in the same cupboard. You didn't love a child in the same way you loved a husband.

Expressing reservation and doubt, Judge Atwill said it was up to counsel. Giotti, who saw the recent event to his advantage, had no objection to LaDonna remaining on the jury. He reasoned privately that this farm woman, most likely a conservative, would be more disposed to the plight of the defendant now that her husband would likely be up on charges. Since any appeal would be his, Giotti's approval mollified the judge. She turned to Mckeen.

The district attorney was in a more serious bind. He had counted on the Dyer woman as one of his. This might still be the case, since he sensed a certain disaffection on her part toward her husband. If she were removed from the jury and replaced with an alternate, which under other circumstances he would have insisted upon, he would almost certainly lose the Hatch woman. He would gamble. One loss was better than two. And the returns weren't all in. He liked her analogy. She spoke in terms his mother used. He hadn't lost the Dyer woman yet. She could stay. It seemed to LaDonna to take forever. "Thank you," she said.

It was Giotti's turn to present his case, and he was ready, armed with notes, a clean white shirt, and a sincere tie, a red and navy rep impeccably knotted by his wife, who made him tuck the ends into his belt. He walked to the balustrade of the jury box, caressing it with his hand, as he strolled from one end of the jury to the other. He told them that the wrong person was on trial. He paused and pointed to the defendant, who sat demurely, her hair braided in little loops. She wore no makeup or earrings, only a white blouse under a navy jumper stark with schoolgirl simplicity. He explained that it was an absolute requirement of criminal liability that the act in question be voluntary, and since Melody Jessica's involvement in this terrible affair was not voluntary she was not a murderer. Instead his client was the stooge of the state's witness, Kevin Clapp, whose testimony they had heard on Friday. Giotti promised to show that she was predisposed to blindly follow such a person, primed from the experiences of her childhood.

He stood before Maggie and engaged her eye. She looked tired, but not from crying. From an all-nighter. Like she had just rolled out of bed. He glanced quickly at his notes, then addressed himself to LaDonna. "You ask yourself, what goes on in the mind of someone connected with such an inconceivable crime? To answer that question, the defense first calls on Dr. Audrey Michaelson."

The court-appointed psychiatrist faced Giotti squarely, directly, giving notice that she was her own person, there to give her own opinion. She confirmed that she had made an evaluation based on interviews, psychological tests, and available records.

"And what were your findings?" Giotti turned his back as if he had no doubt what those findings would be while the expert witness spoke like a Delphic oracle, her words floating on a banner of esoterica. "Melody Jessica Bean is suggestible and immature, extremely susceptible to the domination of older, aggressive males."

Giotti asked her to explain. Most of the jury had never seen a psychiatrist in person, much less been to one, with the exception of the account executive-turned-canner and Bill Hogan's wife, who had been to see a marriage counselor, which anyone would have conceded was close. Some of them looked to her concepts of ego as keys to the puzzles of their own minds. Others regarded her description of instinct with the suspicion they would have reserved for someone who came to sell them aluminum siding.

The jury, however, understood conscience as it related to guilt. Each in his own way had been struggling more or less with both, differing only in degree: Katerina Lodz, because she left her mother in Poland; Hannah Watson, because she hadn't had time to take her sister out of the convalescent home; Amos, because he had run from the draft; and Maggie, because she had been able to blanket sorrow with desire.

The witness explained that while emotional abuse could not be seen as easily as a bruise on the arm or a broken bone on an X ray, it occurred more frequently and was equally devastating. She added that children who were emotionally abused suffered disturbances of attachment with serious consequences for impulse control.

"You've lost me, Doctor," said Giotti with an earnest smile.

"The bond between caretaker and child is improperly forged. Youngsters like Melody Jessica often form shallow, rapid relationships with anyone who promises to nourish their underfed egos. Hence, poor impulse control. And the inability to resist someone who is stronger."

The psychiatrist said that the clinical picture of Joyce Bean was consistent with that of parents who emotionally abuse their children. She spoke of a prenatal attitude of outright denial, of Joyce Bean refusing to buy maternity clothes or to plan where the child would sleep. The postnatal picture was just as bleak. There were reports that the decedent had never held the baby, often leaving her in precarious positions, according to one informant, on the top of a dresser. According to another source, Joyce Hibbert Bean believed that Melody Jessica was a "mean baby" because she kicked so much during her pregnancy.

In contrast, her father, although strict and domineering, was closely involved, taking her sledding, to fairs, to the airport to watch the planes take off. After he had died, her mother, who was busy pursuing one mail-order career after another, exhibited little regard for her, other than to tape written directives on the refrigerator.

Bereft of the one person to nourish her, Melody naturally sought a replacement. She found it in Kevin Clapp. Older, aggressive and self-assured, wiser, or so it seemed to her, and generous with his affection, he was the first person, after her father's death, who displayed any real interest in her. When he mentioned marriage, she submitted herself with reckless abandon to his every wish.

"In your opinion, Doctor," asked Giotti, "did my client understand what she was doing?"

"These kids are like prisoners of war. They can't think straight anymore. When Kevin came along, it was a matter of unconditional surrender, a question of an injured mind seeking its own remedy."

McKeen moved to cross-examine. He seemed sharper, like a blade that had been honed. Maggie saw it in his walk.

"Dr. Michaelson. I am interested in how one gathers evidence about a dead woman who is not there to defend herself."

"It's no different from an autopsy."

"Move to strike, Your Honor."

"The jury will disregard the witness's last remark."

"Please," said McKeen. "Just answer my questions. You mentioned information from neighbors and relatives. Just how scientific is the testimony of lay people who may have forgotten, mixed up their facts, or held a grudge? I would not think that such evidence would be sufficient to form any valid conclusion."

"It's not. Evidence of this sort needs to be corroborated."

"Corroboration from the defendant, who is on trial for murder?"

"Your Honor," said Giotti.

"Sustained."

"I will rephrase the question. Corroboration from what source?"

"Partially from Melody Jessica. Partially from written testimony. I have come across a report written by a public health nurse shortly after the Bean girl's birth, stating that when she entered the Bean household—this was in November—she found the door wide open, the mother in a sweater and the baby in nothing but a diaper. I have it here. Do you want me to read it?"

Jim McKeen was angry with himself for violating a principle canon, that of never asking a question for which answer he wasn't prepared. "That won't be necessary, Doctor. You characterized the defendant as being suggestible and immature. What causes you to reach this conclusion?"

"Her behavior, her comments, her history, and the results of her psychological tests."

When he asked which theory of personality she subscribed to, then asked if it was possible for another expert, using another theory, to arrive at a different conclusion, Maggie was struck by her own subscription to the truth, which seemed to vary with the questioner, and with the light in which it was cast. When Giotti had questioned the psychiatrist on the witness stand, she had sounded reasonable, convincing. Now as McKeen dismantled her testimony bit by bit, asking with what degree of accuracy her diagnoses in the past had proven correct, and if her diagnosis in this case was nothing more than an educated guess, that, too, was convincing and strangely satisfying.

* * *

By the noon break, the jurors were swimming in the testimony of the morning. Deeply ingrained with the concept of free will, most of them were finding it hard to swallow the precepts of the psychiatrist's testimony. The journeyman carpenter, once happy to be on the jury, was now edgy, bored, cracking his knuckles to the annoyance of everyone else, and wishing it were over. He said the psychiatrist was a ball-breaker. He could always tell.

The bank teller argued that Dr. Michaelman's testimony was important, that how he felt about her as a person should have no effect on the evidence she brought to bear, that what she said about Melody Jessica's peers regarding her as a nerd, or that no one other than Kevin ever asked her for a date, was important. It was just as important as Melody Jessica believing that her mother was a stumbling block.

"I don't buy any of that," said the carpenter.

Everyone knew about LaDonna's husband running amok in the supermarket. The news had traveled faster, according to Willard Peterson, than a toad lapping lightning. No one said a word to LaDonna other than the account executive-turned-canner, who asked if she had gotten a lawyer; most avoided even looking at her, except for the first alternate, the wife of the snowplow man, anxious to be part of the real jury, who regarded her as if she were a scab that would not heal.

If they were looking at anyone, it was at Maggie and Amos, who stood before the sideboard without speaking, moving in tandem with the easy accommodation of the intimate. They watched as Maggie helped herself to the bran muffins that lay stacked in a Saran-lined shoebox, and Amos fixed her coffee, the way she liked it, black with two sugars. They saw her bump into his side with a glance of her hip, and peel off to claim a telephone. They heard her dismay when she learned that someone had already left and quickly turned away when she caught them staring.

* * *

"They said they couldn't wait," said Kristen.

Sybil was up to her old tricks. Why did she always do this to her? Always. "They could have made a later flight," said Maggie. "I don't know what the big rush was. She knew I wanted her to wait. I said so in my note. She also knew that I had to go to the police station with LaDonna. She knew I didn't have a choice."

"I don't have any problems with that," said Kristen. "Take it up with Sybil. How many did he kill?"

"For God's sake, Kristen. Now is not the time."

"She left a package for ya. Do you want me to open it?"

"I'll open it when I get home."

Maggie's mood was broken, crazed by old maternal striations that never failed to infuriate her. She searched for LaDonna and found her sitting in a wing chair by the window with her chin in her hands. Maggie was at a loss. They had said all there was to say on the subject of Freeman on their way in that morning, and she would not burden her friend with her own anger. She asked instead if LaDonna had noticed any difference in McKeen. It was as good as anything else. "He doesn't seem as contained, like he's torn off the cellophane. Do you know what I mean?"

LaDonna had no interest in discussing abstractions, particularly those that dealt with tearing off one's wrappings. Her focus was on the concrete, on a strict accounting of the events of the morning, about which she spoke solemnly, mechanically, the way people do when recall is an effort.

"I'm trying to keep the names of all those tests in my mind, Maggie. One always seems to jump off the track. All I can remember is the Minnesota something-or-other. What was the other one?"

"The Stanford-Binet, but I don't think it matters."

"Stanford-Binet," said LaDonna empathically, firmly, as if pressing a cookie cutter into dough. "And the Minnesota test is only forty percent reliable."

"I think that's what she said," replied Maggie. "But

don't drive yourself crazy trying to remember all of it. We're not responsible for every detail." She bent down to smile at her friend. "You're going at this like a bull at the gate."

LaDonna looked at Maggie as if noticing her for the first time. "You're wrong," she said. "That little girl is counting on us to remember every bit we can." She stood up and asked Maggie for a quarter for the telephone, forgetting that she didn't need one.

While they waited for the trial to resume, the jury took the concept of excused responsiblity that they had first rejected and, drowsy with early afternoon, tried it on like a sweater, especially Giotti's analogy that Melody Jessica was a Trilby in the hands of a Svengali or—closer to their experience—a Manson. Each was considering the likelihood of doing something wrong at the instigation of another. Most had been guilty of such an act sometime in their life, usually in their childhood, like Willard Peterson, who remembered putting straws in frogs and blowing them up because his big cousin had told him if Willard didn't do it to the frog, he would do it to Willard.

Maggie, too, was trying another aspect of the morning's concept—doing something someone else wanted you to do—with regard to the people in her life, with regard to herself. Doing something someone else wanted you to do. Sybil hadn't, her father hadn't. Maggie had. She had done what Alan wanted. But that was being a good wife. That was keeping peace. That was insuring stability. And she hadn't always done what he wanted. Sometimes she had done what she wanted. When was that? She sifted through her memories and realized that it had been weeks since she woke up in the middle of the night to reach for Alan.

She caught up to Hogan on the way into the courtroom. "One of the problems with being a widow," she said, "is that you don't get a chance to work things out. It's like garbage that you leave sitting in the kitchen overnight. You know?"

He said he did.

Maggie turned the key in her lock, still thinking of the assistant principal's testimony that Melody Jessica's schoolwork was marginal at best. Preoccupied with the question of why Giotti had taken the entire afternoon to hammer home that point, she was totally unprepared for Rudy's parents, who were waiting in her living room like avenging angels, full of fury and self-righteous rage. They sat with their coats folded on their laps, their wrath puckered in their eyebrows, while Rudy and Kristen sat cross-legged on the floor, like Indians coming to parley.

"You," said the mother at the sight of Maggie bursting in red-cheeked and glossy-eyed from the cold, "are also a mother. How could you do this to another mother?"

"Who are you and what are you talking about?" asked Maggie, skinning her scarf from her neck.

"These are Rudy's parents," said Kristen.

"Are you kidding, lady, or what?" asked the father. "You just waltz through the door and ask who we are? We've been suffering for weeks, going through hell, and you ask, what are you talking about?"

"Someone better tell me," said Maggie. "Otherwise this isn't going to go anywhere."

"They were worried about Rudy," explained Kristen.

"I've been in a courtroom all day," said Maggie. "And I'm really beat. If you have something to say, say it."

"All right," said Rudy's father, rising to his feet, his coat balled up in his arms. "We will. I will. Since when does an eighteen-year-old boy roam the countryside, move in with his girlfriend, in her mother's house, and no one checks whether or not he's allowed to be doing this?"

Rudy did not seem discomfited by the discussion, a detached yet interested observer, as if its outcome did not affect him. It was his reptilian equanimity that caused Maggie to suddenly flash onto the situation. Her words came blasting through her lateral incisors like a winter gale slamming a window frame. "You mean you didn't know that he was here?"

"No, we didn't know," said his mother. "We have him listed as a missing person. They were getting ready to put his picture on milk cartons. The only clue we had was Roger. Thank God for Roger. Roger told us where to find him."

"You know which one he is," said Kristen.

The kid who talked people off. "Yes," said Maggie. She turned to Rudy's parents. "No wonder you're so upset. I'd be pretty wild if Kristen did the same thing." Maggie looked down at Rudy sitting on the floor. "You told me you spoke to your parents and that you had their permission." She pointed to Kristen. "You both told me that. Well, didn't you?"

Reduced to minor status and all that disenfranchisement implied, including having to answer to some parent, Rudy and Kristen hugged their knees to their chests.

"You lied to me, Rudy. You've been staying in my house for weeks on a lie." Maggie revved up. "You've been eating my food, and screwing around with my car, and cluttering up my house, and cutting channels to Kristen's father, and interfering with my life on a lie!"

"You don't cut channels," said Rudy.

"It's been hard on him," said Kristen. "Don't everyone come down on him at once."

"It's not everyone," said Maggie. "It's just me."

Rudy's father put on his coat. "Who in their right mind takes the word of a kid?"

"Is he packed up?" asked his mother. "I'd like to get out of here."

"Not before I say what's on my mind," said his father. "A terrible thing has happened here. Things can't go unsaid." He spread his fingers as if getting ready to tick off a catalogue of grievances.

"I have a better suggestion," said Maggie, surprised that she wasn't trembling. "You listen first to what's on my mind." It came from somewhere, she didn't know where, some unknown taproot, some cache of energy that gave her plenty of breath, ready words as strong as rocks, and a tongue that whipped out like a slingshot.

"He's a lazy, rotten kid. He's a liar and a sponge. He's been nothing but trouble since he got here. Consider yourself lucky that I'm not going to charge you for his room and board, and if this isn't the happiest day of my life, it's up there."

Rudy's father had Rudy by the arm and was dragging him through the door. "I can see there's no reasoning here," he said.

"Don't forget his earrings," yelled Maggie. "All except the gold hoop, it's not his. It's mine."

When the door slammed after them, Maggie laughed hysterically, rolling on the floor like someone threshing out a fire.

"You've lost it," said Kristen. "You've really lost it,"

"This has been a really good week," said Maggie. She rolled and hooted, drawing up her knees and clutching her aching sides. When all that was left was deep, chest-heaving groans, she sat up. Except for Sybil going away so abruptly, it had been a good week. She went to the phone. Sidney answered. Sybil was sleeping. Her hilarity vanished, Maggie sighed the rueful sigh of someone who had found a great radio station, lost it, and couldn't get it back.

"I thought you'd be real mad," said Kristen.

"I am," said Maggie, "but it's still funny."

"Since when do you laugh when you're mad?"

"Since I discovered that it's possible to have two feelings at the same time."

"We *were* going to tell you. We were just waiting for the right moment."

Maggie wasn't listening. She was calling Amos to tell him she couldn't see him. He was disappointed. She heard it in his silence. He didn't press. "Whatever you say, Mag" was his reply.

"You could go over there if you wanted," said Kristen.

"I know."

"Well, why don't you? I'm all right."

"You're almost all right. Except every now and then you slip a cog, like tonight. That's why I want to stay home with you. So we can talk this out. Alone. Just you versus me." Maggie went into the kitchen to make baloney sandwiches. With Sidney and his nouvelle cuisine gone, they were back to basics. "Did you know from the beginning?"

"Not at first."

"You should have told me as soon as you found out."

"I thought since it was just for another few weeks, it wouldn't matter. I don't want mustard on mine."

Maggie ate her sandwich at the sink, where some of the dishes lay soaking. "What about his parents? How they felt? What they went through? Doesn't that matter?"

"I think they overreacted. He kept sending his little brother Creepy Crawlers through the mail. Where did they think they came from? Anyhow, his parents were Rudy's responsibility."

"That's true. But you have a responsibility to me. Don't you see that?" Maggie picked at hardened residue with the point of a knife. "Like these dishes, for instance."

"I know I do. That's why I didn't tell you. I didn't want you to get upset again."

"You don't need to protect me, Kristen."

"Yes I do, that's part of the reason I came home."

Maggie spun around. "Wait a minute, you came home because you were used to coasting in high school and suddenly found yourself up against girls who were willing to work. You came home because you didn't like the food."

"Partly. And partly because every time we spoke on the phone you sounded so lonesome. It was awful."

Maggie wiped her hands on a dish towel, doubting, yet desperately wanting to believe. In a minute she would have to wipe her eyes. She spoke softly, "I can't help how I sounded. I was grieving."

"Maybe, but you should know that it also has an effect on me. I try to picture Daddy sounding like that if something happened to you. And you know what I think? I think he wouldn't make me feel guilty because I was the one who got away."

It was too much to handle. She should have gone out. She should have been with him. Maggie left the kitchen and climbed the stairs.

Kristen followed behind her with the dedication of someone who has gone too far and knows it. "You were talking before to the guy that caught the bats, weren't you?"

"Yes."

"You like him?"

"A lot."

Maggie fell on her bed, exhausted. Kristen flopped down beside her. "Who finishes first?"

Such a conversation would have been impossible with Sybil. For some reason it was less so with Kristen. It probably had more to do with Kristen's state of mind than with Maggie's.

"I'm not sure, Krissie. Let's just say no one goes away hungry."

"No kidding."

They both lay on their stomachs, each leaning on an elbow. "I guess Ranger is right."

"In what way?" Maggie stroked her daughter's cheek.

"Ranger says it gets better for women as they get older."

"Ranger said that? How does Ranger know?"

"He's not a dumb guy, you know. He's very experienced. He's got a twenty-six-old girlfriend. She thinks he's twenty-two. But I want to talk about Sybil. Do you think she still gets it on with Sidney?"

"I would bet on it."

"Then if we go with a simple progression, it has to be better for her than it is for you."

"I don't think so. I think it peaks."

"When?"

"For you, not soon enough for you to worry about. For me, a few months from now." Maggie looked hard at her daughter. "You're so independent," she said. "Could anyone get you to do something that you didn't want to do?"

"You're making me go back to college."

"You can't put it all on me, Krissie. If you really didn't want to go, you know you wouldn't. Be honest. Would you?"

"No."

"I didn't think so." It was then that Maggie knew that even though Kristen's adolescence threatened to do her in, like tonight—comparing her to Alan, or the week before, one minute explaining the strategy of the Pelopennesian War, the next, switching on the Saturday morning cartoons—Maggie had done a fair job. Somehow, with all her uncertainties and insecurities, she had muddled through. Where do you take a child to get her ego measured?

"Tell me about the trial," said Kristen.

Maggie stuck her legs in the air and pulled off her socks. "I can't discuss it."

"But anyone can go into the courtroom. It's open to the public."

"That's right."

"Well, what if I was sitting there? I would have heard everything you did. What's the difference if you tell me or if I see it myself? You don't have to tell me what you think about it. Just tell me what you heard. I'll hear it from someone else anyway."

"Who?"

"Lots of kids know about the trial. Mirabelle Wheatley goes all the time, and Don Haynes went, just to hear Mr. Spaulding."

Maggie took off her glasses and rubbed her eyes. "Would you like to hear some of your assistant principal's testimony?"

"Sure."

"Let's see if I remember. McKeen asked Spaulding why

he had called the truant officer to check into the Bean household. I forgot the date. Spaulding said it was because of the notes. He didn't think an adult had written them. McKeen asked if he checked a home each time he got a suspicious note, and Spaulding said they were too swamped for that kind of follow-up. Then McKeen asked what made him do it on this occasion, and Spaulding said, because there were so many of them, that he tried to call her mother, but Melody Jessica was the only one who ever answered the phone. Then when she told him that her mother had gone to Daytona, he thought it might be a good idea to call the police. He said his concern was desertion."

"Here's something I bet you didn't know," said Kristen, twisting a lock of her hair between her fingers, the way she used to do when she slept in sleepers with feet and Maggie read bedtime stories. "I found out that no one got killed at the food store, but the butcher is critical."

Maggie sat upright. Kristen had the knack for bringing her down with a crash. "I've got to call LaDonna and see how she's doing."

While she was dialing, Kristen asked if she wanted to watch *Halloween IV* on the spook channel. It went on at nine and she would make popcorn. Maggie wondered if that was a loose or a tight association. There was no answer at LaDonna's. She put the phone in its cradle, ready to ask if Kristen had ever forged her signature to absence notes, then changed her mind. "Do you remember making snow angels with me?" she asked.

"No," said Kristen.

"You don't?" Maggie was surprised. The memory was so clear, she could even feel the crunch of snow on her back. "Maybe you were too little. We used to make snow angels in the field behind Letitia's house."

"I never made them with you," said Kristen. "I made them with Jenna."

"It was me. You were just too little to remember," said Maggie, who wondered at the tricks of memory that select certain details to forget and leave others as vivid as yesterday. "You said Sybil left a package. Where is it?"

Kristen returned with an egg-shaped leather box stamped "GOMPERS, PARIS, 28 PLACE VENDOME," and an envelope. Maggie ripped open the envelope and unfolded the letter inside. "My sweet Maggie," it read, "I was waiting for the right time to give this to you. Under the circumstances, now will have to do. Your father gave this to me when you were born. Read his card. I don't know for certain what happened to change things, all I can tell you is that when you were born, this is how he felt about me, about you. Nothing stays the same. You above anyone surely know that by now. All we can hope for are moments. Moments don't change. Moments are forever frozen, like the pond behind your house. This one is yours."

Maggie opened the leather box. In it was something wrapped in a velvet pouch and a little card which read, "With love always to my wife Sybil in her starring role—a great performance—a beautiful understudy."

"Aren't you going to see what's inside?" asked Kristen.

Maggie slid her hand inside the pouch and pulled out a diamond and torquoise-hinged egg on a long platinum chain. She pulled it open carefully. Inside the gilded interior of the locket was a picture of a baby with hair the color of apricot.

"Who's that?" asked Kristen.

"It's me," said Maggie.

CHAPTER 14

Cross Examination

SYBIL HAD BEEN CHATTY and newsy, happy to be back in New York. Even with Sidney? Yes, especially with Sidney. Maggie said the diamond egg was beautiful. She didn't know if she would ever get the chance to wear it, but she would keep it safe in her top drawer, the one you had to step on a stool to reach. Sybil sounded tired, mired in her own breath with excuses enough to cover the deficit of energy and air. The airline had lost her bag, the one with the fittings that contained all her makeup, they had been out late the night before, and another minor upset, she and Sidney had been told at Mortimer's that there was nothing available, when she personally counted twenty-four empty tables. When Maggie asked how she was feeling, Sybil fielded the question with a non sequitur, a recounting of an article in *W* which proclaimed that Shirley Maclaine, Mayor Koch, Prince Ranier and all the Grimaldis, and Pee Wee Herman were out. When Maggie demanded that she answer the question, Sybil played her ace. She had been able—she said this slowly, with style and heightened drama—to obtain the promise of a show for Amos. All he had to do was come to New York and bring his slides.

Why does he have to come in person? asked Maggie. Why couldn't he just mail his slides? Sybil replied that

that was part of the deal, although she neglected to mention that it had to do with the gallery owner, who believed in the privilege of sponsorship and exercised, where it pleased her, the droit d'signorina.

Maggie was sidetracked by her mother's gift to Amos that promised to pull him out of the slippery, depressive crevasse into which he kept sliding. They seem to have traded places. It was she who should have been despondent. I'm the one who's just come out of mourning, who's trying to brush off guilt that sticks like pollen.

"So all you have to do," Maggie explained as they sat in his pickup waiting to enter the courthouse, "is to go to New York with your slides. You could do it on a weekend. I might even be able to go with you. We could drive down in the morning and come back in the evening."

Amos watched a man through the vapored truck window tug on Yancy Scruggs's coat sleeve. "I'm not interested in a gallery show," he said.

She refused to let him bring her down. She was determined to keep him up if she had to hold him by his ankles. "If it's because you don't want to come to New York, maybe you can just send the slides."

"It doesn't have to do with anything. I just don't want it."

Euphoria turned to annoyance with the speed of cotton candy dissolving in saliva. "I don't understand how you can turn down a great opportunity."

"Easy. No damn way."

"Why not? I thought you'd be excited."

"Whoever is making the offer is doing it because of your mother, as a favor, a swap for all I know—not because they think I'm any good."

"She won't do it if she doesn't like your slides."

"I doubt that. It sounds like it's already in the bag. Even if she thought I was okay, she'd still be doing it for your mother."

Maggie let go with both hands. If he slipped down into

some dismal, hopeless fissure, he was on his own. "I thought you wanted to get ahead."

"Not that way."

"This is stupid. Don't you see it's really stupid? You've been complaining that since you're back in Vermont, no one sees your work. Now you have a chance to show your stuff, and what do you do? You turn it down. You know what I think? I think you're afraid of success. I don't think you want to be a known photographer with some kind of national reputation. I'm not sure that you want to be any kind of photographer." It was like ice skating. Once she started to crisscross the frozen surface, it was hard to stop. He stroked the curls at the nape of her neck with his mittened fingers. She brushed away his hand. "I mean, think about it. What do you talk about with me? You talk about laying flat on the curb of a sidewalk for five hours, while some guy fires a machine gun at you from a helicopter. I think you want to be in all that blood and guts, that Central America guerrilla show, running around taking pictures of people shooting each other . . ."

He was looking away from her, staring straight ahead like the face on a coin, his jaws working silently, as if they were clicking into place, the lines around his eyes tightened like gathers that someone had drawn closed. She left off in midsentence, her unfinished thought hanging over their heads like an icicle.

When he spoke, his voice was low, atonal, as flat as the bang on a pan. "Stop playing psychiatrist. You listened to one testify, and now you think you're an expert. Don't ever do that again, Maggie. Stay out of my head and I'll stay out of yours."

How easily he could make her eyes sting with tears. "What do you think I'll see in there?"

"Back off, Mag."

"No one likes a present thrown back in their face."

"That's why I threw it back. You did everything but tie it in a bow."

They sat in silence. He broke it. "What happened to you last night?"

"Rudy's parents came to get him. It was an awful scene. After he left, Krissie and I needed to get some things straightened out between us."

Someone was waving. Amos cleared the frost from the window. It was Hogan, pointing to his watch. "Time to go." Amos fingered her jacket closing. "When we break at noon, don't go into the assembly room. Tell them you have an emergency, some kind of errand you have to run. Meet me at my place."

"Hold it." She pulled away. "You accused me of not knowing the ground rules. This isn't ground rules, it's your rules. You can't declare sections of yourself off limits and then expect me to feel good about you."

"Why not? I feel good about you." He leaned over and kissed her, his hand steady and firm behind her neck.

"I can't," she said. "There's not enough time."

"Sure there is. Thirty-five minutes each way. Gives us fifty minutes."

"I don't know. That's cutting it awfully close."

"It's that or the truck." He slipped his hands under her jacket and sweater, making expert, pill-rolling, pincer-like movements with his fingers on her breasts and nipples.

Her response had nothing to do with principle. He pressed his advantage with another kiss, this one hard, demanding, insistent on her mouth.

It wasn't fair. "All right," she said.

All through the morning's cross-examination of Kevin Clapp, both the witness and Maggie were in a state of unrest. Maggie was filled with erotic ruminations which interfered with her ability to focus on the boy in the witness box, and he, in turn, was preoccupied with a longing to get out of the whole mess, back to the days when he knew Melody Jessica Bean only as a pudgy ninth-grade kid with Dairy Queen Swirl strains on everything she wore.

After Judge Atwill declared Kevin Clapp a hostile witness to the defense, Giotti affirmed Kevin's previous testimony that he had forged his father's signature on a purchase agreement for a used Camaro. That was the easy part. The witness quickly proved hard to pin down, acknowledging only after a persistent, tedious interrogation that he had saved $2,600 from shoveling walks, mowing lawns, and building rabbit hutches.

"Over what period of time," asked Giotti, turning to the jury to show that his patience was wearing thin, "did you earn all that money?"

"I don't remember."

"You don't remember or it didn't happen?"

"I don't remember well."

"What don't you remember well? You seemed to remember well enough when you testified for Mr. McKeen."

"Objection, argumentative." McKeen noticed that the Hatch woman seemed distracted. Had she already made up her mind?

"Sustained," said Judge Atwill, who also noticed that the Hatch woman seemed distracted, and who had just jotted down two issues with which she wanted to be associated, the scarcity of rural housing and the decriminalization of drugs.

"I will withdraw the question and ask another." Giotti steadied his pointing finger like a gun. "Did you make any other purchases at the time you bought the car?"

"Yes." Five pairs of Reeboks, a car stereo with a quick-release system which let you remove the head from the mounting sleeve, a secret code to prevent theft, a Quartz PLL synthesizer, and a super tuner to correct multi-path interference.

Giotti asked Kevin what music he preferred. Kevin acknowledged rock. Was he familiar with Iron Maiden, Slayer, Possessed? Yes. Isn't that called Death Metal? I don't know, Kevin replied. I just like the guitar riffs.

Giotti held up a receipt, which he entered into evidence for the purchase of albums by Megadeth and Anthrax, whose songs, he said, dealt with death, destruction, effective methods of torture and disembowelment, and satan worship.

"I don't listen to the words," said Kevin, "just the beat."

Giotti was attempting a trial within a trial according to McKeen, who had jumped to his feet, saying that it was collateral.

"Objection sustained. Strike the witness's last remark."

Giotti's face became deadly serious. He dropped his voice and asked if Kevin used drugs. Kevin said no, he wasn't into drugs. And even if he was, which he wasn't, you had to go to Burlington to get anything decent. McKeen shook his head. Just answer the questions, he had instructed, no more, no less, and wait, wait, to see if I'm going to object before you answer.

They unhusked each other like ears of corn, stripping away clothing in handfuls as they made love half dressed on the silo sofa, Maggie with a bra dangling from one shoulder and Amos in his socks and boots. It was an avaricious attack, a rolling, thrashing, skirmish. For one brief moment Maggie caught Amos staring down at her in what seemed like vengeful wrath.

Later, as they hurriedly dressed, she recalled the look on his face. "Once," she said, "when I looked at you, it was like you hated me."

"I'm not responsible for what I look like when I'm making love to you."

His disclaimer made no difference. Even if she never saw his face, she felt his fury inside her body. "It didn't always feel like making love. You used your body like a weapon. I thought you were trying to kill me."

"It happens like that sometimes," he said.

It was not until they were on their way back to the courthouse that she spoke again. "There's nothing to read in your house," she said. "How do you keep up?"

"There's nothing I want to keep up with."

"That's stupid," she said. "And smug. No one knows

everything they need to know. You don't have a television set. You don't get the newspaper. What about paperbacks? Don't tell me that they're too expensive. I saw them for a quarter at the flea market. How do you expect to learn anything? Keep up with what's happening?"

"I am the way I am. Take it or leave it."

Inwardly she agreed, even though she was furious. If anything could be said for Amos, it was just that, he was what he was. Romance and its fabricated niceties were not his style. He would have said the same thing before they went to bed.

They were late. Everyone was waiting. The court clerk, standing before them like a stanchion, made no attempt to disguise her annoyance and regarded them both with baleful displeasure, while Hannah Watson remarked to no one in particular and to all, "There's not a lot to see in this neck of the woods, but what you hear makes up for it."

If the jury didn't hear it, they all knew it through the subtle transmissions of a shifting brow, a lowered lid, a furtive glance over an elevated shoulder. McKeen knew, Giotti knew, and so did the judge, who issued a general reprimand. "I'd like to remind the jury," she said, "that after recess, you are all expected at the appointed hour. The reason that we encourage you not to leave the jury assembly room is to insure absolute promptness. Those jurors," she said, looking straight at Maggie and Amos, "who were late in returning this afternoon will make sure that that does not occur in the future."

"Your sweater," whispered LaDonna. "It's inside out again."

The afternoon's cross-examination began in an aggressive, rapid-fire manner. When Kevin Clapp, who now eyed every question with suspicion, became confused and started fumbling, it was clear to most of the jury that the boy was desperately trying to second-guess Giotti and give answers to counter his offensive. And when they saw Giotti breathing deeply through his nose, looking into the distance as he attempted to show the contradiction between Kevin Clapp's prior statements and his present testimony, they knew the defense attorney was trying to control his anger.

"Kevin," asked Giotti, "did you forge a withdrawal slip in the amount of $2,600 from the account of Joyce Hibbert Bean?"

"No, sir. I never did that."

"Who did, then?"

"Objection, calls for speculation on the part of the witness."

"Sustained," Judge Atwill ruled.

Giotti shook his head in disbelief. "Let's go on to something else, Kevin. After you helped dispose of the body—"

Kevin interrupted. "I never said that."

Giotti seemed to be waiting for him. "Let me refresh your memory. Do you acknowledge that this is a copy of the statement you made on October fifth of this year?"

"Yes."

"You were told it might be read in court?"

"Yes."

"Did you swear under oath, just as you did today, to tell the whole truth?"

"Yes."

"This is your signature, isn't it?"

"Yes."

Giotti read it aloud. "I put Mrs. Bean in the backseat. Melody Jessica couldn't do it alone. I used my knee to get her in. Question. Why did you use your knee? Answer. On account of Melody didn't understand the principle of a fulcrum."

"But that's not what you said."

"I see," said Giotti. "If I don't repeat your exact words, then I'm wrong?"

"I didn't understand the question. You messed me up."

"I'll try not to mess you up again, Kevin. Did you continue to see Melody Jessica after the body of Joyce Hibbert Bean was taken to the quarry?"

"No."

Giotti shook his head again and flipped through the pages of the statement before him, then read the portion that contradicted Kevin's last response, making it doubtful to most of the jury that Kevin was telling the truth.

LaDonna didn't clean something, she attacked it. Armed with Murphy's oil soap, a can of Ajax, a bucket and scrub brush, and anxiety, she was on her knees, scouring the oak floor in Letitia's attic apartment with a steady swish-swish.

"Won't that take the stain out?" asked Maggie, also on her knees with a rinse bucket and drying rags, trying to understand how an urgent noontime tryst could have been contaminated with something else, something alien, like sand thrown into a fuel tank.

"It'll take out grime and five years of a senile old man. Any stain that's in there is there to stay. I can still smell him every way I turn. I'm not sure why you want to live here," said LaDonna.

Maggie explained. Her imperative was pecuniary. She couldn't afford to stay where she was. "I don't have a lot of choices," she concluded.

"Sure you do. You could move in with me."

The thought of Freeman hulking in doorways and slamming things so hard he made her jump was an awful one. "Alan would have wanted me to do this," she said.

"How do you know that?"

"He was very close to his mother. Maybe closer than he was to me. He borrowed thirty thousand dollars from her and never even told me. That's the main reason I'm selling the house. Letitia needs her money. Alan would have wanted her to have it. He would have wanted to know that we had a decent place to live. And, he would have wanted Kristen closer to her grandmother."

"Maggie, he's gone. What difference does it make if this is what he wanted if it's not what you want? You can't spend the rest of your life trying to do things the way your husband would have wanted."

"I didn't say it's not what I want." Maggie arched her back. Since when did it stiffen like clothes frozen on a wash line? Is that what happened when you reached forty, things like backs and thighs suddenly falling into disrepair? LaDonna might know something more definitive. "Does your back ever bother you?" she asked.

"I never noticed." LaDonna's focus was narrow. "There's no way you're going to convince me that you're happy about this move."

"I'm not happy about it. It's just that somehow I don't feel as guilty about everything that's happened if I do what I think Alan would have wanted."

"You talking about Amos Stringer?"

"Amos is part of it." Maggie straightened up and touched her elbows behind her, then delivered her confession. "Last night I slept on Alan's side of the bed."

LaDonna didn't seem to appreciate the gradient of mourning that this action represented. She went after a particularly bad stain with a scouring pad, changing the subject to the boy on the witness stand, who she said had been as slick as a hot knife through butter.

Neither noticed the appearance of Letitia at the top of the stairs, standing like an apparition in a cable-knit cardigan. Jenna trudged close behind with thighs that looked strong enough to punch bulging through her riding pants.

Letitia's disapproval of LaDonna was redolent, and it hung in the air with her arrival like heavy, reproachful perfume. She nodded to LaDonna and turned to Maggie. "You're coming for Christmas, Margaret, you and Krissie."

It was a statement, rather than a question, and a clear cue for LaDonna, who quickly determined that Maggie's folk had come for something more serious than Christmas dinner, that someone was going to give someone else a combing out. She rose to her feet, wiped her hands on her skirt, and tucked her hair behind her ears.

Both Jenna and Letitia knew all about Freeman Dyer opening fire on the convenience store. Letitia had even sent a brandied fruitcake to the home of the butcher, who still hobbled from his bullet wounds. Neither, of course, would mention the episode to LaDonna. It was a courtesy, like not talking about cancer in the presence of one who has it. "You're welcome to come along with Margaret," said Letitia. It was the ultimate largess.

LaDonna turned it down. "My girls will be expecting me," she replied. When her coat was buttoned, she turned to Maggie and smiled. "There's something to be said about having lots of space to toss and turn in."

Maggie knew that she was right, that with no one to fight with over the Lone Star quilt there was plenty of room.

After LaDonna left, Jenna chattered about Owen placing a deposit on a new business. He was going to distribute mail-order vitamins. It was a franchise. He had been given all of Vermont and the top half of New York all the way down to Poughkeepsie. How much did he have to put down? Three thousand. Ten percent. Where is he going to get the rest of the money? There was silence, a sudden hush, like that at the drop of houselights in a theater. Jenna and Letitia looked at each other only once.

"We want to talk to you," said Letitia. "I purposely asked Jenna to come along because sometimes you get your back up when I have anything to say to you, and I thought it would be helpful if there were three of us."

Already distressed by a body that was threatening to fall apart, Maggie was in no mood for a slow lead-in. "What is it?" she demanded.

"I wasn't happy about you dating other men so soon after Alan's death, but Jenna convinced me that it was all right. She said that you were still a relatively young woman, and that it was appropriate in today's terms." Letitia glanced at the floor, which was still wet from that evening's scrubbing. "That woman has taken out the stain. Somehow she's got oak to look like pickled pine." She turned her attention back to Maggie. "Especially since you were going out with Justin Herrick. I know Justin. He's a fine man. I knew his wife's family rather well. I know that Alan would have approved of Justin. I think he even met him once or twice."

"But," said Maggie.

"But what?"

"I can tell that you're leading up to a 'but.' "

Letitia stared at the window, as if the answer to her impolite daughter-in-law was hidden under the eaves. "Must you always be so abrupt?"

"That's what it sounds like, Mother Hatch," said Jenna.

"Very well," conceded Letitia. "There is a 'but.' "

"I knew I'd smoke one out."

"Be serious, please, Margaret. This isn't easy for me. I know, we know, that you have been seeing the Stringer boy."

"Amos is a man."

"You've been seeing Amos Stringer, and according to what I heard, you two have become intimate. This is a small community. That kind of news gets around."

"What are you trying to tell me?"

"That you can't know what you're doing, and that you mustn't continue to do it. For your sake, as well as Kristen's."

"It's my business what I do."

"Not in a small town. It's everybody's business. You think that kind of thing can be kept secret?"

Maggie emptied the buckets into the sink. The water swirled slowly into the drain. It was hard to imagine Letitia complaining that since Alan's death, Maggie never came to see her. Yet Jenna never lied, so it must be so. Maggie wondered what words Letitia would have chosen to convey an uncharacteristic message of need. "There's something wrong with this sink. It's clogged up or something. Okay. Let's have it. What's wrong with my seeing Amos?"

"He is a disreputable person, for one. He ran away to avoid the draft. And while his people may be honest, good folk, association is difficult. Not so much from our point of view but from theirs."

"Which is it? Would you like me to be more discreet, or be discreet with someone more to your liking?"

"It's not a question of discretion." Letitia turned on the faucet full force, testing the drain for herself. "It has to do with recklessness. You were late for jury duty this afternoon. Everyone knows it's because you and he were together and forgot what time it was. That kind of behavior is insupportable. I never would have expected it from you."

Jenna nodded in affirmation. "My phone's been ringing all afternoon," she said.

Injustice became a whetstone. "I don't believe this," said Maggie. "You both knew that Alan was seeing Anne. That was adultery. That was all right, but this isn't?"

"It wasn't all right," said Letitia. "I told Alan so."

"She did," said Jenna. "I was there when she told him."

"When did all this happen? How many people were in on it? Where was I?"

"Let's get back to the point," said Letitia. "He's not the sort of person that you and Alan had as a friend. His values are different."

"The only difference I can see is that he drinks beer from a bottle, and Peter Bouchard pours it into a glass. Sideways. As far as friends go, I never really had my own. Right from the beginning, I had to make do with Alan's."

Letitia tried another approach. "What's wrong with Justin Herrick?"

It fell right in her lap and Maggie went for it. "You want to know what's wrong with Justin Herrick? He doesn't turn me on."

"That wasn't necessary," said Jenna.

Letitia's lips were drawn and tight. "We can't get anywhere," she said with lowered voice, "as long as you're combative."

Maggie remembered something McKeen's mother had told her at the flea market. "I heard something about you, Letitia. I heard that when you were young, you wanted to run your grandfather's hosiery mill and that you sued your mother for control."

"Who told you that?"

"What difference does it make? I don't see you checking sources. It seems to be enough that I heard it. Is it true?"

"That was a long time ago."

"Is it true?"

"In a manner of speaking."

"You never told me that," said Jenna.

"It never came up. What's the point to this, Margaret?"

"The point is . . . the point is," Maggie searched for the nail, a blunt one, not too sharp, since Letitia, who had the need for her to visit, was more vulnerable. "Something happened to you to make you think you have the right to tell other people how to live their lives. I'm trying to figure out if it's hereditary, if it's in your genes or if it's environmental, like the rejection of a nineteen-year-old girl's bid to run the family's hosiery mill."

"I find this invasive and off the subject."

"I think it's right on target."

"You're avoiding the issue," said Letitia. "I was hoping you would listen to reason. This reflects badly on all of us and on Alan's memory as well. I'm sure you don't want to see it tarnished."

"What I don't want is to have to polish it anymore."

Letitia shook her head, as if to free an insect. "Jury duty has gone to your head. I don't think there's anything more to talk about." She left.

"You might want to try walnut Minwax on the floor," said Jenna, following after her mother-in-law, "and Mr. Plumber in the drain."

Maggie drove to that evening's aerobics class knowing that everyone in the church basement was talking about her, whether she was there or not, whether she had done anything out of the ordinary or not, just because their cablings were so thick and their connections so intertwined, they were indistinguishable, an agglomerate of women, a single organism of hamlet female, mutually and constantly checking each other's status in the way one's eyes check with one's feet. Maggie thought of the graveyard where Alan was interred and wondered if the stones gossiped to one another across the narrow mounds of snow about those who lay sleeping between them.

She asked herself why she was going to aerobics and decided it was to place something physical between her confrontation with Letitia. Maybe some exertion would ease her anger. She was also going to show them, Anne included, that she wasn't an object of pity like widow Keane, who hadn't opened her drapes for three years. Maggie had friends to see, places to go, and an important civic responsibility to perform. Instead of immolation, she was there to tone up, slim down, tighten her muscles—glutes, belly, thighs, and pelvis—like bow strings. And the principle reason one did that, as everyone with a brain knew, was to look good naked for some man.

Maybeth Chase, an eggplant in maroon leotard and tights, told Maggie about the widow. She was older than Maggie but a wonderful cook and had been seen frequently with Justin Herrick, especially in the last few weeks. "I thought you'd want to know," she said, watching to see the effect of her announcement on Maggie's face.

Maggie pulled a headband over her forehead. Maybeth's message was at odds with the facts. In the last two weeks Justin had called her at least four or five times. They had a date that weekend and plans to meet that evening where Justin, part of an assembly of church choirs, was rehearsing Handel's *Messiah*. In any case, Maggie didn't care about Maybeth's apochryphal information. She had been wondering how she was going to keep a lid on Justin, who had bought—so she had been told by Kristen, who heard it from Ranger, who heard it from his mother, who worked at the travel agency—two tickets to Aruba in February.

"We don't have an exclusive arrangement," she replied.

"That's what we understand," said Maybeth, who had already been told by Pam Daley, as had everyone else, that when Pam's husband had gone to the courthouse to talk to a carpenter about shelves, he had seen Maggie in the cab of a pickup kissing some guy.

They had gone too far and they knew it, past all boundaries of fair play and protocol, and they backpedaled to another topic. Since Hope Dyer, who had injured her knee skiing, wasn't there to take offense on behalf of a second cousin, Drew Pringle asked where the police had taken Freeman Dyer.

"Why ask me?" said Maggie. "Ask Win Dyer. He's his cousin."

"Maggie won't discuss the trial," said Pam with a modest smile, "so there's no point in asking her anything about it, not even about people on the jury."

Anne seemed to be hovering on the periphery, waiting for something, an opening, a lull, her hair slicked back so tight, the tiny pale blue veins on her temples throbbed with her pulse. She whispered to Maggie that she had something to tell her, something that no one else knew. It was currency. A marketable, negotiable instrument. Then she led her aside in the old way she used to do when they were best friends, and stood in front of her with a towel slung over her shoulders like a fur. "Peter and I are splitting up."

Maggie bent to push her leg warmers down closer to her ankles. "That's funny. I saw Peter the other night. He came to my house with the dentist who's going to buy it. He never said a word."

"He's probably too embarrassed."

It was difficult for Maggie to reconcile Anne's view of her husband with her own experience. "I doubt it," she said.

"Don't you want to know why?"

Maggie stood. "The only thing I want to know," she replied, "is why it took you so long."

"Maybe I needed time for things to sink in."

"Are you trying to tell me that you're divorcing Peter because of me? I can't believe that."

"Not because of you, although that might have figured into my decision. Look, I need to talk to you, Maggie. You're the only one I *can* talk to. I know what you must be thinking"—Anne lay light, tapered fingers on Maggie's arm—"and I don't blame you for being angry, even for hating me. But, Maggie, I desperately need a friend. I was there for you when you needed me after Alan died. You know I was. No matter what else happened. I stood by you and looked after you. I was the one who answered your telephone and made you eat something when all you wanted to do was curl up and die. Please. Now I need you. I need a friend who's been there."

"Been where?"

Anne spoke like one stricken. "The single world."

Their aerobics teacher changed the tape. It was their signal to go for their mats.

"I didn't ask to be widowed," said Maggie, marking off her space with a slam of her mat. "And I don't know anything about being divorced. It seems to me they're two different things." The anger was already there. That its most recent source was Letitia was not material. It was handy. "I don't have any advice about being single. It isn't all that great. It's lonely and scary, like being dropped down a dark tunnel. I wouldn't wish that on anyone, not even you. All I know about the single world is what I read in *Self*." She raised her voice just enough so that those on either side of them could hear: "You're supposed to make them use a condom and get them to name all their partners in the last ten years. You're probably safest with a married man."

Anne looked startled, discomfited. She slipped off the rubber band that held her hair, then twisted it on again. There were tears in her eyes. "You're cruel, Maggie. You never used to be cruel."

I never used to be anything, thought Maggie, putting her hands on her hips, switching her head from side to side, from front to back like a fly swatter.

"What is Maggie talking about?" whispered Drew. "Are you and Peter thinking of getting a divorce?"

The music started, loud, raucous, the rhythm of a pounding heart, as their instructor put them through their paces. It was while straining to do leg lifts that Maggie suddenly realized that the three thousand dollars Jenna referred to was ten percent of thirty thousand. A strange coincidence. The exact amount she owed Letitia. Or did she?

Maggie found the choir in musical disorganization in the loft, rattling their sheet music, trying to follow the choirmaster, who had come all the way from St. Johnsbury to direct the complexities of Handel. She recognized Hannah Watson and a woman who looked like Hannah's sister gripping an aluminum walker. Both wore frilly Peter Pan collars and pink lipstick that rimmed their lips. They frowned as the choirmaster, stamping his feet to the beat, told them that one of them was a half step off and that getting them to blend with the other sopranos was like dragging a cat out from under a barn.

Maggie sat and listened to music that was built on an echo, the singers repeating one another's themes under and over like latticework on a pie. At the same time the choirmaster, leading alternately palms up, palms down, told the bass that they did not have enough projection and that he couldn't hear the words. She reminded herself that the next time she spoke to Sybil she would find out what Ranger meant about old people popping pills.

"Every valley shall be exalted," sang Justin. Maggie found him in the third row and was astonished at the depth of his voice.

Liturgical music of trumpet and flute and organ made Maggie sad. It reminded her of Christmas twenty years ago, when Alan had said with some concern, "I don't know if you'll like it there, it's not New York." She had known nothing about where he lived except that it was a place to ski.

Then Alan was on the phone with Letitia, obviously meeting resistance but standing his ground. When they boarded the train at New Haven he told Maggie not to worry, that he would stick to her like glue, and when they stood at the front door to his house he said, "Begin with my father, he's the biggest marshmallow of all." Craggy, unsmiling, more muscular than Alan, his father didn't look like a marshmallow, but his voice was warm, receptive, and he made her feel welcome. "So this is the girl who has our Alan tied up in knots."

He had gotten it backward. It was Alan who had Maggie tied up in knots.

Now suddenly, unexpectedly, it was over, finished as if it had never been, leaving her with awful loneliness and flashbacks of anguish, of an overwhelming terror of loss, and a vivid recall of the moment she had ripped July from the calendar in an effort to go back to the day before it happened.

The minister was a kindly man with pattern baldness that gave his receding hair the look of a tonsure. He slid into the aisle and sat beside her, his wrists hanging over the back of the aisle in front.

"We haven't seen you in some time, Maggie. You've been missed. How are you getting on?"

"I'm fine," she replied.

The minister narrowed his eyes the way Maggie had seen Giotti do when he asked Kevin Clapp why he moved his car from parking lot to parking lot. "It must be lonely for you."

"I manage."

"I know that you're discharging your civic responsibilities despite your loss. Under the circumstances, you are to be commended. Letitia tells me that you're going to move into the apartment over her garage. A fine idea. You can give each other comfort." He put his hand on her shoulder as if holding her in place. "Time flies, Maggie. Just last year at this time, Alan asked me for a character reference. I had no trouble writing that letter, I can promise you. He was a fine man."

"What did he need a character reference for?"

"He was applying for a faculty appointment to the

medical school at UVM. He needed another recommendation to add to his résumé. Surely you knew that."

Alan had couched his intention as a proposition one night in bed, while lying sideways, his hand curled under his pillow. "What do you suppose would happen if I applied?" he had asked. He confided that he would accept even a clinical appointment, which meant prestige without pay. Maggie had no idea that he had actually put things into motion. "He never mentioned it," she said.

"Didn't he? Well, no matter. Husbands sometimes keep things from their wives. They don't want to worry them unnecessarily." They turned to the loft as the choirmaster instructed Schuyler from the Mobil station to hold his book up. "Your eyes," bellowed the choirmaster, "should be on me at all times."

Schuyler said it was hard to follow him when all he did was yell at them like a pig under a gate.

Someone sang, "And he shall reign forever and ev-er," and it echoed from the choir loft, from Schuyler, from Hannah Watson's sister, from Justin, pointing out something on a score to a woman standing at his side. "Justin Herrick is another fine man," said the minister.

"What?" It was the closest to crying Maggie had felt in weeks. She realized how tightly she had knotted herself against the possibility and pulled the strings tighter.

By the time Justin came down, singing, "Unto us a child is born, unto us a child is given," she was sorry she had come at all. It was the music. It carried too much with it. He said he had something to tell her. "If it's about the tickets to Aruba, I already know. You should have asked me first."

"Asked you what, Maggie?" He popped a lemon drop in his mouth and offered her one.

"If I wanted to go."

"There must be some mistake," he said, reaching into his V-neck sweater to pull the knot of his tie. "I didn't buy a ticket for you."

She sighed and turned away. Her thoughts were on

Alan and his longing to teach medical students the use of an arthroscope. He must have been waiting to hear something when he died. Maybe he had already heard and the answer was no.

"What's wrong, Maggie?" asked Justin. "Are you upset?"

They were interrupted by the assistant principal, Maynard Spaulding, who stood behind them with his flute in his hands. "What do you think?" he asked.

"I didn't see you," said Maggie. "I guess the trumpet player was in the way."

"No, I mean about my testimony today. Did I make myself clear?"

"Clear enough," she replied.

"I know you were watching me," said Spaulding. "I caught your eye a few times and knew you were with me a hundred percent."

"Maggie can't talk about the trial," said Justin.

"My wife said I sounded nervous," insisted Spaulding. "I hope I didn't sound too nervous."

When she knocked at Letitia's door, it was late. Letitia was in a woolen robe.

"Margaret, what's wrong?"

"Nothing."

"Well, come in out of the cold and shut the door."

They sat in the living room like strangers in a railroad station. Letitia offered coffee, tea. Maggie declined both. "I hear that the boy is gone," she said.

"Rudy? Yes, he's gone."

"Good," said Letitia. "I never liked him."

"Neither did I."

Maggie pulled on the fingers of her woolen gloves. She would say nothing about the coincidence. That would keep. The other matter couldn't. "I miss Alan," she said. Her lip began to tremble. She couldn't keep it still. Letitia held herself firmly, not giving an inch. "Yes," she said. "I know."

CHAPTER 15

Defendant

WHEN MELODY JESSICA TOOK the stand, she played to a full house. Every seat in the courtroom was taken by spectators who braved a wind-chill factor of minus ten to hear the testimony of the cherub-cheeked fifteen-year-old accused of poisoning her mother.

Her hair skinned back into a ponytail, the defendant was dressed in a navy skirt with a drooping hem, and a navy sweater over a white shirt with a Peter Pan collar. The effect was demure, modest, forlorn. Giotti was pleased, although he tried not to show it, affecting instead, with an uplifted, stalwart chin, an attitude of absolute faith in the justice of his cause.

"Melody," he began, "in your sworn statement, you testified that you saved money out of your own earnings in order to attend cheerleading camp."

"Yes, but Kevin is a liar. I didn't want to go so I could learn backflips. I already know how. I can do liberty heel stretches and everything." Her chirpy, sweet voice confirmed her candid blue eyes. It was what the courtroom expected. The jury was sympathetic when she testified that her mother had not allowed her to attend cheerleading camp even though she had worked hard to earn the money herself. She did not know why.

Giotti smiled gently at his client and asked if being an

alternate felt like being on the outside looking in. When McKeen objected to defense counsel leading the witness, Giotti withdrew the question and asked others. The jury learned that Joyce Bean had locked her daughter out of the house every day until five to do her correspondence-course homework, while Melody Jessica waited in the tool shed, and that Melody's mother would communicate with the girl only through notes taped to the refrigerator.

"Did your mother talk to anyone?" asked Giotti.

Melody looked sideways at Maggie to share her notoriety. "She talked to Jesus."

"Anyone else. Anyone who lives a little closer."

Judge Atwill leaned over her bench. "Mr. Giotti, let's get serious here. We don't need the commentary."

Giotti apologized, then switched his line of questioning and his expression. He appeared sad. "What do you remember most about your father?"

"He had these hairs in his ears." Laughter broke out in the courtroom. Melody Jessica smiled, riding a joke she did not understand, and testified that her father used to think up real good places to go, but that he didn't want her mother along because she would spoil things.

"Melody"—Giotti's voice was soft—"do you miss your mother?"

"Yes, sir."

"What do you miss about her?"

"She cut my hair real good."

Giotti switched his line of questioning to school. The jury learned that schoolwork was always a puzzle for the girl on trial, and she struggled to keep up. Sometimes she expected a really good grade, and when she didn't get it, she never knew why. Maybe they had it in for me, she said. When asked the reason, she suggested that maybe it was because the paint in her house was always peeling and she didn't have Laura Ashley walls like some of the popular girls.

"If you have the opportunity to finish school, what is it

you'd like to do? What do you want to be when you grow up?"

"I don't know. Maybe get a job at McDonald's. I know someone who works the fry machine. It's real easy."

Giotti moved to one side of the jury box and faced the courtroom, as if he were one of them. "Melody, a great deal of money was drawn from your mother's account after her death. Do you know anything about that?"

"Yes, sir." She testified that it had been Kevin who forged her mother's signature and Kevin who used the money to purchase five pairs of Reeboks, a car, and a one-thousand-watt stereo with six speakers, a flex fader and a superbass that cost over five hundred dollars so that when he blasted the bass, his car shook. Giotti asked what kind of music Kevin liked to shake his car with. Kevin liked Dokken. They did the music for *Nightmare on Elm Street*. Kevin was a metal head. Once he had taken her to a headbanger ball.

McKeen had been watching the farmer's wife, sitting morose and distracted, thinking that it might have been a mistake to allow her to remain on the jury. He suddenly caught himself short when he realized that he had almost missed an objection, and thrust his pencil into the air. "Irrelevant, Your Honor."

"Sustained," said the judge, surprised that he had not made his objection earlier. "The jury will disregard the defendant's last remark."

Giotti let his client's testimony sink in before he set out to defuse the question that McKeen would surely ask. "Melody, did you plan to kill your mother?"

"No."

"Who did?"

"Kevin. It was his idea. He said we would get a whole lot of money and get married. He said it was the only way."

"Kevin Clapp testified that it was you who put poison in the tube of denture adhesive. Is that true?"

"Kevin was the one who put it in. I helped him."

"Why did he need your help?"

"Because it was hard to roll back up again. Kevin needed me to press down on the end with a pencil."

Giotti's direct examination of his client took the day. When he asked Melody Jessica how Kevin had gained access to her mother's bank book and the girl looked to the judge as if she were up to her neck in quicksand and replied that Kevin told her to, associations were raised for Maggie that were disturbing, like static shocks from crossing a rug. Maggie for the most part suppressed them, especially when Giotti asked his client if she and Kevin Clapp had ever used drugs and the girl had piped her affirmation in the plaintive treble of a child. When Giotti asked why she used them and she replied that Kevin said she had to if she wanted him to love her, Maggie rummaged through her handbag for a nail clipper.

It was easier to deal with only those associations that related to Sybil. Maggie did this on her way through the parking lot. She had already begun to sort them out, not a full-scale, all-out indexing, but more like tackling a disorganized closet and settling for throwing out the cleaner's wire hangers. That morning when she had called Sybil to tell her that Kristen had tried out for the College Players, her mother had sounded as if she had trouble breathing, and less than keen to learn that her granddaughter shared an interest in the theater. Her response, if anything, was guarded, as if enthusiasm and breath had to be held in the same reserve. She did that when she had been on the stage, working in Vermont or Kansas had been considered banishment—she supposed it was different now. Maggie said that Kristen didn't want to act. She wanted to be a lighting technician.

Sybil said that was a waste, that Kristen had great presence. She finally acknowledged a bad cold. When Maggie asked what she was doing for it, Sybil replied that she was sleeping on three pillows.

Maggie decided that now was the time to confront Sybil

with Ranger's observations. "He said he saw you popping pills, fast. Under your tongue. I knew you were taking medication for your heart. The kind you swallow slowly, with your orange juice. You didn't tell me that you were also taking nitroglycerin. You didn't tell me you had pain."

"I did tell you, Maggie, in a roundabout way. I said it felt like someone sitting on my chest."

"You also said that what you had was a blip on a chart. Someone sitting on your chest and angina are not exactly the same. You misled me."

"You know how I hate spelling anything out."

"If you don't tell me exactly how bad this is, I'm going to call one of Alan's doctor friends and describe the symptoms."

"There's nothing bad about it. I have coronary artery disease. It sounds worse than it is. It just means that my circulation doesn't always get around to my heart. I need to rest. That's all."

Maggie responded with an impulsive commitment that as soon as the trial was over she thought she might come to New York. You hate New York, said Sybil. I do hate it, replied Maggie, who despised the city as much as Alan had. But she wanted to see her mother. It was like having a jar with a missing lid. There was a lot of unfinished business between them, maybe because Sybil had left before Maggie could say good-bye. Maggie inspected what it was she felt, not love—love felt warmer. This was more a connection, vague and shadowy, but not like the tie she felt to Kristen. That was a strong, pervasive tug. This was more like the ring a trapeze artist used, one that you held onto for dear life, that you were afraid to let go, that bit into your hands.

When Maggie went into the village to buy Christmas presents, it was dark, even though it was only four-thirty, and she squeaked over the snow in her boots while lights from the shops washed over the snow-covered pavement in window-wide bands of palest yellow.

Her list was short and the entire excursion took less

than an hour. She bought Owen and Jenna a fruitcake packed in a tin, Letitia an umbrella that she would never use (which didn't really matter, since nothing Maggie gave her had ever been taken out of its box), and an enamel thimble for LaDonna found in the notions store, where the shopkeeper asked if it was true that the Italian lawyer was homely enough to suck eggs. In the only men's clothing store, Maggie met Maybeth, who said she had heard about Anne and Peter. With Maybeth standing over her shoulder, Maggie bought Justin a box of handkerchiefs and Amos a dress shirt with a robin's egg-blue body and a white collar. If he wore it, she would buy him a tie for his birthday once she found out the date. Maybeth did not ask for whom Maggie was buying men's clothing, but she had her guesses. "I suppose you knew about it all along," she said. It took Maggie a moment to realize she was talking about the Bouchards.

Since it was too late to mail a gift to Sybil and Sidney, she decided she could always buy something when she went to New York. The lion's share of Maggie's earnings went for Kristen's gift, a briefcase of cordovan leather with a built-in calculator and a special slot for an appointment book that could be purchased separately for an extra fifty dollars. Maggie decided that the appointment book could wait until Kristen made plans in advance.

That evening Kristen, who had a special technique that relied on cutting mitered corners, helped wrap all the gifts except her own. She said she had been accepted by the College Players. What do you do? asked Maggie. Balance on a ladder, Kristen replied, adding that this Christmas would be the worst of her life.

"I know, baby," said Maggie. "It's bad for me, too."

"Not as bad as it is for me. You can always get a new husband," she said. "I can't get a new father."

Maggie took off her glasses, twisting Kristen's words around as if fingering a ring. This was the first time since Alan's death that she had been able to sit on the sidelines of sorrow and examine its impact deep down in her own breathing spaces.

"You didn't buy something from him, did you?" asked Kristen.

"If you mean from Daddy to you, I wouldn't do that," said Maggie.

"I didn't think you would."

"I wouldn't play those kind of games."

While curling paper ribbons on Letitia's boxed umbrella with a butter knife, Kristen let it slip that Letitia had loaned money to Owen and Jenna based on the money she expected to get from Maggie when Maggie sold the house. Maggie had guessed as much. Letitia must have made the loan right after Owen got Maggie to agree to sign the contract. Alerted, Maggie decided on a casual, offhand interrogation. It promised a better yield.

"It was probably for the deposit on their new business. Did Granny tell you this?"

"No," replied Kristen. "I overheard her tell Jenna."

"What did Jenna say?"

"Jenna said maybe they should wait until the house sale was final."

"What did Granny say to that?"

"Granny said no, the opportunity is now. Owen deserves his chance and he should strike while the iron is hot. I'm willing to gamble." She bent to her task, her long, lovely lashes brushing her cheek. "Why do you want to know what everyone said? Is something wrong?"

"No," said Maggie. "How would you like to go to New York to see Sybil when the trial is over?"

"I don't know."

"And buy clothes."

"You don't have to bribe me to go back to school. I already said I was going. Who are these handkerchiefs for?"

"Justin."

"I thought so."

Maggie smiled. "How did you know?"

"Because they're something you get in a hurry. When you don't care."

Now was the time to ask, when there was a glimmer of understanding between them. Kristen must have tried something. They had talked about it when she went into junior high. Alan had detailed what organ systems were involved, and how she might alter her chromosomes forever. Maggie's approach had been more immediate, the applications more practical. She told her she had a choice of paraplegic or brain dead. "Krissie, do you use drugs?" Her heart beat faster. It was strange that just asking the question could do that.

"When?"

Oh, oh, she thought. "Now."

"Not now."

A parry. "Did you?"

"When?"

It was like pulling teeth. "Krissie, can't you just answer the question? I can handle it, I promise you."

"I tried some stuff."

"Like what?"

"You're going to get upset."

"Not after the testimony I heard today."

"Remember, you were the one who wanted to know. Yellow jackets, reds. Someone wanted to give me acid, but I said no."

One was up, one was down, Maggie wasn't sure which was which. "I'm surprised they're still using acid. Shows you," she said, "how much I know. Did it do anything for you?"

"It's okay. I like being in control better. I'd rather get buzzed on beer."

Maggie would settle for .2 level of Coors Light. She switched on the television set to the evening news and plunged one-half of the lower level into darkness. "Darn," she said, "the fuse blew."

"Should I call Ranger? He's coming over anyway. He could fix it."

"I can change a fuse myself," said Maggie.

"You didn't use to know how to do that. Who showed you?"

"Amos. You have to look at this little copper filament inside. Where's my flashlight?"

"I lent it to Ranger."

Maggie sighed. The new term was only weeks away. "How can you lend my things to other people? I need my flashlight. Now."

Kristen adopted the bee-stung lip of injury. "You don't have to get bent out of shape about it. Daddy didn't need a flashlight to change a fuse. Does Amos?"

"No. He feels his way."

They looked at each other out of the corners of their eyes—the checkpoint, the place where you find out if you've gone too far—and began to laugh with gusty, raucous peals that made them lean upon each other for support.

As soon as Ranger showed up, Kristen ran upstairs to wash her hair, leaving her mother and boyfriend alone in the living room. At first Ranger didn't talk. Instead he waited on the edge of the sofa and swallowed. It was in the middle of a news item about rock throwing in a Palestinian camp that he finally spoke. "They have great scuba."

"Who?" asked Maggie.

"Aruba."

"The ticket's not for me, Ranger," she said. "It's for someone else."

"Oh."

"I met your uncle," she said.

"Uncle Will. He told us. Did you use the screwdriver yet?"

"No, but I'm going to. First chance I get. What I really need is my flashlight."

"Sorry about that. You want me to go home and get it?"

"Next time will be fine."

He looked at the ceiling, searching for connections the

way Ormsbee had searched for termites. "My mother's aunt is a widow. She sold her car."

"Why would she do that?"

He replied that his mother's aunt saw her dead husband sitting in the front seat and couldn't drive with him staring at her on account of he never liked the way she drove. Maggie wondered if anyone was ever satisfied with anyone else's driving.

"You're on a jury," he said. "That's hard, isn't it? You have to pay attention to every single word."

"Not every word. Just most of the words."

"What if you miss one? Like something real important? If I miss anything in class, it's going to be on the test, sure as shooting."

"That's why there's twelve of us. I think the idea is that if someone forgets, someone else will remember."

"I wish we could do that in school. You need me to carry something, get something down from the attic?" he asked.

"I'm fine."

"That's good," he said. "My mother's aunt is going into a home."

If that was a natural sequela of widowhood, Maggie had other plans. "There is something you can do."

"Name it."

"Can you teach me how to shift the M.G. without stripping the gears?"

Maggie waited for Kristen and Ranger to leave before she called Amos. He had changed his mood from the day before and now spoke in mellow, ardent, deep-voiced resonances that one makes to a lover. Was he coming over? No. Silence. Be up front with me, she said. Don't make me wonder. All right. I'm going to Nina's. Maggie was jealous. She hated the feeling. It was an awful recipe of anxiety, heartburn, and doubt. Why did he continue to see his former wife and why wasn't Maggie enough? She knew the answers. She had seen Nina. Nina was beautiful, in the way Kristen and Anne were beautiful and in the way Sybil used to be, with silken, placid-browed, blonde good looks that Maggie would never have.

Her tone sharpened like a pencil. I hope she eats crackers in bed, she said, then realized that he wouldn't care, that his idea of making a bed was shaking it out. Look, he replied. You can't have it both ways. You sandbag me. Tell me, tell me, you say, it's all right. If I don't tell you, you sulk. If I do, you get upset. You box me into a no-win, Mag. When are you going to give me a break? He was getting ready to go out. He would see her tomorrow.

Thoughts of moving in with him or he moving in with her flitted like scudding clouds. The concept was nice, but the illusion was not. Kristen in a silo? Amos in Alan's bedroom? Amos at Letitia's? None of the scenarios was right.

Her loneliness helped her isolate a feeling: the need to work with her hands, to make something out of nothing, to make something whole. She went to the kitchen table to scrutinize the painting of the boy and rooster. It was a problem with a battery of solutions. She decided that before she filled in the cracks with tinted wax, she would soften the paint where it was peeling to try to ease it back into place. It was an easy first step and one that she had taught herself after years of trial and error. A curling iron would do. She found one in Kristen's room (still warm) and returned to the table, where she held it carefully like a wand, gliding over sections of peeling paint the size of a thumbnail.

Some of the paint began to soften and she was able to ease it back into the cracks with the point of a knife when the doorbell rang. It was Justin, uninvited and unannounced. He dispensed with pleasantries, stayed in his jacket, and stuffed his gloves in his pocket. "What's going on?" he demanded. "I thought we had something."

Whatever his problem was, she wasn't up for it, especially after finally getting the paint so old it had probably been made with egg yolks to soften. She unplugged the curling iron. "I'm tired, Justin. I've been in a jury box all day. You should have called me."

"I didn't. I'm here. I know all about him. The other guy you're seeing, the one who sits with you on the jury. He's also a deserter who's two months behind in his rent."

"Amos is not a deserter," she said, "he was never inducted. And how do you know if he's behind in his rent?"

"I know the guy who owns the silo. You sure are one still water, Maggie. I never would have guessed it. You know what I thought? I thought you were frigid. I thought you just needed time. Stupid of me, wasn't it? But that's what I thought."

She sat down, hoping he would do the same. There was no way to handle this standing up. "Take off your jacket." He refused. "I don't know why you're so angry," she said. "Nobody said anything about an exclusive arrangement. You have your Dorset widow. You never told me about her. But I hear that you've been seeing a lot of her."

"That's a different matter. She's a lonely woman. Older than you. No takers to speak of. I'm doing her a kindness. You and I had something to offer each other, not necessarily marriage, but something else just as good, companionship, commitment, if you will."

"I don't know how that works . . . how you can say one thing and do another."

"You did," he countered.

"No, I didn't. I never told you that I felt one way or another about you."

"You showed me. With every move you made. Every time we spoke on the phone. I heard it in your voice. You can't disguise warmth, Maggie, or feeling. With you and me, there was something special, a really good fit. At least I thought there was. You supplied sweetness, a kind of appealing, helpless femininity. I supplied security, know-how. It was yin and yang."

Maggie splayed her fingers on her knees as if they were

fans. "Look, Justin, you're really very nice. You're fun to be with, you know a lot of the same people I do, you're well informed, and you were attentive and kind when I needed a friend. I'm grateful for that."

He interrupted her kiss-off. He had made the same speech often enough and he was not about to be on its receiving end. "This other guy," he said warmly, leaning over to touch her hand. "Let's forget about him." He took off his coat. "Can I get some coffee?"

Maggie was grateful for the truce. She went to the stove.

"You can't throw us away just like that," he said.

"*Us* was never anything" she corrected, putting up the pot. "*We* date. Period. I like you, but I just don't feel anything for you."

"I don't believe that."

"Justin, what do you say to a woman when it doesn't work out? For whatever reason. When it's a no-fault. What do you do?"

"For a minute there," he said, "you reminded me of my wife. Not that you look like her, she was older, and somewhat heavier. It was your hand, the way you held that pot."

She carried two cups to the kitchen table. "I hardly ever hear you talk about your wife," she said.

"I guess I don't talk about her for the same reason you don't talk about your husband. I've never met him, but I would be willing to bet that he would have approved of me."

"Alan believed that Vermont was being dominated by outside interests, the people you represent. I don't know that you would have gotten along."

Justin stirred sugar into his coffee cup. "From all that I've heard about Alan Hatch, he sounded like a reasonable man. I think he might have agreed that change is inevitable. The best you can do is to try to guide it. When people say, 'We won't permit any more people to come into the state,' that's nonsense. They can't stop it. People are coming, just as land values are going up. I hate to see old homegrown industries fall into the hands of a giant corporation, just like anyone else, but it's something we can't stop. It's like standing on a track and seeing a train coming. You can do two things. You can stand still and get run over, or you can hop on the train and try to control it." He jerked his chin toward the painting at the end of the table. "What are you doing with that?"

"Fixing the cracks."

"I wouldn't fool with it, Maggie. You're better off giving it to someone trained in restoration."

Maggie glanced absently at the kitchen clock, wondering if it was broken. He put down his coffee, then reached for his jacket and slipped it on. For a moment he looked stricken. She felt sorry for him "I just don't understand," he said, "why it's him and not me."

She almost relented, only because she was alone and vulnerable, and because he showed her a frailty that she had not seen before. It would have been, she knew, less an act of passion than one of gratitude, as politely offered as a thank-you note. It was because Maggie had always resisted such conventions that she could not bring herself to donate, even before Christmas, her most private self.

After the previous day's face-offs with both Amos and Justin, it was difficult to pay attention to McKeen's cross-examination. Nevertheless, Maggie tried to wipe everything from her mind, the way one rubs an eraser across a blackboard, leaving only traces, undefined smudges of Justin, chalkmarks of Amos, in the corner marked not to be erased, the almanac of Alan, and over everything, the fingerprints of Sybil.

The prosecuting attorney was polite but single-minded, careful not to anger the jury by seeming to attack a defenseless young girl. He asked her to describe the parties she and Kevin had given after her mother's death, his low voice modulated, as if he were asking her to step into an elevator.

The defendant looked up at the prosecuting attorney through lowered lashes and replied that they had watched television as late as they wanted. There was drinking and drugs.

McKeen picked up his pace. "Miss Bean, what is Lamb's Breath?"

"Pot."

"Is that the same as Wacky Weed?"

"No, Lamb's Breath is stronger."

"And Red Hair?"

"That's the strongest pot of all," she smiled.

"Is PCP as easy to get as pot?"

"It's hard to get good PCP."

"What did you tell Kevin about the right way to take a tab of acid?"

"I forget. Maybe it was to spit out the paper."

When McKeen next asked if anyone had had sex with anyone else at those parties, specifically on the decedent's bed, Giotti objected and asked to approach the bench. The three huddled at the side bar with the court reporter, while the jury, only feet away, strained to hear. Giotti said he did not understand the point of the questioning. McKeen argued that it tended to show a lack of remorse. Judge Atwill said she would allow it since it shed light on the state of mind of the defendant.

McKeen repeated the question. "I wouldn't let the others in my mother's bed," said Melody Jessica. "That was only for me and Kevin."

The jury was stunned, as were most of the spectators in the courtroom. Only the attorneys displayed impassive, business-as-usual expressions: McKeen with a what-did-you-expect pucker of the eyebrow and Giotti with a benign, let's-wait-until-we-have-all-the-facts look.

McKeen showed no sign of letting up. "Did you know that your mother was dying?"

"No."

"Well, did she seem the same to you after you and Kevin put the poison in the dental adhesive?"

"She sat around a lot."

"She sat around? Didn't you wonder why?"

"I thought she wanted to watch television."

"I'd like to remind you, Melody, that you're under oath. Did your mother ever complain to you of headaches, sores in her mouth, a lack of appetite? Did she ever say, for example, Melody Jessica, 'I don't feel like eating'?"

"No."

"What did you think was going on when her hands and feet began to swell?"

"I didn't think about it."

"You didn't think about it. Well, what did you think when she was so weak she was no longer able to prepare your supper?"

"I always fixed my own."

Giotti requested another side bar conference. While the judge and the attorneys decided what the jury would be permitted to hear, Maggie was no longer considering guilt or innocence. She was wondering how a daughter could sound so callous about her own mother's death; wondering just how much Melody Jessica would have to hate her mother not to be stopped cold at her death—as she was by Alan's.

At recess, the jury filed into the assembly room, straitjacketed by the judge's admonishment, by their sense of fair play, and by the censuring presence of the clerk popping in and out. The morning's testimony was on their minds on all levels, in their conscious stratum, the thin sliver that dealt with logic and reason. They wanted to discuss it with one another so that they could understand, be reassured about the puzzle of this girl who was, at the very least, a liar, or worse, an aberration. They also wrestled blind, unknowing, with some ancestral memory, an age-old, primitive fear of matricide.

They dealt with it by dealing with the ordinary. LaDonna, who was on the telephone, agreed to babysit for her daughter only if the psychiatric hospital in Waterbury would not allow her to visit on the weekend. Hannah Watson made arrangements with Yancy Scruggs for his aunt to fix lunch for her recuperating sister, who had moved in with her. Trish Robidoux cautioned Hannah Watson that Yancy Scruggs could not be relied upon for anything. The canner distributed a honey-carrot relish. Katerina Lodz, wearing a bracelet that spelled "SOLIDARNOCS," explained to Willard Peterson that it had nothing to do with communism. Amos, working with *L*-shaped guides, cropped photos on the library table, and Maggie, with a shoulder-blade awareness of exactly what portion of the room Amos was in, sought out Hogan.

Hogan was mellow, where the others were not. A weathered, mahogany sage, he seemed to know the way things were. More important, he kept his mouth shut. Maggie spoke her concerns softly, like a ventriloquist who scarcely moves her lips, while Hogan, with his long legs crossed, inclined his ear and listened. He told Maggie that without evidence, there was no loan. Maggie was bound to nothing, he advised. "You're talking about a lot of money," he said. "You got that kind of money that you can just give it away on someone else's say-so?"

"Even my mother-in-law?"

"Especially your mother-in-law. People in families do funny things with each other. Like we heard this morning. You can't just take her word for it."

"Letitia's not the kind of person who lies."

He smiled like a man who had seen a lot of life and then some, a man whose wife of thirty-five years was leaving him. "No one lies, but everyone does it. You'd be surprised what people will do when they're pushed to it. Even if your husband didn't sign a note, there would be other evidence."

"Like what?"

"Bank records. There'd be a deposit of thirty thousand dollars to your account. All you have to do is check your records around the time she was supposed to have loaned him the money. We have a bank teller on the jury. The muffin lady. You don't have to tell her what you're looking for. Just ask her how you go about it. She'll tell you."

"What if there is no record? Couldn't Alan's mother have given the money directly to a contractor?"

"If that's the case," said Hogan, "then she'd have a cancelled check to prove it. Problem is, you never asked her to show it to you."

Maggie thought of demanding proof from Letitia. Would she stand to one side like Giotti, with her arm on some mantel, or would she quietly, resolutely bird-dog it like McKeen? Maybe she would adopt some style of her own. And what was that? Not the head-on collision she had with Amos about the gallery showing of his work. With Letitia, Maggie had to be controlled, her words more carefully chosen, the way you select plums by turning them over slowly in your hand. She rehearsed the possibilities in her head until McKeen resumed his cross-examination and Melody Jessica began to testify that after a pep rally, she and Kevin had gone for a snack at the shopping mall pizza parlor, then rode their bicycles to the murder site to view the body, that Kevin wanted to take pictures but he didn't have a flash.

McKeen took his time. "You testified earlier that your mother discouraged you from becoming a cheerleader. In fact, she told you not to, but you tried out anyway. Why?"

"I wanted to."

"What did your mother say when she advised you against it?"

"She just said, 'Go ahead and do it if you want. Just don't come crying to me someday when you can't have babies.' "

Did all parents do that? Maggie had. It seemed to come so naturally. *Don't come crying to me when you can't get a good job, Krissie, because you didn't finish college.*

Melody Jessica said she did not think her mother was being cruel, just plain mean. The girl's responses were so childish, so artless, yet it was something she reported her mother having said that made Maggie suddenly suspect that the girl was guilty, that she had known what she was doing. It was the moment that Maggie began to look away when Melody Jessica turned to her, as she had from time to time, for confirmation.

McKeen took a moment. He seemed to be studying the defendant, weighing her against some measure in his head. "Why did you feel that you had no other options?"

Melody Jessica looked to the judge as if she didn't know that this question was going to be on the test.

McKeen spelled it out. "You testified that you put poison in your mother's denture adhesive. Did you know at the time what poison does?"

"Yes."

"What is that?"

"It kills people."

"That's right. Poison kills people. If your mother was a serious problem for you, if she was as mean as you say, as unfair, if she made your life so difficult, why kill her? Why didn't you tell other people, your teacher, your guidance counselor, your minister, your grandfather, and ask them for help?"

Melody Jessica's face softened with angelic sanctimony. "I don't go behind people's backs."

McKeen let the enormity of her statement sink in. He faced the jury without a word, as if after her ridiculous inconsistency, there was nothing more to say and gently slapped the balustrade with the palm of his hand. It was an accent, an umlaut, a period. His voice was soft and gentle. "No further questions."

CHAPTER 16

Snow Day

THE DEAL WAS CUT by Kristen, who said she wanted to spend the night with Letitia to help her trim her tree. Kristen had come close, sharing something of herself, then slammed the door in Maggie's face with the same now-you-see-'em, now-you-don't that characterized Sybil. What was more surprising was that it hurt in the same way. Maggie convinced herself that it suited her just fine since she wanted to spend the night with Amos. She told Kristen where she was going, left a telephone number and, in a lip-curling afterthought, added to be sure to share the information with her grandmother.

The snow had begun the day before, spawned by great masses of cold air hundreds of miles across. It had crept down from the polar region, fanning out from Hudson Bay, where it plowed into a block of moist air drifting in from the ocean. Maggie saw the snow drift lazily past the high windows of the courtroom, clumping in clots of soft white crystals like dots on a veil. But she had been too absorbed in Melody Jessica's testimony that it had been the postman she had in mind when she told Chief Hammer that mother's boyfriend was the murderer to pay much attention to the weather.

That night, Maggie and Amos heard only grains like sand which peppered the skylight and the sighing wind which they took for each other. In the morning, when they woke, plaited swollen-eyed and sleep-drugged in each other's arms and legs, it was the hush they noticed first, the silence of deep, blanketing snow.

When all the doorknobs and light switches were white with frost, and Amos couldn't open the front door but could only get out through a window, standing up to his thighs to report that it was still falling and that there was no horizon, they knew it had been an awesome fall. It was one of those few spectacular accumulations that came early in the winter, as if the countryside and all its inhabitants needed to be shut away and silenced.

The night before, Amos had laid out brush on the snow like fishbones picked clean on a white platter. Now the brush was buried deep, folded into an earlier sheeting like a fossil. Amos said it would take hours to free his truck from the drift that reached its hood. They were snowed in. The radio confirmed it. Schools were closed, as were municipal and government offices. Travelers without urgent business were advised to stay at home.

Amos called the courthouse and learned that the day's proceedings were cancelled. Then, after a desperate, near-blind search which yielded her glasses on a windowsill, Maggie called Kristen, who said she was helping her grandmother shovel the walks and couldn't stay on the telephone. It was a free day with no strings attached, a green light conferred by the weather, with no way to be anywhere but with each other. Maggie couldn't remember the last time she had had such a day. Not since she was married. Maybe after Kristen was born, when Maggie sat in a hospital bed, feeling stupid in Sybil's gift of a bed jacket with a pink satin bow tied under her chin. Then she remembered that it had not been a free day at all, that Jenna had come smelling of alfalfa, bearing a box of birth announcements printed overnight as a courtesy to Letitia, a sheet of stamps, and a list of names and addresses and instructions from Letitia to please have them done before she left the hospital. Before Alan? That was a lifetime ago.

She couldn't remember nor did she particularly care to. Those were the times she had hurried away from, as far as she could, as soon as she could.

After coffee and stale doughnuts in front of the blazing wood stove, they climbed the ladder back to bed, where they spent the morning in deliberate and lazy passion, with all the time in the world to express it. Amos taught her an East Indian technique he had learned in the Arctic. It was an exercise in control in which he was more successful than she. Let it build, he said, keep still. By the time he began to move, she was as delirious as when she was twelve and had the chickenpox.

Later, Maggie wanted to ask why he continued to see his former wife, hoping his explanation would be something she could live with. She could not find the right moment, the special slot in time into which such a question might be artfully slipped. Instead she rubbed his back and described the painting she was trying to restore until he told her that she could ruin it if she didn't know what she was doing. Then he told her that his father had gotten him an apprenticeship with a stone-wall builder. He was thinking of taking it. It wouldn't be until March, when the ground thawed.

"Aren't you a little old to be an apprentice?" she asked.

"It's never too late," he said.

"What would you be building, culverts, field walls, stuff like that?"

"No," he replied. "This would be mostly for people from the city, summer people who want gardens and terraces, retaining walls that are fitted, faced. There's money in it. My dad's friend Carl says that he's got more orders than he can handle."

Amos's announcement gave Maggie a philosophical problem which she wrestled with by doing leg lifts. A photographer, even a poor one, was an artist, a vocation she could easily reconcile with her value system. An apprentice stone mason, on the other hand, could not even be called a craftsman. He was a laborer. "Is this something that you want to do?" she asked incredulously.

"Not particularly," he replied.

"Then why do it?"

"For the same reason you're moving in with your mother-in-law."

She thought of him hauling great slabs of rock. "It sounds like awfully hard work," she said.

"All you need is a jeep and a chain. Carl has both."

Maggie turned to lie on her stomach with her hands folded under her chin, and asked Amos why he didn't want to reconsider the idea of a gallery show. He said he had work to do in the darkroom and left the bed.

Maggie rolled over on her back to stare at the snow-covered skylight and wondered if it had been like this for Alan and Anne. She doubted it because of Alan's constant preoccupation with hip replacements or knee-joint repairs. Not even Anne could have broken that concentration. She turned her attention to her body, particularly to the plane of her abdomen that dipped concave and hollow between her hipbones, the lean and spare pelvic cradle no longer endlessly rocking. Alan had convinced her that one child was enough. One was all she could handle at that time. She could still have a baby. There were women of her age having their first, although, according to Alan, they used to be considered obstetrically elderly.

Maggie became restless. She put on a faded work shirt that hung from the back of a chair, climbed down the ladder from the loft, and roamed about the silo looking for something to do. Other than the magazines she had already seen and given to Amos, there was nothing to read. Since it was not her house to keep, there were no projects to finish, to mull over, or to write off. There were also no closets to clean, no drawers to empty, no cracked, leathery painting found in some junk shop that needed restoration, no casseroles to defrost, no clothes of Kristen's to mend, no journals of Alan's to stack. She caught herself. She had forgotten that she had cancelled Alan's subscriptions.

Had she cancelled Alan as she had his journals? It was a painful question. Then she reassured herself, marshaling reason the way one frantically stockpiled canned goods, that she hadn't canceled Alan, only her grief. She knocked on the door of the darkroom, entered, and closed the door behind her. The garnet-lit cubicle smelled like onions. Water gurgled in the trays while Amos dusted proofs with a can of air, closeups of men and women with craggy, careworn faces who looked as if they had the answers but weren't going to give any away. He clipped the pictures to a line and came behind her, lifting his shirt up to her waist. "This is bad," he said. "I want you all the time."

He lied. He wanted her only for a moment. He dropped the shirt soon after, settled it indifferently as if settling the flap on a tent, and went back to work without a word. Maggie left the darkroom and began to drift around the silo, picking up things and putting them down, thinking of yesterday's testimony in abstracted pieces, like biting off pieces of candy. She wanted to call Sybil, but was anxious not to add long-distance charges to Amos's bill, then decided to check in with LaDonna.

It took several rings for LaDonna to answer. When she did, her labored replies made it apparent that she was dispirited. "He's pulling me down with him, Maggie," she said, "one way or another. I thought I could fight him off, I thought I had power."

"What kind of power?"

"You know, making babies well, that sort of thing. It gives you the idea that you can do anything. I was wrong."

Maggie didn't like where this was going. It had the feel of a no-win argument, with LaDonna stacking the cards in advance. "How were you wrong?"

"I didn't have enough strength, not the real kind. If I did, he wouldn't be where he is."

"Are your girls saying that to you?"

"They don't have to. I reasoned it out for myself."

Maggie asked what evidence she had to support such a conclusion. LaDonna became testy and told her to leave the lawyering to the courtroom. Maggie lightened the topic as if adding milk to coffee. She said that a lot of people hadn't finished their Christmas shopping, and asked if LaDonna wanted to sew on Saturday and take a booth at Sunday's flea market.

"No point, Maggie. It takes energy to thread a needle. It's all I can do to dress myself. Besides, I said I'd watch Janine's baby."

Worse for Maggie than the hopeless feeling of being depressed herself was the equally helpless feeling of not being able to pull a friend out of it when she knew she had the answers, when all LaDonna had to do was to take her advice and do what she said.

It was after her conversation with LaDonna that Maggie began to take notice of things about Amos that she did not like, such as his habits of wearing the same socks over and over—leaving them sour and crumpled in his boots to put them on again—brushing his teeth with salt instead of toothpaste, and not being bothered by the teetering, crusted stack of dishes in the sink. Maggie told herself that she was stupid to let such things annoy her. If she did, she was not much better than Letitia, whose meticulous, pluperfect standards she considered fussy beyond belief. Maggie would try to control trivial conventions that had nothing to do with the growing feelings she and Amos had for each other. It was difficult and it didn't last.

"How come you don't have a washing machine?" she yelled into the darkroom.

"They cost money."

"Where do you wash your clothes?"

"You mean *when*, don't you? The answer is, when I go to see my folks." Should she offer to take a bundle home with her? He would think her pushy, interfering, taking over his life. But, she thought, isn't that what people in love did, rampage through each other's lives like looters?

Maggie decided that since she had nothing else to do, she would tackle the kitchen. There were no dish towels, no paper towels, no sponge, no scouring pads, no rag, no liquid kitchen soap, no laundry soap, only a slippery ring of bath soap that fell apart at the touch. Maggie used her fingernails, wishing she were back in the courtroom listening for discrepancies in Melody Jessica's story. She wondered what she was going to do with her time when the trial was over and Kristen was back in school. Judging by all that Hogan had said, closing arguments were next on the agenda, and then the jury would be sent to deliberate. She had a few days, a week at best, and it would be all over. She felt troubled. It had only a little to do with losing a legitimate reason to see Amos on a daily basis, although that was part of it. There was something else about being a member of the jury. It was purposeful, responsible; it was belonging.

She yelled to Amos that she was going to call the bank. They might open later in the day once they got the roads open because it was the week before Christmas. She wanted to check certain things, certain records. She did not elaborate. Then she asked if he noticed anything different about her? Like what? *Like the fact that I'm stronger.*

"For example, that I've changed in any way." Depending on his response, she might tell him about Justin.

Amos emerged from the darkroom to give Maggie his answer. "It's called an ice-out," he said as he began his diagnosis. "You know what that is?" She did. Ice-out was a phenomenon of early spring when the water, fed by melting snows, rises above the ice and one hears the ice cracking and groaning beneath the surface. Finally, enough of the ice breaks away and begins a chain reaction, plowing its way downstream. It catches here and there, loosening more ice, until with a rush, the whole stream seems to break up at once.

"You're like an ice-out," he said. "You began to break out when you first came on the jury, and now you're like tons of water and ice careening downstream without direction. I've seen it overrun trees, flow across roads, take away fences." He looked steadily at her. "Bulldoze its way the way you rode over me the other day in my truck about being afraid of success. Even all those magazines that I didn't ask for. You couldn't leave it at that. You had to underline the articles I'm supposed to read. You have to be careful with ice-out, Mag. Once the main channel clears and the energy's gone, there's nothing left but chunks of ice on some farmer's meadow."

It still bothered him, that business about the gallery show and what she left unsaid. "You're still angry about that, aren't you?"

"Angry? No way."

She put a hand on his shoulder. "You're still talking about it, so it must have made you feel something. Look, I didn't say it to make you angry or to hurt your feelings. I only wanted you to see how it looked to me."

"I don't let that kind of thing get to me." But he had. It was clear in the way his shoulder rippled away her hand.

Maggie changed the subject to the trial. The ground was safer. Amos thought the Clapp kid was smart, so much smarter than the defendant that it was clear that he had masterminded the whole affair. She was a dippy kid with a mother who didn't care whether she lived or died. It was easy to see how it happened.

Maggie said she had problems with that, gnawing problems, like gnat bites that made it difficult to accept. What kind of problems? Well, she said, her name for one thing. It's a pretty name. A fanciful name. You don't call a baby Melody Jessica that you don't have good feelings about. That you didn't want.

He didn't buy her reservation. Okay, he challenged. What do you call a baby you don't have good feelings for?

Margaret, she replied.

He said she was focusing on the wrong facts. In any case, it wasn't worth arguing about. Life was too short. If she thought about it, she would eventually see it his way. In the meantime, he was going to dig out the front door and his truck.

She was supposed to see things his way, but he didn't have to take her views into account. Maggie climbed angrily, hand over hand. Whether or not Amos had any ideas about going back to bed, or to the clumsy clawfoot tub that always overflowed, she was going to get dressed in her own clothes. How could they be so close on one level and be so far apart on another?

She was on her knees rummaging under the bed for her other shoe when she heard the door creak open and shut and the sound of voices below. Amos had visitors. Maggie leaned over the railing and recognized Nina, red-cheeked from the cold, her eyelashes frosted with snow, holding a little boy by the hand and scooping her long blonde hair over her coat collar with the other.

Nina looked up, arrested as people are by a flicker of movement, a rustle of sound, the prickle-neck sensation of the presence of someone staring at them. "Hi," she said, then turned her attention to Amos. The roads were open but bad. Luckily, Smitty had a four-wheel drive. He was waiting outside. They were going to Troy to Smitty's brother's house. Smitty's brother had bought a second-hand snowmobile and if they got it to work, they were going to try it out. Smitty didn't want to take Sam.

"I knew you wouldn't be in trial today." She looked up again at Maggie. "You're the one drove past my house, aren't you?" Maggie could only nod. "I recognized you by your glasses." She made it sound as if Maggie were the only one in the world who wore them. Then she dropped the hand of the child, who stood immobilized in his padded snowsuit with his arms held stiffly at his sides, and blew him a kiss. "Be a good boy, Sam, and do what Amos tells you." It was "Amos," not "Daddy."

"I have to be in the courthouse on Monday," warned Amos.

"Don't worry." Her laugh was young, girlish, a trill of adolescence belied by her tired eyes. "We'll be back in the morning."

"Where are his clothes?" asked Amos.

"He's wearing clothes, honey. He doesn't need any

others. He'll only mess them up anyway, won't you, Sam?"

Maggie was bothered by the prior claim that "honey" implied. The child looked like his mother. "Who is Smitty?"

"I told you before. Only you forgot. He's the guy she lives with. He works part-time at the lumber yard."

"Is Smitty his father?"

"No," he said, bending to pick up the child.

"He doesn't resemble you at all," she said. It was a shot in the dark.

"No reason he should."

"Then he's not yours?"

"He's hers. He's the reason I came home."

There was a bruise on Sam's lip. "How did you get that, big fellow?" Amos asked. Sam didn't know. Amos did. "That's not true. Smitty's the reason I came home." Maggie tried to conjure an image of a man who wanted to spend the day on a snowmobile and only got as far as Ranger.

"Are you concerned about her?"

"She can take care of herself."

Sam was responsible for Amos's unexplained comings and goings. It wasn't other women, at least not all of the time. It was concern for the child. Maggie was relieved, suddenly weightless from the slough of unreasoned jealousy.

Amos explained that Sam had been born after their divorce. His paternity was a cloudy affair, which made no difference to Amos, who was hooked from the moment that six-week-old Sam grabbed his finger and wouldn't let go. Why he continued to see his former wife was also cloudy.

"How come you get to be the baby-sitter?"

"I think I'm lucky to be the sitter. Aren't we lucky, Sam? You and me? We sure are two lucky fellows." Amos picked up the child, who continued to stare at him with solemn eyes. "This is Maggie. Maggie's my friend. See all that red hair. Looks like it's on fire, doesn't it? When autumn comes around again, I'm going to take pictures of her against the leaves. That's when you go to kindergarten. Say hello to Maggie."

They drove to the bank over the freshly plowed, cindered road, with Sam seated silently between them. Mailboxes flew by, appeared instantly in the swirling, blowing snow. Maggie reflected on Amos's reference to fall. It seemed so far away. Almost a year. A year ago she had still slept next to Alan, her face nestled against his strong, reliable back, and borrowed his razor when he wasn't looking. How did it happen that one could lose a husband, be devastated by the loss, and less than five months later lie shivering in another man's arms? Where would she be a year from now? No longer in the home she had come to love. That much was plain. Would she and Amos be together? And was she the only one who wondered?

"You're supposed to have a car seat for a little kid," she said. Amos made no response, instead, cleared the windshield with his arm.

"Does he talk?"

"He will," said Amos, "as soon as you're out of the car."

The teller was waiting for Maggie. Maggie recognized her bran muffins stacked in a tissue-lined shoebox in front of the Christmas Club window. She told Maggie that she would have to go into a back room to look at the microfiche. The search might take hours. Maggie asked if she could watch. I'm really not supposed to, she replied, but since they were on the jury together it would probably be all right.

It was tedious reading. What she saw was a ledger of her marriage in debits and credits, checks to the mortgage company, the hardware store, the auctioneer, the tree surgeon; other checks from Sybil, from the hospital, from patients, from insurance companies, from a visiting lecture series. Each check and entry increased in size and number as their income and responsibilities grew.

Maggie rubbed her eyes. She had been there since three o'clock. It had been almost four hours. There were no checks of thirty thousand, no large checks deposited in the account in close proximity to total that amount, and nothing to indicate a loan from Letitia or anyone else. How about Letitia's cancelled checks? They'd be there, the teller said, somewhere in the archives of the bank, but she couldn't review them just like that. Mrs. Hatch had to request those herself. The teller dropped her voice. What do you think? she asked. Do you think she's guilty? I don't know, said Maggie. How could she be? replied the teller. She's not responsible.

It was dark when Maggie called to ask Kristen to pick her up at the bank. Much later in the evening Maggie realized that the teller's reference to guilt had been directed at Melody Jessica.

Kristen accused Maggie of sticking her with the problem of a broken clothes dryer and of being careless with the French braid that she had so carefully contrived the night before. Fooling around was no excuse. "Someone had to pull out all the pins."

Maggie ignored both charges and announced that she wanted to return to Letitia's house. She had something private to say to her that would only take a minute and she wanted Kristen to wait in the car.

"Why?"

Maggie was tired. She couched her response in uncharacteristic homily. "The farmer waits to fix his fence until he hears frogs. That's because they're both waiting for the ground to thaw—so the frog can come out of hibernation, and the farmer can drive in his fence posts."

"What does that have to do with anyone except farmers."

Paydirt. "It has to do with picking your time before you make a move."

* * *

Maggie found Letitia rewiring a picture frame. She would give Alan's mother every opportunity, even a cue. "Did you give him the money in dribs and drabs?"

Letitia gave the wire a sharp twist. "What are you talking about, Margaret?"

"The money you loaned to Alan."

"The money was a loan to both of you."

"And the answer is?"

"All at once, I suppose. I don't remember." She carried the portrait of some bewhiskered forebear into the center hall.

Maggie followed behind her. "Show me your cancelled check. That's all I'm asking."

"It's been over fifteen years," said Letitia. "That's unreasonable. I don't keep records that long."

"The bank does," said Maggie. "Ask the bank for a copy. Call them."

Letitia turned to face her, no less obdurate and forbidding than the day she had shaken Maggie's trembling, nail-bitten, nineteen-year-old hand. "You just have to take my word for it."

Becoming Sheena wasn't easy. The queen of the jungle swallowed hard. "I'm not prepared to do that."

"There is no limit to your rudeness, is there? It explains how you could have sent the message you did with Kristen about that man's telephone number, although it is beyond me how you can care so little for your own daughter. What I absolutely don't understand is, why are you doing this? For what purpose?"

"For thirty thousand dollars."

Letitia sighed with a deep exhalation that seemed to deflate her body of all its support. "I hope you are not going to delay giving me what is mine. Owen and Jenna have signed on a note. They are committed, as am I. Owen is forty-eight years old. This is his only chance. I don't know if you know what that means. If you had two children, with one more gifted than the other, you would understand that I am saying."

"I don't see what this has to do with how many children a person has."

Letitia set her ancestor sideways. "Come to the point, Margaret."

"Without proof, I guess you'll have to take me to court."

"If you're talking about a lawsuit, that's something I would never consider."

It was irresistible. "What made you change your mind? You were ready to sue your own mother."

"Leave the house, Margaret, before I say something I will regret."

"You've been saying things to me you should have regretted for twenty years." Maggie felt good. The exchange had been like riding a bike through heavy traffic with no hands.

"What happened?" asked Kristen. "I'm frozen stiff."

The feeling continued heady and groggy like a brandy drunk. "The only thing I'll tell you is that I don't think we'll be moving in over Letitia's garage."

"You found out about the leak, didn't you? I don't know what you're upset about. It's very tiny. And Letitia is getting it fixed in the spring."

The drive was contentious, with Maggie peering over the windshield in an effort to find the road and Kristen grabbing at the wheel at every lurch. Maggie said she wanted to go through Kristen's things for a teddy bear that she remembered and an old pair of pajamas with feet so she could take them to Amos's place. There was a little boy she wanted to give them to. Kristen complained about donating the teddy bear to some kid she didn't know. "You haven't looked at it in years," said Maggie, anxious to do something for the doleful, lonely child who had been left with Amos, just as anxious, though she would not acknowledge it, to be reassured by Amos that he was as wild about her as she was about him.

"What if I don't want to go to his house?"

"I would like you to come. It's important to me."

"Why?"

I can't breathe when he's not around, and I'm out of breath when he is can't be told straight out and unvarnished to one's child. "I care about him. A lot," she said gently.

"I still don't want to go."

Maggie heard the snap of someone's driveway marker under her wheels. "Listen, I put up with Rudy trashing my house for weeks, I even let him borrow my earrings."

"Watch out! You're trying to kill us. You can't forget that, can you? How come I never hear you say anything about him fixing the M.G.? Okay. But only because you're making me feel guilty. I wish you'd let me drive."

Kristen liked the silo and everything in it—the ladder to the loft, the loft, the darkroom, the glossies of bandannaed carbine-carrying mestizos that lined the walls and the wood-burning stove. She even liked the solemn little boy who stayed, like Silly Putty, wherever you put him. What she didn't like was Amos and she made no attempt to hide it. She followed him with her eyes without turning her head, answering his brief questions with even briefer answers and refusing the Dr Pepper he offered. He, on his part, made no move to curry her favor, and while he didn't exactly ignore her, simply dropped her from his line of sight.

When Amos carried Sam, wearing Kristen's yellow pajamas, upstairs, Maggie took Kristen home.

Kristen waited until they stamped their way into the mudroom. "I don't think it's going to work out between the two of you, and it has nothing to do with that little kid."

"Why not? What makes you think that things, whatever they are, won't work out?"

Kristen faced her squarely. "He needs too much."

"Not everyone can have money." Maggie went into the kitchen where the oil painting of the boy and rooster lay waiting on the card table. Tinted wax had already been pinpricked into the remaining cracks. She would begin with the feathers. She squeezed out a dab of raw umber and a speck of carmine, checking the shade against the faded canvas.

"I don't mean money. He doesn't have it together. It would never be fifty-fifty. You would always have to be the giver, you know? Like tonight, you ran over in an awful storm to bring pajamas. He never thanked you. It was like that's what you were supposed to do. And you were the one who was always smiling at him. He hardly ever smiles at you."

Maggie poured a drop of linseed oil onto the paper plate palette and mixed it with her paint. The framer had said he wanted to see it when she was done. He said there was money in it if she was any good. How much? she had asked. He said they were not talking about museum restoration, that was mega-bucks. This was small potatoes, maybe one or two hundred bucks. "Daddy expected me to do things for him. He seldom thanked me."

"That was different. You were married."

How did she get so smart? "Couples are seldom fifty-fifty. Isn't Ranger always the giver?"

"That's not true at all. I pulled him through math. He wouldn't have graduated if it wasn't for me. Besides, I'm a lot of fun to be with."

Maggie held a magnifying glass over the painting and began to follow the direction of the original strokes. She wished the framer hadn't raised her hopes. It made her nervous. "You said he didn't have it together. Maybe I don't have it together, either."

"That's why it worked out with Daddy. He had everything, didn't he?"

Ayup. Even a girlfriend. "Your father was great."

"You ought to look for someone like him."

Smart, but not that smart, Maggie thought to herself.

Later, with the smell of linseed oil on her hands and the only sounds the creaking of the ceiling beams, Maggie dredged up desire. Along with desire was the leaden weight of guilt, creating a cumbersome twisted set of feelings, impossible to unravel, as tangled as she had been with Amos. Lovemaking in Amos's silo was one thing, but remembered passion in the kitchen of Alan's house was another.

She also knew, as she feathered the rooster's tail with light, timorous brush strokes, that she would never make plans with Justin again—not for any reason, not even pity. If it meant that she was not invited to share the society of the coupled, then she would stay home and sew lace onto sweaters, or rub a ragged canvas with an oily wad of cotton until the color shone as bright and as lucid as the day it was painted. And if she had any doubts, all she had to do was remember the simple covenant to be made beneath the skylight of a loft.

CHAPTER 17

Rebuttal

SUDDENLY IT WAS NOT just the society of the coupled that was closed to Maggie, it seemed to be the entire village. More than the partial exclusion of a widow, this was a closing of the ranks. A community's back had turned against her in a single weekend, including the postmistress, who wouldn't let her in to buy stamps only minutes after closing; Jenna, who hung up on her when she called to tell her side of the story before Letitia did; Schuyler, who forgot to check her oil, and her own daughter. All this because she had asserted herself against Letitia Hatch. The facts were not material. What was relevant was that Letitia had been there before her, not only Letitia, but Letitia's father's grandfather. It was a full house. There was no way to beat it.

Maggie even got a call from Woody Pringle, who advised her that since the contract was signed by both parties, she had to go through with the sale of the house, no matter what she planned to do with the money, so he didn't know what she was gaining.

Thirty thousand dollars that is probably mine and Kristen's, she told him. She asked Woody if he knew about the loan.

"It was before my time," he replied. But that was not

the point at all. No one, he said, has ever questioned the word of Letitia Hatch.

The only show of support came from Anne and LaDonna. Anne had left a note attached to a red-ribboned holly plant, urging her to please get in touch, and LaDonna called to ask if Maggie would go with her to the state hospital, which didn't really count since LaDonna who lived in the county, was already an outsider.

Maggie's first inkling came when she went to take her laundry down from a hastily rigged wash line. The clothes had been stiff, frozen in rigid attitudes when Maggie, thinking that wash smelled better outside, even frozen, forced them into the basket. Nathan, the man who lived on the next property, made one of his rare appearances. Usually he brought eggs from his henhouse. This time he flapped across the yard on snowshoes to complain about Maggie's folks, who had taken him to task for not removing his boulders from his own property. Old folks like me, he said, have no business sledding in the first place. Then Nathan turned and said, quite out of the blue, that Letitia Hatch was the finest woman he knew, and that while Maggie might have saved at the spigot, she lost at the bunghole. Maggie was trying to deal with what he might have meant when Amos pulled into the driveway in his pickup with Sam jouncing beside him in the front seat.

Amos rolled down his window to say that he was on his way to his sister's trailer to deposit Nina's boy. Did Maggie want to come along for the ride?

"He needs a seat belt," said Maggie, balancing her basket on her hip, the place where she used to carry Kristen. She asked why Nina hadn't returned when she knew that Amos had to be in court in the morning. He didn't know.

"She's pretty irresponsible," Maggie said.

Amos put his hand on the knob of the gear shift. "Nina does things her way," he replied.

His quick defense rankled as did the fact that she would have to wait a week to get her dryer fixed. Maggie shifted the basket to her other hip as she also tried to shift aside her annoyance, and said she couldn't go, that she wanted to but she had already promised LaDonna that she would drive with her to the hospital where they were holding Freeman. Then she told him what her neighbor Nathan had said earlier about Letitia. "I'm not sure what he means. It's possible, although I don't see how, that he knows something about the money."

Amos said to give it a rest, to stop thinking so much of the whys and wherefores. It didn't make any difference. What was, was. Knowing about it didn't change it. Sometimes you were better off not knowing. He backed up the truck, about to pull away, when she grabbed the door handle.

"I don't believe that," she said. "About not knowing. Staying in the dark is good for mushrooms, not people. Tell me something, Amos," she called into the cab, "when Nina does things her way, does that include sleeping with you?"

"Jesus, Mag, her kid's right next to me." The truck spun out of the driveway, kicking small pebbles behind it to pockmark the snow.

Maggie called New York. Sidney said Sybil was sleeping. Maggie asked him how her mother was doing. She said she knew all about her condition, so it would do no good to lie. Sidney, as she had guessed, was not as good at equivocation as his wife. He was direct. Sybil was facing bypass surgery. They were going to strip her leg arteries to bypass the clogged highways around the heart. Not immediately. She had used up whatever reservoir of energy she had. She needed to get some of it back before the doctor would perform surgery.

Maggie thought that her mother had seemed too frail for a brutal invasion of her rib cage, and was comforted when Sidney explained that it was not likely in the next few weeks. At least not until Sybil was stronger.

At least, Maggie said, the trial will be over by then. How will they determine when it's time? she asked. Sybil was scheduled to check into the hospital for tests the following week. That would give them a better idea. Will she talk to me? She's not up to it, Maggie, maybe tomorrow, he replied, and Maggie felt a knot around her own heart.

Maggie expected McKeen's rebuttal witness to be a psychiatrist. LaDonna said she hoped it was someone from Waterbury, so she could ask about Freeman. They waited to file into the courtroom, many girded against the testimony as one would prepare against a catechist from a strange religion. They were surprised when McKeen called Renfrew Hibbert to the stand.

They had seen Melody Jessica's grandfather in the rear of the courtroom. Sitting in the last row with his neck pulled into his coat collar, he seemed wizened and shriveled, yet when he stood he was lean and lanky, a rangy, somber-faced man with a strong stride, who glanced only once at his granddaughter in dispassionate appraisal, as if assessing a natural phenomenon like drought.

Giotti was as surprised as the jury, and when he objected, Judge Atwill asked both attorneys to approach the bench. Giotti flapped his tie as if it were another tongue and argued to exclude the witness, claiming that under rules of discovery he should have been informed. McKeen countered that he needed Hibbert to rebut material he could not have anticipated while Giotti argued that the defendant's grandfather had been sitting in the courtroom throughout the trial, against all practice of excluding witnesses from the proceedings. The jury heard none of this. They only knew that Giotti did not want the old man to testify.

The courtroom listened as Renfrew Hibbert related with flawless memory, and in gruff, halting tones, that he had come to Vermont at the age of seventeen from Massachusetts, to work for a dollar a day in a CCC camp on the outskirts of Brattleboro. He had been one of President Roosevelt's tree army. Maggie wished that Kristen was there to hear how he and a hundred others like him had planted trees, cleared miles of firebreaks and forest trails, and built a road through the Green Mountain National Forest by cutting through rocks and boulders by hand. Then, remembering how angry Kristen was with her, how infuriated, she changed her mind and listened carefully to Renfrew Hibbert recount how he had been bussed to a square dance in a union hall, where he met his wife, who stuck out like a blackberry in a glass of milk.

After he married, Hibbert went to work for the fish hatcheries unpacking trout eggs, which had been shipped in moss and ice, and setting them on a screen. He and his wife had one child, Joyce, a dutiful, devoted daughter who always bought beautiful cards for Father's Day and birthdays, all handpicked with real nice sayings, and never missed a one.

"Did you approve of your daughter's marriage to Dacey Bean?" asked McKeen.

"Dacey did the best he could. It's not his fault that it wasn't very much."

Shaking her head in protest, Melody Jessica whispered angrily to Giotti, while McKeen strolled to the witness box and leaned on his elbow. It appeared to be a friendly chat among neighbors. "Was your daughter, in your opinion, happy in her marriage to Dacey Bean?"

"No."

"Objection. Leading. Move to strike."

"Sustained."

The witness's response was stricken from the record as if it had never been spoken. Maggie thought how convenient it would be to be able to do that with her own words, like those that she had said to Amos about not wanting success, or worse, what she had asked the day before in the driveway. She would not, however, want to have disregarded what she had said to Letitia. To repudiate that would be to repudiate herself.

"Do you know whether or not the deceased ever wanted children?"

"I can't say. She never talked about such things with me."

"How did you learn that your daughter was pregnant?"

"She brought me a picture from a catalogue of a cradle made out of some kind of net, like a hammock. 'Can you make this for me, Daddy?' she asked. That was all she said about it."

"Let's move closer to the present, Mr. Hibbert. How would you describe the relationship between the deceased and the defendant." McKeen pivoted to face Melody Jessica and to point in her direction. The move was a reminder to the jury that she was on trial.

"Touch and go. Jessie never knew what the girl was going to do. She'd be quiet, then wham, she'd tear off to do something she wasn't supposed to."

"You said Jessie, sir. Didn't you mean Joyce?"

"Did I say Jessie? I meant Joyce."

"Did the defendant ever run away from home?"

"Yes."

"Objection," said Giotti. "Beyond the scope of rebuttal."

"Overruled."

"Did she ever steal?"

"She stole all the time. From her mother's pin-money tin. Once she stole two packages of Reese's peanut butter cups from the five and ten."

"How do you know that?"

"I was the one who went to pay for the candy."

He bought her a baby doll. She threw it into the trash bin. She wanted the kind with boobs. She wanted what she wanted *when* she wanted it. She was always that way.

Some of the jurors wondered how a grandfather could testify against his own grandchild. Apparently he did not understand that his testimony could sentence her to prison, and that he would probably be dead before she got out.

It was a strong rebuttal.

That morning, Sidney had handed the telephone to Sybil, saying, "Here's your mother," in the same brisk tone of transfer in which McKeen said, "Your witness." Sybil picked up the phone in her old way, with the lilting, infectious cadence that Maggie never knew was real or performance. She was feeling better. She was getting rest. When Maggie asked if surgery had been scheduled, Sybil replied that she was waiting to talk to her doctor. Don't put it off any longer, cautioned Maggie. Sybil promised that she was not planning to do that.

Maggie told her about her confrontation with Letitia. It had cost her Kristen, for the time being anyhow. Kristen had demanded to know if Maggie's assault on her grandmother had anything to do with the fact that Maggie no longer wore her wedding ring. "Don't think I didn't notice," she had said. Sybil had no trouble with the revelation that Kristen was angry, giving it less attention than a broken nail. At certain times, she said, it didn't make sense to do what your children wanted if it wasn't what you wanted. Besides, it was a question of two people being unhappy versus only one. You had to do what was right for you. It worked out, usually, to be the best for the child. Maggie decided not to challenge that remark and told her mother that when the trial was over, which looked like it might be very soon, she was coming to New York. Maggie's motivation, which was partly unfinished business and partly a desire to just get away, remained unspoken.

This was not the time to validate insights—that while Maggie had been an attentive mother and Sybil had not, the results seemed to be the same. Kristen was doing exactly as she pleased, choosing a path that felt right for her, just as Maggie before her had done what she thought best. What it boiled down to was that no matter the style, a mother was just a curator and the exhibition, if things had been done the least bit right, moved on.

LaDonna stood by the window of the jury room, still wearing the hospital visitor's pass. It was pinned above the Christmas ornament to the dress she had worn the day before, a gray wool she said she wore from mill to meeting. Maggie unpinned the visitor's pass. "You don't need this anymore," she said. "It's only good for one day anyhow."

"He looked good, didn't he, Maggie?"

Freeman had looked bewildered, but Maggie didn't say that about the man who sat hugging his arms in the solarium. "He looked like he's being well cared for," she replied instead, "so you can relax on that score."

"What he did," said LaDonna, "anyone can do. If you pushed a person far enough, anyone."

"Maybe," said Maggie. She did not want to argue.

"He doesn't belong in that place," said LaDonna.

"No one does," said Maggie, remembering that Freeman had cried when they left. She talked of what they would do when the trial was over. Wouldn't it be nice, she asked, to just sit at a kitchen table and have coffee with no place to rush to and nothing to do except visit?

LaDonna agreed that it would be nice, but her thoughts were on her husband sitting puzzled in a place that smelled of urine and Lysol, like a man who could get lost in his own sap orchard.

Giotti began his cross-examination as if he were rushing the net. He asked Renfrew Hibbert about his days in the Civilian Conservation Corps. Hibbert testified that he wore green army surplus uniforms, was awakened by reveille at six, did calisthenics before breakfast, usually push-ups, forty of them.

"You testified before that you had to scratch away at rocks with a pick and shovel. That's something I'm also trying to do, sir, in a manner of speaking," said Giotti, with the deference due a witness to whom the jury was sympathetic. "You also testified," continued Giotti, "that Melody Jessica ran away from home before your retirement. When did you retire, sir?"

"Five, no, six years ago."

"Six years ago Melody Jessica was nine. Are you saying she ran away from home before the age of nine?"

"Guess not. Must have been after."

"So you are not certain of the dates?"

"No," he replied, and the jurors shifted in their seats.

"You said the defendant had tantrums as a young child. How would you describe these tantrums?"

"Joyce took you down steady, like sandpaper."

Giotti paused, showing his puzzlement to the jury. "Joyce? You mean Melody Jessica, don't you?"

"Yes, sir. Jessie."

"Mr. Hibbert, how would you describe the relationship between your daughter and your granddaughter?"

While the witness hesitated, the door to the courtroom opened. Justin Herrick settled on a bench at the rear in time to hear Hibbert reply, "My daughter put up with a lot. Joyce is a stubborn girl. She won't let you say no to her."

Giotti spoke softly. "Who is a stubborn girl, Mr. Hibbert, Joyce or Melody Jessica?"

Hibbert seemed annoyed. "Jessie," he replied, "try to get it straight."

"A few minutes ago," said Giotti, "I asked a question relative to your retirement. Do you remember the question?" Giotti waited, there was a pause while Hibbert strained to connect the dots of his recall.

"Can't say that I do."

"You met with the state's attorney prior to this morning?"

"Yes."

"Sir, what is the state's attorney's name?"

"I know it. As well as my own."

"It begins with an M."

"Objection. Badgering the witness."

Judge Atwill's focus was keen and made even more acute by the objection. The night before she had come off badly during a television spot when she had tried to explain her position on decriminalizing drugs to a hostile interviewer. She rubbed her hand across her brow and sustained the motion.

"How much social security do you receive monthly, sir?"

"Three hundred eighty-five dollars."

"Do you know the amount of your daughter's estate?"

"Not to the penny. It isn't much, I know that."

Giotti read from a slip of paper. "The exact amount, including her insurance and what is left in the bank, totals exactly $15,042. Are you aware, sir, that under state law, if one is convicted of taking the life of another, he or she may not inherit from the person whose life he is convicted of taking?"

"No. I didn't know about that law you're talking about."

"You are under oath, sir."

"I said no, and no it is."

Judge Atwill's voice was acid. "The witness has answered the question, Mr. Giotti."

"I'm sorry, Judge. I apologize to the witness. Are you aware, sir, that you, as the only surviving relative of Joyce Hibbert Bean, stand to inherit this money if Melody Jessica is found guilty of the crime for which she is charged?"

"I object to the question," said McKeen. "It is a collateral issue. The defendant is the one on trial here, not this man."

"Overruled," said the judge, and Maggie wondered why.

The jury filed sadly into the jury room, sickened by the demolition of the old man on the stand, by Giotti trying to impeach Hibbert by showing that his memory was faulty. A few on the jury were beginning to forget names. They could identify with the deficit. Maggie felt sorry for him, as they all did, yet she was determined not to let that affect her evaluation of his testimony, just as she was determined not to let Kristen's angry glances change her mind about not handing over thirty thousand dollars to Letitia.

Maggie returned Anne's call from the jury room. Anne said she needed to talk to her in person. Maggie replied that if it was some kind of apology, she was not interested. If it was some question about single life, Anne would have to find out for herself, the way she did. Maggie said she was no tour guide.

Anne explained it was something else, something confidential that she could not discuss over the telephone. Then she asked if Maggie knew about Maybeth's brother, Harold, who was being investigated for insurance fraud, and if Maggie had taken in the holly plant.

Maggie didn't know anything about Maybeth's brother, Harold, although she did know that Alan would never give him any insurance business. She had taken in the plant, but said not to attach any significance to her action since she wouldn't allow any plant to freeze if she could help it, even a plant that she didn't ask for, even a plant with poisonous berries.

She was in no mood for Justin, who was waiting for her in the parking lot. He told her that he had come to take her to supper. His attention made an awkward situation more so. She was hoping to be able to talk to him on the telephone, to tell him that she thought it would be a good idea if they didn't see each other any more. It certainly would have been easier than the face-to-face confrontation they were sure to have. But it also would have been gutless, at odds with the confidence she was beginning to feel, leaving it back on the gantry where it belonged. At the very least, Justin deserved a turn-down in person.

Justin said he had to get to choir rehearsal by seven o'clock. That gave them two hours. He was hoping to see her after dinner as well. He took her to a tavern. They were the first customers in the dining room. The tavern, he told her, had been a terminal on the underground railroad. The room they were sitting in had been the waiting room where runaway slaves had sat on benches waiting for the wagons that would carry them to Canada. A few of the benches, grooved on their seats and arms by impatient fingernails, still lined the walls.

Maggie ordered dinner although she was not hungry, waving away Justin's attempt to order for her. When the waitress left, she announced that this was as good a time as any.

"You want to talk?" he asked.

She nodded. He hung their jackets and sat across from her, then reached for her hand as he offered observations of the trial. "That old man's mind is like a sieve. His testimony, as far as I can see, is worthless."

She faced him squarely. "You know I can't talk about the trial. You know it. Why do you insist?"

"Loosen up, Maggie. I'm only trying to help. Sometimes an outside perspective on a situation is all it needs to make something clear. Were you surprised to see me?"

"Yes."

"I like to be spontaneous when I can. It livens things up." He took off her glasses and cleaned them with his handkerchief. "What would you like to talk about?"

"Us."

"Maggie"—he settled her glasses over her ears and spoke softly—"I told you early on that I was not interested in anything more serious than being loving friends."

"I know."

"And you'd like to change that."

"You might say so." She held up her hand. "It's this. I don't want more of a commitment. I want less. I guess what I want is no commitment at all."

He leaned back in his seat, trying to get a jump ahead of this latest development and trying to figure out her next move before she figured it out herself. That was the trick with women as far as he could see. You had to stay a step ahead. He asked about the other guy.

"His name is Amos," she said. "But I don't know how much this has to do with him. I think if I would feel this way even if I didn't know him. I'm sure I would." That was a revelation, even to herself. And she realized that it was also a large part of the attraction to Amos, who offered at best a free-floating, marginal commitment which matched her need to *be*, and her need to get back sensation and feeling, without the constraints of definition.

"He's a one-way street, Maggie."

"What is that supposed to mean."

"He can't do anything for you."

"Maybe I can do something for him."

"You know what I think. I think you're still in mourning. You're still grieving. It's getting close to Christmas. Emotions get all tangled up this time of year. Take it from someone who knows. It's been a few years since I lost my wife and it's still happening to me."

Maggie thought about what he was saying and knew that some of it was true. The lid was coming off. Feelings that she had locked out of sight were becoming more difficult to suppress.

When the waitress brought rolls and butter, Maggie asked about the widow from Dorset. It was a tactical ploy, a way of shifting focus, showing him where his strengths lay. "I'd like to hear more about your friend. I hear she's a great cook."

"Emily is more than just a good cook. More than a little old lady in tennis shoes if that's what you're picturing. Emily is strong, resourceful. She was part of the group that drove to Connecticut to protest testing suturing devices on dogs. I'm surprised that you don't seem to know her. She apparently knows a good bit about you."

Maggie became wary. Something in his glinting smile told her to be careful. She approached his remark gingerly, cautiously, the way she had once trod with Alan through Nathan's trap-laden back ten searching for Kristen's lost cat. "Like what?"

He wiped his mouth with his napkin. "I don't know if I should tell you this."

"Tell me."

"She claims that you're the cause of the divorce between Anne and Peter Bouchard."

Maggie was outraged. "That is absolutely untrue!"

"That's what she heard." The defense rested, having implied and left hanging an accusation, like Giotti asking

Renfrew Hibbert if he knew he stood to inherit his daughter's estate if his granddaughter was convicted.

They ate the rest of the meal in a silence that was punctuated by only the most courteous remarks. The argument resumed out in the parking lot. He could not believe that she was calling it off, especially since they were so good together.

"Let's stop this," he said. "It's some kind of reaction. Maybe guilt. I don't know. But it's not what you want. I know you better than you know yourself."

It was the ultimate arrogance. Maggie wished at that moment that she was strong, muscle-bound like Ranger, with biceps and deltoids pumped up with snaking veins, strong enough to knock Justin down and when he struggled to his feet to knock him down again.

"Let me change your mind," he said. "I'm a patient man. I'll wait."

"Don't make a move on me, Justin. Just don't do it."

"All I want is a chance to straighten this out."

He grabbed her, yanked her to him, and kissed her, while she pushed out of his embrace like an insect struggling from an outworn carapace.

"You kiss like a dental hygienist, Justin. You ever been told that before?"

That seemed to do it. Justin drew on his gloves and opened the car door. They drove back to her car in silence while Maggie thought that this is what it had been like when she turned down Peter: the same silent, angry response, the same contempt. For one moment she thought that Alan would be pleased. She also realized that there was a good chance that Amos would say he didn't care one way or another.

CHAPTER 18

Closing Arguments

THEY MET IN THE pancake house. Anne ordered grapefruit juice and black coffee. Maggie ordered a waffle with pecans which she heaped with whipped cream and dollops of butter, great heaping spoonfuls that plopped when they fell and melted on contact. Maggie knew the personal cost of self-denial to Anne, a career dieter with a keen appetite, and when she caught the greedy glint in Anne's eye, she poured maple syrup on the waffle, making lazy, elegant, amber-colored rings.

Anne made an offering, a votive gesture of inside information about Maybeth's brother, Harold. Considering that Harold was a selectman, it had come as a terrible shock to everyone; nevertheless, his wife was standing by him. No one could believe it. Hope Dyer said that her husband said that the thing that Harold worried about most was homosexual attacks in prison, but that didn't seem much of a likelihood since Harold was grossly overweight and quite unattractive.

Maggie blew out the candle. She said her stepfather, Sidney, told her that they liked fat men, that when they got one, they tied a rope around his middle and pulled it tight so he looked like a woman.

"That's not funny," said Anne.

"I have to get to the courthouse," said Maggie. "What do you have to tell me?"

Anne leaned forward and pulled in her lower lip. "I know all about the business with Letitia."

"Who doesn't?"

"The point is, Mag, I know about it, and I think you're right."

Maggie waited, holding her loaded and dripping fork lovingly to her lips.

"You have to be careful with waffles," cautioned Anne. "Six hundred calories at the very least is something to think about."

"It depends on what else you've got going on in your head."

"What I have to tell you isn't easy," said Anne. She spoke in a whisper, checking first to see who was seated nearby. "Alan talked about you. A lot. In fact, sometimes all he talked about was you. You may not believe this, but that used to upset me."

"No one would believe this conversation."

"I thought that would make you feel better, about me, Mag, that I was jealous of you." Anne folded her hands on the table, an indication that everything was above board, a variation of the handshake, the ancient function of which was to show the absence of weapons.

"Alan worried about you. He didn't think you could manage alone. He thought about the effect on Kristen and Letitia. In fact, he wanted to wait until Kristen finished college, but you were the main reason he couldn't consider a divorce."

"That makes me feel great." The rheostat of Maggie's mood turned from disbelief to anger. "Maybe he didn't want a divorce. For any reason. Maybe that was just the excuse he gave you. Maybe Alan didn't want to marry you. Ever." *Don't strike that from the record.*

Anne accepted the sting with the grace of a true penitent. "He told me everything about you, Mag. I know that the hospital bookkeeper kept your accounts because Alan didn't trust you with the checkbook. I even know you argued over whether or not Kristen was sleeping with Ranger. Incidentally, I want you to know that I agreed with you on that. I know some things even you don't know. Once you made a harvest figure. Alan got Kristen to tear it down because everyone kept telling Letitia it was flashy."

So Alan had told Kristen to pull out the stuffing. How unfair to put an eight-year-old in that kind of bind. On the other hand, maybe she had liked the assignment. "Okay. He told you everything. So what?"

"Here's the point. Here's what I'm leading up to. Alan told me everything about the two of you. Himself included. We talked about everything. I know when he increased his fees and how much. I know how much he spent on your birthday present."

"According to my mother," said Maggie, "it couldn't have been very much."

"It was seventy dollars, not including tax. I'm not telling you this to hurt you but to prove that I know what I'm saying. He would have told me about the loan if there had been one. I know he would. Besides, he wouldn't have kept a loan of that size for that length of time. He would have found a way to pay it back. It would have bothered him. He never said anything about it. That's why I don't think there was a loan, in case you have any doubts. Although, frankly, I would not like to be quoted."

Maggie set down her fork. She wasn't hungry anymore. She felt sick, like when she used to spin on a piano stool until the seat fell off. "How long did it go on, between you and Alan?"

"Ten years, more or less."

"Ten years! That's like a marriage."

Anne's eyes became slick with brine. "Not exactly," she said. "It's more like living in the freezing compartment of the fridge, always on ice, always waiting for the next time you see one another alone, waiting all week for ten minutes, a half an hour, once in a blue moon, a morning, a late afternoon, usually in some sleazy place with plastic mattress covers. Most plans cancelled by a phone call—someone's shoulder needed to be set, something with Kristen, with you, with Letitia, afraid to dial out in case he was calling in. It was just one long wait on top of another. The time we actually spent together probably totaled no more than a couple of weeks."

Anne began to cry, her chest bellowing great heaving, silent sobs. It was unexpected. Maggie watched, at first with the unblinking appraisal of a lizard, then realized that Anne was still doing heavy-duty grieving, which Maggie had begun to replace with the keloid of a duller, less finely honed sadness. It was easy to figure out why. Maggie's feelings for Amos had begun to cover her sorrow, like gravel heaped upon a casket. More significant, Anne had experienced no betrayal to jolt her out of it. For Anne, it was just another long wait. Someone had told Maggie that the word "widow" in Sanskrit meant empty. If that was true, then it was Anne who was the widow.

Maggie left her side of the booth and slid in beside Anne, then put her arm around her jerking shoulders while the waitress dipped over them with a pot of steaming coffee and a cheerful, unenlightened grin.

"I want you to know," sobbed Anne, "I agonized for months before actually sleeping with him. The worst thing, Mag, is having to keep the most important person in your life in a closet."

The crying stopped with a deep sigh. All that remained was a freshet of tears that glossed Anne's cheeks like dew. "What's he like?" she asked. "The guy you're seeing. The one on the jury with you."

"He's not like anybody you know," replied Maggie, amazed at the transparency of Anne's dynamics, the association to keeping someone in the closet, glistening beneath the surface like a fish. She thought of Sunday when Amos had taken her to the abandoned granite quarry, hidden in the hushed woods, bordered with piles of granite and eerie, sheer walls. They had come upon it suddenly, the crime scene which they weren't permitted to see, spanned by a trestle and filled with frozen spring water and snow melt. Amos showed her where old railroad ties poked up beneath the snow like ribs. When the trial was over, he was coming back to shoot in the late afternoon when the shadows were the longest.

She hadn't wanted to go on two counts. The jurors had been instructed not to do so, and even more of a deterrent, it had been the scene of death. Why was that more chilling than a curtained hospital bed? Maybe it had something to do with the silence. Hospitals were noisy.

"We're not supposed to be here," she had said.

He had looked at her strangely. "You really believe that they hand out rewards for playing by the rules, don't you?"

She had gone to please him, but it still had not been enough.

Anne dried her eyes and lifted her head from the cradle of Maggie's shoulder. "I hear he's a hunk."

"He's good-looking. My mother says he looks a little like Alan, but I don't see it. Alan was taller, crisper, starchy like his lab coats. Alan smiled more. Amos looks disheveled, troubled, like he's been buried alive. And he's younger, but not by much."

"Do you love him, Maggie?"

Maggie had skirted that question. Now she fingered it carefully, like a garment for sale on a hanger. "I don't know. I think about him all the time. I feel alive when I'm with him, most of the time anyway, and miserable when I'm not." She did not tell Anne that he was never really there when she needed him or that he was guarded and cautious. Nor did Maggie confess that she had to be careful what she said to him and that she didn't know much more about him than when they had first met.

"Do you want to marry him?"

"I can't think of him in those terms. Not yet, anyway."

"Can't he commit?"

"It's not something we discuss."

"It's funny how some women go for the same type."

Alan and Amos were not the same type at all. Alan spoke with authority, supported by evidence, logic, and the persuasion of charm. Amos was full of muddled facts. Whenever he started to talk about anything serious, Maggie felt her ears hum. In a strangely proprietary way, she was annoyed at the comparison and returned to her own side of the booth. "He may look a little like Alan, but he's nothing like him. Alan liked to talk about things. He liked to take them apart, examine every aspect, and put them together again, like he did with his patients. Discussions were big with him—actually they were more like lectures, with me taking notes. We talked about everything. We even talked about you and Peter."

"Really? What did he say about me and Peter?"

"I think he said that he thought Peter had a bigger sex drive than you did." Maggie pulled it out of her recall, a rabbit she had forgotten she had.

"Alan said that?"

Maggie brushed it aside as unimportant, too insignificant to have been anything but the truth. "I think so. I don't really remember. Anyway, Amos is different. He holds back, keeps things in. I don't always know what he's thinking."

"Maybe you only think he holds back. Maybe he has nothing to say. Maybe you're smarter than he is."

Maggie had thought about it, but had put it aside. She had suspected that their mental fit was bad, mainly because she had to pretend to be less in order to please him; she had to bite her tongue to keep from correcting him. But she would not give that to Anne.

"You mean the smart one talks and the dumb one listens?"

"Don't be defensive with me. Please, Mag. Not when we were beginning to fix things between us."

Maggie knew they would never again be like they used to. Betrayal stood between them. So did the sobriety of responsibility.

They sipped coffee and talked about Peter. He was out of the house, renting a converted barn near the mountain. He had a steady girlfriend that he was seeing openly, a twenty-five-year-old ski instructor from Montreal. Anne said she was told that because it was no-fault, the divorce would not take long. She added that she had put up with Peter as long as she had Alan. Alan made it bearable.

"They're blaming me," said Maggie. "Can you believe that?"

"I can't imagine who started that, Maggie, but I set the record straight where I can," replied Anne. "Things are bound to get twisted."

"You didn't help any." Maggie asked why Anne had been so angry and had given her such a bad time when she must have known all along what had really happened between her and Peter. Because, replied Anne, it sounded like it could have been true. Besides, if she didn't try to play the injured wife, there were bound to be suspicions. She had to lay them to rest.

"Don't you see?" she asked.

"No," said Maggie. "I don't." But she did. It was far more basic than even Anne suspected. Everyone had made a fuss over Maggie when Alan died, babied her, petted her, pitied her for her loss. No one had said poor Anne.

"Did he ever say anything to you about a faculty appointment to the med school?"

"He was hoping for one," replied Anne.

"He told me that he was thinking about it," said Maggie. "I just found out that he actually applied." The next question was hard to ask, but the information was more important than the loss of face. "Did he ever hear anything, one way or another?"

"He was being considered," said Anne. "You'll be happy to know that he made the short list. He was very excited about that."

Maggie tried to remember Alan's behavior in the last few months, weeks, looking for signs of zeal, however bridled. How could he have kept excitement hidden from his family? More to the point, why?

"If you're wondering why he didn't say anything to you," said Anne, "the reason is, he didn't want you constantly asking him if he had gotten it. That's very difficult for someone waiting on tenterhooks for anything. This way, he would be able to surprise you with good news if he got it. If he didn't, well then, you wouldn't have worried over nothing."

Maggie signaled for the check, writing in the air the way Alan used to, and asked if Anne was dating.

Anne smoothed her hair back into its bow. "In a manner of speaking. The problem is that there's not a lot out there that I would consider."

Maggie smiled. "I know someone I could fix you up with," she said. "You've met him." Then she stood, pulled on her parka, and jammed her hair into a woolen hat.

"Call me tomorrow?" asked Anne.

"I can't. We're going to be sequestered."

Informed by the clerk to prepare for an overnight stay at the Paradise Motor Inn, Maggie lugged the soft-sided weekender that she had ordered by mail from a U.S. Air catalogue into the courthouse. The jury room looked like a bus depot, its oak floor littered with valises, boxes tied with string, shopping bags, garment bags, duffel bags, hampers, and anxious jurors making frantic last-minute phone calls as if they were being forced into exile.

Maggie found LaDonna repacking her valise. Maggie wanted to tell her about her breakfast with Anne. She began by asking about Freeman. LaDonna refolded a blouse and said that she had spoken to the charge nurse that morning. Freeman was still under observation. He would be there for weeks. Then LaDonna carefully packed each garment as she talked in an obsessive monotone about the days when the baby—that was Janine—had ridden in a backpack while LaDonna balanced a zinc pail between her knees and milked. Sometimes LaDonna didn't have the time to fix her hair, but Freeman never seemed to notice.

"We worked together side by side, sixteen hours a day," she said. "We were a pretty good pair, planning, scrimping . . . Freeman said we pulled together as good as his Clydesdales."

Maggie decided that this was not the time to ask a friend on the edge what she thought about anything. "Hang in there," she said. "Today's the closing arguments. Today or tomorrow we go into deliberation. As soon as we come back with a verdict, you'll be able to visit with him whenever you like."

"Then what?" asked LaDonna. "It won't ever be the same after what he did."

It won't be the same after what Alan did, either. "Nothing stays the same," Maggie replied. "That's for sure." They both had suffered heartache, both had felt the iron grip of its tetany. The difference between them was its resolution. LaDonna didn't expect things to get better. Maggie did. But why?

McKeen seemed more somber than usual, his voice as metallic and silvery as he was. Where before he had been only courteous, now he was deadly serious. "You already know what I'm going to say," he began, "but I want to repeat it. I promise not to take much of your time."

He knew that the jury was anxious to finish their deliberations before Christmas. He confronted their impatience head-on, coming so close they could see the extra crease that had been ironed into his shirt collar.

"Sometimes you need to ask the jury to be hard-hearted because the law demands a seemingly cold and heartless choice. But if you studied law as I have, you would know that laws are designed to protect the rights not only of society, but of individuals. Joyce Hibbert Bean is not here to fight her battle. The law, and you, are here to do it for her."

While the judge rocked in her chair, the state's attorney

stuck to the issues, knowing that the jurors considered an attack on opposing counsel the weak and desperate act of a poor sport. He told them that the testimony of a psychiatrist had no validity in a murder case because the descriptive phrases she used were too speculative. One could allude to almost any adolescent as being susceptible to suggestion without making a case for diminished capacity. When he said that the case she made against the deceased was largely a guess, based on bits and pieces of gossip, Maggie was reminded of all the gossip that had kept everyone in the village as vulnerable as clams without shells.

McKeen was saying that Kevin Clapp had given them a unique inside view of what had happened, the only person besides the defendant who could have told them. "I'll agree," said McKeen, "that he is not an admirable kid. But I am asking you to believe him because his testimony makes sense in light of all the other evidence."

The prosecutor turned to face Melody Jessica with a knit of his eyebrows. "You heard testimony as to how this defendant led school officials and neighbors to believe that her mother went to Florida. You don't cover your tracks unless you think you have something to hide."

McKeen concluded his summation with a reference to Renfrew Hibbert's testimony against his own granddaughter, asking the jury to think of the pain that must have caused him and to ask themselves if there was any motive but the truth that could have brought him to the witness stand.

Maggie turned to Melody Jessica, only a few yards away. The girl, who returned her gaze with pouting hostility, was getting a pimple on her forehead. She had had an unpleasant childhood at best. Kneeling on rice and salt was not the punishment Maggie would have meted out. Sitting beside her counsel, she looked so helpless, so vulnerable. It was difficult to believe that she had committed anything more serious that sticking gum under a table as she now did. Maggie thought of one's hands and feet suddenly swelling from failing kidneys and turned away. What an awful way to die. Alan had been only forty-three. That was awful, too. Maggie frowned in an effort to close off the tears. She thought she was through with totally unreliable emotions that spewed like a faucet without a washer.

Giotti looked neater, slimmer, and squared off, as if he had been pressed between the pages of a book. He checked his notes, made that morning on a yellow pad, and began by urging the jurors to find Melody Jessica less than competent, without the capacity to fend off Kevin Clapp's murder plan or to appreciate the consequences of her actions. He reminded them that his client had taken the witness stand, which she was not required to do, and asked them to recall the answers she gave.

"Melody Jessica," he said, "was not rational a week before her mother's death, she was not rational a week after. What is the first thing she did after Kevin Clapp arranged to dispose of the body in the quarry? She forged absence excuses so she wouldn't have to attend school. Kevin Clapp? He had an indictment hanging over his head. You have a right to question his motive, to weigh whatever Kevin Clapp said in the light of the deal he made with the state's attorney.

"You heard the testimony of my client's grandfather. What made him come to court? A simple motivation. Money. How much credence to give his testimony? You heard his confusion, his memory lapses. I leave that choice to you."

Giotti strode from the juror's box to where Melody Jessica sat and put a protective arm about her shoulder. He told them that when they examined the evidence, they would find that this was not a murder but a manslaughter lacking deliberation, premeditation, malice, and the voluntary will necessary to all three states of mind. He concluded with his hands clasped as if in prayer as he told them that the presumption of innocence and the requirement that a person be proven guilty beyond a reasonable doubt was a priceless heritage. "If you have any doubts at all about guilt in this case," he said, "you are bound under your oath to resolve the doubt in my client's favor. Hundreds of people are lined up against her. We are all that stand between Melody Jessica Bean and a vengeful society, twelve of you and one lonesome lawyer. I will take those odds. I believe I can depend on you to see that Melody Jessica Bean gets a fair trial."

The attorneys sat at their tables like team players at halftime, hunched over their benches. Someone behind Maggie whispered that McKeen got one last turn at bat. Maggie wondered if either of them had been sincere or only acting—like Sybil.

Amos had something to tell her. He grabbed her wrist and pulled her toward him with his characteristic muffled urgency. Even a tug on the wrist had an erotic effect. Conditioned by a long-term marriage to carefully thought-out foreplay, Maggie was certain she was losing it.

He was enthusiastic, as much as she had ever seen him be, not a rolling-boil enthusiasm, more like a bubble that blips to the surface of a simmering pot. He had gotten a call from the American Folklife Center. Someone there—a folklorist, an anthropologist, he wasn't sure—had seen his photographs: ice fishing, tag sales, old men in suspenders, young women with long, straight hair snapping rubber bands over canning labels, and one that Maggie had not seen of Willard Peterson and his bees. They wanted his prints. The pay was not high because the prints would be available without cost from the Library of Congress. Amos didn't care that photographers received no residual income from sales of stock photographs. His work would live in the library's collections. It was a major break.

They wanted to meet him and were willing to pay his expenses for the opportunity. He was planning to leave for Washington, D.C., as soon as the trial was over. His good news made Maggie feel unsettled, formless, like

Jell-O unmolding too soon. Amos was ephemeral at best. Success, however limited, gave him wings that Maggie was not prepared to deal with, just as she was not prepared for the feeling of panic because the accommodation between them, the balance, had just been upset. She told him that she planned to go to New York as soon as the trial was over and that after she saw her mother she could take the train to Washington and meet him.

"I don't know if that would work out," he said.

"Why not?"

"What if I'm done meeting with the people at the Folklife Center and you're not ready to leave New York? I'd have to wait around and twiddle my thumbs. Or the other way around. You've had it with New York, you're ready to come to Washington, and I have to hang out at the Folklore Center. Either way it's a hassle."

"We're not talking about a long-term engagement here. We're talking about meeting in a motel room." With a bed that has top sheets, she wanted to add.

"That's the point, Maggie. It wouldn't be in a motel room."

"Then where?"

"I'd be staying with a friend."

"What friend? A guy? A woman? Why do you always do this? You just can't be open with me, can you?"

He wondered why she always had to nail everything down. Why nothing was ever enough. "You don't mean open, Mag. You mean a lock."

A woman. Anne was right. He couldn't commit.

When McKeen stood for his closing rebuttal, Maggie was still angry and still trying to understand Amos. She attempted to concentrate on McKeen, who was saying that the state would have been happy to have six selectmen as witnesses, but that the state didn't get to choose its witnesses, that it was the defendant who had chosen Kevin Clapp.

"Is it rational," asked McKeen, "to forge your mother's

signature on absence notes after you have murdered her? You bet it is. To call Kevin Clapp a replacement for Dacey Bean is insulting to Dacey Bean as well as to your intelligence. The defendant had a built-in replacement for her father, someone who was there all the time, her grandfather. As to his memory, those of you who are getting up in years know how easy it is to forget, from time to time, a name or a date. It doesn't mean that the person doesn't have all his marbles. It doesn't mean he's not sharp.

"The saddest thing of all is that Joyce Hibbert Bean, a widow with a child, tried to earn money in the only way she could. For that effort, she has been villified as an uncaring, abusing mother. How many men and women in this courtroom," he asked, "would have earned the same label given the same criteria?"

McKeen wrapped up. He told the jury that the process of deliberation had required an appreciable time to elapse between the formation of the plan to kill and the fatal act. He reminded them that this was no impulsive shooting or stabbing, but a methodical, slow delivery of poison, resulting in weeks of painful dying, a dying by inches, totally inconsistent with any notion of suicide, and that when the defendant saw her mother weaken, heard her complain about lesions in her mouth, headaches, dizzy spells, saw her hands and feet swelling because of failing kidneys, she had plenty of time to stop it. Still she did absolutely nothing to get medical help.

Maggie thought of how Sybil's feet had swollen at the end of each day. The next time they spoke on the phone she would tell her to watch her salt, then realized that salt had little to do with a heart muscle that would fail without surgery. She remembered walking behind Sybil once into The Four Seasons. Sybil had just been turned down for a part in a new show. Making Maggie follow after (it would not do to advertise a daughter who was almost fully grown), Sybil strutted in on four-inch spikes as if she owned the place. Maggie realized that it was not *what* that made the difference between her and LaDonna but *who*, a mother who looked life in the eye and winked.

McKeen came close to the jury, facing them squarely, and asked that they and their common sense act on the evidence and return the only just verdict in this case in the name of the people of the State of Vermont—guilty on all three counts.

The alternates were excused. Nervous and apprehensive, the remaining twelve jurors glanced about at the eagles that mounted the chandeliers, at the spectators crammed in benches that looked like church pews, at exits through which they could not leave. Willard Peterson's sciatica acted up. He adjusted his seat cushion, hoping that this would not take much longer, while Hobart Straw hooked his thumbs under his suspenders.

Judge Atwill, relieved that this portion of the trial had concluded without error, dismissed from her mind the phone call in which she had been asked to list her assets and outside investments, which meant that she had a good shot at the party endorsement and gave the jury its instructions.

"The question for you to decide," she said, "is whether there has been generated a reasonable doubt as to the defendant's intentional state of mind, whether the prosecution has proved beyond a reasonable doubt that the defendant did, in fact, act with premeditation, deliberation, and malice."

When she was through, the jury was swimming in judicial guidelines and rules of law. Most of the jurors understood little of what they had been told. They were led by a uniformed sheriff's deputy and a court officer into the brittle winter sunshine to a waiting school bus. Amos told Maggie that her hair shone like copper in the light, but she didn't hear him. She was trying to juggle everything she had been told, including what was meant by a preponderance of the evidence and a voluntary state of mind, the distinctions between murder and manslaughter, and the judge's last instructions that the testimony of an accomplice be scrutinized with care, and that motives be considered in determining how much weight and credibility such testimony be given. She compacted information into her head just as LaDonna had done earlier with the contents of her valise, and as she had crammed for exams twenty years before.

It might have been the crisp, fresh air that cleared Maggie's head or the trial that had shown her the two parts to truth. Perhaps it was McKeen's last question of the jury that had allowed her to jettison hostility toward Sybil in a single pitch, that let her see that while it was true that Sybil had left her alone for weeks on end like a plant you give a neighbor to water, a habit that once made Maggie wish that her mother looked like Imogene Coca, it was also true that Sybil was someone special. The contrail of her glamour still wisped, proof that she was born to light up a stage or a life, if only in a bit part or a walk-on, trailing a feather boa or a skinny, owl-eyed child behind her.

CHAPTER 19

Deliberation

JUDGE ATWILL APPOINTED HOGAN to be the foreperson. She did it for three reasons: his educational background and managerial experience suggested that he might be a good discussion leader; his behavior during the trial showed interest without intensity; and he was black, the only black on the jury and one of a handful in the county. It was a way of expressing judicial impartiality, hoping that by her example, the jury would be likewise moved.

When the bus discharged the members of the jury at the entrance to the motel, they were led to their rooms, which were all on one side of a single wing that smelled of carpet freshener. Except for Trish Robidoux, who insisted on private accommodations according to Hannah Watson because she didn't want anyone to know that she wore false teeth, everyone doubled up. LaDonna and Maggie shared a room, and Amos shared one with the carpenter. After a surf-and-turf supper with the sheriff's deputy and the bailiff at a long, polyurethaned table made of seashells and lobster traps, they returned by bus to the courthouse to begin their deliberations.

Hogan suggested that they try to get agreement on some of the facts. "I think we're going to spin our wheels unless we stick to some kind of agenda," he said, reminding the jury that they were fact finders, which Maggie thought inaccurate. If they were truly fact finders, why hadn't they been privy to all of the facts, some of which seem to have been managed by the lawyers and the judge, deciding among themselves, through some series of private codes, what the jury could and could not hear.

Not everyone spoke. Several jurors, like LaDonna and the canner, kept silent and deferred to the others. A few, like the bank teller and Maggie, checked with those around them, searching out affirmation in eyes and mouths. Others, like Hannah Watson, were off the mark, tangential, skirting the issues like fringe. For the most part, the jury understood their charge, yet they seemed to assume no personal responsibility toward its resolution.

Certain jurors had trouble with the meaning of "voluntary." Hogan handed a written request for a definition to the waiting bailiff. When the answer came back—that to be voluntary an act must be the result of a person's conscious choice—Willard Peterson leaned back in his chair with his arms folded across his chest. He had made up his mind. He had made it up in the first week of the trial. The defendant was as guilty as sin. Slicker than goose grease despite her girly ways. Period. End. All the talk of consciousness or unconsciousness, as far as he was concerned, was a waste of time.

His resistance led the jury to attempt to decipher the ideograph of emotional abuse. It was too vague for most, and they were getting tired. Bruises could be seen. Emotional abuse was something you had to accept on faith, like fossil bones. Even worse, what they were doing was gathering evidence against a dead person.

The bank teller stirred sugar into her coffee and timidly reminded them that the psychiatrist had said that examining behavior was no different from an autopsy. Katerina Lodz admonished her. They were supposed to disregard that remark.

"I can't pretend I didn't hear it," replied the teller. She sipped her coffee. "What about the report from the public-health nurse? That was pretty condemning as far as I'm concerned."

When Amos said there was plenty of evidence of Joyce Bean's indifference, Hobart Straw argued that locking a kid out of the house wasn't so bad. He and his wife kept their kids outside lots of times, especially when they were evaluating items for the Thursday night auction.

"What about sticking notes on the refrigerator?" asked Amos.

"I do that sometimes," said Maggie.

"It's not the same. You talk to Krissie all the time. The Bean woman hardly ever spoke to her kid."

It was the first time Maggie and Amos had addressed each other openly, and it confirmed what Hannah Watson had whispered around weeks ago, that these two were as thick as wool.

Trish Robidoux broke the silence that followed. "She may not have been the warmest person, I'll grant you that, but that doesn't mean someone else has the right to poison her to death."

"The right to kill isn't the issue," said Hogan. "It's whether the mother caused a defect of mind that would make the defendant susceptible to the suggestions of another."

"I think it's pretty obvious that the kid is out of it," said Amos. Hogan asked him to be more specific.

Amos tipped back in his chair and folded his hands behind his head. Before he could answer, Maggie cut in: "I disagree. She had a goal. She worked toward it by washing cars all spring. That means she knew how to plan to get what she wanted, and it demonstrates to me the kind of resourcefulness you don't associate with anyone who's out of it."

The clench of Amos's jaw told her that he was angry. She wished she had not interrupted him. What was the hurry to speak? While Hogan suggested that it might help to think of diminished capacity as a kind of sliding scale just short of insanity, and that they take a poll before they called it a night, Maggie tried to assure herself that Amos's refusal to meet her eye was only his way of safeguarding their privacy.

She tried to talk to Amos alone, tell him she hadn't been showboating, but there was no easy way to get to him without attracting attention. If the other jurors weren't poking their heads in and out of doorways like turtles to see if anyone had razor blades or change for the candy dispenser, the sheriff's deputy sitting on a chair in the hall had his eye on every door. She finally found him at the ice machine. She said she hadn't meant to put down what he was saying. She had gotten caught up in the discussion and it just came out. His response was not the assurance she sought. Instead he said that it wasn't the first time she had put him down. She left with an empty paper bucket, puzzling over the fragility of their relationship.

LaDonna's preparations for bed included Scotch-taping her bangs to her forehead and folding her bedspread down to the foot of her bed in neat accordion pleats. "Men don't like women who best them," she said, as Maggie lay staring at the ceiling, berating herself for not letting Amos finish what he was saying, even if he was wrong. Maggie suddenly felt trapped, wishing she could use the phone to call out, to talk to Kristen to see what she was doing, to Sidney or Sybil, whoever answered the phone, to find out the results of whatever tests were taken, specifically how soon a by-pass could be scheduled. She hoped that Kristen had remembered to let the varnish dry before she took the oil off the boy and the rooster to the framer.

LaDonna tucked herself in bed, folded her hands on the topsheet, and said she had been selfish. She hadn't asked Maggie about her mother and she asked to be forgiven. Her daughter, she explained, had gone to see Freeman. He didn't speak, wouldn't even talk to the doctors. Worse, he refused to walk, although there was no reason why he couldn't, and Janine had to push him around in a wheelchair.

LaDonna turned out the lights. They spoke in the dark across the empty space between the beds. Maggie said she was worried about her mother and that her daughter, like Freeman, wasn't speaking.

LaDonna's thoughts were elsewhere. "Hannah said that the Clapp boy liked devil music," she murmured in the drowsy voice of one about to fall asleep. "As if that was important. It doesn't prove a thing. When my folks found out I liked Elvis Presley, they thought I had gone to hell and back. That same Sunday the organist's wife stuck these flannel figures on a board and taught us how Satan tricked Eve into eating the apple and God took off her clothes. I know she was talking to me on account of Satan had Elvis's face pasted on him."

"Did you think I came on too strong?" asked Maggie.

"Which time?"

When the jury reconvened the next morning they were argumentative and combative, railing against one another for both the enforcement of their responsibility and the impossibility of their task. It was the first time since deliberations had begun that LaDonna volunteered anything. She spoke softly. The others strained forward in their seats to hear her definition of manslaughter. "It's where you kill someone without wanting to," she said. "In a way, it's an accident."

The canner shook his head. "I don't know," he said. "If her mother turned mean all of a sudden, like a change-of-life sort of thing, and they had a quarrel and the girl shot her, I could buy manslaughter. But the girl was involved every step of the way."

"I thought we had all this down last night," said Yancy Scruggs. "We're getting buried under shavings. At this rate, we'll be here all year."

They folded back upon themselves like a Möbius strip to the testimony of the psychiatrist. Willard Peterson said he didn't set much store in all that gobbledygook. The teller, on the other hand, argued that the prosecutor had accepted Dr. Michaelman as an expert witness. He couldn't have it both ways just because her testimony went against him. Either she was an expert or she wasn't, and if she was, they had to take seriously what she said. Trish Robidoux said that the reason McKeen didn't use a psychiatrist was that he didn't believe in them, either.

"Maybe," said Amos. "Or maybe that's what he wants us to believe so we won't give too much weight to what she said."

That led to a discussion of how the assistant principal's testimony had dovetailed with that of the psychiatrist. When Amos reminded them that Spaulding had testified that the Bean kid did what she was told, Maggie wanted to argue that, of course, that's what Spaulding would say. It showed that he was doing his job. He couldn't very well stand up and admit that kids don't behave in his school. Instead she kept silent and picked off a cuticle.

Willard Peterson shook his head. He had no such compunction. "Folks who see a little helpless sweetheart in there should take the blinders from their eyes and try thinking of her as a smart cookie instead. As two-faced as a double-bitted ax."

Katerina Lodz changed the subject. She announced that she believed the grandfather.

"I don't know how you can do that," said Amos. "He wasn't just mixing up their names, I think he was confusing his daughter with his granddaughter. Besides, the old man had a motive to lie."

Maggie sighed. She was certain that Hibbert, who thought enough about his granddaughter to pass forward a handkerchief, would not have made that trade.

The conference table grew quiet, then the canner spoke carefully, as if picking up a broken string of beads. He suggested they return to diminished capacity. Hobart Straw said that the girl had covered her tracks. You don't do that, he explained, unless you have something to hide. Amos got up and stretched, then said that if Straw was talking about the postcards and the absence notes, the girl had done what the Clapp kid told her to.

When each became convinced that the others were stubborn, unreasonable, and selfish, they became angry, with an all-stops-out annoyance that eliminated politeness and allowed them to carp and rail at one other, take the last plastic spoon, the last packet of sugar, or the last drop of coffee with no excuses, no apologies. It wasn't until the teller argued that the defendant had to have diminished capacity—how else could she have killed her own mother? —that Maggie resettled her frames on her nose and spoke again. "It's not logical to think that because the crime was horrible, the person who did it has to be crazy. All murder is insane."

"Insanity isn't the subject," said Amos, "diminished capacity is." He directed this to Maggie. His tone made it clear to her that he was still galled from the night before.

Maggie's brakes were losing their lining. She didn't tackle Amos head-on. Instead she turned to Hobart Straw. "You said something about the defendant covering her tracks. I agree. Like her chewing gum. She's been sticking it under her table every day since the trial began when she thinks that no one is looking. I think she's capable of knowing what to conceal and when it's time to conceal it."

"That's not admissible evidence," said Hogan, who then called for an open ballot. Maggie changed her vote from undecided to murder two. Her reason: Melody Jessica's testimony that her mother had not wanted her to go out for cheerleading because it might affect her ability to bear a child. The result was three votes for murder in the first degree, three votes for murder in the second degree, and six for both categories of manslaughter. Hogan asked the jurors to explain their positions.

Maggie didn't think that her reason, which was based on a guess of a dead woman's values, was enough to persuade others to change their votes. While the jury cajoled, shouted, and kept injured silences until, like pieces of nutshell lodged between their teeth, the issues of *malice* and *intent* emerged central to their disagreement, she ruminated over the questions of whether Amos had contested her because of principle or ego. Was he angry because she had contradicted him, or because she had made a good point?

They were interrupted by the bailiff, who asked if progress was being made toward consensus. Hogan informed him that while there were shifts in positions, they were no closer to a consensus than they had been the day before.

Judge Atwill had them brought back into courtroom, having just been assured by a physician at Columbia Presbyterian that the Hatch woman's mother was not critical. Relieved that she did not have to make a judgment call, she explained malice and intent, then instructed the jury on the meaning of a deadlock and how to avoid one.

The jury returned to their assembly room, refilled their coffee mugs, and, except for Yancy Scruggs, who had begun to pace, took their seats around the table. They were determined to look for some piece of evidence that would allow them to change their minds in a way they could live with. Hannah Watson said it would be on her conscience if the defendant hurt someone else. That was why she was changing her vote.

"Why didn't you change your vote this morning?" asked Trish Robidoux. "You might have saved us some time."

Hogan said there was nothing wrong with letting something sit for a while. Changing their minds was the only way they could ever hope to come to a unanimous position and that no one was accountable for when or how late in the game they changed it.

The teller reminded them that a defendant does not have to take the witness stand. No lawyer, she insisted, would have put his client there unless he was certain of her innocence. Katerina Lodz said the reason he had put her on the stand was to show how stupid she was.

They continued to sit in self-centered, isolated silence, which was broken only by grudging opinions and an occasional confrontation. When LaDonna said she could live with murder two if a diminished-capacity defense meant that complete acquittal was not an option, a fourth ballot was taken. It resulted in ten votes for murder in the second degree, with Willard Peterson holding firm to murder in the first degree and Amos fixing himself to manslaughter.

Hogan handed a note to the bailiff which said that while progress was being made, they might have to stay overnight, while the remaining jurors moved to convince the two holdouts to adopt the majority position.

Willard Peterson had said he didn't have any doubt at all. He had known from the first. The jury jumped on him. He had promised under oath to make up his mind only after he had heard all the evidence. "All right," he said. "I'll change my vote if someone can give me a convincing argument, but so far all I've heard is a wagonload of potholes."

Hogan asked if he could honestly support the position that the defendant was able, maturely and meaningfully, to reflect on the consequences of her acts.

"She knew right from wrong," insisted Peterson.

"We're not saying she didn't know right from wrong," argued the teller. "We're saying she wasn't very good at it." Then she said that Peterson had heard the same evidence they had. What more did he want?

With the herd's instinct that their quarry was weakening, the jury moved on to Amos. He stood firm. The girl was missing a piece. She had acted under the boy's sway and it was not her fault. He really felt the verdict should be involuntary manslaughter. He was willing to consider voluntary manslaughter, but that was as far as he would go.

Maggie had kept herself in check long enough. She knew it by the ragged hangnails she had picked. "Her grandfather said the same thing the boy did," she said, "that Melody Jessica was headstrong. She knew what she wanted and she went after it." Like I'm doing now, she thought. Amos was glowering. She didn't care. The truth was more important. So was her ability to tell it. Her rising voice squeaked like sled runners on snow: "You're picturing her as some kind of taffy head, and she's not. She's pretty definite about a lot of things. How about watching your mother die inch by inch? You don't think it takes malice to be able to stand by and watch that happen?"

"Maybe," he said.

"And what about having sex on your dead mother's bed?"

"I don't think I could get into that."

Hobart Straw and Yancy Scruggs laughed. Hannah Watson pursed her lips. "I find that in very poor taste," she said, "and I know I speak for the rest of the jury."

Trish Robidoux leaned across the table, putting her face within inches of Amos. "Don't you believe in going along with the majority?" she asked. "How can eleven people be wrong?"

"Ten," said Willard Peterson. "I haven't said I'd change my mind."

Maggie hesitated, reluctant to put Amos down again, but equally reluctant to sit on her thoughts. "Why is it so hard for you to imagine," she asked, "that Kevin Clapp took orders from Melody Jessica? What if she had said to him, 'I want to kill my mother. I want to poison her, but I don't know with what. You're good in chemistry. How do you poison people? What do you use?' "

Amos tucked his thumbs under his chin and regarded her with steady caramel eyes. "Her lawyer asked her that on the witness stand. 'Why use poison? It seems like a lot of trouble to go to.' And she said, 'I don't know, maybe you better ask Kevin.' "

Maggie thought that dependency wasn't always a need. Sometimes it was a habit, like the thousands of jars that Alan had opened for her even after she got the hang of knocking their lids on the counter.

Amos was still speaking, something about women being like that when they were in love, following a guy to places they really don't want to go, or doing things they didn't really want to do. Was he talking to her or thinking of Nina? "The law provides an escape hatch for this kid," he said.

"Not an escape hatch," said Hogan. "Just a reduced sentence. She's not off the hook."

"A reduced sentence even if they caught you red-handed?" Willard Peterson shook his head. "That's what I can't see."

"It's not something I invented," said Hogan. "The law says that under certain circumstances, a person is not held completely responsible."

"It seems to me we can negotiate this thing," said the canner. "You're talking about degree. The rest of us just think she's a little more responsible than you do."

"I'm having the same kind of problems that Mr. Peterson is," said Maggie. "I guess that's because I think it's a weak defense to begin with. On top of that, her lawyer tries to make it stick with flimsy evidence. Some of it I buy, but most of it I don't. You stare at the ceiling of a motel room long enough, and you realize that there are no hard facts to support the notion that her mother abused her emotionally. He made me do this, she made me do that. The bottom line is, that it's all just a cop-out. Everyone has an excuse. All of us. And it's usually someone else. You made me spill that because you were talking to me; you robbed me of my independence because you took over; I killed her because she didn't love me enough; I ran away to Canada because it was the only way out."

Oh, God. It was what she had started to say in the pickup. Maggie fought back tears by blinking hard and thrusting out her chin, while LaDonna rested a hand on her shoulder. "If Maggie's short as pie crust, it's because her mother is in the hospital."

Amos stood up to peer through the frosted window at the sleet. "Where else did you see malice?" he asked.

Maggie spoke to no one in particular. "They rode out on bicycles to see her mother's body. It was an outing. They even went to a pep rally first. They were going to take pictures, but it was dark in the quarry, the way it gets in the late afternoon, and Kevin didn't have a flash. If taking your friends to see your own mother's decomposing body isn't an act of malice, I'd like to know what is."

"How do you know how dark it gets in the quarry?" asked Trish Robidoux.

Maggie felt her face radiate. "I was there once," she said.

Amos turned and faced her. His look was one of injury, of contention. "What about free will?"

"Her mother told her not to try out for the cheering squad. She did it anyway. That's not being docile and obedient. That's being willful."

"You weren't there during the trial, were you?" Trish Robidoux persisted. "Because if you were, it's something we should all know."

Amos came to stand behind his chair, rubbing the palms of his hands along its wooden rung. "I'm ready to change my vote."

"If Mr. Peterson will go along," said Hogan, "that makes us unanimous." Willard Peterson paused before he cast a ballot for murder in the second degree.

When Hogan informed the bailiff that they had reached a verdict, some of the jurors expressed remorse. Hannah Watson said that she didn't know how she was going to look at that sweet, trusting face, and Yancy Scruggs wanted to explain to Melody Jessica that this was the best they could do.

Maggie, on the other hand, felt the numb, exhausted victory she had felt when she had swum across Lake Catherine on a dare from Alan and had hoisted herself, sputtering and blind, from the mossy shallows.

They filed into the courtroom, where they took their seats for the last time beneath the furled state flag with the words "freedom" and "unity" inscribed over the emblem of a cow and three bales of hay. It was dark outside.

Sleet scratched the tall, narrow courthouse windows, which were now black and shimmering with winter starshine. The day before, the courtroom had been packed. Now only the principals, a handful of spectators scattered like birdshot, and Melody Jessica's grandfather remained.

"Ladies and gentlemen of the jury," said Judge Atwill, "have you reached a verdict?"

"Yes, Your Honor," said Hogan. "We have."

The judge instructed Hogan to hand the verdict to the clerk. The clerk in turn handed the verdict to the judge for scrutiny before publishing to the court the jury's finding of murder in the second degree.

Giotti requested that the jury be polled. As the clerk called jurors by name, Renfrew Hibbert rubbed his eyes as if trying to pull them toward the bridge of his nose, while his granddaughter glared at the jury in hurtful surprise, then returned their perfidy by retrieving a wad of gum.

It was a difficult moment for Maggie. She had to stand apart from the other jurors and acknowledge that the verdict was her own. She met the girl's wrath head-on, trying to smooth her own face into an impassive, objective mask, not realizing that this was what Letitia did.

Judge Atwill thanked the jury for their labors and apologized for removing them from their normal lives. Before discharging them, she invited any jurors who felt troubled by their decision to meet and talk with her. It was over. Giotti slapped his folders together with the verve of a man already planning his appeal. The court reporter snapped off her paper ribbon. And Melody Jessica Bean, stopping to adjust her banana comb, was led away by the sheriff's deputy.

Judge Atwill was proud of this jury, as she was of most. Deprived of their usual supports, they had been plunged into a disturbing, intense experience from which they could not turn away. Yet they had come through. She recognized a representative of the Grange waiting in the rear of the courtroom to speak to her about the problem of erosion. Sidetracked for a moment by the downside of candidate accessibility, she continued to watch the jury file out. She was gratified that LaDonna had stuck it out during difficult circumstances, but partial to Maggie, who had brushed herself off during the course of the trial like someone whisking cobwebs from their eaves. She waited to see if Maggie would turn back, a sure sign of guilt, of wavering, of the timid waffling characteristic of certain women. *Don't do it,* she urged, *keep going,* as Maggie paused, took off her glasses to wipe them on the edge of her sweater, and walked out, not even stopping to fall in beside the Stringer fellow as she had done every day for the last few weeks.

Except for Katerina Lodz, who kept her distance, everyone in the jury room hugged or patted one another's backs, and promised to keep in touch. Maggie avoided Amos. She shook hands with Hogan, and waited to embrace LaDonna on the steps of the courthouse. "Will you be all right?" she asked.

"Just being able to make it through without falling apart was a big thing," replied LaDonna. "I'll be okay."

McKeen came down the steps with his briefcase in his hand. He thanked them both, said that his mother had a box of lace for either one of them, and asked Maggie if she was in the telephone book. He knew she was. It was his way of telling her he was going to call. Maggie said she was still listed under her husband's name, but that in the new book she would be listed under Maggie. Somehow she had been expecting it. Now, perhaps because she just wanted to get into a hot, steamy tub, she was only mildly interested.

After he left, Maggie remarked that she had been awed by McKeen until weeks ago, maybe even days, until she noticed that he had lint on his socks. She told LaDonna that she would call her tomorrow and that they would see each other soon.

"I'll understand if you don't," replied LaDonna. "You

have your own life. I guess I have one, too, except I'm kind of packed between straw in the icehouse until they decide what to do with him."

It was bitter and windy. Maggie pulled her woolen hat down over her ears. "One of the best things about this trial was getting you as a friend."

"And him," said LaDonna.

"Maybe," said Maggie. "I don't know."

"I do." LaDonna smiled and began to pick her way carefully over the ice as Renfrew Hibbert tramped stiffly down the steps, muffling his neck against the cold.

"He's the one I want to say I'm sorry to," said Maggie.

Amos came up behind her. She didn't hear him. "Talking to yourself is the first sign," he said. "Come on, I'll drive you home."

Maggie jammed her mittens into her coat, realizing that of all the things she had said, the reference to running from the draft was one likely not to be forgiven. "What I said about Canada," she said, "it just slipped out."

"Don't reel yourself in, Mag."

"I'm not. It's what I really feel. I'm just sorry if I hurt you in any way." She stepped closer, relishing the familiarity of the wood scent that lingered on his mustache and the erotic jump start that followed. "What about you?" she asked. "What do you feel?"

He played with the fringes of her woolen scarf before he spoke. "I guess I love you," he said, then drew her to him, pulling her by her scarf, ignoring Giotti, who hustled down the steps.

Why were the words so necessary? They were only a collection of sounds, but as satisfying and complete as the seal on an envelope. Yet there was no question that she and Amos were a mismatch. It was like the way the locals dressed, a discordant, defiant, haphazard put-together, even those well fixed, as distinguished from the tourists and second-home people who coordinated their handbags, shoes, tops, and bottoms, even their hiking gear, with conscious dedication.

The simple truth was that they didn't belong together. She had been raised in the city, he in the country, not the town squire enclave that Alan had enjoyed, but pig-worming country. She had enjoyed some privilege, he had grown up in a family that scrambled for a living. The only thing Maggie and Amos had going for them was bed, and they couldn't make love all the time. What was left? Conversation was not like it had been with Alan, not that Amos didn't follow what she was saying. He just wasn't interested in turning everything upside down, preferring instead to touch base with a proprietary clutch at the back of her neck. Yet he wasn't boring. He wanted to show her things. It wasn't his fault if she didn't much like ice fishing, and it was not as if she could predict his thoughts, at least not all the time. He wasn't as urbane as Alan or Justin. On the other hand, he had little of their arrogance. The simplest truth was, they were interested in each other, electroplated with each other's image, spun together in some magnetron neither of them understood. They had reached a crucial threshold, had cracked a door from which there didn't seem to be any turning back.

There was no one home when they stomped their way into the mudroom after a check of the garage. Maggie wanted to test the M.G. It started fine despite the fact that the engine had been turned over only once since Rudy left. Amos said it was not a good choice for a year-round car. Maggie said she knew. She had been driving the sensible choice for fifteen years.

They pulled off their boots and shook the sleet from their coats. "What would have happened," she asked, "if they had found out about the quarry?"

"Who knows? A mistrial, maybe. Maybe not. It didn't happen. Forget it."

Then she stopped at the landing and turned. "Did you really change your mind, or were you rescuing me?"

"I don't know."

"Which one was it? I want to know."

"Nothing is ever black or white, Mag. I have a thousand proofs in every shade of gray that will tell you that." He buried his face in the pleats of her slacks and wrapped his arms around her. She felt his need and the warmth of his mouth through the flannel. Nothing else seemed to matter. Not even finding out how Sybil's tests went. It was too late to call in any case. That could wait until morning.

Later, he cursed the bed. While it had served for immediate need, it would not do for any sustained activity. The thing could not be fixed. He had already tried to brace it once, after his forage into Kristen's room for the almond oil. There was no way he was going to have that stupid canopy wave over his head. Maggie was equally intractable. It was too cold to go downstairs into the study. Besides, she had stripped the sheets from the pullout sofa and was too tired to put them back. The only answer was to get Alan's tools.

Amos was dismantling the canopy when Kristen opened the bedroom door. She said she had seen the light on from outside, then gave Amos a grudging nod, and asked if the trial was over.

Maggie said it was. She was as astonished at her daughter's radiant good looks as she always was after a separation, and was reminded for an instant of lying in a bed with Bo Peep painted on the headboard—it must have been a crib, there were slats to peer through—and Glinda the Good, in a pouf of Bal de Versailles and spangled pink, smiled in on her in a halo of hallway light. Maggie thought of something else. Something vague and blurry, like trying to see through frosted windows, something about snow angels and Glinda the Good. Then it became clear. It was Sybil who had held her hand and fallen into the snow beside her, perhaps in Central Park, who knew where; it was Sybil and she who had made snow angels with their outstretched arms. That was why Kristen didn't remember.

Kristen appeared to want to say something more. With her hand on the doorknob, she said that Sidney had called to say that Sybil was worse. She asked if that meant that Maggie would have to go to New York.

"When did he call?" asked Maggie, who was now bolt upright, wrapping herself in a sheet.

"An hour ago. At Granny's."

"Sybil's your grandmother, too, Krissie. Why is that so hard for you to get?" Maggie instantly regretted the transaction. It had been two days. She could have put a lid on it. But then, so could Kristen.

Kristen looked aggrieved. "What is my almond oil doing in here?" she asked.

Maggie looked to Amos, who was still tinkering with the bed. "I thought you put it back."

Kristen grabbed the bottle from her mother's dresser. "Get your own," she said, with the same lift to her chin that Sybil used as an exit line.

CHAPTER 20

Verdict

AFTER A NIGHT OF staring into the dark and lying curled against Amos like a spoon in a drawer, Maggie made arrangements to take a late-afternoon flight to La Guardia. That way she could still make visiting hours, yet attend to errands that had been neglected while she was on jury duty, like mailing a second insurance claim to Alan's surgical society with a copy of his death certificate and picking up the boy-and-rooster painting at the framer. While the framer wouldn't say that her restoration was good, he said that it was not bad, and he wanted her to try to repair another primitive oil for one of his customers, a couple from New Hampshire whose attic-stored painting had been ravaged by bat droppings.

It was a hurried breakfast with frequent interruptions like Maggie bolting from the table to pack something she suddenly remembered to take; a telephone call from Anne to say that Justin had called to ask if she was as calculating as she looked, and to ask if that was his standard opener; and by Kristen, who ran downstairs to tell Amos that her toilet was clogged.

While Amos sprinted upstairs with the plunger, Maggie squeezed her eyes into pinpoints to slip a safety pin through her broken glasses. She told Kristen that she had decided to give her the Datsun and she could plan to take it to school in January.

Kristen swooped some of her pale blond hair behind an ear. "What about you, Mom? How are you going to get around without wheels?"

Maggie breathed on her glasses. "I still have the M.G."

For an instant Kristen's expression was like that of Melody Jessica's when the verdict had been read. "You don't know how to drive the M.G."

"You said the same thing about the Datsun," said Maggie. "If I have to choose between which one I can't drive, I pick the M.G. Besides, I do know how. Ranger taught me."

"Ranger? When did Ranger teach you?"

Maggie taped a note to the lid of the dryer. "Make sure the repairman sees this. When did he teach me? I don't remember. I think you were washing your hair."

Kristen was injured was on two counts. It was not clear which she thought worse: her boyfriend's perfidy or her mother's selfishness. "Granny gave it to Daddy. You hardly ever drove it. You hated it."

That was true. It was also true that part of the reason she had hated it was because it had been a gift from Letitia, just as it was true that Letitia had given everything to Alan. If Alan's mother had made an equitable distribution between her sons, Maggie was not aware of it. Alan, the younger, was clearly her favorite and, to the extent that Maggie's stiff-necked mother-in-law permitted herself any display of affection, she adored him.

Maggie bent to put the wet clothes in the laundry basket and remembered something that McKeen had said—that in every case there is a piece of evidence that comes out and bites you, like the chewing gum that Melody Jessica stuck beneath the defense table. What bit Maggie was that Letitia had had every reason to believe that she would die before her sons. Since Letitia had not asked for the money, especially in the last ten years when Alan's earnings had increased substantially, it was possible that she never had any intention of getting it back. It was only with Alan dead, and the realization that she could survive both sons, that her efforts, possibly out of guilt and remorse, turned to Owen. Like the crime picture that Hogan had asked the jury to reconstruct, it was a scenario most consistent with a reasonable doubt and with the facts as Maggie knew them. But the facts also included a picture of Letitia propped up by lifelong principles so rigid she could not have lied to Maggie. It was not in her repertoire. Neither were a heart fatally bent on mischief, an evil intent giving rise to an unlawful act, or an action flowing from a wicked motive—the judge's definitions of malice.

Kristen still wore the disgruntled frown of someone who had been betrayed. "I asked you for the M.G. first," she said.

"I know," said Maggie. "And I'm not giving it to anyone else. Just me. And don't forget to hang these up."

Kristen complained that the whole washload was stained because Amos had left a Magic Marker in his shirt pocket. "How come we're doing his stuff anyway?" she asked.

Before Maggie could answer, Amos thundered downstairs. The sound was a familiar one. It was nice to have it back. "I think it's okay," he said. "It wasn't clogged. The float was stuck. All I did was bend it back."

Maggie thought that men must be born knowing such things. Kristen was less impressed but grateful. "You're good with toilets," she said, "but my Vermont Granny can wire stereos."

Maggie controlled an impulse to smile and collected her belongings. She put on her Manhattan winter coat, a hated Lanvin leather trimmed at the hood and cuffs with Mongolian goat—a gift of Sybil's—then hugged Kristen, who wrinkled her nose at the fur and said that it looked like it had been crinkled with a curling iron.

"You can still come with me," she said.

"I hate hospitals," replied Kristen. "They smell funny and they're noisy. I'd rather come next week."

Maggie felt a lurch, a jolt in the solar plexus at the memory of the last time she had been in a hospital. Noise was what had kept her together when Alan died. Noise and the crush of people in the corridor. "You're not supposed to like hospitals."

"How soon do you think they'll send her home? I need to know so I can buy my ticket."

"I'll call you as soon as I find out."

Kristen handed Maggie a roll of paper bound in rubber bands. "Tell her the lighting cues are highlighted with yellow marker."

"I don't know if Sybil is up to a script."

"It's not a script. It's a prompt book. She said she wanted to see it."

"When did you talk to her?"

"Last week. I called her on the phone."

"Let's go, Mag," said Amos. "We've got a lot of ground to cover."

Kristen looked over her shoulder at her mother's boyfriend. "I don't know if my dad would have liked you," she said. "I'm trying to decide."

He smiled. "I don't know whether my dad would like you either, so we're even."

"I know he doesn't like me," added Maggie, pulling on her gloves and smoothing each finger into place.

"Why do you think she did it?" Kristen asked.

"She's talking about Melody Jessica Bean."

"Don't ask me," replied Amos. "Ask your mother. We don't think alike on this."

"Why not? I thought you had to. I thought it had to be unanimous."

Snow fell like granola in fat, wet flakes quilting the ground in cushy pads of white. Maggie had to be helped into the front seat of the pickup. She said it was the coat's fault, then said there was an advantage to having a kid who was too young to ask questions.

Amos slid in beside her. "If you mean Sam, he asks questions all the time. He just doesn't ask them around you."

Maggie said that her first stop was Letitia's. She had to settle something between them, and asked if he wouldn't mind waiting in the truck. He said it was fine as long as she didn't take forever. He turned on the heater, then rubbed his nose in her hood, and said the fur was turning him on.

"Stop it," she said. "You're getting it all wet."

"Yeah," he replied in an escalating sigh.

Letitia was standing on a dictionary in front of her bedroom mirror, while Jenna, wearing an unlikely apron tied around her riding pants, was on her knees basting her hem. Jenna, whose outrage had been tempered by her sense of family, turned to nod to Maggie. "I didn't hear you come in," she said. "You look tired. You must be worried about your mother."

Maggie acknowledged that she was both tired and worried, and that was the reason why she was going to New York. When Jenna reached into her apron pocket for a spool of thread, bit off a piece with her teeth, and wet its tip with her tongue, Maggie thought that ties of family were like Jenna's apron strings: two strands of love and guilt that held everything together.

Letitia asked to be remembered to Sybil and said that it must have been a difficult trial. She would never ask Maggie anything more specific. It was part of her cultural reticence, the same brakes, in addition to arthritic changes, that prevented her from swinging her hips when she walked.

Maggie slipped off her hood and said that it hadn't been all that difficult, thinking that for weeks the jury had been her cornerstone. She was sorry in many ways that it was over. She worried about Melody Jessica and the sentence she would receive, yet like Letitia, she was not about to reveal a bit of it.

"In any case," said Letitia, stiffly executing a half turn, "you can feel gratified that you performed your civic duty despite your loss."

"I thought you didn't like fur," said Jenna.

Maggie's reply was for Letitia. "I don't like it, I don't hate it. The same way Letitia feels about me. Isn't that true, Letitia? Isn't that how you feel about me?"

Letitia sighed. "Not true. I always thought you made little effort to take hold, but I never disliked you. Why push this, Margaret? What does it accomplish?"

Jenna told Letitia to unclasp her hands. It made the hem uneven.

"You told Alan not to marry me."

"Maggie," said Jenna. "For heaven's sake. How am I going to ever get this thing straight?"

"Whatever I said," replied Letitia, "I acted in Alan's best interests. You're a mother. You should understand that. I said you were city-bred and that you were young. I said that you would find it difficult to be separated from your mother."

"That was the easy part," said Maggie, sorry she had spoken even before the words were uttered.

"Actually," said Letitia, "I remember that your alienation from your mother was a consideration. I felt it would affect our relationship. It worried me." She stepped down from the dictionary. "We included you in everything, Jenna and I and Owen, and Alan's father. You lived with us for two years, for heaven's sake. What more did you want?" Letitia stepped away from the mirror. "We'll do this later, Jenna. I would like you to tell me, Margaret, what more did you want?"

"For you to call me Maggie."

"Is that all? I find that hard to believe."

"That's all," said Maggie, asking herself if there were any truth to what Letitia had just said. Maggie wondered if she had transferred disaffection from one mother to another, as Letitia implied.

"I'll try to do that, Margaret. Certainly. If that's all you wanted, why didn't you ask me ages ago?"

"Maggie."

"Maggie."

It was an empty, barren victory. Letitia's Maggie was not the Maggie that Maggie wanted. She pulled back the curtains. Amos still waited in the pickup below. "I came to tell you something. The money is yours, the amount that you asked for, as soon as the check clears from the sale of the house."

Letitia stepped closer, one hand touching a scarf pin. Although her slate-gray eyes glistened, there was no spillover. Maggie didn't expect any. "Thank you," she said.

Maggie put on her hood. A wisp of fur fell across her eyes and she blew it back.

"Then you'll be moving into the apartment?"

"I don't know yet."

"When will you know?"

"Maybe by mud season. I want to see how bad the roof leaks. I want to see if I can find someplace I like better."

"With him?"

"I don't know."

Jenna stood. Her hips shifted like saddlebags as she rose to her feet. "Let us know if you need anything," she said. "When you're ready to move, Owen and I want to help."

"Sure," said Maggie, wondering how Owen and Jenna were going to make any money from vitamins. "I can always use help."

"It would be nice if you stayed close by," said Letitia. She asked for any other of Alan's things that Maggie wasn't going to keep. Then she asked, almost as an afterthought, if Maggie still felt Alan's presence in the house.

"No," said Maggie. "I used to, but I don't anymore. I know he isn't there." Maggie didn't tell them that what she felt was that somehow Alan had deserted her. With him she had been shielded by everything society said was good, and suddenly his protection was gone, like a fence that has been torn down. She wondered if she could ever disconnect from the event, be anything but its victim or ever be able to separate the sound of "death" from its meaning. She wondered why being someone's widow and someone else's lover were not mutually exclusive. Then, in a kind of afterthought, an insignificant, soon-to-be-forgotten tag like a rag on a kite string, it occurred to her that Letitia was also a widow.

The framer occupied a converted carriage barn, the walls of which were covered with chevrons of wood and metal. A disbarred attorney from somewhere in Pennsylvania, he dressed like a woodsman in a checkered flannel shirt, down-filled vest, and hobnailed boots that gave away their owner's urbanity by their high gloss shine.

Clicking like a tapdancer, he carried the painting from the back room and tore off its wrappings. It appeared to be an early eighteenth-century scene of William Penn making a peace treaty with Indians garbed like classical Greeks. The brush strokes were coarse as if laid on with the tail of some animal.

Maggie searched for the signature, already planning in which corner she would begin her slow, careful rotations with solution-dipped cotton balls and razor blade, cleaning in a seamless glide, then mending the holes with canvas patches and muting her palette to match the umber tones. It was her own special skill, a combination of methods that she had learned from someone else and techniques that she had developed on her own. The result was a gift, handed to her as if on one of Letitia's silver platters, a way to earn a living doing something she loved. It wasn't the same as sewing lace onto pillows. That was therapy. This was making something right again; this was restoration.

She asked him if it would be all right if she didn't begin

working on it until after Christmas because she was going to New York to see her mother.

He replied that it would be fine as long as she didn't take longer than two weeks to finish it and added that if she was going to do it professionally, that she should see about getting insurance in case she ruined anything. He reminded her that he expected a finder's fee, and then told her he knew she was going out of town.

"How did you know?" she asked.

"Nobody ever wears a coat like that around here. That's what I love about this place."

Amos and Maggie arrived at the airport two hours early, then settled at a back table in the coffee shop next to a noisy group banked with an entrenchment of ski boots and duffel bags.

"Come back soon," he said. "And bring your hood."

"You're kinky, you know that?" She slipped off her coat and draped it over a chair.

"I'm not kinky, your hood is."

They talked about the trial in fragments, like dogs worrying a bone, laying it down, then picking it up again to nibble somewhere else. Then Amos changed the subject. He was going to pick up Sam on his way back from the airport and keep him for a day or two.

A waitress wiped the rings from their tabletop and slapped down menus. Amos ordered coffees.

"Is that all?" she asked.

"You got it."

"You should have taken counter seats if that's all you wanted."

"We didn't want the counter," he replied. "Is there some problem?"

She flounced away, holding the menus over her head.

"What are you going to do about him?" asked Maggie.

"There's nothing to do. Sam's not mine, so custody is out. See him when I can, that's all I can arrange."

"She's beautiful," she said.

He knew whom she meant. "Yeah. Nina's real pretty."

"There's a good program on television tonight—CBS or NBC, I don't remember which—something about enrichment programs for preschoolers."

"Stop trying to educate me, Mag. I know how to read the TV guide."

Maggie was frustrated. He made it difficult to share experience. "Stay cooped up in your stupid darkroom, then, and never come out."

"Can't do that. I'm going to Washington next week, remember?"

She did. This time she refused to ask whom he was planning to stay with. "That's doesn't mean you can't lift up your head long enough to see what else is going on around you."

"You remind me of this guy," he said. "A long time ago, when we had ten square blocks choked off around this induction center, scrimmaging for hours against hundreds of cops, our faces smeared with Vaseline and our pockets filled with ball bearings. We were disconnecting distributor caps, letting air out of tires, knocking over barricades, then this guy comes by and shouts, 'You're defeating the movement, you're going to kill us with the public.' Hell, I was having a good time, feeling like maybe I was doing some good. And then he comes along and tells me how I'm supposed to see it. He tried to make it for me what it was for him. It wasn't my view of what was happening. It's what you do sometimes, Mag. You try to make me use your viewfinder. When I want the serious side of anything, I'll find it myself."

A skier at the next table leaned over to take one of their chairs. Amos waved his permission, then slipped his hand over Maggie's. "Most times between us it's pretty good. But you've got to let me be. I don't mess with your head, Mag. Don't mess with mine."

She thought about the things he had told her for her own good, like the time he compared her to ice-out, but she decided to leave it alone. "What did you do with the ball bearings?"

"Scattered them in the street."

"And the Vaseline?"

"Protection against Mace."

The skiers at the next table were getting noisier. One of the women stared frankly at Amos. "He was right," she said.

"Who?"

"That guy. It did kill you with the public. You had to go to Canada."

"You never quit when you're ahead, do you?" He withdrew his hand and turned to stare out the window at mechanics de-icing the wings of a 747.

They sat for a while, not speaking, draining their coffee cups and idly rummaging over the tabletop with their fingertips, trying to find rapproachment on the Formica. She told him not to wait. He should get home before the roads iced up, especially if he wanted to pick up Sam. He moved to kiss her good-bye. There were too many eyes and she pulled back.

"Not here," she said.

He shook his head and asked when she was going to stop looking for Brownie points. She said she didn't know, then reminded him as he walked away to put the painting on top of her pantry cupboard. She thought that she loved him, a false-positive perhaps, but it didn't matter, not did the problems between them, which were no more or less than those between her and Alan, just different.

Maggie stood at the magazine counter, deciding what to take with her on the plane, thinking that she could discuss Amos with Sybil, who was good at this sort of thing. She noticed that the trial had made the front page of two newspapers, one edition with a picture of Melody Jessica being hustled into a waiting van, the other with a studio shot of McKeen, looking as silvered as he did in person. She went over her reasoning, assuring herself through a careful check that she had done the right thing. She was not personally responsible for what happened to the girl. The verdict was not her fault; it was a unanimous decision and Amos had changed his own mind. She was thinking of McKeen, figuring out what to say to him when he called, if he called, when she heard the page. At first she couldn't find the airport telephone and ran racing past the ticket counters until a Delta clerk pointed out a red house phone on the wall.

It was Sidney. He was crying. He wanted to prepare her before she made the trip. Sybil was dead. It had happened an hour before. It was awful. She was gasping for breath. She had the best doctor. He was even written up and he came with the best recommendations. Nothing could be done. Congestive heart failure. Sybil had waited too long.

"Because she came to see me," said Maggie. "Why did she have to do that? Why? It could have waited."

"Maybe not. She postponed it once before. If anybody's to blame, it's me. I knew. I should have insisted. I should have made her go through with it two, three months ago."

It was a punch in the stomach that Maggie wasn't ready for, and it went through her viscera to slam against her spine. She thought of Sybil, whose dicta included always stepping through a doorway with your right foot, and who had been mentioned once in Walter Winchell's column. She had things to tell her, things to ask her about, things to give her, like a Christmas present from Kristen and a partial apology, she hadn't argued her final point, she hadn't said good-bye. She remembered something that Kristen had said. *You can always get another husband. I can't get another father*. Kristen's experience may have been different, but it didn't matter. It was what Amos had said about his father on the ice. *He's the only one I've got*. It was the paucity of the allotment that made it so dear. Maggie could have more daughters, but Kristen had only one mother and so had Maggie.

"I'm coming anyway," she said, "you need help making arrangements."

He didn't seem to hear her. His voice cracked as he spoke. "I don't know what I'm going to do without her," he said.

She didn't tell him the answer. Instead she said, "Try to get some rest. I'll tell care of everything as soon as I get there. You can count on me."

It was as effortless as riding an escalator. Maggie had moved up a generation while waiting in an airport. She showed her boarding pass to the flight attendant and entered the jetway.

"Great-looking coat," said the flight attendant.

"It was a present from my mother," Maggie said, hating the coat but loving the gift. She wondered for one impulsive moment what it would be like to strip it off and give it to the flight attendant, then stepped into the cabin as Sybil would have done, her right foot first, with a look that challenged anyone who didn't like Mongolian goat to take a flying leap.

About the Author

EVELYN WILDE MAYERSON is the novelist-in-residence at the University of Miami. She's the author of five other novels, including the highly acclaimed *No Enemy but Time and Sanjo.* When she's not teaching in Miami, Florida, she lives in Manchester, Vermont.